PRAISE FOR
THE *Not So* NEUTRAL ZONE

"Chloe and Brody are so realistic. Both have relatable family situations that haunt them. And the complications are perfectly timed to keep me turning pages, breathless for the resolution. When you can wrap characters to root for into believable scenarios with just the right sprinkle of a faith journey, you've hooked me. Thanks Sarah and Susie May!"

—SHARON, GOODREADS

"I didn't know that 'hockey' was a genre, but if *The Not So Neutral Zone* is an example, give them all to me! This novel has everything I love: steamy-but-clean romance, strong writing, realistic characters, important lessons, and redemption.."

—AMY, GOODREADS

"A sweet clean rom com with hockey players and swoon worthy romance. Loved it! can't wait for more of this series."

—LILY, GOODREADS

"A well written story with vivid characters who are dealing with real struggles. Brody and Chloe have great chemistry and a tender romance. This uplifting story touches on themes of family, faith and forgiveness. I recommend it to readers who enjoy clean, heartfelt stories."

—RD, GOODREADS

THE *Not So* NEUTRAL ZONE

THE BLUE OX BOYS

THE NOT SO NEUTRAL ZONE

THE BLUE OX BOYS

THE *Not So* NEUTRAL ZONE

SUSAN & SARAH MAY WARREN

SUNRISE PUBLISHING

The Not So Neutral Zone
The Blue Ox Boys, Book 1

Soli Deo Gloria

"My grace is sufficient for you, for my power is
made perfect in weakness."

2 CORINTHIANS 12:9 NIV

BRODY

Six Months Ago – Barcelona

THERE ARE ABOUT A HUNDRED REASONS why I shouldn't be here now, and most of them are stuffed in my backpack.

To start, my hockey team's PR department would have a collective aneurysm if they knew where I was—or what I was about to do. Secondly, I'm carrying enough cash to buy a luxury car or fund a small criminal enterprise. And thirdly, I hate crowds. But here I am, drowning in a sea of tourists on La Rambla in Barcelona, and I've got nobody to blame but myself.

Well, myself and my father, but we'll get to that disaster in a minute.

The late-afternoon sun beats down on the tree-lined promenade, turning everything gold and hazy—very picturesque, very *Insta-worthy*, and very much wasted on me right now. Palm trees tower overhead, their fronds rustling in the Mediterranean breeze that carries the smell of salt water mixed with roasting chestnuts and something sweet—likely from those sugar-dusted pastries the vendors are hawking from carts. And if I were here for anything close to resembling a vacation, I'd be soaking it in. As it is—

My phone buzzes in my pocket for what has to be the thirtieth time in the last hour. At this point, I don't need to check it to know who it is.

Dad.

Again.

I pull the brim of my baseball cap lower and keep my head down as I weave through the chaos, shouldering past flower stalls exploding with roses the size of my fist—reds, yellows, pinks so bright they hurt to look at. A guitarist sits on a folding chair near a café, his fingers moving over the strings with the kind of easy confidence that says he's never had to bail his father out of a gambling debt.

Must be nice.

I break through the crowd and keep walking, leaving the square behind me.

Me, on the other hand, I'm here because my father gambled away fifty thousand dollars he doesn't have—*again*—and now he owes it to people who don't exactly accept IOUs or sad stories about "next time, I swear." I'm here to bail him out with cash I can't afford to give, cash that's currently sitting in my backpack like a ticking time bomb. To clean up his mess, make sure no one finds out, and get him on a plane home before the press catches wind of any of this.

Because if they do? If one single journalist gets a whiff that Brody Kane's father is a gambling addict who just went on a three-day losing streak at an underground poker game in Spain?

Career over. Image shattered. Contract renewal? Might as well frame it and hang it on the wall next to my childhood participation trophies.

So yeah. No stopping to smell the roses.

My phone buzzes again—because apparently the obvious thing to do when you're waiting to be bailed out from a potential knee-capping is to send thirty-seven text messages back-to-back—and this time I yank it out just to make it stop.

Dad
____

Where are you? The guy's getting impatient. Brody, PLEASE. I need you.

The screen is too bright in the sunlight, making me squint, a bead of sweat trickling down my back in the Barcelona sun.

You always need me, Dad. That's kind of your brand.

I swipe back to my map. Almost there. The meeting point is ten minutes away—some shady back-alley casino tucked into the Gothic Quarter, where my father's been hemorrhaging money like it's an Olympic sport and he's going for gold. I just need to get there, pay off whoever needs paying, pour my father into a taxi, and vanish before anyone recognizes me.

I set out to do just that, taking one last glance at the picturesque square before starting down the next street. So far, so good.

Stay invisible. Keep your head down. Don't let anyone see you.

It's basically been my mantra since I turned pro. On the ice? I'm untouchable. Calculated. Controlled. Perfect. My teammates call me—and I'm not kidding, this is actually a thing—"Candy" Kane, because apparently I'm so *sweet* and polished and media-friendly that I might as well be made of sugar.

I hate that nickname. Every time someone calls me Candy, I die a little inside. At this rate, I'll be completely dead by playoffs.

But off the ice? I'm a ghost. No scandals. No mess. No cracks in the armor. Because if people see the *real* me—the guy with the train-wreck father and the hidden dyslexia and the fear that no matter how hard I work, it'll never be enough—they'll know the truth.

I'm not made of candy.

I'm just a guy pretending to have it all together while everything falls apart in slow motion.

I sidestep a group of tourists taking a selfie in front of a flower stall—matching "Barcelona Babes" T-shirts, matching fanny packs, the whole nine yards—and catch a glimpse of my reflection in a café window. Baseball cap pulled low. Faded gray T-shirt with a small tear near the hem. Dark jeans. The post-season haircut—shorter on the sides, longer on top—hidden under the cap.

Generic. Forgettable. Exactly what I'm going for.

Good.

I take a breath and adjust the straps on my backpack. The weight of the cash inside feels heavier than it should. Fifty thousand dollars. I can't believe I'm bailing him out. Again—

Someone slams into me.

Hard.

The impact sends me stumbling forward, my sneakers skidding on the smooth cobblestones, and I barely catch myself. Smooth, Brody. Real smooth. I look up just in time to see a guy in a dark hoodie sprinting past me. Dark hoodie. In Barcelona. In the late afternoon. In the heat. Because that's not suspicious at all.

He's weaving through the crowd like he's got somewhere *very* important to be, which—spoiler alert—usually means he's running *from* something, not *to* something.

What the—

And then I see her.

A woman—mid-twenties, maybe—standing about ten feet away. Her hand is still outstretched like she's reaching for something that's no longer there. Her face is frozen in pure shock.

She's wearing a sundress, blue with tiny white polka dots, and flat sandals. Her purse strap is broken, dangling uselessly from her shoulder.

Oh.

Oh.

Hoodie guy just stole her purse.

And I don't think. Which is probably for the best, because if I thought about it, I'd remember I have fifty thousand dollars in cash on my back and a father waiting for me and approximately zero time for heroics.

But something about the look on her face flips a switch in my brain.

And I run.

The backpack bounces against my spine—*fifty thousand dollars, Kane. You're running with fifty thousand dollars in cash*—but I ignore it. My sneakers pound against the cobblestones. Years of hockey training kick in—muscle memory, reflexes, all the countless hours in the gym and on the ice finally paying off in the form of . . . purse-chasing.

The thief is fast, but I'm faster. I vault over a café chair—someone yelps—dodge a family with strollers, and nearly take out a flower display. Petals scatter everywhere, and I mentally apologize to the vendor, who's shouting something that definitely isn't "good job, American tourist."

The street musician stops playing. The silver statue breaks character to watch. Tourists scatter.

And honestly? This is the most alive I've felt in *months*.

Which says something deeply concerning about my life, but we'll unpack that later.

The thief darts into a side alley—narrow, lined with graffiti—and I follow. The alley smells like stale beer and poor life choices.

He stumbles over a trash bag.

I grab the back of his hoodie and slam him against the wall.

Not hard. Just . . . *encouragingly*.

"Bad idea, man," I say, breathing hard.

He stares at me for half a second, then throws the purse at my feet.

Smart kid.

Then he bolts.

I let him go. I don't care about him. I pick up the brown leather bag and check the contents. Wallet. Phone with a daisy case. Keys on a keychain shaped like a tiny Eiffel Tower.

I jog back toward La Rambla, because apparently, I'm doing this now. I'm the guy who chases down thieves while carrying fifty grand in cash and ignoring increasingly frantic texts from his disaster of a father.

Somewhere, my agent is getting a stress migraine and doesn't know why.

I round the corner back onto La Rambla, and there she is. Still standing in the same spot, one hand pressed to her chest.

I walk up, slightly out of breath, and hold out the purse. "I think this is yours."

Her gaze lifts to meet mine, and—

Up close, she's . . . wow. Freckles scattered across her nose. Brown eyes—warm, the color of melted chocolate—currently doing this thing where they're welling up but also crinkling at the corners like she can't decide whether to cry or laugh.

She looks at me.

Then at the purse.

Then back at me.

And then she *laughs*.

Not a polite chuckle. A full, slightly hysterical laugh that makes her shoulders shake.

"Oh my goodness," she says, taking the purse and clutching it to her chest. Her voice is warm, slightly breathless. "Oh my *goodness*. You—you got it back. I can't believe you—" She stops, presses a hand to her forehead. "Thank you. *Thank you.* I don't even—who *are* you?"

"It's nothing," I say, which is a lie because—you know, 50K in my backpack and all. "Are you okay?"

"Am I—" She stares at me. "You just chased that guy down

and rescued my purse like you're Batman, and you're asking if *I'm* okay?"

When she puts it like that, it does sound a little ridiculous.

I shrug. "Just making sure."

She opens her purse—the zipper sticks—and starts riffling through it with shaking fingers. And then she pulls out this worn, battered sketchbook. The cover is soft leather, faded and creased, with coffee stains near the bottom corner.

She flips through it quickly, her lips moving silently.

And for just a second, it falls open.

I see it.

Drawings. Whimsical, detailed, *beautiful* drawings. A dragon with fierce, expressive eyes and intricate wings. Handwritten notes crammed in the margins.

It's . . . incredible.

She notices me looking and snaps the sketchbook shut, shoving it back into her purse. Her cheeks flush pink.

"Sorry," she mutters. "Just . . . making sure everything's there."

I want to ask about the drawings. Want to tell her what I just saw was amazing.

But something in the way she's holding the purse now—close, protective—tells me that topic's off the table.

So I don't say anything.

But I don't forget it.

"And?" I ask.

She nods, still looking dazed. "Yeah. Everything. Even my—" She pulls out her phone and lets out a shaky laugh. "Even my phone. Which is a miracle, because I am *so bad* at keeping track of things." She glances at her watch, and her eyes widen slightly. "Oh. I should probably—I mean, I have some time, but"—she looks up at me—"can I at least buy you a coffee? You literally saved my vacation. That has to be worth at least a cortado."

I find myself smiling. "Aren't you going to be late?"

"Late for—" She checks her watch again, and her face goes pale. "Oh. *Oh.* Yes. Very late. Extremely late. My sister's going to kill me." She groans. "I got so distracted I completely lost track of—"

"Where are you headed?"

"Port Vell. The cruise ship. It's leaving at six, and I have no idea where I am right now."

I glance at my own watch. It's just past five. "I know a shortcut," I hear myself say. Followed by a very bad idea . . . "I can walk you."

"You don't have to—"

"It's fine. I'm heading that direction anyway." (I'm not. Not even remotely close. But I tell myself it's just a small detour. And then back to help Dad.)

Her face lights up. "Are you for real right now? Because you'd be literally saving my life. Again. That has to be some kind of record."

"Glad to help."

"I'm Chloe," she says, sticking out her hand. "Chloe Dawson. And you are officially my hero."

"No hero, just Brody," I say, taking her hand, her soft fingertips brushing my callused palm.

"Brody," she says like she's testing it out. "That's a good name. Fits the whole vigilante-in-a-baseball-cap vibe you've got going."

I laugh despite myself. First genuine laugh I've had in weeks.

"Come on," I say. "Let's get you to that ship."

We start walking, and she falls into step beside me. The crowds thin slightly as we move away from the densest part of La Rambla. The buildings here are older, painted in faded yellows and peaches, balconies overflowing with plants. The air smells like jasmine.

She's babbling—something about getting lost looking for a vintage shop and wandering through the Gothic Quarter taking photos—and I'm only half listening.

Because the other half of me is noticing things. The way she talks with her hands. The freckles on her shoulders. The fact that she doesn't recognize me—doesn't know I'm Brody Kane, professional hockey player.

She's looking at me like I'm just . . . Brody.

Some guy who rescued her purse.

Just Brody.

I can't even remember the last time that happened.

My phone buzzes again. The weight of the backpack tugs against my shoulders, a reminder of where I should be, what I should be doing.

I silence it without looking.

Just ten minutes, I tell myself.

Dad's kneecaps probably won't get busted if he waits another ten minutes. Besides, it might be good for him. A night in the "clink," so to speak.

Ten minutes before I go back to being the guy who fixes everything.

What's the harm in that?

CHLOE

Okay, so here's the thing about being rescued by a ridiculously attractive stranger in Barcelona: It does *not* happen to people like me.

People like me—Chloe Dawson, chronic overplanner, professional people pleaser, girl who once got left behind at a rest stop on a family road trip for *two hours* before anyone noticed—do not get swept off their feet by handsome heroes who chase down thieves to help them.

And yet.

Here I am, walking down a cobblestone street in one of the most beautiful cities in the world, next to a guy who's giving off major

Captain America-in-hiding vibes with that baseball cap pulled low over his brow. And sure, he's handsome, all tall and broad-shouldered with dark hair, a little stubble around the edges. But it's his eyes that keep catching me off guard. Gray-blue, like storm clouds over the ocean, with this intensity that makes me feel like when he's looking at me, he's actually *seeing* me. Not looking through me or past me, but *at* me.

Which is . . . new.

And slightly terrifying.

Or maybe it's just the adrenaline working its way out of my system. That would explain why my heart is still doing that weird fluttery thing and I got all weak in the knees at the way his voice softened when he asked if I was okay.

Yeah. Definitely the adrenaline.

The street we're on now is quieter than La Rambla, the buildings pressing close on either side, painted in faded peaches and buttery yellows. Wrought-iron balconies spill over with geraniums and trailing ivy, and someone's laundry hangs from a line overhead, white sheets fluttering in the breeze. I tuck a strand of hair behind my ear, willing it to stay put for once.

Come on, hair. Hot guy here, work with me.

"So you planned this whole trip?" he asks, breaking into my self-deprecating dialogue, and I startle.

"Oh—yeah. I mean, I'm an event planner," I say, waving a hand. I can't help the way I gesture when I speak, no matter how much I try. I stopped fighting it a long time ago. "Well, *trying* to be an event planner. I just started my own company a couple months ago, Ever After Events—super cheesy name, I know—and my sister's wedding is kind of my big debut." I shrug. "This whole bridesmaids' cruise thing was my idea. A Pinterest-worthy "bridal-cation," if you will. Barcelona to Mallorca, with every gorgeous stop in between." A quiet laugh escapes me and I add, "I think I might be better at *planning* other people's experiences than actually *participating* in them."

I'm rambling. I know I'm rambling. It's what I do when I'm nervous. Or excited. Or existing.

Brody's mouth quirks up at the corner. Not quite a smile, but close. "Sounds like a good idea."

"Tell that to my sister when I show up late." I adjust the strap of my purse—my miraculously recovered purse—and feel my face heat up. "I got a little sidetracked at the Mercat de la Boqueria . . ."

"That doesn't sound like a bad thing."

"It does if I miss the cruise ship departure."

He glances at me, and there's something in his expression I can't quite read. "How late are you?"

I check my watch, and my stomach does a little flip. "Um. Pretty late. But the ship leaves at six, and it's only five thirty. So . . . I've got time. Probably. Maybe. Thanks to my superhero tour guide." I glance at him, my face burning. I cannot believe I said that. But he's still smiling, shaking his head with a chuckle in a way that gives me an ounce of reassurance that maybe, just maybe, he sees me as charming—not chaotic.

We turn onto a wider street, and the sun pours over the old cobblestone, sifting through the trees that line the buildings. The shadows almost look like works of art themselves, blending with the art of the ancient city. It's enough to steal my breath away.

"Your sister must be excited," Brody says. "About the wedding."

"Oh, she's *Thrilled*. Capital T. She's marrying this hockey player—Derek something, I can never remember his last name—and apparently, he's a big deal in the sports world, which means the wedding has to be '*perfect*.'" I make air quotes with my fingers, nearly smacking a passing tourist in the process. "Sorry! Perdón!"

The tourist—an older woman with a sun hat the size of a small planet—glares at me. Fair.

"Anyway," I continue, words pouring out of me. And I know,

I know, I'm oversharing. But this guy—nope, the adrenaline, remember?—makes my heart race, and I just can't seem to stop. "My sister has very high expectations. For the wedding, for this trip, for . . . everything, really. That's her fun thing. You know, that thing everyone's got going for them. Oh, not the high-expectations part. The living-up-to-them part. She's smart and successful, and she's got her life together. And I'm the one who—" I stop myself before I say something pathetic about being overlooked. "Anyway, she's just . . . she's great."

"You sound like a good sister."

The comment catches me off guard. I glance at him, and he's looking straight ahead, but there's something genuine in his voice that makes my chest feel tight.

"And you?" he asks.

"Hmm?"

He glances at me, turning my little heart into a pathetic glob in my chest. "What's your fun thing?"

"Oh . . . um . . . I'm"—a chronic people pleaser? An absolute disaster?—"*great* at impressions."

Brody casts me a skeptical look. "Really?"

"Oh yeah. One hundred percent."

"So let's hear it."

"Okay . . . but you asked for it." I cup my hands over my mouth, breathing heavily with a little *coo-choo* as I inhale. "Luke . . . I am your father!"

Brody's brows lift dramatically. "That was . . . terrible."

"What?! No." I try my best to hold a scowl. "That was *America's Got Talent*-worthy. You don't know what you're talking about."

And then he laughs. The sound is warm and genuine and does absolutely nothing to help my "this is just adrenaline" theory.

I wait for him to catch his breath before asking, "What about you? What's your thing?"

"I play—" He stops, like he's reconsidering what he was about to say. "I'm . . . between things right now."

"Between things. That's delightfully vague."

"What can I say? I'm a man of mystery."

"A mysterious man who knows Barcelona and has the reflexes of a parkour expert. Very suspicious."

"Maybe I'm Batman."

I laugh—a real laugh, not the polite one I use at family gatherings. "Barcelona Batman. I'd watch that movie."

"It'd be very confusing. Batman, but with tapas."

"*The Dark Knight Rises* . . . to get second breakfast."

He grins, and the expression transforms his whole face. When he actually *smiles*—not that half-quirk thing but a real, genuine smile—his eyes crinkle at the corners, and there's this warmth that makes him look younger, less guarded.

Stop it, Chloe. You're staring.

We turn another corner, and suddenly the port opens up before us, the massive expanse of Port Vell stretching out with sailboats bobbing in their slips, their masts clinking softly in the wind. The water is blue—unreal blue, like a dream—dotted with white sails and the occasional yacht. The wooden boardwalk stretches ahead, lined with restaurants and shops.

And there, in the middle of the harbor, is a very large cruise ship.

A very large cruise ship that is *moving*.

My heart drops into my shoes. "Oh no."

"What?"

"That." I point with a shaking finger. "That's my ship. That's . . . it's *leaving*."

The cruise ship is pulling away from the dock, massive and white and utterly indifferent to the fact that I am NOT ON IT. Its horn sounds—a deep, mournful blast that echoes across the water.

And I don't know why, because there's no way I'm catching that boat, but suddenly I'm running.

And I can hear Brody calling something behind me, but I'm too busy sprinting toward the pier, weaving between startled tourists and a man selling balloons who yells something as I nearly take out his entire inventory.

The sun is hot on my shoulders. My hair whips across my face. The smell of salt water and diesel fuel from the ship's engines fills my nose.

I reach the end of the pier just as the ship clears the dock. There's a gap of water between the ship and the pier—not huge, but definitely too wide to jump unless I've suddenly developed superpowers in the last thirty seconds.

Which I haven't.

I stand there, breathing hard, the rough wooden planks warm under my sandals. The breeze coming off the Mediterranean is cooler here, lifting my hair, carrying the cries of seagulls circling overhead.

And then I see her.

My sister—tall, blonde, perfect even from a distance—standing on the upper deck with the other bridesmaids. They're all holding colorful drinks with little umbrellas, their dresses fluttering in the wind. She's waving. As though this is a fun little mishap and not a complete catastrophe.

"CHLOE!" Her voice carries across the water, bright and unconcerned. "We'll meet you there! Don't worry!"

Don't *worry*?

I slap on my best event-planner smile and wave back as I watch my carefully planned bridal-cation float away, mimosas and all.

"Okay!" I call out, my voice hitting that register that's way too cheerful to be genuine. "See you in Mallorca!"

The ship keeps moving, its wake spreading out in a V shape that rocks the smaller boats in the harbor. The bridesmaids keep waving—a little cluster of pastel colors against the white railing. Someone's taking a selfie.

Of course they are.

Brody appears beside me, slightly out of breath. "Did you just—"

"Miss my cruise? Yup." I lower my hand, letting my arm drop to my side. My shoulder aches from waving. "Watch my sister and her friends leave without me? Also yup."

"They didn't seem worried."

"They're not." I turn to face him, and I can feel the weird smile on my face—it's my people-pleaser smile. "Don't worry about it. It's . . . it's fine. Super fine. She's happy, that's what matters."

There's something in his expression that looks almost like . . . sympathy? Understanding? I can't tell, and I don't want to look too closely, because I'm approximately five seconds away from doing something embarrassing, like crying.

"I'm so sorry," I say, pressing my hands to my warm cheeks. "You were trying to help me get here on time, and I was babbling the whole way, and now I've wasted your time—"

"Hey." His voice is gentle. "This isn't your fault."

"It kind of is though—"

"When's the next stop?"

"What?"

"The cruise ship. When does it stop in Mallorca? There has to be a schedule."

Oh. Right. Problem-solving. That's a thing I can do. That's literally my job.

I pull out my phone—miraculously unstolen, still in its chipped daisy case—and pull up the cruise itinerary. "It gets to Palma de Mallorca tomorrow morning. Around ten."

"Okay." Brody nods, like this is a perfectly solvable problem and not the end of my carefully orchestrated plans. "So you need to get to Mallorca by tomorrow morning."

"Right. Which means I need to . . ." I scroll through my phone, squinting at the screen in the bright sunlight. "I need to figure out how to get there. There has to be a ferry or a flight or—"

"Or you could stay here tonight."

I look up from my phone. "What?"

"In Barcelona. You're already here. The ship doesn't get to Mallorca until tomorrow morning, which means you have"—he checks his watch—"about eighteen hours. You could get a hotel room, catch a flight or ferry tomorrow, meet up with your sister."

"I . . . guess?" My brain is trying to process this, but it's still stuck on the image of that ship disappearing into the distance. "That makes sense. Logistically. I should probably . . ." I walk over to the port authority booth—a small white structure with a faded blue awning and a bored-looking attendant inside, visible through the smudged window. The booth smells like stale coffee and cigarette smoke.

I knock on the glass.

The attendant looks up from his phone, his expression suggesting I've just interrupted something very important. "¿Sí?"

"Hi—*hola*—do you speak English?"

"Yes." And he sounds thrilled about it.

"Great. Um, I just missed that cruise ship." I point at the rapidly shrinking vessel, now just a white speck against the blue horizon. "When's the next boat to Mallorca?"

"Tomorrow morning. Ferry departs at seven, arrives at ten thirty."

"Perfect. Can I buy a ticket?"

"Not here. You buy online or at the ferry terminal." He gestures vaguely in a direction that could be anywhere from here to Portugal.

"Okay. And where's the ferry terminal?"

He gives me an address in rapid Spanish that I immediately forget, then goes back to his phone.

Right. Super helpful.

I turn back to Brody, who's leaning against the railing, the sun turning his hair almost gold at the edges. Behind him, the harbor is alive with activity—boats coming and going, tourists strolling along the boardwalk, a street performer juggling near a fountain.

I suppose, in the grand scheme of things, there could be worse places to get stranded. Maybe this won't be a disaster so much as a . . . handsome—I mean, scenic—detour.

"So," I say, walking back over. "Ferry tomorrow morning. I just need to find a hotel, figure out where the ferry terminal is, not lose my purse again—"

"What if I showed you Barcelona?"

I stare at him. "What?"

"You're stuck here for the night anyway." He shrugs, but there's something in his gray-blue eyes that makes my heart do that fluttery thing again. "I know the city pretty well. I could show you around. Make sure you actually make it to the ferry terminal tomorrow."

"You don't have to do that."

"I know."

"Don't you have somewhere to be? Something to do? A life that doesn't involve escorting tourists around?"

He pulls out his phone, and I see the screen light up with what looks like a dozen notifications—texts, probably, from whoever's been trying to reach him all afternoon. He looks at the screen for a long moment, his jaw tightening slightly.

Then he deliberately puts the phone away.

"Nothing that can't wait," he says.

I should say no. I should absolutely say no. I don't know this guy. He could be anyone. And I have a business to run, a sister to catch up with, a very carefully planned schedule that's already in shambles.

But he's looking at me with those eyes, and he just chased down a thief for me, and he walked me all the way to the port even though he clearly has somewhere else to be, and—

"Okay," I hear myself say.

"Yeah?"

"Yeah. I mean—" I laugh, running a hand through my wind-tangled hair. "Why not? I've already missed my cruise and given my sister a great story to tell at family gatherings for the next decade. Might as well make the most of it."

His smile, that real, full smile, appears again, and something in my chest does a little flip. So . . . maybe it's not just the adrenaline.

"All right, then." Brody turns and gestures back down the dock. "After you."

Brody falls into step beside me, and I'm hyperaware of everything—the way he adjusts his stride to match mine, the way his hand almost brushes mine and then doesn't, the way he's actually *here*, present, not distracted or checking his phone or rushing ahead.

For the first time in longer than I can remember, I feel . . . noticed.

Not invisible. Not like the sister who gets left behind or the planner who works behind the scenes.

Just . . . seen.

"So," I say, glancing up at him. "What's the first stop on this impromptu Barcelona tour?"

"Patience," he says, but he's smiling. "You'll see."

And despite everything—the missed cruise, the disrupted plans, the fact that I'm wandering through a foreign city with a man whose last name I don't know—I find myself smiling back.

This is definitely not the sort of thing that happens to girls like me. But maybe, just for today, it is.

"What kind of work?"

Danger zone. Redirect.

"Nothing interesting," I say. "What about you? You said you're an event planner. How'd you get into that?"

She makes this little sound—half laugh, half sigh. "Honestly? I kind of fell into it. I've done a lot of things—retail, restaurant work, tried being a receptionist for about five minutes before I got so bored I thought I'd lose my mind. But event planning . . ." She pauses, tucking a strand of hair behind her ear. "I'm good at details. Good at making things run smoothly. And I like making people happy, you know?"

"Sounds like you found your thing."

She plays with the strap of her purse, her eyes on the street below. "Maybe. My sister got engaged last year and asked me to help plan her engagement party. It's been going so well, and I enjoyed helping her. So I thought, why not?" She shrugs. "I started Ever After Events, and now I'm just trying to figure out if I can actually make a living at this."

"Her wedding's the big test?"

"Exactly. I figure if I can pull off a destination wedding for my sister without major disasters, maybe it's feasible. And if I mess up . . ." She trails off. "Let's just say the pressure is on."

I can't help it. I give her a little nudge with my elbow. "You won't mess it up."

She glances up, those eyes catching mine, all bright and beautiful. "You don't know that. You've known me for, like, an hour."

"An hour in which you've shown remarkable problem-solving skills and the ability to remain calm under pressure—"

"I literally ran screaming after a cruise ship."

"—which shows dedication and commitment."

She laughs, and I find myself smiling. I could get used to this.

We turn another corner, and the buildings open up slightly. Modern glass-fronted shops appear between the older structures—a jarring contrast of centuries. The sidewalk here is crowded with café tables, their striped umbrellas casting shadows across the pavement. The smell of coffee hits me first, rich and dark, followed by something savory—grilled seafood, garlic, olive oil.

"So where are you from?" Chloe asks.

"I was born in North Dakota."

Her eyebrows shoot up. "Really? That's so . . . flat."

"Very flat. And very cold. The winters are enough to make any-one wonder who thought it was a good idea to live there."

"But you don't live there anymore?"

"No. My parents moved away when I was in middle school." When my world started falling apart. "But you know, I like to think those early years shaped me. Even in my job now, I—" I cut off abruptly, wincing.

"Ah, the mysterious work you won't tell me about," she muses over her shoulder.

"It's really not that interesting."

"See, now I'm convinced you're a spy."

"If I were a spy, would I tell you?"

"That's exactly what a spy would say," she says with mock sus-picion.

"Well great, you caught me." I toss up my hands. "Now I gotta kidnap you."

"What?"

"You know too much."

Chloe laughs again, stumbling as the street slopes gently down-ward. I reach for her elbow, steadying her, and she stills, her laugh-ter settling into a smile. My pulse rushes. *Zero business, Brody. Get ahold of yourself.*

I step back, clearing my throat before gesturing onward.

"What about you?" I ask. "Where are you from?"

"Minnesota, actually. Small town you've never heard of."

"Try me."

She names a town that I absolutely have heard of—we played a charity game there two years ago—but I keep my face neutral.

"You're right, never heard of it."

"See? Nobody has. It's the kind of place where everyone knows everyone." She pauses. "What about you? What was it like growing up in North Dakota? Besides cold."

"Quiet. A lot of space to think." I pause, choosing my words carefully. "Spent a lot of hours shooting pucks in the hockey net in my parents' driveway."

"Did you play in school?"

"For a while. It was something to do." All technically true, just . . . edited. "What about you? Any sports?"

"*Oh* no. I'm what you call athletics intolerant. Trust me, you don't want me going anywhere near a sporting event. I'll curse the whole thing."

I chuckle, trying to imagine this girl on the ice with me.

We're quiet for a moment, just walking. The street is emptying out as people head indoors for dinner.

"So, your sister's marrying a hockey player?" I ask.

She pulls in a breath. "Yeah. Derek something. I really need to remember his last name." She laughs. "My parents are *ecstatic*. They're huge hockey fans. Growing up, they dragged me and my sister to every game—my brother's high school games, college games, you name it. I spent a good chunk of my youth fighting off frostbite from the stands."

"So . . . not a fan, then?"

"Not even a little bit. I mean, I get that people love it, but to me it's just . . ." She shrugs. "It's never been my thing. And honestly, most of the hockey players I've met through my sister are exactly what you'd expect. Big egos, lots of swagger."

My stomach tightens. "Maybe they're just confident."

"There's a line between confident and arrogant." She glances at me, her eyes going wide. "Oh no, you're not a hockey guy, are you? Shoot—I feel bad."

"No, you're good." I answered that maybe a little too quickly.

"Oh, thank goodness," she breathes.

We round another corner, and suddenly the Sagrada Família towers above us—all organic curves and soaring spires.

Chloe stops dead.

"Wow."

Wow is right. The warm sun kisses her cheeks, highlighting those freckles, and I know—I know—I'm staring, but . . . this girl. She is completely herself. Completely unselfconscious, her gaze taking it all in greedily.

When was the last time I got excited about anything?

I can't remember.

She's still staring up, her eyes tracing each line as though she means to memorize it. "It's wild to think Gaudí knew he'd never see it finished."

There's something wistful in her voice. A breeze trails a whisp of hair across her shoulder.

"You sound like you get that," I say.

She glances at me, startled. "What?"

"Building something bigger than yourself."

She frowns for a split second, her lips parting, considering, and then, "What about you?" She changes the subject. "What was your childhood like?"

All right, mystery girl. Keep your secrets.

"I spent a lot of time alone," I say, careful with my answer. "My mom worked a lot. My dad wasn't always around." *Or ever.* I pause.

We start walking again, circling the cathedral. The streets around it are busy with tourists and vendors, but somehow it doesn't feel crowded. It could be just the two of us out here, for all I care.

"If you could do anything, what would it be?" I ask after a while.

"You mean besides planning other people's weddings?"

"Yeah."

She's quiet, and I can see something churning in her expression. Her gaze travels the ancient lines of the cathedral walls. "I don't know. Travel, maybe? I've never really been anywhere . . . well, except here. So . . . maybe not a great omen for my future travels." She drags her gaze away, turning it toward me. "How about you? What's your dream?"

The question catches me off guard.

"I don't have one," I hear myself say.

She stops walking. "Everyone has a dream."

"Not me."

"I don't believe that."

"Believe it."

"There has to be *something*. Something you want that you don't have."

The honest answer? I want to stop feeling like I'm drowning. I want my father to get his life together. I want to be more than just the image everyone expects.

But I can't say any of that.

"Maybe I just haven't found it yet," I say finally.

She studies my face, then nods slowly. "Okay. But when you do find it, I hope it's something good."

I paste on a smile. "Yeah. Me too." But I look away, because suddenly I'm in too deep, and the way she's looking at me, all full of hope, as though she expects that dream to come to me any minute now—it's too much. I run a hand over the back of my neck, adjust my hat. "Hey. You hungry?"

"Are you kidding? I just missed the boat to my never-ending shrimp buffet. I was saving up an appetite for that."

I can't help but chuckle as I grab her hand on instinct, redirecting our path. "Come on."

Twenty minutes later, we're at La Boqueria market, and Chloe is practically vibrating with excitement.

The market is an assault on the senses. Stalls overflow with fruit so bright it looks painted, like Hollywood props—strawberries the size of small apples, mangoes glowing orange-gold. Legs of jamón ibérico dangle from hooks. Fresh seafood sits on beds of ice, still smelling like the ocean. The air is thick with competing scents: spices, fresh bread, roasting nuts, sweet fruit.

Chloe stops at every stall, taking photos, exclaiming over everything.

"Look at these tomatoes!"

"They're tomatoes."

"They're *perfect* tomatoes!"

I'm smiling without meaning to.

We stop at a flower stall—massive bouquets of sunflowers and roses. Chloe reaches out to touch a sunflower, her thumb brushing over the velvety petal. The vendor catches my eye with a knowing smile, and before I can second-guess myself, I'm sliding two euros across the wooden cart. The woman plucks out the sunflower and holds it out toward Chloe.

"What's this for?" she asks.

I lean in. "Consolation prize. For missing your cruise."

Chloe glances at me over her shoulder with a shy smile. Her cheeks flush. "Thank you. No one's ever bought me flowers before."

I frown. "Really?"

"Really. My sister used to get flowers all the time. But me?" She tries to play it off with a shrug. "I guess I must give off a too-practical-for-flowers sort of vibe."

The notion is so wrong, I almost laugh. Nothing could be further from the truth.

She tucks the sunflower carefully into her purse, and we continue on, coming to a stop at a juice stand. Chloe orders in Spanish—halting but confident—and I'm impressed.

"You speak Spanish?"

"Un poco. Enough to order food and ask where the bathroom is." She grins. "The important stuff."

Our drinks arrive. She takes a sip and makes this sound that does something strange inside me. She really has no idea how adorable she is.

"This is amazing. Here, try it."

I take a sip. Sweet, tart, tropical.

"Good, right?" she says.

"Really good."

"Better than boring orange juice," she says, glancing pointedly at my drink.

"Hey now," I scoff. "Orange juice is classic."

"*Classic* is code for 'boring.'"

I laugh despite myself.

The light filtering through the market's windows is turning rose-gold with the sunset. We keep walking, and I realize I can't remember the last time I did something this simple. Just walking through a market with someone. No agenda. Just easy.

We finish our juices and head toward a tapas bar tucked into a corner—standing room only, chalkboard menu entirely in Catalan. Chloe orders confidently.

"What did you order?" I ask.

"Patatas bravas, croquetas, and pan con tomate—bread rubbed with tomato and olive oil. And Manchego cheese if they have it."

"You know your tapas."

"I did my research."

The bartender slides plates across—golden croquetas, potatoes in spicy red sauce, thick bread slices glistening with tomato pulp and olive oil. The smell alone makes my mouth water.

We eat standing up, sharing plates.

"This is so good," Chloe says. "Why doesn't food taste like this at home?"

"Because you're eating it in Barcelona."

"Fair point. Everything tastes better when it's slightly irresponsible."

The bartender brings more food—grilled octopus, peppers—and we keep eating. The bar is getting busier, crowds gathering to watch a European football game on the TV overhead. Someone makes a goal and the bar erupts.

Chloe flinches.

"Wow, you really don't like sports at all," I say, chuckling.

She blushes, crinkling her nose. "Between you and me? Most of the athletes I've met are exactly what you'd expect. It's exhausting."

I think about my teammates. The locker-room talk. The swagger.

She's not entirely wrong.

"Not all of them," I say.

"Maybe not. But enough." She pauses. "Sorry. I'm probably being judgy."

"Little bit," I tease.

She tucks a strand of hair behind her ear, looking down at her hands. "I don't mean to be. It's just not my world."

And there it is. The reminder that if she knew who I was, she'd probably put me in that exact category.

We finish eating, and despite her protests, I manage to snag the bill. The sun has set, and the streets outside are dark except for the glow of streetlamps. There's a warm breeze, and for a moment we simply stand there, soaking in the evening.

"Walk?" I suggest.

"Lead the way."

We walk through the Gothic Quarter, where the city feels timeless, where layers of history stack on top of each other. Past shops closing and restaurants opening. Under archways that have stood for centuries.

The air is cooler now, pleasant. Music winds through the old streets—a guitar, slow and melodic. The city smells like flowers and garlic and the sea.

And with every step, I'm thinking: *Maybe this is it. Maybe this is the dream I didn't know I had.*

Which is ridiculous.

But it doesn't feel ridiculous.

It feels like the truest thing I've thought in years.

CHLOE

I am absolutely, completely, maybe falling for someone I met a few hours ago.

Which is insane. I mean, clinically, certifiably insane.

It's the kind of thing that happens in movies . . . but not to people like me in those movies. Not to the extras.

Which brings me back to the first point—you know, the insanity. Maybe none of this is real. Maybe I fell off the dock, chasing down the ship, and hit my head. Maybe this is all some sort of coma-induced fever dream, because there's no way this is real.

The evening is in full tilt now, the old city all aglow. After leaving the tapas bar, we kept walking, taking in the sights between easy conversations until we wound up here, at this tiny restaurant tucked under one of the archways of Plaça Reial.

The restaurant is small—maybe ten tables, half inside and half outside, where we are, under the stone archway. Edison bulbs strung overhead cast this warm, vintage glow that makes everything look like a movie set. Candles flicker on the tables in little glass holders, their flames dancing in the evening breeze.

Brody smiles at me, making my stomach do that swooping, sudden-drop flutter, and heat rushes to my cheeks. I have to admit, it feels pretty real.

He's taken off the baseball cap, and I can see his face properly now. Dark hair that's slightly messy. Gray-blue eyes that seem to shift in the candlelight—storm clouds one second, ocean the next. A small scar above his eyebrow. The shadow of stubble along his jaw that I definitely should not be thinking about touching.

The waiter drops off our food, and it's incredible. The fish is flaky and tender, tasting like the ocean but in a good way, not a fishy way. The vegetables are caramelized and sweet, with crispy edges that crunch between my teeth. The bread is warm and crusty, steam rising when I crack it open. I take a greedy bite and actually die a little bit.

"This. Is . . ." I chef's kiss my fingertips.

Brody chuckles, shaking his head slightly.

"What?" I say, covering my mouthful of the life-changing fish with my hand.

"Nothing." He shrugs, but he's full-on grinning now, his eyes crinkling at the corners. "Just you."

I still, my heart catching for a moment, but he continues as though he hadn't said anything.

"Tell me something," he says, taking a sip of wine. "Something you haven't told me yet."

"I've basically told you my entire life story at this point. You know more about me than most people I've known for years."

"Then tell me something small. Something nobody knows."

Okay, Mr. Suave. I think about it, swirling my own wine and watching the candlelight reflect off the surface. "I guess . . . if you must know—"

"I really must," he says, inclining his head.

"When I was in college . . . I got a C in my required physical credit. Not because I didn't try . . . but because I was just *so* bad at it."

Brody's lips quirk. "What was the class?"

I hide behind my hands, my cheeks blazing against my palms. "Badminton."

Brody coughs a laugh. "Wait. Seriously?"

"Don't laugh! I was the only person in the class who didn't get an A. It haunts me!" Even now, the memory of flailing around the gym only to get popped in the eyeball by a plastic birdie is a little too much to think about.

And he's full-on, eyes-watering, face-red laughing.

"Brody!" I feign upset, scowling at him.

"I'm—I'm sorry, Chloe," he says, catching his breath. "I shouldn't laugh."

I give him my most stern expression. "No, you shouldn't."

He reaches across the table, his fingertips brushing my wrist, and my gaze snaps to his. "I'm sorry. Please forgive me."

My little brain is empty. All thought has left the building. What was I even pretending to be upset about? Badminton? All I can think about is the way his fingertips trace over my wrist and curl into my hand, trailing electricity that seems to have completely short-circuited me. "It's okay," I think I hear myself say.

"Your turn," I manage, my voice coming out slightly breathless. "Tell me something nobody knows."

He's quiet for a moment, his thumb still moving across my knuckles in that slow, mesmerizing way. The world around me turns to white noise as I watch his eyes sweep over our hands, the blue churning.

"I have this dread," he says finally, his voice low. "That I'm going to end up like my father. That I'll spend my whole life trying to be someone I'm not. That I'll wake up one day and realize I've been performing for so long that I don't know who I actually am anymore."

I swear I stop breathing. That was not what I expected. His thumb stills against my fingers, and I give his hand a gentle squeeze. "Do you feel like you're performing right now?"

He looks at me, and something changes in his expression—something raw and unguarded. "Not tonight."

And now my heart is absolutely thundering in my chest. I'm pretty sure you could hear it if not for the music in this place—and I'm pretty sure my hand is sweating in his, but I don't pull away. Because if I pull away, this moment ends, and I don't want it to end.

The waiter clears our plates, asks if we want dessert. Brody looks at me, and I shake my head because I'm too full and too nervous and too aware of his hand holding mine to think about food.

"Just the check," Brody tells him. He turns that intense gaze on me, and my pulse flutters. "We should probably head toward your hotel. Wouldn't want to get you home too late. Where are you staying?"

I pull out my phone, swiping the screen to my hotel confirmation and the little map below with that red pushpin. Brody takes a glance and nods. "That's not far. Come on, the night's still young."

And then it's just us and the candlelight and the distant sound of guitar music drifting from the plaza.

The music gets louder—or maybe I'm just paying attention to it now—something slow and romantic, the notes floating through the warm evening air like they're made of honey.

"Do you hear that?" I ask.

"The music?"

"Yeah." I glance toward the archway, where I can see the edge of Plaça Reial—the twinkling lights of those gorgeous Gaudí lampposts, the fountain lit from below, people moving in the glow. And couples. Dancing couples, swaying to the music.

I watch them for a moment. An elderly couple moving in perfect synchronization, a younger couple laughing and stumbling, a middle-aged pair holding each other close. And something in my chest aches.

I want that.

I want to dance with Brody under those twinkling lights and

pretend for just a little longer that this is real, that tomorrow isn't coming, that this isn't going to end.

But I can't ask. That's too much. Too forward. Too—

"Want to dance?"

I turn back to him, startled. "What?"

"Dance." He's smiling, but there's something nervous in his expression, like he's not sure what I'll say. "With me. Out there."

My brain short-circuits for a second. "You want to dance? With me?"

"That's generally how dancing works."

"Oh . . . no, I'm terrible at dancing. Like, catastrophically bad. I once stepped on my prom date's foot so hard he had to go to urgent care."

I'm still babbling about broken toes and lifelong limps when Brody stands, pulling out his wallet to pay the check. He tosses some cash on the table and turns back to me. "I'll risk it."

I take his offered hand and stand, my legs slightly wobbly. The wine, probably. Or the handholding. Or the way he's looking at me like I'm the only person in the entire city. Brody—mysterious, guarded, ridiculously attractive Brody, with his storm-cloud eyes and the way his T-shirt stretches across his shoulders when he moves—wants to dance with me.

In Barcelona.

Under twinkling lights.

Best coma ever.

He leads me through the archway, into Plaça Reial, and my breath catches. It's even more beautiful than it looked from the restaurant. The fountain in the center sparkles, water catching the light and sending tiny rainbows dancing across the cobblestones. And those lampposts—those gorgeous, ornate Gaudí lampposts with their twisted iron and multiple glowing lanterns—cast everything in warm, golden light that looks like captured fireflies.

A street musician is sitting near the fountain, his guitar resting on his knee, fingers moving over the strings with the ease of someone who's played for years. He's older, weathered, his shirt wrinkled and sleeves rolled up, and his case is open at his feet with a few coins and bills inside. He's got his eyes closed like he's lost in the music, and the notes he's playing are so beautiful they make my throat tight.

There are maybe a dozen couples dancing, and Brody pulls me into the fray, wrapping an arm around my waist as he takes my other hand in his warm, steady palm. I feel completely safe. Like even though we've only known each other a few hours, there's something starting here today. Like this is the first dance of many. And I want to melt into it, memorize it.

We start to move.

And for .2 seconds, I manage not to hurt anybody, and then—

"Sorry!" I gasp.

"*Oof,* you weren't kidding."

"I warned you!"

"I thought you were exaggerating."

"I never exaggerate about my complete lack of coordination."

He's laughing now, and so am I, and we're still moving even though I'm pretty sure we're not exactly dancing so much as shuffling in a vague circle while I assault his feet.

But then, somehow, we find a rhythm. His hand tightens slightly on my waist, steadying me. My hand on his shoulder relaxes. We stop thinking about it and just . . . move.

The music swells, something slow and romantic, and suddenly we're not stumbling anymore. We're dancing. Actually dancing.

The candlelight from the nearby café tables flickers across his features, catching on the sharp line of his jaw, the curve of his mouth, those eyes that are suddenly looking at me like I'm something worth looking at.

He pulls me closer, leaning in until his breath grazes my ear.

"See?" he says softly. "Not catastrophic."

"Yet. The night is young."

"Ever the optimist."

"It's one of my many charms."

He pulls back, laughing again, and his smile fades slightly. His eyes drop to my mouth for just a second before coming back to my eyes. My stomach does that swooping thing again, and I'm suddenly very aware of how close we are, how his hand is splayed across my waist, how I can smell whatever soap or cologne he uses—something clean and slightly woodsy. I can feel the warmth of him through our clothes, can feel his heartbeat against my palm where my hand rests on his chest.

Or maybe that's mine. It's hard to tell when they're both racing.

"Chloe," he says, and his voice has this rough edge to it that I haven't heard before.

"Yeah?"

He doesn't answer. Just looks at me for a long moment, like he's trying to decide something.

And then he glances around—at the couples dancing, at the people sitting at café tables, at the general publicness of where we are—and makes a decision.

He takes my hand and leads me away from the dancing area, toward a quieter corner of the plaza, where string lights drape between orange trees. We pause beneath the branches, the trees creating the illusion of privacy, just far enough from the crowd that the music feels like a distant dream.

Brody's still holding my hand, and he's looking at me with this intensity that makes my knees weak.

"I've been wanting to do this all evening," he says, his voice low. "Can I—"

"Yes," I say before he can finish, because I know what he's asking, and the answer is absolutely, definitely, *yes*.

And then he kisses me.

And—

Oh.

Oh, this is what all those romance novels were talking about.

His mouth is warm and soft and sure, and his hand comes up to cup my face, his thumb brushing my cheek, and I make this embarrassing sound—half sigh, half something else—because this is *happening*, this is real, Brody is kissing me and it's perfect and overwhelming and—

He pulls back suddenly, his eyes wide.

"Sorry," he says, breathing hard. "I shouldn't have—I didn't mean to—"

"I'm not sorry."

He blinks. "What?"

"I'm not sorry." And before I can talk myself out of it, before my brain can catch up with what my heart is doing, I grab the front of his T-shirt, the fabric soft and warm under my fingers, and kiss him back.

And this time, when he makes a sound, it's not an apology.

His arms go around me, pulling me closer, one hand sliding into my hair, the other pressed against the small of my back. I can taste wine on his lips, and his stubble is rough against my skin in the best way, and—

He pulls back again, but this time he doesn't apologize. He just looks at me, his forehead resting against mine, both of us breathing hard. His hand is still in my hair, fingers tangled in the strands.

"I have to tell you something," he says, his voice rough. He lifts his head off mine and the cold rushes in.

"Okay."

"I—"

But then he goes still. His whole body just . . . stops. He's looking over my shoulder at something, and his expression changes—from open and vulnerable to closed and tense in the space of a heartbeat.

His hand falls away from my hair. The arm around my waist loosens.

"What—" I start, but he's already stepping back.

"I'll walk you to your hotel," he says, and his voice is different. Distant. Polite.

"What? Why? Did I—is something wrong?"

"No, it's just—" He's not looking at me anymore. He's looking at whatever he saw, and his jaw is tight, a muscle jumping there. "It's late. You should get back."

"Brody—"

"Come on." He takes my hand—but it's different now, perfunctory instead of intimate—and starts walking.

And just like that, the evening is over.

We leave the plaza, stepping into one of the narrow streets that branch off into the Gothic Quarter. The street is darker here, lit only by occasional streetlamps that cast pools of yellow light with long shadows between them. The buildings press close on either side, their balconies overhead creating a tunnel effect. Laundry still hangs from some windows, ghostly white in the darkness.

The air is cooler, almost cold now, away from the plaza—the stone walls holding on to the chill. It smells like old stone and dampness and faint cigarette smoke from somewhere nearby.

Our footsteps echo on the uneven cobblestones—my sandals making soft scuffing sounds, his sneakers a dull thud. The rhythm is wrong, out of sync.

And it's silent.

Painfully, awkwardly silent.

I don't know what happened. One second we were kissing and everything was perfect, and the next, he saw something and shut down completely.

"Brody," I try again, my voice small in the quiet street. "What just happened back there?"

"Nothing. It's fine."

"It's clearly not fine. You just—you went from kissing me to looking like you'd seen a ghost."

"I'm just tired. It's been a long day."

Tired. Right. Yes. Me too . . . No, I'm not. I'm so unbelievably awake, there's no way he's tired.

"If I did something—"

"You didn't do anything." His voice is still polite, still distant. Like we're strangers. Like we didn't just spend the entire evening together. Like he didn't just kiss me like I mattered. "I just think we should call it a night."

We keep walking. Past a couple speaking softly in French, holding hands, looking at each other the way Brody was looking at me five minutes ago. Past a group of loud British tourists heading to the bars, their laughter echoing off the stone walls. Past a cat sitting on a doorstep, watching us with unblinking yellow eyes.

Every step feels wrong. Like I'm walking toward an ending I don't want, and I can't figure out how to stop it.

My sunflower bobs sadly from my purse, the bloom drooping now, petals soft and curling inward.

"For what it's worth," I say, trying to keep my voice light even though my throat feels tight, "I had a really good evening."

"Yeah. Me too."

But he doesn't sound like he means it.

We turn a corner, and suddenly we're at my hotel—a small boutique place with a weathered yellow facade and wrought-iron balconies. I'd called earlier to extend my stay for another night, told the receptionist I'd missed my cruise. (Left out the part about wandering the city with a stranger who makes my heart do stupid things.)

There's a small plaza in front of the hotel—more like a widening of the street, really—with a tree in the center casting shadows across the cobblestones. The air here smells like the potted geraniums on someone's balcony, mixing with the musty scent of old stone.

We stop under the tree, and Brody finally looks at me.

Really looks at me.

And there's something in his eyes—conflict, longing, pain—that makes my chest ache.

"Do you want to come up?" I ask, even though I know the answer. "I mean—not like that—just to talk or—"

"I can't."

"Okay." I'm trying not to cry. I'm trying *so hard* not to cry. "Can I at least get your number? Your last name? Some way to . . ."

My words drift off at the look on his face. Anguished—that's the only way to describe it.

"I know this is a bad idea," he says, and his voice is rough again, raw.

"What is?"

And instead of answering, he steps closer and kisses me.

One more time.

This kiss is different from the others—desperate, almost frantic, like he's trying to memorize the feel of my mouth against his. His hand cups my face, and I can feel him shaking slightly, and I'm kissing him back just as desperately because I know—I *know*—this is goodbye.

When he pulls away, his forehead rests against mine for just a second. I can feel his breath on my lips, warm in the cool night air.

"Take care of yourself, Chloe," he whispers.

And then he's gone.

Just—gone.

And I'm standing on a cobblestone street in Barcelona with a wilting sunflower in my purse and absolutely no answers.

Story of my life, honestly. I knew it was too good to be true.

BRODY

Present Day

SIX MONTHS AGO, I WAS A TOP-FIVE DEFEN-
seman in the league. Now I'm getting burned by rookies who
probably spend more time scrolling TikTok than on the ice.

Six months ago, I met Chloe Dawson in Barcelona.

Six months ago, I left her standing under the twinkling lights
without an explanation.

And here's what I know about regret: It's the one thing you can't
block, can't check into the boards, can't shake off, no matter how
many laps you skate. It follows you. Stays with you. Whispers in
your ear during the third period when you're already exhausted
and the game's slipping away.

You left her standing there.

You ran.

Coward.

The practice facility is smaller than our usual digs, more utilitarian—one rink, wooden stands that seat maybe a few hundred, Blue Ox banners hanging from the rafters.

We're here because they're updating our main arena. Renovations, new sound system, upgraded locker rooms—all the things that make the front office feel like they're investing in the future. It's better than driving up to Maple Lake, where the minor league plays, and there's something almost nostalgic about it. This is the kind of rink where we all started—before the NHL contracts and endorsement deals, when hockey was still just a game.

The Zamboni just finished its rounds, and the ice is perfect. Freshly layered, smooth as glass, reflecting the industrial lights overhead. Smells like rubber and exhaust and that crisp scent of possibility.

Used to be, practice felt like home.

Now it feels like an audition I'm failing in slow motion.

The ice burns my lungs with every breath, but that's not what's killing me. It's the silence. The space my teammates leave around me in drills—like I'm contagious, like whatever's rotting inside me might spread.

Some might call it a slump.

Coach Jacobsen, Blue Ox's head coach, blows his whistle—sharp, cutting through the sound of skates and pucks and the low hum of conversation. "Two on one! Blake, Munson—you're up. Kane, you're defending."

Of course I am.

Justin "Blade" Blake is twenty-two and built like he runs on Red Bull and pure confidence. Kid's got speed I remember having once—before I started to overthink my every move. His blond hair is too long, sticking out from under his helmet, and he's grinning like this is the best part of his day.

Derek Munson glides up beside him—six feet of lean muscle and overpriced hair product. Even in practice gear, he looks camera-ready. Helmet gleaming, brand-new gloves (who gets new gloves mid-season?), custom skates that probably cost more than my first car—maybe even more than my current car. He skids to a stop, ice spraying across my skates, and smirks.

"Try to keep up, old man."

I'm twenty-eight.

But in hockey years? I might as well be collecting social security.

They take off. Blake has the puck, Derek skating stride for stride with him, their movements synchronized like they've been running this play for years instead of weeks. I backpedal, trying to read their eyes, their shoulders, the angle of Blake's stick.

My game is off—weight distribution wrong, stick position too high—and I know it even as I'm setting up. My legs feel heavy, reaction time lagging like I'm moving through water.

Blake fakes left.

I bite.

Stupid!

Blake cuts right with that cocky rookie speed, and my skates tangle like I'm back in Peewees, learning to stop. He's past me before I can recover, puck sliding clean toward Wyatt Marshall in goal.

Wyatt—thirty-one, father of one, goalie with reflexes like a cat and a wife who could hack the Pentagon before breakfast—makes the save. Barely. The puck catches his glove, and he cradles it, then looks at me over his mask.

His brown eyes are concerned. Worried.

Yeah, yeah. I know. I'm a mess.

The coach's whistle shrieks across the rink, echoing off the boards and wooden stands.

That's the third time this practice.

Good.

Great.

Fantastic.

I skate to the boards, grip my stick too tight. The tape on my blade is starting to fray—I should've retaped last night, but I was too busy staring at my ceiling and not sleeping—and my knuckles go white against the shaft.

Around me, the rest of the team keeps moving.

Tyler "Torch" Anderson—stocky, redheaded, freckled, the kind of guy who'd give you the shirt off his back and then give you a hard time about looking better in it than he did—is running drills with Kalen Boomer. They're laughing about something. Probably me.

Derek glides past backward. "Nice one, Candy. Maybe try smiling at the puck next time. Might slow it down."

I wrench my jaw shut. Because if I open my mouth right now, I might say something that ends up on SportsCenter, and Rick will have my head.

"What's wrong?" Derek adds, loud enough for everyone in a ten-foot radius to hear. "Losing your sweetness?"

Someone snickers. I don't look to see who.

Tyler skates closer, bumping Derek with his shoulder as he passes. "Ignore him, man. It's not worth it."

Easy for him to say. He hasn't spent the last six months as the team joke.

Coach skates over. Doesn't yell—never does. He played enforcer for fifteen years, still built like a tank. Despite his salt-and-pepper hair and a nose that's been broken so many times it sits crooked on his face, the man knows how to make silence hurt more than shouting ever could. He stops in front of me, arms crossed over his Blue Ox windbreaker, studying me like I'm a play he can't figure out.

"Kane." He jerks his head toward the bench. "A word."

Here we go.

I follow him off the ice, skates heavy on the rubber mats. The fluorescent lights above are too bright, bouncing off every surface—ice, boards, glass—making my head pound.

Coach leans against the boards. Doesn't sit, just waits until I'm looking at him.

"Your head's not in the game."

It's not a question.

"I'm fine, Coach." The words come out automatic. Smooth. The same tone I use with reporters when they ask about contract negotiations or trade rumors. *I'm just focused on the team. Taking it one game at a time. You know how it is.*

"Save the media training for the press conference." His voice is flat. "I need my top defenseman sharp. Focused. Whatever's going on off the ice, figure it out. Or you're riding the bench next game."

My jaw tightens. I can't afford to be watching from the sidelines while Blake and Derek and every other hungry kid on the roster prove they can do my job better than I can. Can't afford for the front office to start asking questions about my contract renewal.

As far as what's going on off the ice . . . If I knew how to shake it off, I would have done it months ago. But I can't tell him that.

"Yes, sir. Won't happen again."

"See that it doesn't." He pauses, and something almost like sympathy crosses his face. The same look he gave Conrad Kingston a year ago when Con was spiraling. "You're better than this, Kane."

My pulse thickens. I used to be.

Coach steps back onto the ice. "Pull it together." Skates away, leaving me behind. Just me, the bench, and those words that sound an awful lot like my next headline.

Used to be.

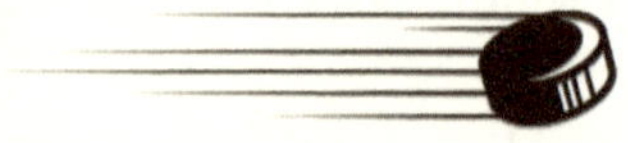

My gear hits the floor of my stall with more force than necessary as I peel each piece away. Helmet, gloves, shoulder pads, elbow pads, shin guards. My jersey is soaked through—dark blue with white trim, number seven on the back, KANE spelled out in block letters that feel like they're getting heavier every game.

Around me, the team is in various states of undress and chaos.

Steam from the showers turns everything humid and soggy, and someone is playing one of those trendy pop-music songs, just loud enough to be annoying.

Tyler's arguing with Kalen about one of the practice plays.

Wyatt's sitting on the bench, unlacing his skates. His goalie pads are stacked neatly beside him—white, barely scuffed, because his glove side is legendary. Mine look like they've been through a war.

Derek's holding court near the showers, talking about wedding plans. "Maya's going crazy over Valentine's Day details. Florist, photographer, cake tasting—it's nonstop. But she's happy, so . . ." He shrugs like he's doing everyone a favor by getting married.

Someone mutters, "Valentine's wedding? Bold choice, man."

Derek grins. "What my baby wants, my baby gets."

My stall is in the corner. Away from the main cluster. Used to be a choice—I liked the space, the quiet, the ability to get in and out without getting pulled into every conversation. Now it just feels like isolation.

The nameplate above my stall gleams under the fluorescent lights: *KANE #7.*

And below it, engraved in smaller letters, is *"CANDY."*

I learned a long time ago to brush it off. Ignore the grating in my mind every time I hear the name. I didn't hate it so much at first. The first time I heard the nickname plastered on some sports headline—*Brody "Candy" Kane, Sweet-Talking His Way Through Post-Game Interviews and Melting Hearts Across the Twin Cities*— it was funny. But then the name stuck, worked its way into the locker room and onto the ice.

Now, the nickname feels like a game I'm playing. And given my most recent tabloid splash, I'm losing.

Tyler comes over, hands up like he's approaching a wounded animal. He's already out of most of his gear, wearing compression shorts and a Blue Ox hoodie, his red hair sticking up in seventeen directions. "Hey, man. That drill was rough, but we all have off days."

I don't look up. Just keep unlacing my skates. "I'm fine."

"You sure?" He sits on the bench across from me, not quite close enough to be in my space, but close enough to be annoying. Torch has this thing where he thinks if he just keeps showing up, keeps trying, eventually people will let him in. It's worked for him his whole career—he's the glue guy, the one everyone likes. "We could grab food after this. Decompress. Talk—"

"I said I'm fine, Torch."

The temperature in my voice drops about forty degrees, and Tyler rocks back, brows lifted.

"All right." He stands, shoves his hands in his hoodie pocket. "I'm just trying to help. The Candy I know would have snapped back by now, given me a hard time already about"—he shrugs—"I don't know, my hair looking like I stuck my finger in an outlet or something. This isn't you."

"Well, maybe you don't know me as well as you think."

The words come out colder than I intended. Tyler's face hardens, and he walks away without another word.

Great.

Add him to the list of bridges I'm burning.

Someone clears their throat behind me. I cast a glance over my shoulder. Conrad Kingston leans against the doorframe, arms crossed. Con's been in the league longer than most of us have been alive—or at least, it feels that way. Six foot, broad shoulders, dark blond-reddish hair and beard.

His fiancée is Penelope Pepper—better known as Penny, the murder podcaster, which means nothing goes under the radar with her around. Which also means Con definitely knows about the tabloid situation.

Great.

"Listen, Kane." His voice is calm. Measured. "This thing'll blow over. Until then, you gotta keep your head down and in the game."

I want to tell him to mind his own business. Deflect. Anything to get him—and everyone else—off my back. Instead, I do exactly what he says. I keep my head down and nod.

Con waits a beat as though expecting something more, then walks away.

I head for the showers before anyone else decides to weigh in on my performance today.

The water is scalding. Steam fills the space, turning everything hazy. I press my forehead against the tile, close my eyes, and try to drown out the headlines in my head.

Brody "Candy" Kane's Sweet Talk Hides Cold Heart, Says Victim
Is This the Real Candy Kane? Woman Exposes Dark Side of Hockey Charmer

My mind flashes again to Chloe, standing alone on the steps of her hotel, hurt etched in the lines of her face. Maybe the headlines are right.

By the time I emerge, most of the guys have cleared out, and I almost let out a sigh of relief as I pull on my dark jeans, a gray sweater, and leather boots. I look like I'm headed to a photoshoot instead of a parking lot confrontation.

Image. Always image. At this point, it's probably the only thing that can save me.

I grab my keys and head for the door, walking through the narrow hallway back toward daylight.

Time to face the next disaster.

The parking lot is brutal. Blistering cold that hurts your face, gray, hopeless sky, snow piled in dirty mountains along the edges of the lot, wind that cuts through every layer.

And my car is parked—you guessed it—in the back. The black Ford Mustang Shelby GT500 gleams darkly against the ashy sky. Nothing fancy, but fast when I need it to be.

I'm almost there when someone steps into my path.

Rick Castellano. My agent.

Fortysomething, always in a suit that costs more than most people's mortgage payment, carrying his iPad like it's the tablet Moses brought down from Sinai. Today's sartorial selection is charcoal gray, perfectly tailored, and he's wearing Italian leather shoes that have no business being in a Minnesota parking lot in January. He's not even wearing a coat.

"We need to talk. Now."

I don't slow down. "Not in the mood, Rick."

He falls into step beside me. "I don't care. Look at this."

He shoves the iPad in my face, and I stop walking, because I don't have a choice.

The screen is filled with headlines:

Is Candy Kane's Charm Just an Act?

Hockey's Nice-Guy Image Shattered: Kane Faces Heartbreaker Allegations

Below the headlines are more photos, boosted, probably from Ashley's Instagram account. I shrug. "It'll blow over." I hope.

"It might, if it weren't for these." He scrolls down the page and shows me more photos. Blurry, zoomed-in, clearly taken from someone's social media and enhanced until they're almost unrecognizable—but unmistakably me. And unmistakably *her*.

Chloe.

Six months ago. In Barcelona.

My chest tightens. "I thought that was taken care of." Meaning Rick contacted the photographer, got an NDA, and the photos were taken down.

"Yeah, well, regardless how they got them, it's not a good look, Brody. And now this Ashley girl is threatening legal action for emotional distress—"

"I barely talked to her!" I can feel my blood pressure rising. "We met at a gala. She said she was a professional sports blogger. I was being polite."

"She said you were flirting. That you gave her your number—"

"Because she was going to send me her blog for approval." I reach my car, set my duffel in the trunk. "She's the one who's been stalking *me*—"

"I know." Rick holds up his hand. "Listen. There's no doubt her legal case is weak—"

"Weak? I didn't do anything!" And now there's no candy left in my voice, and he looks around, just in case people are watching.

Let them. I'm so done playing the part while this girl tries to ruin my life over a smile.

Rick waits a beat, his eyes asking *Are you finished?* "It doesn't matter, Brody. True or not—and you know I believe you—the team called. They want answers. Your performance is slipping, the press is having a field day, and management is losing patience."

He looks behind me and lifts a hand. I turn. Oh goody, there's a small crowd gathering near the fence. Fans. A family—two adults, three kids—wearing Blue Ox gear, all holding their phones.

"Candy! Hey, Candy Kane!"

"Can we get a picture?"

"Sign my jersey!"

I stare at Rick. "This. This is my life."

"No, Candy. *This* is your life." He holds up his phone and keeps scrolling, showing me comment after comment. *Fake. Player. User. Just another athlete who thinks charm is a substitute for character.*

"It's tabloid garbage." My voice sounds distant even to me. "It'll blow over."

"It won't." He stops on an article from ESPN. A think piece about performative masculinity in professional sports. My face is the thumbnail. "Your charm offensive worked for years—the smile, the perfect quotes, the fan engagement. But now they're digging deeper. They're calling you fake, Brody. A performer. Someone who uses people for image management."

I want to argue, but the words stick in my throat. "What do you want me to do?"

Rick stops scrolling. Looks at me like I'm particularly slow. "You need damage control. A girlfriend—real or fake, I don't care—to prove you're not just a charming smile with nothing behind it. Someone stable. Genuine. Makes you look human."

I laugh. It comes out bitter, sharp. "You want me to *hire* someone to prove I'm real? You see the irony, right?"

"I see a client who's about to lose his contract renewal because his head isn't in the game and his reputation is in the swirl." His voice goes flat. Hard. The kind of tone that means he's done negotiating. "You have until Valentine's Day. That gives you five weeks. Find someone, make it convincing, get through the season with good press. The charm's not gonna do it for you this time."

Something in my chest cracks.

The fans are still calling. "Candy! Please! Just one picture!"

"And if I don't?" My voice is barely above a whisper.

Rick just looks at me.

"Never mind," I say.

"Good." He turns and walks to his Mercedes. Black, sleek, idling near the exit like a getaway car. He pulls away without looking back.

And I'm left standing in the parking lot with the wind cutting through my jacket and voices calling my name like a Greek chorus of disappointment.

I don't wave. Don't smile. Don't turn around.

Just get in my car and drive.

I drop my gym bag by the door, hockey tape and sweaty base

layers and the smell of the rink gear spilling out across the hardwood of my South Minneapolis penthouse. It's the only mess I allow. The only proof that I live here.

The rest of the apartment looks like a hotel room. You know, magazine-worthy.

Kitchen: spotless. Granite counters gleaming. No dishes in the sink because I haven't cooked a meal in this place since I purchased it two years ago. The fridge hums quietly, filled with takeout containers I'll probably throw away without eating and a six-pack of beer I never drink.

There's a stack of unopened mail on the counter—bills, probably, mixed with promotional stuff from sponsors who think I'll endorse their protein shakes or razors or whatever.

Living room: black leather couch—expensive, uncomfortable, barely sat on—facing a massive TV mounted on the wall. I use it for game tape. That's it. No streaming services, no movie nights, no friends over for playoff games.

No friends.

I trudge through the apartment, every muscle aching, and sink onto the sofa.

My phone buzzes. Multiple missed calls. All from the same number.

Dad.

I should ignore it. Delete the voicemails without listening. Cut him off like I've threatened to do a hundred times.

Instead, I sit on my couch—leather creaking under me, cold even through my jeans—and press Play on my voicemail.

His voice fills the apartment. Slurred but warm. Friendly, even. The version of my father that shows up when he's three drinks in and feeling nostalgic.

Please let him not be in a casino.

"Hey, buddy. It's Dad." A pause. Ice clinking in a glass. "I know you're probably busy. Big game coming up, right? You're doing great, son. Really great. Your mother would be so proud."

My throat tightens.

"Listen, I need a favor. Small thing. There's this . . . situation. Gambling thing. You know how it is." He laughs, like we're sharing a joke. Like calling your kids to bail you out is totally normal. *Come on over, son. We'll play some catch, you can watch me get banned again from another casino. It'll be good times.* "I got in a little over my head. These guys, they're not messing around. I need maybe ten grand. Fifteen, tops. Just to smooth things over."

I close my eyes. Shoot. Ten grand. Fifteen. *Tops.*

Last month it was eight. The month before, five.

And of course, the fifty large ones from Barcelona. He wasn't too happy with my little detour. But I managed to bail him out, kneecaps intact. In fact, by the time I arrived, he'd managed to wheedle a loan out of the house and was back on a winning streak.

At least one of us was. It lasted all of an hour.

So I guess the fifty grand came in handy after all.

"You know, you got your charm from me. Your mother used to say you could talk your way out of anything. Just like your old man." His voice gets softer. Almost tender. The tone he used when I was a kid and he'd tuck me in at night, back when he was still Dad and not just a collection of problems I can't fix. "Before I . . . well. Before I messed everything up."

There's a long pause. More ice clinking. The sound of him taking a drink.

"I love you, Brody. You're a good kid. Always have been. Just . . . call me back, okay? Please. I'm counting on you."

The message ends.

I sit there in the silence, staring at the gray sky outside my windows.

You got your charm from me.

Just like your old man.

Yeah, the kind of charm that gets you called "Candy" until you forget your own name.

I delete the voicemail.

The silence in my apartment is suffocating. The gray January sky presses against the windows. My phone sits on the coffee table, screen dark, offering no answers.

I need something. Anything. A distraction. A solution. A way out of this mess that doesn't involve becoming my father.

My laptop is sitting on the coffee table. I flip it open without really thinking about it.

Instagram loads.

I shouldn't look. I know I shouldn't look.

I look anyway.

I don't even have to type it into the search bar. It pulls up in my history as if to say *Ah, back to this again.*

@everaftereventsco

I scroll through the usual posts—beautiful event setups, color palettes, behind-the-scenes shots of her work. She's good. Really good. I can't help but wonder why she's not booking every event in the Twin Cities instead of her small town of Maple Lake.

Then I see it.

Posted twenty minutes ago.

It's *her.* Sitting at a table, giant chocolate chip cookie in a skillet in front of her, whipped cream melting over the top. Her sketchbook is open beside her, and she's smiling. Not for the camera, just . . . content. Happy.

The caption:

Sometimes you need to find peace in the storm 🌧️ ☕

The location tag: Ironclad Desserts

I stare at the photo.

Twenty minutes ago.

She could be there. Right now.

My stomach growls. I haven't eaten since this morning, and that giant cookie looks like exactly what I need . . .

And, oh hey, she'd be there too.

Before I can talk myself out of it, I'm grabbing my keys. Pulling on my jacket. Heading for the door.

My brain is screaming at me that this is a terrible idea. That I should let her have her peace. That showing up is creepy and desperate and exactly the kind of thing a guy who's losing his grip would do.

But my feet are already moving.

Because giant cookies might not be the answer to all my problems, but maybe—just maybe—it's the cure for six months of regret.

CHLOE

Don't look at the Instagram post. Don't look at the likes. Don't refresh to see if anyone cared.

I'm doing it anyway. Obviously.

Three likes. One from Jessa (obligatory best-friend support), one from my cousin, who likes everything I post without actually reading it, and one from a bot account selling teeth whitening.

Cool. Great. I flip my phone face down on the table and stare at what's left of my chocolate chip cookie skillet. The whipped cream has fully melted now, pooling around the edges in a way that looks sad and almost metaphorical.

The twinkle lights at Ironclad cast everything in the kind of soft glow that reminds me of Hallmark coffee shops and old bookstores—the kinds of places that usually manage to romanticize the chaos of my life. She's not late for a meeting and forgot to brush her hair, she's fabulously busy and windswept. She's not stuck on a proposal, she's just letting the creative juices flow over a warm cup of coffee . . . and a pile of crumb-covered napkins. This is just the glamorous life of an event planner. She's not avoiding her life and eating her feelings in a cookie dessert shop, she's . . . um . . . Okay, that's exactly what I'm doing.

But it's fine! Everything's fine! I've got my sketchbook open to the seating arrangement (which we only need in order to avoid the very real possibility of Great-Aunt Muriel winding up in fisticuffs with Uncle Stew in front of the ice sculpture—two hockey sticks crossed over a heart, gag me) for the wedding. And I'm trying to find a unique napkin-fold design, which of course led me to Pinterest, which led to Instagram, and suddenly I'm doomscrolling past everyone else who's actually got their life together and not just pretending. And now I've got something to prove, so I'm posting photos of my Obsidian Luxe Chip cookie.

See, look! I'm a successful, spontaneous girlboss who's soaking up life to the fullest. Not a broke loser whose mom is so desperate to fix me that she tried to set me up with the waiter from Olive Garden.

It's fine.

I'm fine.

My phone buzzes. Text from Maya.

Maya

Mom mentioned you're bringing a date to the meet and greet. Who is he? Do I know him?

I make a small noise that's somewhere between a laugh and a whimper. An older man with a laptop looks up briefly.

Look away. Trust me on this.

Before I can formulate a response that doesn't sound completely pathetic, my phone rings.

Jessa. Thank You, God.

I pop in my earbuds and answer. "Hey! How's your day going? Is it great? Because mine's great too! Super great!"

"That bad?" Jessa says without preamble.

"Define *bad*."

"On a scale from minor inconvenience to hiding in a coffee shop eating your feelings, where are we?"

I look at my decimated cookie skillet. "I don't know what you're talking about. Cookies are brain food. I'm hard at work on Maya's wedding designs!"

"Chloe."

"Jessa."

"What happened at dinner?"

And there it is. The question I've been trying not to think about for the past hour while I stress-sketch and stress-eat and stress-post to Instagram like a well-adjusted person.

"Nothing! It was fine! Maya loved my napkin-fold design!" My voice is doing that thing where it's too bright, too enthusiastic, like I'm a children's TV host discussing something deeply upsetting. "She thought it was super cute!"

"That's . . . good?"

"And then she asked if I could 'maybe consult with someone more established' to make sure it's sophisticated enough for her venue." I'm smiling while I say this, even though Jessa can't see me. "You know. Someone who's done this before. Someone professional."

The word *professional* sticks in my throat a little.

"She didn't."

"Oh, she absolutely did! In front of everyone." My parents. Derek and his parents. Even the waiter. I take another stab at my cookie, shoveling a spoonful of crumbs into my mouth. "It's fine! It's totally fine! She's the bride. She gets to want what she wants. I'm just here to help make her day special."

Jessa is quiet, but I think I can almost hear her eyes rolling. "So what did you do?"

I look down at my napkin. At the swan fold I'd originally designed. "Oh, I invented a client emergency to escape, which everyone knew was a lie because I have exactly three clients, Jess. Three. In six months—all from Maple Lake. Which I'm starting to get a sneaking suspicion my mom had something to do with." I flatten the napkin again. "And then I came here and got a cookie, so I'd call that a win."

"Stop."

"Stop what?"

"The thing you do where you make everything sound cheerful so people won't worry about you."

I open my mouth to deny it, then close it. "I don't do that."

"You absolutely do that. You've been doing it since college." Jessa's voice goes gentler. "How are you really? The truth."

The truth.

The truth is I have five days to pay rent, and about sixteen dollars left in my bank account after paying for my twelve-dollar cookie. My student loans are in collections because I haven't been able to make payments in three months, and I'm living off dog-sitting money and the occasional dog-walking gig, which pays approximately enough to keep me in instant ramen and creative bankruptcy.

The truth is, I'm terrified I'm going to have to give up and ask my family for money, which means admitting I failed at the one thing I was supposed to be good at.

But I can't say any of that, because Jessa already worries, and she's got her life together—steady job working for an online magazine, benefits, a 401(k)—and I can't be the friend who's always drowning.

"I'm okay," I say, aiming for somewhere between honest and not completely alarming. "I'm just . . . adjusting to the entrepreneurial lifestyle! You know how it is! Ups and downs!"

"Chloe, I love you, but you're a terrible liar." She pauses. "Listen, I know you're a little behind on groceries money this month. I've seen the fridge. Have you been eating regularly? Real food, not just Ironclad cookies?"

Oh. That kind of question.

"Define 'regularly,'" I hedge.

"That's not an answer."

"I had cereal yesterday! And a banana!" Both true. The cereal was the last of the box and the banana was extremely brown, but still. "I'm fine."

"You're a professional event planner living off dog-walking money."

"It's called a diversified income stream," I say with as much dignity as I can muster.

"You could ask your family—"

"No." The word comes out sharp. Too sharp. I try to soften it. "I mean—that's really sweet of you to suggest. But I can't. They're already helping so much! Maya hired me for her wedding! At a discount! That's incredibly generous!"

"She hired you for a discount and then criticized your work in front of everyone."

"She's paying me to do a job, and she wants it done right. That's reasonable! That's normal!" I'm smiling again, even though she can't see me. My face hurts. "Besides, if I ask for money, it's just . . . My dad already introduces me as 'our daughter who's trying the event planning thing.' *Trying.* Like it's a phase. Like I'm not drowning in debt trying to make this work."

There's a long silence on Jessa's end.

"What?" I say.

"Nothing. Just . . . you matter, Chloe. Your work matters. Maya's opinion doesn't define your worth."

Something in my chest cracks a little at that. "Yeah, well. Tell that to the four clients who rejected me this week."

"Four?"

"Technically, three rejections and one ghosting, but I'm counting it." I shake out the napkin again. "I got another email right before the dinner from hell. The couple I was really excited about? The New Year's Eve wedding?"

I don't have to pull up the email to remember the headline. I've heard enough of them to commit to memory. "'Thank you, but we've decided to go in a different direction.' Which is corporate speak for 'You're not good enough.'"

"That's not—"

"It's okay." Too bright again. Too cheerful. "Rejection is just redirection! That's what all the Instagram motivational quotes say. Every no gets me closer to a yes! Growth mindset!"

"You don't believe that."

"I'm trying to!" My voice cracks slightly. "I'm really trying, Jess."

The young couple in the corner booth is laughing about something, feeding each other bites of whatever dessert they're sharing. They look so happy.

And suddenly I'm thinking about him. The Man I Will Not Mention.

Yeah, that guy. From Barcelona. The one who—

Nope. He doesn't deserve space in my brain.

Oh, who am I kidding? I could draw him in detail on my sketchpad. Again.

"You're still thinking about him," Jessa says, because she can read my mind.

"No."

"Chloe."

"Fine. Yes. Sometimes." I look over at my sketchbook, my fingers tracing the sketch of the Barcelona café. The outdoor tables under twinkling lights. The warm glow of votives. What can I say? It makes for a good seating plan. "I'm pathetic. It's been six months, and I'm still trying to figure out what I did wrong."

Jess pauses. "You didn't do anything wrong," she says gently.

I'm quiet for a moment, staring at the Barcelona sketch. At the memory of twinkling lights and genuine smiles and dancing like nobody was watching.

An idea hits me.

"What if . . ." I say slowly, shaking out the napkin. I start to fold it into something that looks like gathered petals, something blooming. Beautiful and elegant . . . like Barcelona.

"I think I figured out the napkin design."

"Of course you did. Babe, I gotta go. See you at home?"

"Sure thing."

Jess hangs up, and I smile, looking at my design. This is good. I pull out my phone and snap a picture. I catch the time in the corner of the screen. Almost nine. The January darkness is deep outside, the twinkle lights reflecting in the window.

I slide from the booth and pack up my things—sketchbook, laptop, fabric swatches that are now covered in eraser shavings, colored pencils that are mostly broken. I leave cash on the table and grab my coat, juggling everything while trying to check my phone one more time. Maya's text glares at me as I walk toward the door.

Maybe I just ignore it, pretend I didn't see it . . .

I'm so focused on my screen that I don't see the door opening.

Don't see the person walking in.

Don't notice anything until I'm walking straight into someone and suddenly there are hands on my elbows, steadying me, and my phone is flying and my sketchbook is hitting the floor and I'm making an undignified squeaking sound—

"I'm so sorry, I wasn't—"

"No, that was my fault, I—"

We're both talking at once, both reaching for my scattered things, and I look up—

And everything stops.

It's *him.*

Barcelona Brody.

He's staring at me with the same expression I probably have on my face. Recognition. Shock. And then that . . . that smile. That devastating smile that made my brains leak out of my head six months ago.

What? No—

I make a sound. Not quite a word. Not quite a breath. Something between a gasp and a wheeze.

And of course, those eyes are just like I remembered, deep and stormy.

And all I can think is . . . run.

So I do.

BRODY

I PROBABLY SHOULD HAVE LISTENED TO THE voice in my head telling me this was a bad idea. Because if there's anything that says "I want nothing to do with you, dirtbag," it's having the girl of your dreams literally flee at the sight of you.

"Chloe!"

It's too late. She's already out the door. The wind sweeps through the restaurant as she vanishes into the street.

Stupid. Stupid. What did I think? That I'd just show up, buy her a cookie, and we'd, what? Pick up where we left off? I scoop up the remainder of her things, stuff them in the satchel she left behind Cinderella-style, and debate going after her. Of all the idiotic ideas—

The door swings open again, and my head snaps up.

Chloe stands just inside. Her hair, now wind-tossed, hangs over her shoulders. She looks . . . just as gorgeous as I remember. Those freckles across her nose. Flushed cheeks, nose pink from the cold.

And those big brown eyes . . . which I realize are staring at me like she's seen a ghost.

That's fair.

She draws in a breath, waits for a waiter to pass, and then marches back through the café, her gaze turned anywhere but me.

She comes to a stop in front of me, the top of her head barely reaching my chin, but she doesn't lift her head. "I need my things."

I hand over the disheveled bag, trying to duck into her line of vision. My voice comes out rough. "Chloe, please. Could we just talk?"

She reaches for the satchel, but I don't let go just yet. Our fingers brush.

"Please," I add softly.

Chloe finally meets my gaze, and something in her eyes makes my heart stutter.

"Wow! It's Candy Kane!"

The voice comes from behind me—young, female, way too enthusiastic for the havoc it's about to wreak on my life.

No.

No.

Not now. Not here. Not when I finally—

I turn slightly and pull Chloe a little closer to me—it's a reflex, really—but it manages to tuck her next to me as I face a girl in her early twenties, who is standing there, phone already out, eyes wide with that particular brand of fan excitement that means this is about to become a whole thing.

She's wearing a Blue Ox hoodie. Great. One of mine.

"I can't believe it's really you!" She's bouncing slightly. "Can I get a photo? Please? My friends are never going to believe this!"

I feel Chloe stiffen beside me.

My brain does that thing it does under pressure—rapid calculation, risk assessment, exit strategy formation. In about two seconds, I catalog:

– We're in Ironclad (cozy, local, witnesses)

– This fan has her phone out (already filming? Taking pics?)

– Other people are starting to notice (three customers turning to look)

– Marcie behind the counter is watching (concerned expression)

– Chloe is about to bolt, again (I can feel it in her posture)

– If I say no to the photo, fan gets pushy, scene escalates

– If I say yes, one photo, done, we can leave

Simple math.

Except nothing about this is simple.

I take a breath. Feel my shoulders roll back—automatic, years of training. The mask slides into place like a second skin I hate but can't take off.

"Sure," I hear myself say. Smooth. Easy. Candy Kane, reporting for duty. "Always happy to meet fans."

Liar.

The girl beams. Looks at Chloe. "Is this your girlfriend? Can she be in it too?"

And here's where I make the decision that's going to haunt me.

Here's where I choose performance over truth.

Here's where I become exactly what Chloe's going to think I am.

I don't hesitate. Don't think. Just react—the same instinct that made me chase down that purse thief in Barcelona, the same protective reflex that got me into this mess in the first place.

"Yeah," I say. "She is."

Chloe makes a sound. Like a gasp, or maybe she's taking a breath before she bolts.

So I slide my arm around her back—gentle, not possessive, just *there*—and she doesn't pull away.

All right, she's not exactly leaning in either. But it's something.

"Smile," I murmur. Not for the photo. For her. Apologizing without apologizing, because I don't have time to explain and I don't know how to anyway.

This is why I ran in Barcelona. The photographer, taking our picture après kiss. And, as it turned out, during said kiss. Admittedly, I panicked.

But now, I'm in the game and smiling with that signature Candy Kane smile, because that's what I do.

The fan is grinning, phone up. "You guys are SO cute together! Okay, ready?"

I pull Chloe a little closer—it feels too good, feels too much like Barcelona, feels like everything I've been missing—and she's looking up at me with wide eyes and that expression, that *trust* she had six months ago before I destroyed it, and I hate myself a little more.

No flash. Just the soft click of a phone camera that's going to blow up my life in about thirty seconds.

"Thank you SO much!" The fan is already looking at her screen, probably already posting. "You two are perfect!"

Perfect.

In my wildest dreams.

"We need to go," I say, hand still on Chloe's back, already steering her toward the door. My voice has dropped back to normal— clipped, urgent, real Brody instead of Candy. "Now."

Chloe's moving on autopilot, still too shocked to argue.

The air hits like a slap. Single digits, clear sky, that Minnesota cold that makes your lungs hurt. Our breath comes out in clouds between us.

I get her around the corner, away from the windows, away from witnesses. My Mustang is parked down the block, black against the dirty snow.

Finally, some privacy.

Except now I have to explain, and I don't know where to start.

Chloe pulls away from my touch. Steps back. She's breathing hard—cold air, shock, anger starting to break through the surface.

"What—" She stops. Starts again. Her voice is sharp, cutting. "What the . . . what was *that*? Did you just tell a stranger I'm your girlfriend?"

"I panicked."

She stares at me. "Panic? That was *not* a panic response. No, panic is telling them I'm your cousin, or better yet, a stranger you've never met in your life. Panic is telling them I'm another one of your fans—a fan of what, I'm not super sure, but we can get back to that after you explain why exactly *your* brand of panic turned us *Instagram official* when I don't even know your last name!"

"There were people watching, and I didn't want to make a scene—"

"Oh. Right. Sorry. Because body-slamming me didn't draw any attention." Then her expression changes and . . . oh no—"Did she call you Candy Kane?"

The way she says my nickname, like it's something distasteful, hits harder than it should.

"Chloe—"

"Brody . . . Kane." I watch in horror at the exact moment it clicks into place. "You're Brody *Kane*. Derek's teammate. The guy he complains about literally every time my sister mentions hockey, which is constantly."

She didn't know.

She *really* didn't know who I was.

And somehow that makes everything worse and better and more complicated all at once.

"You're Maya's sister," I say.

She shrugs. "Mystery solved." She turns, hiking the satchel on her shoulder.

"Wait—"

She glances back. "Why? So you can ghost me again?"

Ouch. "I can explain—"

"Can you?" She crosses her arms. "Because I've spent six months trying to figure out what I did wrong. What I said. What was so terrible about me that you had to literally vanish without a word."

"You didn't do anything wrong—"

"So why, then? Why bother spending the whole evening making me fall for you, only to change your mind?"

A thousand explanations run through my mind. My dad. My image. My disastrous . . . everything. My lips part, but nothing comes out.

"Really, Brody? Even now?" She gapes at me for a moment and then, eyes rolling to the sky, flops her arms dramatically. "Unbelievable."

My phone starts ringing in my pocket.

Ignore it. Ignore it.

It keeps ringing.

Chloe's lips press together. "You should get that. Sounds important."

"Chloe, wait—"

I pull out my phone. Rick's name is flashing. I hit Ignore and look up, but she's already walking away.

"Wait—" I start after her, catching her elbow.

She stops. Turns. And the look in her eyes makes me let go.

"Don't," she says. Not angry. Just tired. "Don't call me. Don't follow me. Don't show up with some charming excuse and expect me to smile for another photo."

She turns and walks away.

This time, I let her.

I answer on the third ring.

"What." Not a question. A warning.

"Who is she?"

"Who is—"

"Your photo is trending!" Rick sounds like he just won the lottery. "Brody, this is—where are you? Who is she?"

I frown. "Who?"

"Hang on." A moment later, an image flashes through my text messages. I pull the phone away to look at it, and my heart plummets. It's Chloe. And me. From five minutes ago.

The cold wind bites at my neck, and I lift the phone back to my ear.

"This is exactly what we needed, Brody! 'Hockey's Candy Kane spotted with mystery girlfriend'—it's everywhere! The comments are overwhelmingly positive. This could save everything!"

Could save everything.

Could.

I look in the direction Chloe went. She's long gone, disappeared into the darkness like she was never there at all.

But I know she was, because in my heart is a gaping wound again.

"I have to go," I tell Rick.

"Wait, don't hang up. We need to strategize. Can you get her to come to your next game? If we can get another photo, maybe something more couple-y—"

"Rick."

"What? I'm trying to help you here!"

"I'll call you back."

I hang up. Stare at my phone.

Three notifications already. How can the photo be everywhere? It's been, like, a minute and a half? X, Instagram, fan accounts I didn't know existed.

The image loads.

There we are. Me looking down at her. Her looking up at me with those wide eyes, surprised, but with something else—I can't unpack it. But my arm around her back, the warm glow of Ironclad behind us . . .

We look like a *real* couple.

And the comments are rolling in:

@renodaisy: Oh my word, they're so cute!

@Letsgoblue: Candy finally found someone!

@LuvCats39: She's gorgeous! Who is she?

@NHLOnline: Hockey's heartbreaker is off the market! 😍

My phone buzzes. Text from Tyler.

Tyler
DUDE. Who is she?! Way to go!!!

Another from Kalen.

Kalen
Bout time you settled down, Candy!

Team group chat exploding with questions.

And then, at the bottom of my notifications:

Rick
Management will love this. Keep it
going. This is exactly the image we
needed.

I pocket my phone. Look down the empty street where Chloe disappeared.

Someone explain to me how, within the last ten minutes, I've somehow:

    — found the woman I've been looking for;

    — claimed her as my girlfriend without asking;

    — got a viral photo taken;

    — made her think I orchestrated the whole thing;

    — let my phone call prove her worst assumptions;

– confirmed I'm exactly the fake, performative person she thinks I am.

Solid work, Kane. Really stellar.

The wind cuts through my jacket. My breath comes out in clouds. My hands are cold, shoved deep in my pockets.

What am I doing?

The smart move: Go home. Leave her alone.

The Rick move: Capitalize on this. Make it work. Get her to play along somehow.

The right move: I have no idea what the right move is anymore.

But if I do nothing, she's going to find out about the photo from Barcelona from someone else. From Maya. From her own phone blowing up with strangers asking about "Candy's girlfriend." From her face being tagged in posts she never consented to.

And that's not fair to her.

I pull out my phone. Stare at it. But I don't have her number. Never did.

Barcelona was perfect and anonymous, and I ruined it before I could get the details that mattered.

I could probably set up camp at the Ironclad.

Or.

I could go after her right now.

Chase her down the street like I chased that purse thief. Risk making everything worse. Prove I can't take a hint and don't understand boundaries.

The January wind makes the decision for me.

I start walking.

Even if I'm crossing a line I have no right to cross.

Even if this is the worst decision I've made since leaving her in Barcelona.

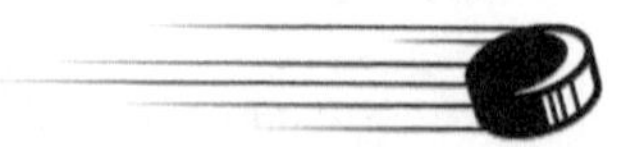

CHLOE

Don't run. Don't cry. Don't look back.

I'm speed-walking down Hennepin, which I'd say is pretty risky, considering the icy state of the sidewalks combined with my track record for clumsiness. But a girl's gotta do what she's gotta do, and right now, all I can think about is putting as much distance between me and Ironclad as humanly possible before my carefully constructed composure shatters into a million pathetic pieces.

Two blocks to the bus stop. Just two blocks.

My phone buzzes in my pocket. I don't even bother looking. It's Maya. I know it's Maya because that's the way my life goes. When it rains, it pours, and Maya will be there to see it. And I can't deal with that right now. Nope. Right now, I have the exact emotional capacity for one thing and one thing only—catching the Number 10 so I can fall apart in the privacy and discomfort of a dimly lit vinyl bus seat.

"Chloe, wait!"

No.

His voice behind me. Footsteps getting closer—the quick rhythm of someone taller, faster, not emotionally destroyed.

No no no no no.

"Please, just—give me five minutes!"

I don't stop. Don't turn around. Just keep walking because, if I look at him, if I see those eyes that made me feel—what was that word that Jessa used? oh, *special*—for one perfect night in Barcelona, I'm going to lose it completely, and I absolutely cannot handle a public breakdown on Hennepin Avenue in the dead of winter.

The bus stop appears ahead. Glass shelter. Metal bench. That useless digital sign that never works right.

Route 10 – 4 minutes

Four minutes until escape.

I can do four minutes.

I reach the shelter and finally—*finally*—turn around. Arms crossed. Chin up. Game face on. Never mind that my game face probably looks more "about to cry" than "unbothered." Red-rimmed eyes or not, I'm not going to break that easily.

An older woman is sitting on the bench, bundled in a puffy purple coat, shopping bags at her feet. She glances up, sees us, and immediately looks back at her phone with the expression of someone who's witnessed exactly this kind of drama before and knows to stay out of it.

Smart woman.

Brody stops a few feet away, breathing hard. His breath comes out in white clouds between us. Not from the running—he's a professional athlete, this is nothing—but from something else. Stress? Desperation?

Can't be that.

Doesn't matter. I'm a stone wall, remember?

The cold is already vicious. Single digits at least, maybe lower. That Minnesota cold that bites through thin coats and reminds you that winter doesn't care about your problems.

"I said don't follow me." My voice comes out steadier than I feel, which is a small miracle.

"I know." He runs a hand through his hair. The wind immediately messes it up again. "But you need to hear this. What happened in Barcelona—"

"I don't need to hear anything." I pull my coat tighter. The fabric is thin, not nearly warm enough. I should've replaced it last year, but rent took priority. "You made your choice six months ago."

"Someone took our picture." The words come out fast. Urgent. "That night. At the café. And . . . I panicked." He stops. Breathes. More clouds between us. "I didn't want to drag you into my drama."

Wait. "What drama?"

He hesitates. There's something in his expression—shame,

maybe, or exhaustion—that makes him look less like "Candy Kane, media-trained hockey star" and more like the guy from Barcelona who told me about his fear of letting people down.

"My dad was in a big poker game. And he . . ." He sighs, and it works its way into my body like a hot-oil massage, letting down my guard. "He owed money he didn't have to people who don't exactly take IOUs. I had to bail him out, literally and figuratively, and"—his voice drops lower, and it sort of sinks into me—"I didn't need the press knowing about my life."

Oh.

That's not what I expected.

I was prepared for excuses. For charm. For some smooth explanation that would make me feel stupid for caring in the first place. But this?

This feels almost . . . real.

Don't fall for it, Chloe. You are a stone wall. A STONE WALL. This is Brody "Candy" Kane, notorious charmer, hockey-world sweetheart. It's his job to protect his image. Do. Not. I repeat, DO NOT fall for it.

But there's this tiny, traitorous part of my heart—the part that felt that pitter-patter when he said *girlfriend,* the part that's been wondering for six months what was so wrong with me that he had to vanish—that is whispering: *Maybe it wasn't about you not being enough.*

Stop. *Stop.*

"So what? You panicked, and you just left?" I'm trying to keep my voice level. My hands are shoved in my pockets, fingers already numb. "Without a word. Without—"

"I'm sorry." He steps closer. Not crowding, just . . . closer. I can smell his cologne now—something expensive and woodsy that brings back Barcelona in a rush. "I know that doesn't fix it. But I am."

My phone buzzes again. Insistent. I pull it out with stiff fingers.

Maya calling . . .

Perfect timing, universe.

I look at Brody. At the phone. At the digital sign. *3 minutes.*

"I have to . . ." I gesture with the phone. "It's my sister. She'll keep calling if I don't—"

"Answer it."

I swipe to accept, turning slightly away for some semblance of privacy, even though we both know the older woman and probably half of Hennepin Avenue can hear everything.

"Hey, Maya, I'm kind of in the middle of—"

"Derek just saw a photo." Maya's voice is tight. That particular tone that means she's upset but trying to sound reasonable. "Of you. With *Brody Kane.* Chloe."

"What?" My mind is swirling. A photo of me . . . and Brody? Heat rises to my cheeks as I think back to the picture of us captured in Barcelona. "What photo?"

"It's you and Brody inside what looks like a restaurant. From today."

I let out a sigh of relief and immediately suck it back in. Oh no. *Is this your girlfriend?* the girl inside had asked. Oh . . . no, no. "It's . . . complicated."

"Complicated?" Her voice climbs. "He's Derek's teammate. They don't exactly get along. And you—" She stops. Recalibrates. "I just want to make sure you know what you're doing."

There it is. The subtext I've been hearing my whole life, wrapped in sisterly concern. I'm over my head, out of my league. Tell me something I don't know.

"And he has a reputation," she says, almost whispering it, like we might be in a hair salon, talking behind a copy of *People* magazine.

"A reputation for what, exactly?" I know I shouldn't ask. I already know I won't like the answer.

"For dating models. Influencers. You know—" Another pause. More delicate. "You're not exactly his type, Chloe."

No duh. He's standing there, looking away from me, his hands in his pockets, and she's right. He's gorgeous, with those shoulders, and dark hair and blue eyes. And then there's me . . . flyaway hair tangled around my shoulders, chin turtle-tucked into my jacket collar, fully aware that I look ridiculous, bundled up like the Michelin Man. Maybe he had a touch of heatstroke that day in Barcelona.

"I'm just worried about you getting hurt. And"—the real concern surfaces—"I don't want anything to mess up the wedding."

There it is.

Don't mess up my perfect wedding with your poor life choices, Chloe. Don't embarrass us by being with someone out of your league. Don't exist too loudly.

My free hand clenches in my pocket. The cold metal of the bus shelter presses against my back.

"Wow. Thanks, Maya. But I think I can handle myself."

"Can you? Because this seems really sudden, and with the party this weekend—"

I've already lifted the phone away from my ear. "I gotta go. I'll call you later," I say into the icy wind and hang up before she can respond.

Then I stand there for a second, phone in hand, trying to remember how to breathe. The exhaust from a passing truck hits me, diesel fumes mixing with the metallic smell of cold air.

The digital sign changes. *2 minutes.*

"Your sister?" Brody asks quietly.

I laugh. It's not a happy sound. "Yeah. Apparently, I can't be trusted to date without supervision."

Brody frowns. "She said that?"

My gaze lifts at the tone in his voice—clipped. He almost sounds . . . defensive, which would be crazy because he doesn't know me well enough to be angry for me.

"Not . . . exactly that."

Brody tilts his head, that protective look deepening. The thought sends a wave of heat rolling through me. "What *did* she say?"

"That you have a reputation for being charming." I'm going for light sarcasm. It comes out harsh, almost bitter. "That I'll get hurt ... that I'm not exactly your type. That she's worried I'm going to—" I stop. Can't quite say it out loud.

Ruin her wedding. Embarrass the family. Prove I'm exactly who they think I am: the sister who can't get her life together.

"I wouldn't believe everything you read about me on the internet," he says.

"This may come as a shock to you, Brody"—I stuff my hands deeper into my pockets as a shiver runs through me—"but I actually don't spend my evenings catching up on the latest hockey drama. It's my sister's fiancé, Derek. He's not a huge fan."

Brody is still, standing at my side, his warm gaze searing through the side of my head. A gust of wind scatters the snow off the top of the bus stop. Icy crystals glitter against the inky darkness. Finally, he turns toward the road, tucking his hands into his own jacket as though he intends to join me on the bus.

"I heard her mention a party," he says nonchalantly. "This weekend?"

"It's a meet and greet, actually."

Brody raises a brow. "What is a meet and greet?"

"Exactly what it sounds like. It's a party for everyone involved in the wedding, the families and wedding party, to all meet prior to the wedding."

"Sounds like a fancy way to waste money."

I gape at him. "That's ..." Not entirely wrong. But you'd never catch me saying it. "Yeah, well ... it's still happening." And why not tell him everything else? After all, according to him—and everyone else on the internet—he's my *boyfriend.* "And my mother wants me to bring a date. She's been trying to set me up with literally anyone who crosses her path. I narrowly avoided getting traded to an Olive Garden waiter for unlimited breadsticks earlier today. I had to lie and tell her I already had a date."

Brody chuckles, the sound taking me right back to Barcelona. To the warmth and sunshine. The bus is visible down the street now. Headlights cutting through the darkness, that familiar rumble of diesel engine.

1 minute.

"I could be your date," Brody says softly.

My head snaps his direction. "What?"

"To the meet-and-greet party." He pauses. "Your sister's marrying Derek, right? I'm invited anyway. Teammate obligation. I could—*we* could go together."

Something in the way he suggests it—the offer coming out too easily, too eagerly. My heart hitches as something clicks into place. The one thing Derek's always complaining about: Candy Kane's image.

He needs PR. "You need this." The words come out slow, understanding dawning. "You need a girlfriend, don't you? That's what this is about."

He looks startled—like I've caught him at something he wasn't ready to admit. His mouth opens. Closes. Then he seems to consider it, really consider it, and something shifts in his expression.

"Yeah." Finally. Honest. Direct. "I need help." His mouth makes a tight, perfect line. Good grief, even his lips are perfect. "It's complicated." He takes a breath that clouds white between us. "But it sounds like you need help too. With your family. With"—he gestures vaguely—"all of it."

"So we help each other." My voice sounds strange. Distant. "A fake date. For the meet-and-greet party."

He lifts a shoulder.

"And then what? We have a fake fight and fake breakup?"

His mouth opens, then, "On second thought, I probably need to be your boyfriend through the entire wedding."

I raise an eyebrow.

"It's a contract thing."

And I don't know why, but those words have the power to spear through me, take me out, right there on the grimy sidewalk.

Still. "There are five big events—the meet-and-greet party, the couples shower, then three events over the weekend wedding in Maple Lake. You'd have to go to all of them."

He nods, grimacing as though I'm the one proposing this grisly idea but he's up for it. What a champ.

"And then what? Part ways like it never happened?"

"If that's what you want."

The bus pulls up with a hydraulic hiss. Brakes squealing. Doors opening with that pneumatic sound. The older woman gathers her bags, stands slowly—arthritic joints, careful movements—and gives me one last look that might be sympathy or might be judgment. Hard to tell in the harsh fluorescent light.

"Wait. Are you taking the bus?" he says, as if just figuring it out.

I glance up at him, my chin tucked into my jacket. "One too many shots to the head there, hockey boy?"

"Let me drive you home," he says, ignoring the jab.

I should say no. I should get on this bus and go home and forget this entire insane conversation, crazy fake-relationship plot and all.

But then I think about showing up to Maya's party alone. About my mother's pitying smiles. About being the overlooked sister at five different wedding events while everyone else is coupled up.

And I look at Mr. Candy, standing there in his expensive leather jacket with his blue eyes, those broad shoulders, and suddenly all I can think is . . .

This is completely insane, but also—

It might be exactly what I need.

"Come on, Chloe," he says, those blue eyes catching in the light. Oceans again. "It's just a ride. Let me help you."

A teenage boy has run to catch the bus and now stomps up the stairs, hood up, backpack, that particular smell of teenage body spray and weed and winter sweat. He looks at me. Looks at Brody. Recognition flashes across his acne-marked face. "Hey! It's Candy Kane!"

Brody—er, Candy smiles and nods.

And that's enough for my pride to find its feet, even though my brain is screaming *Just say yes. It's subzero. You're going to freeze on this bus.* "I can take care of myself."

"I know you can." His voice is gentle. Matter-of-fact. "But you don't have to."

"Lady?" The bus driver sounds impatient. His voice carries that end-of-shift exhaustion. "On or off?"

I look at Brody. At the warmth and ease he's offering.

Then I look at the bus. At my escape route. At my dignity.

"I'll think about your offer."

It's not an agreement. It's not a no. It's somewhere in between, which is probably the most honest thing I've said all day.

I pull out my phone with numb fingers. Open a blank contact and hand it to him.

He enters his number and hands it back to me, his gaze meeting mine with intensity. "I'll wait for your text."

Heat flushes my cheeks, but I nod, step onto the bus, and leave him standing there on the sidewalk, hands in his pockets, breath clouding in the cold. Not moving.

But something on his face looks . . . almost content. Hopeful.

The bus pulls away with a jerk, the engine rumbling as the darkness envelopes me. I sink into the seat, my body swaying with the familiar route I've taken a hundred times since selling my car.

Brody Kane.

Two words that represent everything complicated about the last twelve hours.

Really, I should forget the offer. Forget the whole conversation. But . . .

I think about Maya's voice: *You're not exactly his type.*

I think about showing up to the wedding events with Brody Kane as my date.

I think about my family's faces.

And then I think: *Maybe I'm tired of being overlooked.*

Maybe I'm tired of playing it safe.

Maybe this is the worst idea I've ever had.

Maybe I'm going to do it anyway.

You're an idiot, I tell myself.

But my thumb is already moving. Already typing.

Already making the choice my heart wants even though my brain is screaming warnings.

And hitting Send.

CHLOE

CHLOE! YOU'RE ALL OVER THE INTERNET!"

Jessa's voice carries from her bedroom down the short hallway, loud enough to jolt me out of the half-sleep state I've been in since approximately three a.m., when my brain decided to replay every mortifying moment from yesterday on an endless loop.

I pull my pillow over my head. The morning light seeps through my curtains—that pale January sunlight that's bright but offers no warmth. My room smells like the lavender candle I forgot to blow out last night and the faint mustiness of the radiator that clanks but doesn't quite heat properly.

"Go away. The internet can wait."

"No, seriously, you need to see this!"

My door flies open. Jessa stands there in her pajama pants covered in little hockey pucks and her oversized University of Minnesota hockey sweatshirt, phone in hand, eyes wide, long blonde hair in a sleep-mussed bun.

"It's bad, isn't it?" I sit up, my own Golden Gophers sweat-shirt—the soft gray one I've had since freshman year—twisted around my torso. My mouth tastes like stale late-night coffee and regret. "On a scale of 'mildly embarrassing' to 'pack your bags, you're moving to Canada,' how bad?"

"Actually?" Jessa's mouth quirks into a smile. She crosses my room, socks padding on the hardwood floor, and hops onto my bed. The whole frame shakes. "It's sort of amazing."

I squint at her suspiciously. "What do you mean by that?"

"Just—look." She thrusts her phone at me.

The screen is too bright for my barely awake eyes. I squint at it, and there we are. Me and Brody at Ironclad Desserts. Him, looking amazing and handsome. His arm around my shoulders. My eyes doing that deer-in-headlights thing. The photo is everywhere—X, Instagram, hockey forums, Reddit. I wouldn't be surprised to find it on the Maple Falls Facebook page.

My heart sinks as Jessa reads out the headlines. "'Candy's Mystery Girlfriend,'" Jessa points out over my shoulder. "And this one: 'Hockey's Heartbreaker Finally Has a Heart.' Oh, here's a good one: 'Blue Ox Defenseman Spotted with Adorable Girlfriend—Fans Approve.'"

"They called me adorable?" My voice comes out as a pitiful squeak.

"Of course they did." Jessa waves a hand as though that point should have been obvious. "They love you. They're trying to figure out who you are. Someone thinks you're a Vikings cheerleader. Another person swears you're a grad student at the U."

I take her phone, scrolling through the comments. The radiator clanks loudly, hissing steam that smells faintly metallic. Outside my window, I hear the muffled sounds of the city waking up—car doors, distant traffic, someone scraping ice off a windshield. But none of that compares to the sound of my thundering heart or the blood now rushing through my ears.

This can't be real.

"This picture was taken last night. How are you seeing this now?" I check my own phone on the nightstand. "It's nine thirty in the morning."

"I set a Google alert for Blue Ox news." Jessa shrugs at my raised eyebrow. "What? I write about hockey. I need to stay informed."

Right. Jessa's hockey blog. Because I'm apparently the only person in the world whose life doesn't revolve around sports, who wouldn't have recognized Candy Kane back in Barcelona if he'd been wearing a name tag and a hockey jersey. I let out a groan and toss the phone away.

"Nope." I fling myself back down and toss the blankets back over my head.

Jessa leans in, her voice muffled on the other side of the covers. "What do you mean, nope?"

I peek back out. "I mean, NOPE. This isn't happening. It's a bad dream."

Jessa laughs, completely oblivious to my torment. "You're ridiculous. I would have loved to meet one of the Blue Ox players. Even Brody Kane."

I close my eyes again. Coffee. I'm gonna need coffee before I tell her the rest of the story from last night.

I toss back the blankets, and my feet hit the cold hardwood. I pad down the hallway toward the kitchen, Jessa following.

The living room opens up, pale morning light through the window showing off my attempts at making this place homey: throw pillows on the secondhand couch, string lights along the bookshelf, my event planning vision board, covered with swatches, sample invitations, and venue photos, leaning against the wall.

I cross into the kitchen—galley-style with white cabinets, gray countertops. Dishes (mine) litter the sink. A small window looks out onto bare tree branches and the brick wall of the building next door. A great view if you're into the whole starving artist (or in my case, event planner) aesthetic. I reach for the coffee maker, then remember with a sinking feeling.

"We're out of coffee." I stare at the empty machine.

"Tragic." Jessa leans against the counter. "But also? Not the biggest problem. You're viral, Chloe. Thousands of comments. And they're mostly positive."

"Fantastic," I say, opening the cabinet to confirm: no coffee. Just empty space where coffee should be.

"You're being . . . very weird about this." She sets her phone down. "What aren't you telling me?"

I close the cabinet and lean back against the counter, the gray surface cool through my sweatshirt.

"Remember Barcelona guy?"

Jessa's eyes go wide. "Mystery man who disappeared? That Barcelona guy?"

"That would be the one." I wrap my arms around myself. The apartment is cold, the radiator doing its best but not quite keeping up with the single-digit temperatures outside. "Turns out Barcelona guy is Brody Kane."

The silence that follows is so complete, I can hear the building pipes creaking.

"Brody Kane," Jessa says slowly. "Brody 'Candy' Kane. Number seven. Defenseman for the Blue Ox. *That's* your Barcelona guy?"

"That's the one."

"How did you not know who he was back in Barcelona?"

"I don't follow hockey! I didn't recognize him. He was just this guy. This normal, sweet—very handsome—guy, who chased down a purse thief and then spent the evening with me. We talked about everything except hockey. He never mentioned it . . . well, actually . . ." The memories I've been trying (not trying) to get out of my head come crashing back. "He talked about playing hockey in high school. And *I* talked about hockey players . . . and how much I can't stand them . . ." My words trail off as the horror sets in.

"And then he disappeared," she says.

"And then he disappeared." The words still sting.

Jessa crosses to where I'm standing and pulls me into a hug. She smells like sleep and her coconut shampoo and that particular Jessa scent that means safety and home. "I'm sorry, babe. I wished I'd known." She pulls back. "So what happened last night?"

"I was ambushed. We just ran into each other, and someone took our picture. They assumed we were an actual couple." I drag a hand over my face. "Which we're not. Obviously. Because he ghosted me six months ago, and I've spent all that time convinced there was something wrong with me."

"There's nothing wrong with you." Jessa's voice is firm. "If he disappeared, that's on him. Not you."

"I know that. Logically. But"—I gesture at my phone—"feelings aren't logical."

My phone buzzes.

We both look at it.

<u>Brody</u>

I'm outside. Can I come up? I want
to talk about the deal.

Jessa's eyebrows shoot up. "How does he know where you live? And more importantly . . . what deal?"

My face heats. Here it comes. "I gave him my address so we could talk. It's not a big deal. It's just, last night he mentioned an arrangement. Something about the photo. Helping each other out with—" I stop, suddenly mortified. Because how do you say *He wants to fake date me for PR purposes* without sounding completely pathetic?

You don't.

"An arrangement?" Jessa looks at me like I've grown a second head. "What kind of arrangement?"

"I don't know!" I shrug dramatically. "That's why he's here. To explain."

"Oh, I can't wait to hear this." She heads toward the door.

"What are you doing?"

Jessa glances back at me. "I'm letting him in so he can *explain*."

What?—No. I grab her by the elbow. "You can't be here. You have to go."

Jessa gapes at me. "You can't be serious. I'm not letting Brody Kane in here so he can sweet-talk you into forgiving him."

I give her a wide-eyed look. "Please, Jessa. I'll fill you in on everything afterward. Please just . . ."

Jessa lets out an exasperated breath. "Fine." She's already heading toward her room. "But I'm listening. To everything. Just so you know." She pauses at her bedroom door. "But seriously, Chloe? Whatever he's proposing? Ask the hard questions. Don't let his charm get to you."

A knock at the door.

Jessa disappears into her room, and I'm alone in my Golden Gophers pajama pants and coffee-stained sweatshirt. I catch my reflection in the microwave. Hair in a disaster bun. No makeup. A faint pillow crease still visible on my cheek.

This is fine. Everything is fine.

Another knock.

"Coming!" My voice comes out higher than normal.

I cross the living room and put my hand on the doorknob. Take a breath.

You can do this.

I open the door.

Brody Kane stands in my hallway in dark jeans and a gray Henley under a black wool coat, beanie in one hand, two to-go cups in the other. His dark hair is slightly messed where the hat was, and his blue-gray eyes meet mine with an expression that's equal parts nervous and sheepish. There's a faint flush on his cheeks—from the cold, probably, but maybe also from embarrassment.

"Hi," he says very charmingly. Handsome smile. And then the words start pouring out. "Um. Good morning. You look . . ." His eyes travel over my haphazard appearance, his lips tugging at the corners. "You look great." He pauses a moment and starts when he looks down at the coffee in his hands, as though just remembering it was there. "Oh. I brought coffee . . ." He starts to hand it over, then pulls back, looking for the label. "I . . . don't know what kind this is—I didn't know what you'd like. Had to guess." He thrusts it toward me. "Sorry. I'm . . . I'm not super great at this kind of thing."

I think it's the least suave thing he's ever done. And it's probably the most adorable.

I take the cup, and our fingers brush—barely a touch, but I feel it everywhere. The smell of the coffee hits me—rich, dark, with hints of peppermint and chocolate. The cups have the distinctive logo I'd recognize anywhere: the small brass plaque design from Brew & Rumor.

"You went to Brew & Rumor?" Surprise colors my voice. "I love that place."

He shrugs a little.

"Is this candy cane mocha?" I take a sip. It's perfect. Exactly what I'd have ordered myself, the peppermint and chocolate and espresso mixing in that way only Brew & Rumor manages. "How did you—"

His cheeks get redder. "I, uh, your business page. It links to your—" He clears his throat. "I may have looked at your Instagram. After yesterday. Just to—" He runs a hand through his hair, clearly mortified. "Wow, that sounds creepy. I swear I'm not a stalker. I just wanted to make sure you were—" He stops. "I'm making this worse, aren't I?"

"You stalked my Instagram," I say, but there's no heat in it. More like wonder.

He attempts a smile, self-deprecating and embarrassed. "Is that bad? You post about that place a lot. The typewriter. The vintage teacups. It seemed . . ." He shrugs helplessly. "I wanted to get it right. The coffee. As an apology. For—everything."

I don't know what to say, so I take another sip. The warmth spreads through my chest.

He looks relieved I'm not slamming the door in his face. He shifts his weight. "Can I come in? I'm starting to lose feeling in my extremities."

From down the hall, I hear Jessa's door creak open slightly.

I step aside. "Yeah. Okay."

He enters with visible relief, and suddenly my small apartment feels even smaller. He's tall—taller than my memory of Barcelona allowed—and his presence fills the space in a way that makes me aware of every secondhand piece of furniture, every bill on the counter, every sign that I'm barely holding my life together.

I close the door. The click sounds loud.

He sets his cup on my counter, carefully, away from the wedding files and the stack of bills. His eyes flick to the overdue student loan notice on top. I see the moment he registers it, but he looks away quickly.

"Nice place." His eyes take in the string lights, the gallery wall, the vision boards. "Very—" He stops himself. "Actually, I guess I don't know you well enough to say what's very you. But . . . I think it is."

"It's okay." I move to the couch. He stays standing. "It is very me. At least, the version of me that's trying to make something work on a shoestring budget."

"You left Maple Lake for this," he says quietly. "To start your business."

"I moved in with Jessa two years ago." I wrap both hands around the cup. "Did odd jobs to get by. But it wasn't until I started planning Maya's wedding that I even considered event planning as a job. So I scraped together my savings and decided to go all in on that."

"Is it working?"

The honesty slips out. "I'm here, aren't I? Still trying. That has to count for something."

His expression softens in a way that makes my chest tight. "It counts for a lot."

The radiator clanks. Outside, the wind rattles the window.

"I thought about you," he says. "After Barcelona. I thought about trying to find you. But Maple Lake seemed far, and I didn't have your last name, and I convinced myself it was better to just—" He stops. "Let you go."

"But you didn't let me go. Because here you are."

"Here I am." He finally sits—not on the couch next to me, but in one of the mismatched chairs across the coffee table. Maintaining distance. "Turns out you were forty minutes away this whole time."

"Not in Maple Lake after all."

"Not in Maple Lake." He leans forward, elbows on his knees, hands clasped. "I'm sorry I hurt you, Chloe." He says my name like it hurts. And for a moment, he's just Brody again, the charming man I met in Barcelona. Sweet. Safe.

The moment stretches between us. Heavy. Real. The space filling with that kind of meaningful silence that makes your heart race and your skin tingle.

Then Jessa's voice carries from her bedroom. "What about the deal? Didn't you come here to propose something?"

Brody's expression shifts. Like a door closing. The vulnerability disappears, replaced by something more guarded.

"Right." He clears his throat, sits back. "The deal."

And just like that, we're not talking about Barcelona anymore.

"My agent thinks this could work. The photo. You and me. The response has been good. Really good. It helps my image, which I need right now."

"Why?" I ask. "Why do you need help with your image?"

He hesitates. "Team stuff. Contract renewal coming up. It's complicated. But having a girlfriend, having stability—it looks good."

"More marketable."

"Yeah." He doesn't sound happy about it. "And you need a date to your sister's wedding events. Five of them? Starting this weekend."

"Saturday," I confirm.

"So we help each other." He's looking at me, but also not. "I get good PR. You get a boyfriend for the wedding season. Clean. Professional. Mutually beneficial."

"No strings," I hear myself say.

"No strings," he agrees quickly. Too quickly. "No romance. Just an arrangement. Five events. We show up together, act like a couple, and when it's over, we're done."

My heart is doing something painful. Because a minute ago, he was apologizing, being real, admitting he looked me up online. And now we're talking business transactions.

"And to make it worth your time—" He pauses. Glances at the counter. At the bills he saw but didn't mention. Back to me. "I'll pay you."

The words fall on me like icy water.

Pay me? The student loan bill burns on the counter. The rent due in three days. The business barely surviving. The life I can't quite hold together.

He's offering me a solution.

Wrapped in the most humiliating, complicated package imaginable.

From the hallway, Jessa's door creaks open another inch.

I look at Brody Kane. At the candy cane mocha he brought me

from my secret coffee shop. I don't understand what's happening. I don't understand what he really wants or if any of this is a good idea.

But I'm out of coffee, out of money, and possibly out of options. And he's sitting in my living room offering me all three.

BRODY

The silence after "I'll pay you" stretches like the last seconds of a tied game in overtime. Uncomfortable. Tense. Everything riding on what happens next.

Chloe's face gives me nothing. She's staring at her coffee cup—the candy cane mocha I spent twenty minutes in line for at some speakeasy coffee shop I found by stalking her Instagram like a creep—and I can't read her expression. Her roommate's door is cracked open. She's definitely listening. I sound like a jerk. I know it.

I should say something. Clarify. Make this sound less like I'm trying to buy her affection and more like a mutually beneficial business arrangement between two adults.

"I know how that sounds," I start. Professional. Matter-of-fact. Like I'm negotiating a lease, not asking someone I ghosted to pretend to love me. "But I'm serious. This would be a legitimate arrangement. My agent will draw up a contract. Clear terms. Professional boundaries."

Chloe finally looks up. Those eyes—the ones I remember from dancing under twinkling lights in Barcelona—are guarded now. Calculating.

"How much?" she asks. Direct. No games.

I respect that.

I also hate that I saw the student loan bill on her counter. Three months overdue. The number made my stomach turn. I don't know the full extent of her situation, but I know desperation when I see it. I've been wearing it like a second skin for weeks.

"Twenty thousand." The number comes out steady. Not so high it seems like I'm trying to buy her. Not so low it's insulting. "Ten up front. Ten after the last event."

Her eyes widen slightly. She wasn't expecting that much.

Good. Neither was I until the words came out of my mouth.

From the bedroom, her roommate's voice cuts through. "What are these events? What's he asking you to do, Chloe?"

Chloe glances toward the hallway. "Jessa—"

"No, it's fine." I lean back, trying to look relaxed even though my shoulders are tight enough to snap. "She should know. You both should." I look at Chloe. "All five events. Starting this Saturday."

"All of it." Chloe sets down her coffee. "You sure?"

I nod. "I'm sure."

"What events specifically?" Jessa again, from the other room.

Chloe looks at me, waiting.

"I don't know," I admit. "I'm not the wedding expert here. You tell me."

Chloe hesitates, then lists them on her fingers. "Meet-and-greet party. Saturday night. We're hosting it in a party room at a bowling place."

I raise an eyebrow. "Okay. Saturday. What else?"

"Couples bridal shower in two weeks. Then three days for the destination wedding, Valentine's Day weekend. Rehearsal dinner, the wedding ceremony, and the reception."

I wince. That's right. The wedding is on Valentine's Day.

Because God has a sense of humor.

"All right. So I show up, play the part of a devoted boyfriend, make you look good for your family, the whole song and dance."

"That's the idea."

"What's in this for you?" Jessa's voice is louder now. Closer.

"Besides fixing your image and keeping your precious contract? Why Chloe specifically?"

Chloe turns her gaze back to me, the question echoing in her eyes.

The question I've been dreading.

The one I've been thinking about since she left me in a cloud of diesel on the sidewalk last night.

She . . . isn't impressed by me. And I know that sounds crazy. But I made her laugh six months ago in Barcelona, and she let me kiss her, and she didn't have a clue who I was, really.

Or maybe she saw the real me, and that's just a little bit addicting. Which is why I'm here, with coffee, and I know it feels creepy with the money on the table, but I saw the overdue bill on the counter and did a little math. She's broke. So, I could lie. Say she's convenient. Already in the viral photo. Has the wedding dates I need.

But if I don't put a little skin in this game, she's going to walk. Or run. Or I guess, since this is her place, kick me out onto the street. She can't be the only one sacrificing some pride for this win.

So I give her just a little of what I owe her. Honesty.

"Because I trust you," I say. "I trust you not to sell this story to the tabloids. Not to use it against me. Because—" I stop. Regroup, because the way she's looking at me now, all big brown eyes . . . I can't think straight. "There was an incident."

"What incident?" Chloe leans forward slightly.

I brace myself.

"About a month ago, I went to a charity gala. Met someone—a woman who seemed nice, normal. We talked for maybe twenty minutes. I gave her my number because she said she worked for a social media magazine and wanted to do an article about me. I was being nice."

"Of course you were," Chloe says, but it doesn't sound like judgment. Huh.

"Turns out she was an aspiring influencer looking for her big break."

Chloe's brows lift, soften. Not quite sympathy. More like recognition. Like she knows exactly where this is going.

"She posted our entire conversation online—DMs, texts, everything—claiming we had this intense romantic thing and I ghosted her. Painted me as this serial charmer who uses women and throws them away."

Because that's not at all what I did to the woman sitting across from me six months ago. Completely different situation. Totally.

The irony is not lost on me.

"Did you?" Jessa asks flatly from the doorway. Arms crossed. Pajama pants with little hockey pucks on them, which would be funny if she wasn't looking at me like I'm a suspect in an interrogation room.

"No. I literally talked to her for twenty minutes. But after that night, we shared a few texts."

Silence.

Jessa raises a brow.

"I . . . Okay, I flirted a little." I don't look at Chloe. "I was . . . charming." Heat sears my neck. "It's what I do with members of the media. But I was never inappropriate. And I never led her on. She asked about my game, wondered if we could meet for dinner. It was light. *Polite.* And then she started asking if she did something wrong and why I was ignoring her. Asking why I was rejecting her, because she thought we had a connection—"

"And you answered her?"

"At first. I tried to let her down easy. But eventually . . ."

"He told her not to text anymore," Jessa says, now holding up her phone. "I've seen the post." She glances at Chloe. "I'm a little surprised *you* haven't. Even outside the sports realm, it went viral."

I run a hand through my hair. "Yeah, and then she went on some podcast talking about how I led her on. It got completely blown out of proportion. I've got this reputation—I'm friendly, I smile for photos, I'm good with fans. So when someone claims I'm secretly a player who charms women and disappears . . ."

Jessa makes a face, reading off the headline. "'Kane's Contract Renewal in Question Amid Personal Conduct Concerns.'"

Yeah. That.

"And now she's threatening to sue me."

"For what?" Chloe says, frowning, and oh, I like that tone. It's nice to have someone on my side about this for once.

"Intentional Infliction of Emotional Duress. For five hundred thousand dollars . . ." I trail off. Watch Chloe's face carefully.

Her eyes flick away. Down to her coffee cup.

Yeah. She's probably thinking it too. The charmer who disappears. That's exactly what I did to her.

"So you need a girlfriend to prove you're not a heartbreaker." Jessa pockets her phone. "Interesting strategy, considering your track record."

There it is. Of course she knows all about Barcelona. And she's not letting me off the hook for it.

Chloe's shoulders tense. She still won't look at me.

"Yeah, well." I meet Jessa's stare. Try for casual. Land somewhere around defensive. "That's why it has to be someone who won't sell me out." I glance at Chloe, willing her to look up.

The silence stretches.

Jessa is watching me like she's waiting for me to confess to murder, while Chloe studies her coffee, which apparently has become very interesting.

"And your contract renewal?" Jessa presses. "What happens if you don't fix this?"

"I don't get renewed. Maybe get traded. Maybe get dropped altogether." All because I can't seem to convince people I'm capable of being a real person.

Chloe and Jessa exchange a look.

"And you thought," Jessa says slowly, "that asking Chloe—who you ghosted six months ago—to fake date you was a good solution to this problem?"

"I didn't say it was a good solution. I said it was the solution I have."

"Why?" Chloe asks again. Quieter this time. "Why not someone else? Why me?"

"Because you're real. You don't care about the hockey thing. You didn't even know who I was. And I—"

I what? Miss you? Think about you constantly? Spent six months trying to forget you and failed spectacularly?

"I just . . . trust you," I finish lamely. "And I don't trust people. So. Yeah. That's why you."

The apartment fills with a different kind of quiet. Not the warm, intimate quiet Chloe and I shared minutes earlier. This one is heavy. Almost insurmountable. Suffocating.

"Chloe," Jessa says carefully. "Can I talk to you for a second? Privately?"

"No." Chloe doesn't break eye contact with me. "Whatever you want to say, say it here."

Jessa huffs but moves into the room properly, sitting down on the couch next to Chloe. United front. Great. Honestly, I'm glad Chloe has someone to stand up for her. I wish she didn't feel like she had to stand up for Chloe *against me,* but still.

"If she does this," Jessa says, looking at me now, "there are conditions."

"Okay."

"You don't even know what they are yet."

"Doesn't matter. If they're reasonable, I'll agree."

Jessa's eyebrows rise. "You're that desperate?"

"I'm that desperate."

She studies me for a long moment. Then nods, like I've passed some test. "Five events. Like I said, you show up to all of them.

You play the part of devoted boyfriend convincingly enough that Chloe's family believes it."

"Done."

"You don't embarrass her. You don't make her look stupid. You treat her like she's the best thing that ever happened to you."

Something in my chest tightens. "Done."

"After the end of the last event, the wedding on Valentine's Day, you two have a big, public fight. Chloe's the heartbroken one. You're the jerk who couldn't commit. Her family rallies around her, stops trying to set her up, and leaves her alone."

I hesitate. That one stings. Being the villain again. Hurting her publicly after hurting her privately in Barcelona. And doing it on Valentine's Day, because apparently, I'm destined to be that guy.

But what choice do I have?

"Okay," I say quietly.

"And one more thing." Jessa's voice is hard now. Final. "You don't talk about Barcelona—not outside of your official story. Sure, you can tell everyone how you two met and how you swept Chloe off her feet. And how you spent an evening together. But that's it. No googly-eyed stories about kissing under the orange trees. That's her story, and you don't get to use it. And you don't get to make her relive being left behind without so much as an explanation. You got that, Candy?"

I look at Chloe. She's staring at her hands. Not meeting my eyes.

She wants to pretend our kiss never happened.

Which means it mattered to her. Which means it still hurts.

Which means I did exactly what I was afraid of—I hurt her so badly she wants to erase it.

"Fine."

Chloe finally looks up. "And physical boundaries. Handholding is fine. Kissing on the cheek if necessary for photos or family. But no—" She stops. Clears her throat. "No real kissing. Nothing more than what's needed to sell it."

The way she says *real kissing* does something to my stomach. Because that kiss can still undo me.

"Understood."

"And when this is all over, you let her be. No contact," Jessa says.

I just found her again, and already I'm losing her . . .

My teeth click shut, holding back the objection as I nod. "My agent will have a contract drawn up."

Chloe won't meet my eyes. Her cheeks are pink, highlighting her freckles. I want to reach out, brush my thumb over them, reassure her that I would never do anything to hurt her . . . but I already have. And I've got no right to act like I didn't.

Her eyes lift to the frosty window. "So, we make our big entrance at the party this Saturday."

"I can pick you up," I offer. "We should arrive together. Makes it look more real."

"The party starts around three," Chloe says. "But I'm supposed to be there early to set up, because, you know, I'm the event planner."

"No problem. I'll pick you up early. Help you set up."

"You don't have to—"

"I want to." The words come out before I can stop them. Too honest. Too eager. I dial it back. "I mean, it might earn a few points with your family. Make it more believable. Devoted boyfriend helps with party setup. It can't hurt."

Jessa's watching me with narrowed eyes. She doesn't buy the casual act.

Smart woman.

"Saturday morning," Chloe says. "Eleven a.m."

"I'll be here."

"And you'll pay her ten thousand before Saturday?" Jessa, the shark, isn't letting this go. She could have a real future in agenting.

"I'll have it transferred to her account by Friday night. Is that acceptable?"

Jessa looks at Chloe. "Is that acceptable to you?"

Chloe's quiet for a long moment. I can see her thinking. Calculating. Weighing the money against whatever reservations she has about this insane plan.

I feel gross.

Finally, she nods. "Okay. I'll do it. Five events. Fake girlfriend. Professional arrangement." She stands up, extends her hand across the coffee table. "It's a deal."

I stand too.

I take her hand. Her fingers wrap around mine, and there it is again—that electric shock from earlier when I handed her the coffee. The one that reminds me this is a terrible idea for about seventeen different reasons.

Her eyes meet mine.

We shake. Professional. Clean. Businesslike.

Except her hand is warm and fits perfectly in mine, and I remember how it felt to dance with her under those lights in Barcelona, and this is absolutely not going to be as simple as a business transaction.

Not even close.

I release her hand. Step back. Try my best to look normal.

"I should go, but I'll text you the contract when my agent sends it," I say. And I can't help it . . . I need her to look at me. So I duck my head into her line of sight. Her eyes lift, those deep, beautiful brown eyes find mine. Worth it. "I'll see you Saturday morning."

Jessa stands. "I'll walk you out."

Oh, this will be fun.

She opens the door and steps into the hallway with me, pulling it mostly closed behind her.

"If you hurt her again," she says quietly, "I will personally destroy your career and your reputation so thoroughly you'll never play hockey in this country again. Are we clear?"

One way or another, this arrangement is going to ruin me. It's either going to end my career or destroy what's left of my heart.

I nod to Jessa and turn away toward the elevator.

I'm not going to break Chloe's heart.

She's going to break mine.

And I'm going to let her.

Because five weeks with her—even fake, even ending badly—is better than the rest of my life without her.

BRODY

THE XCEL ENERGY CENTER LOCKER ROOM smells like sweat, wintergreen balm, and desperation—and tonight I'm contributing to all three.

Around me, guys are going through their own routines: Tyler's got his headphones in, nodding to whatever pump-up playlist he's running. Wyatt's methodically taping his goalie stick, the rip of athletic tape punctuating the low hum of conversation.

I'm lacing up my skates for the third time because my hands won't stop shaking and I keep getting the tension wrong. The familiar ritual—cross the laces, pull tight, double knot—feels foreign tonight.

Professional. Controlled. Candy Kane doing his pregame routine.

Except my phone keeps buzzing in my equipment bag, the vibration rattling against my helmet, and I can't stop checking it.

Three days since she agreed to the deal. Two days until I have to show up at her sister's party and convince an entire room full of people that I'm the devoted boyfriend, while Derek—her sister's fiancé, my teammate—watches every move I make, as if looking for cracks in the performance. He's got a burr under his jersey, and for some reason, it's me.

"Kane." Coach Jacobsen's voice cuts through my spiral like a blade on ice.

I look up. He's standing in the doorway, arms crossed over his Blue Ox–branded quarter-zip, already disappointed. He's got that look—Jacobsen's been coaching for twenty years, has a Stanley Cup ring from his playing days, and can smell weakness from across the rink.

"Yes, sir." I flash the smile. The one that's gotten me out of trouble since junior hockey. "Ready to go."

He studies me for a long moment, gaze narrowing. Yeah . . . he's not buying it.

I'm not sure I would either.

"Your defensive play has been off for two weeks. Tonight's the night you fix it. We clear?"

"Crystal."

He walks away, and of course the locker room goes quiet as a church. Oh goody, everyone heard that.

I finish with my skates, and when my phone buzzes again, I pull it out.

Rick
____

Contract ready. Need you to review
before I send to her. Call me after
the game.

Something in my chest tightens. The contract is ready. The contract that turns this crazy plan into something legally binding. Something real.

I wish.

There's no time to look at it though. I toss my phone into the locker and head for the tunnel. The muffled roar of the crowd echoes off the cinderblock walls, the cool rink air seeping in, and with it, the distinct arena smell—ice, popcorn, beer, and possibility.

The arena is maybe half full. It's a Thursday night game against the Seattle Firebirds, a team we should beat easily. The seats are a patchwork of Blue Ox jerseys peppered with some of the black-and-orange of the Firebirds. A handful of dedicated fans bang on the glass during warm-ups, their faces pressed against the plexiglass like kids at an aquarium.

I warm up with the team, take to the box, listen to the coaches. And most importantly, absolutely, definitely, one hundred percent do not think about the contract. Or about Saturday. About walking into that party with Chloe on my arm. About Derek's scrutiny. About her family's questions.

No sir. I'm not thinking about any of that.

I'm on the first line, of course. The puck drops with a hollow *crack* that echoes through the arena.

I'm supposed to be marking their center, Jenkins, a journeyman player who's been in the league for eight years. Instead, I'm half a step behind, thinking about the contract burning a hole in my phone.

Jenkins blows past me like I'm standing still. His skates spray ice crystals, and I turn to see him shoot—a wrist shot that sails toward the net. Wyatt makes the save, but barely, his glove hand flashing out at the last second.

"Kane!" Coach Jacobsen's voice from across the ice, cutting through the organ music and scattered applause. "Wake up!"

I grit my teeth and reset, taking my position at the blue line. Bang the ice with my stick.

Focus! Contract or no, you're gonna be out of a job if you can't get it together.

But two plays later, their winger is open because I drifted too far left, chasing a pass that was never coming. Derek has to cover for me, abandoning his position to prevent a breakaway.

The other defenseman, Conrad Kingston (King Con—why didn't I get a name like that?), skates past me during a line change, catches my eye as we tap gloves. The look is clear: *Get your head in the game.*

The period ends scoreless, but we're being outshot 11–7.

In the locker room, the mood is tense. Guys strip off their gloves, grab water bottles from the coolers, towel off sweat. The coaching staff huddles near the whiteboard, drawing up adjustments with squeaky markers. Coach Jacobsen pulls me aside.

"What's going on with you?"

"Nothing. I'm fine." I take a long drink from my water bottle, avoiding his eyes.

"You're playing like your head is somewhere else."

"Just an off night. I'll adjust."

He looks at me like he's deciding whether to bench me or give me one more chance. In the background, the assistant coaches talk strategy.

"Fix it." It's not a request.

I sit down at my stall and drop my head, sweat beading across my neck. My phone rattles across the locker, setting my nerves even more on edge. That contract's going to be the death of my career before I even get a chance to look at it.

I can't stop myself. I grab the phone.

New text from Rick:

Rick
____

Sent you the contract. The Blue
Ox management had an update to
Section 7. It's important. Read it
after the game.

After the game, Brody. Now's not the time.
Not a chance.

I open the attachment. The PDF loads slowly. Legal language, clauses, payment schedules. I scroll to Section 7, and my stomach drops like I've just hit a patch of bad ice.

Section 7: Morality and Conduct Clause

Both parties agree to maintain the appearance of a genuine romantic relationship through all wedding events. Upon completion of the Wedding (Event #4), both parties will execute a staged public breakup at the Wedding Reception (Event #5), with Party B (Chloe Dawson) initiating the breakup and Party A (Brody Kane) positioned as "at fault," followed by a mandatory thirty-day no-contact period. Any premature breakup, exposure of the contractual nature of the relationship, or other deviation from this termination plan will result in forfeiture of all benefits: Party A loses NHL contract renewal, and Party B forfeits all payment and owes financial penalties.

Furthermore, in the event that Player's relationship with Ms. Dawson is proven to be fraudulent, staged, or undertaken primarily for publicity purposes, the following penalties shall apply immediately:

(a) Contract termination without severance

(b) Repayment of signing bonus in full ($547,000)

(c) Forfeiture of all future salary obligations

(d) Two-year non-compete clause preventing Player from signing with any NHL team

I read that all again. Then a third time.

This isn't just losing the contract. This is losing my *entire* career.

If anyone proves the relationship is fake—Derek, a reporter, anyone—I'm done with professional hockey. For two years minimum. Two years is an eternity in sports. Players retire, teams rebuild, opportunities disappear. I'd be thirty when I could come back. Ancient in hockey years.

"You good, Kane?" Tyler has grabbed up his helmet. His hair is plastered to his forehead with sweat. "You look like you're gonna blow chunks."

"I'm fine." I lock my phone, force the smile. Completely fine. "Let's get back out there."

The second period is worse.

I'm cataloging every way this could blow up. What if Chloe sees the contract and panics? Or a reporter asks too many questions at the meet-and-greet party.

I miss an assignment. Their winger—Martinez, a rookie with a wicked slap shot—is standing alone in the high slot, exactly where I should have picked him up. The pass comes across, clean and hard. He one-times it.

Goal.

The red light behind Wyatt explodes in rotation, sirens wailing. The goal horn blares—that deep, resonating sound that means failure. The visiting team celebrates, gloves and sticks raised, while our home crowd groans in disappointment.

Coach calls a timeout. Glares at me across the ice. The team huddles around him at the bench, but his eyes are lasered on me the entire time he's talking strategy. Then, as I get up—

"Kane, you're done. Anderson, take his spot."

I've been *benched.*

Seriously?

Conrad catches my eye from the ice during a stoppage. *We're talking after this.*

Fantastic. Now I've got a pep talk to look forward to from Coach *and* King Con.

Third period. Coach doesn't put me back in. I watch from the bench as the game slips away—another Firebirds goal at 8:34, then an empty netter with thirty seconds left when we pull Wyatt for the extra attacker.

We lose 3–2.

The final buzzer sounds like a death knell. The arena empties quickly, disappointed fans filtering up the stairs, leaving behind scattered popcorn containers and crushed beer cups. The ice is torn up, scarred with the record of the game.

In the locker room after, nobody looks at me. Guys strip off their gear. Shin guards hit the floor. Jerseys get tossed into the laundry bins. The usual post-game energy has been drowned out by tense silence. The only sounds are zippers, Velcro, and the occasional muttered curse.

Derek glances at me from two stalls down. "Congrats on the new girlfriend, Kane. Interesting timing."

I look up, my chest tightening. "What's that supposed to mean?"

"Nothing." He pulls off his jersey, revealing the compression shirt beneath, dark with sweat. "Just noticed you've been off your game for weeks. Then suddenly, you've got a *girlfriend*."

"My personal life is none of your business."

"It is when it affects the team." He crosses his arms. "And when it involves my fiancée's sister."

Oh, this will be fun.

"Maya showed me the photos. From Ironclad." He's watching me too carefully. "Funny thing . . . Chloe's never so much as mentioned dating. And now she's your girlfriend?"

The question hangs in the air between us, loaded with suspicion.

He walks away before I can respond.

I finish changing in silence. Pull on my usual tailored look—tonight it's a Gucci crewneck sweater, pressed slacks, and a wool Burberry jacket. I thread my Rolex through my cuff.

The parking lot is nearly empty when I finally head out, the

January wind cutting to the bone and my breath clouding in the security lights. Frost crackles as I pry open the door of the Shelby and slide in. The leather seats are freezing even through my slacks. I sit in the dark and defrost the windshield while the engine warms up.

I pull out my phone, the screen nearly blinding me as the contract fills the screen.

Section 7 stares back at me, the words highlighted.

Two-year non-compete clause.

Do I really want to do this?

Someone knocks on my window.

I jump, nearly lose my phone.

Conrad's standing there with his fiancée, Penny Pepper, beside him. Penny Pepper . . . the murder podcaster.

Fantastic.

If anyone can see through me, it's her.

Maybe it's not too late to peel out of here, make a break for it before she picks up on anything. If I stick around, it'll be the murder of my career she covers next.

I roll down the window. Cold air rushes in, stealing what little warmth had built up.

"Everyone's heading to Sammy's," Conrad says, his breath creating clouds with each word. "You coming?"

Sammy's, the team's usual haunt, sits about three blocks away. It's usually a great place to down some wings and a couple beers. Not tonight.

"Not really in the mood."

Penny leans down. "You looked rough out there tonight."

"Thanks for the support."

"She means—" Conrad starts.

"I know what she means."

Conrad glances at Penny, and she nods slightly, understanding something unspoken. I guess that's how it is when you're dating someone.

"I'm an ice cube," she says. "So I'm getting in the car. But Conrad's not leaving until you talk, so for everyone's sake, just talk to him." She squeezes Conrad's arm and saunters off toward his car, a few spots away.

Conrad, meanwhile, heads over to my passenger door, opens it, and drops into the seat with a grunt. He waits all of one second before cutting to the chase. "What's going on?"

I stare for a second, then, well, why not? If anybody could understand, it's Conrad. "I'm in a situation."

"I'm listening."

"Made a deal that seemed simple, but the stakes are higher than I thought."

He waits.

"And if I screw it up, it could end my career. So . . . that's great."

Conrad's looking out the windshield at the empty parking lot and the distant lights of downtown St. Paul. "Been there."

". . . And? What do I do?"

"You show up. You play with everything you got. And you leave the rest to God." He shrugs, a gesture that seems too casual for the weight of what he's saying.

I blink at him. He can't be serious. "That's it?"

"That's it." He turns in the seat to face me more fully. "Someone told me once, faith isn't knowing it'll work out. It's doing the thing anyway. It's showing up when you want to run, believing that God is with you."

His words fill the darkness, settle over the silence like a thick, heavy blanket.

A beat passes and Conrad sighs, slaps a hand on my shoulder. "Hang in there, Kane. I've been where you're standing. But sometimes faith takes a leap." He holds up a fist. "See you at Sammy's."

I tap it. He gets out, his words still caught in the clouded breath, lingering.

God is with you.

Hardly. God left the day I buried my mother.

I turn on the defrost, the windshield clears, and I pull out.

Not toward Sammy's. And not toward home. No … Somewhere between the Xcel Center in St. Paul and my downtown Minneapolis penthouse, I end up on Chloe's street.

I didn't plan it. At least, I tell myself I didn't.

Her apartment building is in the Crocus Hill neighborhood, an older area with tall trees and historic homes converted into rentals. It's a classic St. Paul structure—red brick with white trim, probably built in the 1920s. Second-floor unit on the right side. Lights on in the windows, warm yellow against the winter darkness.

I park down the street, under a massive oak tree. I sit there, engine purring. I should go home. Get some sleep. Review the contract properly. Call Rick back. But I keep looking at her front door … willing her to text me, ask me if I'm up. I know it's crazy— she's the last person I should want to talk to about the contract— but what I wouldn't give right now to talk it out with her, with someone who doesn't see me as just Candy Kane … or who didn't.

Maybe she does now.

I let out a heavy breath. I shouldn't be here.

You have her number. You could text her.

Right. And say what? *Hey, crazy thought … you wanna hang out and talk fake-relationship contracts? No? That's cool. Me neither.*

Looks like I'm on my own.

I palm the shifter and—

The front door opens.

Everything stops.

Chloe steps out onto the exterior stairs, and I swear time does that cheesy, slow-motion thing they do in movies. She's wearing gray sweatpants, the well-loved kind with frayed hems, and an oversized Gophers sweatshirt—the same one from the other morning. Her brown hair's piled in this messy bun situation with little wisps escaping around her face, catching the porch light.

She's taking out the trash.

Taking out the trash.

And somehow, it hits me all over again. She's the most beautiful thing I've ever seen.

Drive. Drive now. Before she sees you and calls the cops.

My hands won't move. I'm frozen like an idiot, watching her hustle down the stairs, breath clouding in the cold air. No coat. Just speed-walking to the bins at the side of the building with this little bounce in her step that makes my chest physically ache.

DRIVE, YOU CREEP.

I force myself to shift into gear, foot heavy on the clutch, pull away before she can glance up, before she can notice my car lurking in the shadows. Before I can manage to scare her away and mess things up even worse than they already are.

White knuckled, I pull back onto the freeway, head toward home.

All right, Brody. A few rules if you're gonna go through with this.

First, no more letting it get into your game.

Second, no more creepy stakeouts.

And finally, absolutely, one hundred percent, no falling in love with Chloe, for both your sakes.

I pull into the underground garage of my apartment building and kill the engine.

Five weeks of pretending.

Five weeks of Chloe.

I close my eyes, drop my head against the steering wheel.

I absolutely do not "got this."

But here goes.

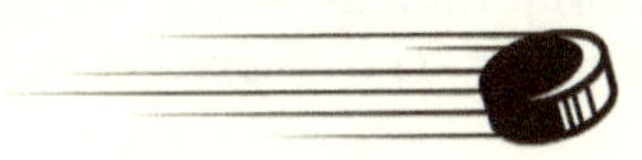

CHLOE

This is a bad idea.

Section 7 of the contract glows on my laptop screen. I've read it maybe fourteen times since yesterday, and it still makes my hands shake.

> Furthermore, in the event that Player's relationship with Ms. Dawson is proven to be fraudulent, staged, or undertaken primarily for publicity purposes, the following penalties shall apply immediately:
>
> (a) Contract termination without severance
>
> (b) Repayment of signing bonus in full ($547,000)
>
> (c) Forfeiture of all future salary obligations
>
> (d) Two-year non-compete clause preventing Player from signing with any NHL team

Two years.

His entire career.

Everything.

I slam the laptop shut as though doing so will trap the scary words inside. Keep me from letting my disastrous life seep into Brody's. My gaze lands on the dress hanging at the end of the bed, and I let out yet another heavy breath.

Okay. List time. Lists fix everything.

> *1. Get dressed. In clean clothing.*
>
> *2. Meet Brody at 11 a.m. Be cool. Don't embarrass yourself. We're going for Sandra Bullock from The Proposal, here. Not Sandra Bullock—Miss Congeniality. Poise. Professionalism. Altogether put-togetherness. You get the picture.*

3. Align our stories, coordinate our watches, you know the drill.

4. Pick up flowers.

5. Decorate the venue.

6. Change into party dress. (Take off the Goodwill tag.)

7. Convince my entire family I'm in love. (Honestly, this is the easy one.)

8. Don't get your heart broken. I think it's important to keep this on the list, don't you?

My phone buzzes. I grab it too fast, nearly fumble it onto the floor because I'm graceful like that. Maybe I should take the whole *poise* thing off the list . . .

Brody
On my way. Coffee first?

My heart does a little flutter that I refuse to attribute to the idea of a fake coffee date with my fake boyfriend. Attribute it to indigestion, if you will. Lack of sleep. Caffeine withdrawal. All great alternatives to the truth.

Chloe
Yes. Brew & Rumor?

Brody
Perfect. See you in 20.

Twenty minutes.

Perfect. Just enough time for me to get dressed, throw on some makeup, and talk myself back off the ledge. This is fine. I'm fine.

I pull on jeans and an oversized cream sweater that makes me feel approximately three percent less like a disaster. Hair in loose waves because I tried for "effortlessly pretty" and landed somewhere around "gave up."

My party dress hangs on the back of my bedroom door—a

simple black sheath, January-appropriate, elegant. I bought it on clearance three years ago, and it's been to exactly two events. I think you'd call that *mint condition*.

I grab my tote and shove in the essentials: party dress, party shoes, makeup bag, deodorant, Tylenol, double-sided tape, scissors, pliers, glue gun—hey, you never know what you'll need in an emergency. I'll be darned if Maya's party is a flop all because I forgot my glue gun.

I scramble through the apartment in search of my keys, flipping over piles of unpaid bills and zero-balance bank notes.

No wonder Brody offered me money. Wow.

My phone buzzes again.

<u>Brody</u>
Outside.

Oh.

Okay.

This is happening.

Deep breath. Coat. Bag. Stairs. Oh—I spot my keys and toss them into my tote. I'm ready.

The Shelby idles at my curb.

Brody gets out when he sees me. Opens my door.

He's wearing dark jeans, a sky-blue Henley under a black jacket, and he looks—

Well, shoot. He looks downright delicious. When I catch my reflection in the window, I half expect to find myself with full-on Looney Tunes heart-shaped eyeballs. I mean . . . Awooga!

He looks like every book boyfriend I've ever fallen for. A real-life rom-com hero. He even rests an elbow on the door, leaning in that perfectly bookish-boy way.

"Morning," he says.

"Hi." Honestly, I'm surprised I managed that. "Thanks for picking me up."

"Of course." He steps back, waits until I'm settled before closing my door and walking around to his side.

Very gentlemanly. Very "contractually obligated to appear like a good boyfriend" of him.

Oh, Chloe. We're enjoying this too much already.

The inside of the car smells like leather and light cologne. It's clean too. No crumbs in the seat cracks, no wadded-up McDonald's wrappers between the chairs . . . I feel underdressed just breathing in here.

"So," Brody says, pulling away from the curb, one lean arm passing over the other as he turns onto the street. "Ready for today?"

"Absolutely not." *Ope! Chloe! That was an inside thought.*

He laughs. The warm, real sound does something terrible to my heart and fades too quickly. "Yeah, me neither."

I glance at him. His shoulders are relaxed, a slight smile touching his lips. But his jaw's tight. Hands gripping the steering wheel a little too hard.

I wonder for the first time how he feels about this whole thing. Is he nervous? He has way more to lose than I do. If we're found out, I just lose money I've already mentally spent on rent and pretzel M&M's. He loses his entire career.

No pressure or anything.

"Did you watch the games?" he asks suddenly. "Thursday and Friday?"

I freeze.

Okay, so here's the thing. I wasn't *going* to watch. Because watching him play hockey felt weird and invasive, like reading his diary or stalking his Instagram at two a.m., which I *definitely* haven't done. But then Jessa came home Thursday night with Thai food and turned on the game, and I was going to say no, but there he was on the screen—all intensity and focus and athletic grace that made my stomach do this swoopy thing—and I was *riveted.*

Like, couldn't look away, forgot to eat my Pad Thai, accidentally elbowed Jessa in the face when he got slammed into the boards.

And then he got benched. Just sat there on that bench looking like a kicked puppy, trying to maintain his dignity, and my heart sort of . . . broke?

But I'm not telling him any of that.

"A little," I say.

He waits for me to expand. I don't.

"And?" he prompts.

"And . . . you're very good at hockey." It was that or *You look great in hockey pads*, and that didn't seem like the right direction for my first date with my fake boyfriend.

His shoulders tense. "Not lately."

"So you got benched. It's not like that happens all the time. Well, actually, I have no idea if that happens to you all the time—"

"It doesn't."

"Right. It doesn't." I continue with my weird and probably very unhelpful pep talk. "So, it was just a bad game. You'll . . . knock 'em dead next time. Is that a phrase? For hockey?"

Brody glances at me, the tense lines of his face melting away. He chuckles softly, shaking his head. "No, it's not . . . but thanks."

I try my best for a reassuring smile, and thankfully, his eyes are back on the road.

The rest of the drive is quiet. But it's nice. Comfortable.

He parks on the street, gets out, opens my door before I can beat him to it.

"You don't have to do that," I say.

"Do what?"

"Open my door. Be"—I wave vaguely—"all chivalrous and stuff. I mean, it's just us. No one's watching. You can save the Prince Charming routine for when we have an audience."

"Maybe I want to." He grins, and it transforms his entire face, his blue eyes warm, his smile white and what looks genuine, and bam, it's like a bomb of confetti goes off in my chest. Oh, no wonder they call him Candy. "Practice, right? Devoted boyfriend behavior."

Right.

Practice.

This is practice. He's practicing. You're a practice dummy. A very well-compensated practice dummy who needs to stop reading subtext into every little thing he does.

I follow him down the unmarked stairs to Brew & Rumor's basement entrance. The small brass plaque reading "B&R" is the only hint this place exists.

Inside, it's like walking into a 1920s speakeasy, if speakeasies served oat milk lattes and had decent Wi-Fi. Exposed brick, Edison bulbs, the rich mahogany bar that now serves coffee instead of bootleg whiskey. Mismatched vintage leather armchairs sit alongside velvet sofas in deep jewel tones. Floor-to-ceiling bookshelves are crammed with mystery novels and yellowed newspapers.

The rumor wall—covered in typewritten anonymous tips and conspiracy theories—takes up the entire back wall. Someone's added a new one since last week:

> The truth about the Blue Ox losing streak:
> cursed hockey sticks or poor conditioning?

"This place is incredible," Brody says, looking around like he's stumbled into Narnia, except with better coffee.

And I wonder . . . He brought me coffee from here just days ago, so why does he act like he's never been here? Or maybe he ran through the drive-thru?

Anyway, "I know. I've been coming here since college." I point to a corner table tucked between bookshelves. "That's my spot."

We order lattes for both of us and egg bites. The barista, Marcus, recognizes me and winks. "Special occasion?"

"Work meeting," I say, maybe a little too quickly.

Marcus raises an eyebrow but doesn't comment.

We settle into the corner. The vintage lamp casts warm light across Brody's face, highlighting his jaw, the tired shadows under his eyes, and it hits me.

He didn't sleep well.

Join the club. I've been awake since four a.m. running worst-case scenarios like my own personal horror-movie marathon.

"Okay," I say, pulling out my phone and opening my Notes app. "Basics first. Timeline. How we met. How long we've been together. We need our stories to match, or Derek's going to smell blood in the water."

"Right." He stretches his impressive legs out. His knee bumps mine under the small table. "Maybe we should just . . . stay close to the truth?"

"All right . . . so . . ." I try not to look at him. Jessa did say we could use the story in an official capacity. "Barcelona?" The word sticks to my lips.

Brody's brows pinch, hesitation heavy between them, but he gives a nod.

Okay. We're doing this. I tap the screen of my phone again and type:

Met six months ago in Barcelona.

He leans into my space, peering at the notes over my shoulder, and I swear I can *feel* his body heat setting my shoulder on fire. But like . . . don't lean away just yet. "Ran into each other again two weeks ago."

"At a coffee shop," I say.

Brody frowns, his head tilting. "Not Ironclad?"

The explanation slips out without a thought. "We told that girl at the shop we were dating. It wouldn't make sense for that to be our first time seeing each other again."

Huh. Maybe I'm more equipped for this whole lying thing than I thought.

I don't want to think too hard about what that means about me.

Brody's lips part. "Ah. Smart. Okay, so we met again at the coffee shop."

"Classic Hallmark meet-cute. The spilled coffee, hands touch, the whole goopy thing," I add, already typing it down.

"And realized we still had—" He pauses, his gaze lifting from my phone to meet my eyes.

"Chemistry." I say it like it's a fact. My brain just spits it out. And now it's too late to take it back, so I double down. I type it. Try to ignore the fact that every single one of my brain cells is collectively screaming because his knee is touching mine. It's very loud inside my head right now. "And we've been seeing each other for two weeks. Casually. Taking it slow because we're both busy professionals who don't rush into things."

"Seeing where it goes," he adds.

"Right. Just . . . seeing if there's something there." I add a note:

Keep it vague. Don't oversell.

"Is there?" He's looking at me now. Not at my phone. At *me*.

"Is there what?"

"Something there."

My brain short-circuits, and for a moment, all I can do is blink. "We're—I mean—for the story—"

"I'm asking for the story." But his eyes say something else entirely.

And there goes my heart again, and I have to remind myself that he's literally an image pro. He probably wrote the book on meaningful eye contact. *How to Appear Sincere for Publicity Purposes*, Chapter 7: The Smolder.

"Yes," I manage. "For the sake of the story, there's definitely something there."

"Agreed." He takes a drink. Doesn't break eye contact. "So, how'd it happen—our meeting in Europe?"

Oh, thank goodness. Back to facts. Heartless, feelingless facts.

We both know how we met. He chased down a thief. We spent the evening together. Danced. Shared a life-changing kiss. And then he left me standing outside my hotel, wondering if I somehow made the whole thing up.

But that's not the story we're selling.

That story makes me look pathetic. *Girl falls for charming guy, guy disappears, girl agrees to be his fake girlfriend for money six months later.* That's not a Hallmark rom-com. That's a Lifetime movie. And not even a good one.

"Your sister's—what'd you call it? Bridal-cation?—still works," Brody says. "You were there with bridesmaids. I was visiting the city. I still chased down the purse snatcher. We still spent the evening together. I still walked you back to your hotel."

"And we didn't exchange numbers because—"

"—it felt like a vacation moment. Something perfect we didn't want to ruin by dragging it into reality."

No dance by the fountain. No kiss under the orange tree. As agreed, those parts of the story stay off the table.

I stare at him for a beat. "Yeah," I say. "That works."

The air between us feels thick, but that's probably just the humidity from the espresso machine. I clear my throat. "Um, right. So, two weeks ago. Coffee shop collision. We recognized each other immediately."

"And it was like we never lost touch." The corner of Brody's mouth tilts upward, sending warm fuzzies all through me.

"It's the classic event-planner-meets-hockey-player love story," he says.

I chuckle. "I'm not sure anyone would call that a classic."

Brody scoffs. "Sure it is! It's the whole 'They come from different worlds but—'"

"'—make each other laugh.'" I shrug, smiling into my drink. "Yeah, okay."

The sound of grinding coffee fills the air, and Brody leans back, draping an arm over the back of the booth. "We should probably know basic stuff about each other. Your family's going to ask questions. Speaking of, who am I meeting today?"

"My parents, my brother Devon and his wife Melissa, and of course, Maya and Derek and a flock of their friends and extended family."

"I might need a list."

"And who should I know on your side?"

His face changes, just like that—goes a little white, and he swallows. "No one."

I raise an eyebrow. He looks away.

And my chest sort of caves in, remembering his story about his father.

Okay then.

He looks back at me. "Favorite color?"

"What?"

"Favorite color. Come on, that's kind of basic couple knowledge. Isn't it?"

"Oh. Um—" Why is this harder than coordinating our fake backstory? "Green. Forest green. Sunlight-on-the-leaves-in-summer green. Christmas green. Not lime green. Or Sage. Or that icky brownish green." *For the love, Chloe, stop using the word* green.

Brody quirks a brow, but he types it into his phone. "Favorite food?"

"Pasta. Any kind. But especially carbonara. I'm very boring and predictable." I pull up my notes. "You?"

"Blue. Steak."

"That's very . . . aggressively on-brand for a hockey player."

He lifts a shoulder, but his smile is cute.

We keep going.

Guilty pleasure TV. (His: cooking competitions—I can't help but love that for him. Mine: K-dramas. Don't judge.)

Dream vacation. (His: somewhere remote with good fishing where people leave him alone. Mine: anywhere with old bookstores and questionable Wi-Fi. And now I'm envisioning us honeymooning in some small town in the Land O'Lakes . . . Bad. Bad Chloe.)

Biggest pet peeve. (His: people who don't rerack gym weights. Mine: people who dog-ear library books.)

With each answer, I learn something new about him. He's funny—dry humor that catches me off guard in a good way. Thoughtful—listens when I talk.

It's not long before we've melted from business conversation into honest-to-goodness get-to-know-you-because-I-could-love-you conversation, and it's like I'm standing outside my body, screaming at myself not to get attached. It's not real!

We're not friends. We're not dating. We're business associates who happen to be coordinating a very elaborate lie for money.

Professional. This is professional.

Even if it doesn't feel that way.

I check my phone. 11:45 a.m. Where did the time go? "We need to get going. I still have flowers to pick up and the room to decorate."

Brody stands, offering his hand like we're in a Jane Austen novel.

I take it, and he helps me up, pulling me close. Close enough that I can see green flecks in his gray-blue eyes.

"Ready?" he asks.

For what? The flowers? The party? Pretending to be in love with him when I'm starting to suspect the pretending part is going to be way harder than the being-in-love part, which is absolutely not what I signed up for and is definitely going to end badly for me specifically?

"Ready."

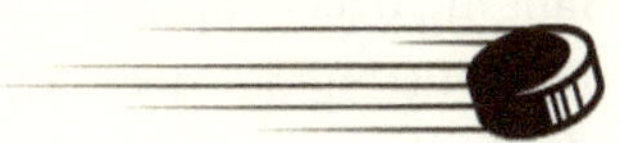

After a quick stop at the florist—and an awkward conversation about how the flowers aren't for *our* party, where I blush so bad that I worry I might have second-degree burns—we pull up to Pinstripes.

The building is gorgeous—an upscale bowling alley slash venue. Polished wood floors, sophisticated lighting. Floor-to-ceiling windows overlooking a courtyard that's currently covered in snow.

The bowling lanes are pristine. The dining area is set up with round tables draped in white linens. The event space is empty when we arrive—just us and the venue coordinator, a woman named Lisa, who shows us where to set up.

"Guests arrive at three?" Lisa confirms, checking her tablet.

"That's correct," I reply, dropping a box of decorations on the nearest table. "Oh, and I spoke to the caterers yesterday. They'll be arriving at two instead of two thirty. Will you be ready for them?"

Lisa notes it down with a quick nod. "We'll be ready. Let me know if you need anything else."

"Thank you, Lisa!"

Brody and I get to work. He carries in the flower arrangements while I start on the photo backdrop—a full greenery wall made of 20 x 20-inch boxwood panels framed with silk flowers to match the real ones on the cocktail tables, and a custom neon sign that reads *She said yes!*

"Where do you want these?" he asks, gesturing to a particularly large centerpiece that looks like it weighs more than me.

"Set it down beside the welcome sign, I think."

We work in silence for a while. It's actually kind of nice. Comfortable. Like we've done this before, even though we absolutely haven't.

Arranging flowers. Hanging backdrops. Setting up the small gift table near the entrance. Putting out decorative dessert trays for when the caterers arrive.

Brody sheds his jacket, rolls up his sleeves.

I try very hard not to notice his forearms.

I fail spectacularly.

"Chloe?"

I jerk my attention back to his face like I've been caught stealing. "What?"

He's grinning. Like, knows-exactly-what-I-was-doing grinning. Busted. "I asked where you want this banner."

"Oh. Um—" Think. Words. Use them. String them together in a coherent fashion. "Above the gift table?"

"You okay?"

"Fine. Just . . . concentrating."

"On my arms?"

My face goes nuclear. Like Chernobyl levels of meltdown. "I was not—you're very—I mean—shut up."

He laughs. The sound reminds me of that ocean color in his eyes, like waves crashing on the shore. Loud, exciting. I need to hear it again.

"You're cute when you're flustered."

"I'm not flustered."

"You're flustered."

I spin back to my work, focusing very hard on the precise placement of the dessert trays. "Are you going to hang that banner or just stand there being smug about your stupid attractive forearms?"

"I can do both." He gets the ladder from the storage closet Lisa pointed out and sets it up.

I watch him climb up, reach for the banner, secure it to the wall.

"Toss me the other end?" he calls down.

"I got it." I grab the banner's opposite corner and climb on a chair, because I'm helpful like that.

"Careful," Brody warns.

"I've got it."

Deep down, I'll admit that I should have known I don't "got it." But in this moment, all I'm thinking is *Look at us, we're so cute working together.*

I reach too far, trying to line up the banner with the hook. The chair wobbles, and I have a brief moment of clarity where I think *This is it. This is how I die.*

And suddenly, I'm in Brody's arms.

We're pressed together. My hands on his shoulders. His arms around my waist. His face inches from mine.

Neither of us moves.

"You keep doing that," I hear myself say.

Brody frowns. "Doing what?"

"Swooping in to save me."

He chuckles, but his voice is rough, deeper than normal. "Anytime."

We should pull apart. Step back.

We don't.

Music starts playing overhead. The venue's sound system—Lisa must be testing it.

And I know this song.

Oh no.

Classical guitar. Soft and romantic and achingly familiar.

Barcelona. The outdoor café. Dancing under the twinkling lights before he disappeared and broke my heart.

Brody's eyes widen. He knows it too.

We stand there, frozen, while the music swells around us, my heart thundering in my chest as his grip on my waist tightens slightly.

I should say something. Acknowledge it. Ask him if he remembers or if I'm just being delusional and reading meaning into random coincidences.

But Jessa negotiated, and I'm bound by the whole "no reliving Barcelona" rule.

The song ends. A different one starts—something upbeat and completely wrong for whatever just happened.

The spell breaks.

Brody clears his throat, steps back with the kind of careful distance that feels deliberate.

I step back too, tucking my hair behind my ears with trembling hands, and glance at my watch. Shoot. It's almost two thirty. "I should change," I say, breaking the moment. "Party starts soon." I grab my bag and head to the bathroom, trying not to run like I'm fleeing a crime scene.

A few minutes later, I emerge from the bathroom, brushing out the silhouette of my black sheath dress.

And freeze.

Maya and Derek are standing near the entrance, talking to Brody.

They're early.

Of course they're early.

Maya sees me first. "Chloe! Oh my goodness, the place looks beautiful!"

Okay, I'll take that.

"I can't believe you and Brody did all this!" Maya gestures around like we just built the Taj Mahal rather than arranging a few flowers and hanging things up. "It's gorgeous."

"It was a team effort," I say, which is technically true.

Brody appears at my side. His hand finds the small of my back automatically, like we've practiced this—which we haven't, but apparently our bodies have decided to coordinate without consulting our brains.

"Your sister's very talented," he says to Maya with the kind of sincere smile that could sell ice to Minnesotans in January. He's very good at lying.

I need to remember that.

"I know! She's the best." Maya beams at me.

Really? *Really?*

But wait. Her expression shifts, goes curious. "So. I've been dying to ask—how exactly did you two meet?"

Here we go.

Game time.

BRODY

THE QUESTION HANGS IN THE AIR LIKE A puck suspended mid-flight, and I've got maybe two seconds to decide if I'm going to catch it cleanly or let it drop and shatter everything.

How exactly did you two meet?

Maya's looking at us with genuine curiosity—the kind that comes from sisterly love, not suspicion. But Derek is right beside her, arms crossed, expression unreadable. He's not curious. He's testing.

Chloe's body goes rigid under my hand. I can feel her heart racing through the thin fabric of her dress.

This is it. First real test. Don't screw it up.

I smile—easy, charming, the one that's gotten me out of trouble since I learned to talk. "Funny story, actually."

Maya leans in, already invested.

Chloe leans into me. "You remember Barcelona guy?"

Maya's eyes go wide. "Wait—that was you? The mystery guy?"

Chloe nods and I chime in. "Hold on, you know this story?"

Maya turns her gaze on me. "Of course I do!"

And I prepare myself for the obligatory you-hurt-my-sister look, but it doesn't come. Huh. Maybe Chloe never told her about the ghosting part.

"So, you know how we decided not to exchange information," I continue. "The evening felt like this perfect thing we didn't want to ruin by dragging it into reality. So we just"—I shrug—"let Barcelona stay in Barcelona."

Chloe and I share a look before going on. "So, two weeks ago, we ran into each other in a coffee shop. Literally. I crashed into him, spilled coffee all over him." She turns those gorgeous brown eyes on me. "Completely ruined that suit you were wearing."

"Worth it," I say, my hand instinctively tightening against her waist, and I feel her relaxing slightly against my side. We're in this together. A team. And for a second, I almost forget we're lying. Because the way she's looking up at me, the small smile playing at her lips—it feels real.

Maya clasps her hands together like we just performed a Broadway musical. "That's so romantic! It's serendipity!"

Derek says nothing. Just watches us with those calculating eyes.

"Something like that," Chloe says.

Maya's buying it completely—she's already tearing up, which seems excessive for a two-week relationship, but I'm not complaining.

Derek's still not convinced. But he's not calling us liars either. So, small victories.

The next hour is a blur of handshakes, small talk, and me pretending I'm not cataloging every threat in the room like I'm preparing for a playoff game.

Chloe's parents arrive—James and Patricia Dawson, normal

people from a small town. Her dad's wearing a casual polo, and her mom, a sweater over slacks.

"Brody Kane!" James pumps my hand enthusiastically, grinning like he just won the lottery. "This is incredible. My wife and I have been following your career for years. That defensive play you made in Game Six against Chicago last season? Unbelievable."

He remembers a specific play from last year's playoffs?

I relax slightly. "Thank you, sir. That was a good game."

"Good game? You shut down their entire power play in the third period!" He turns to his wife. "Patty, remember? We were screaming at the TV."

Patty laughs, squeezing Chloe's shoulder affectionately. "James wouldn't stop replaying it on his phone for a week. Our son Devon played hockey in high school—left wing." She gestures across the room toward a man with dark curly hair and the petite blonde tucked under his arm. Devon and his wife, presumably. "Not professionally, of course, but we've been hockey people forever. Small-town Minnesota, you know. Friday nights at the rink."

"Maple Lake, right?"

"That's right! You been there?"

"The Blue Ox minor league team practices there."

James lights up and claps me on the shoulder. "Come on up sometime. We'll show you the real Maple Lake."

Patty is beaming at Chloe. "Sweetheart, you didn't tell us he was *this* Brody Kane. When Maya said you were bringing a hockey player, I thought—well, I don't know what I thought, but certainly not this!" She laughs. "We're just so happy you found someone who—"

She stops herself, but I catch the end of that sentence.

Someone who . . . ?

"We're just getting to know each other," Chloe says softly, and I hear the careful hedge in her voice—protecting herself, managing expectations.

"Well, you picked a good one," James says, winking at his daughter. "Anyone who can handle Derek's ego in the locker room deserves a medal."

I laugh. "Derek can be competitive."

"That's a polite way of putting it." James leans in conspiratorially. "But he knows what he wants. Can't fault him for that. Maya's a catch."

And just like that, I see it. The dynamic that's shaped Chloe's entire life.

Her parents aren't the problem. They're warm, genuine, excited to meet me—not because I'm famous but because they love hockey and they love their daughter.

But they're also completely swooning over Maya's world.

Maya's wealthy fiancé. Maya's destination wedding. Maya's perfect life.

Chloe's parents fit into that world the way I fit into a tuxedo—uncomfortable, out of place, trying their best.

And Chloe has spent her whole life watching her parents try to keep up with the life Maya built, while her own quieter dreams got overlooked in the chaos.

Not because they don't love her.

Because Maya's life is just . . . louder.

Chloe catches me watching her, and for a second, our eyes meet.

She sees that I see it.

Something changes between us.

"Chloe did a great job on all of this, don't you think?" I gesture around the room at the flowers, the lights, the perfectly arranged tables. "The decorations, the setup, the coordination. She's got an incredible eye for detail. You must be so proud."

Patricia blinks. "Oh. Yes. Of course."

But she wasn't thinking about it. Wasn't acknowledging it.

Chloe's contributions are invisible to her own mother.

I feel something crack open in my chest. Protective. Angry.

I shift on my feet, sliding from the easy, comfortable conversationalist to something . . . harder. Just because we've only been "dating" for two weeks doesn't mean I'm going to let anyone walk all over her. Not my girl.

I'm in the game now.

James Dawson, still wearing that cheery expression, takes a sip of his beer and jumps back to the topic of hockey. "You know, Brody, I know you've had a rough season, but you've got a tough position to fill. Defense—not an easy job."

Oh good. Here we go. I brace myself for the usual unsolicited advice. But something in his gaze softens.

"It's an important position. Lot of responsibility." He glances at Chloe. "You've got to be reliable. Steady. Not too flashy."

Is he talking about hockey or relationships? I can't tell.

"I try to be all of those things."

"Good. Chloe needs someone steady." He says it like she's fragile. Breakable. "She's had a rough go of it lately. Business struggles, you know. Not everyone is cut out for entrepreneurship."

My jaw tightens. Chloe's staring at her shoes.

"Actually," I say, maybe too firmly, "I think Chloe's business is pretty impressive. Event planning is brutally competitive, and she's built something from the ground up. That takes guts."

James looks at me like I just said something mildly interesting but ultimately irrelevant. "Well . . . she's had a pretty great example to learn from. Maya's always been the go-getter in the family."

And there it is again.

Everything leads back to Maya.

I glance down at Chloe. She's smiling—the kind of smile that doesn't reach her eyes. The kind that says *I'm fine, I'm used to this, it doesn't bother me anymore.*

Except it does. I can see it in the way she's holding herself. Small. Invisible.

Her parents drift away to greet other guests, and Chloe exhales like she's been holding her breath. "Sorry about that," she mutters. "They're—"

"A lot?"

"Enthusiastic about Maya's wedding." She's deflecting. Making it about the wedding instead of admitting her parents barely see her.

I want to tell her *They should see you. You're right here. You're incredible.*

But I can't. Not here, with everyone watching. And not privately, where too much of my heart would be in it.

So instead, I say, "You should be really proud of what you did here today. They all should."

She looks up at me, surprised. Like she wasn't expecting the compliment.

"Thanks."

And I realize—she's not used to being seen.

The murmur of the crowd dies down as Derek announces the bowling tournament at four o'clock, and I immediately regret every life choice that led me to this moment.

"Couples competition!" he says, grinning like this is the best idea he's ever had. "Prizes for the top three teams. Bragging rights for everyone else."

Chloe glances at me. "You bowl, right?"

"Define 'bowl.'"

"Oh no."

"I'm sure it's fine. How hard can it be?"

As it turns out, it is not, in fact, fine.

My first ball careens into the gutter so fast it's almost impressive. The second one follows its predecessor like they're magnetically attracted to failure.

Tyler Anderson is in the lane next to us with his girlfriend, Ava, and he's laughing so hard he has to lean on the ball return.

"Kane!" he shouts. "You're supposed to hit the pins, man!"

"Thanks, Torch. Super helpful."

Chloe is trying not to laugh. Failing spectacularly.

"It's not funny," I mutter.

"It's a little funny."

Derek appears at our lane, arms crossed, that smug captain smile plastered on his face. "Thought athletes were supposed to be co-ordinated, Kane."

"Different skill set," I say through gritted teeth. "Very different."

"Clearly." He turns to Chloe. "You should probably teach him. Before he breaks something."

Chloe picks up her ball—a sparkly purple thing that looks like it belongs in a kid's party—and steps up to the lane.

She bowls a perfect strike.

The pins explode like she just fired a cannon at them. The crash echoes through the venue.

Everyone stops. Stares.

"Holy—" Tyler starts.

"That was incredible," I finish.

Chloe turns around, grinning—a real grin, not the careful smile she's been wearing all day. "I was in a league in college."

"Of course you were."

Derek's smirking. "Looks like your girlfriend is carrying the team, Kane."

"I'm aware."

But watching Chloe light up like this—confident, happy, un-selfconscious—is worth the humiliation.

She walks back to me, still smiling. "Want me to show you?"

"Please."

She picks up my ball, demonstrates the approach, the release, the follow-through. Her hands move confidently, precisely. This is her element.

"Now you try," she says.

I step up. The ball feels heavier than it should. I focus on the pins, visualize the path—

Gutter ball.

Chloe's laugh is pure and bright and completely unguarded. "Okay, we need to try something else."

She steps up behind me, her hand on my arm, adjusting my stance. "Loosen your grip. You're strangling it."

"That's what it feels like."

"And follow through—like this." Her hand guides mine through the motion.

We're standing close. Too close for the performance. But it doesn't feel like performance.

It feels—

Real.

I try again. The ball wobbles down the lane, clips three pins.

"Progress!" Chloe cheers like I just won the Stanley Cup.

"I knocked down three pins. That's not—"

"It's three more than last time!"

And she's so genuinely excited for my terrible bowling that something in my chest tightens.

This girl. This girl who gets overlooked by her family, who makes herself small, who accommodates everyone else—she's cheering for my pathetic three-pin knockdown like it matters.

Like I matter.

We lose the tournament. Spectacularly. But we're laughing the whole time, and when the photographer—some professional Maya hired—captures us mid-laugh, covered in the glow of the overhead lights, it doesn't feel staged.

It feels like the most real thing I've done all night. Until my phone buzzes in my pocket.

Rick

Don't forget social media posts.

Right. I almost forgot.

I pull out my phone and swipe to the camera. Debate warning Chloe what I'm about to do, but Derek is watching me. I can feel his eyes tracking every move I make, every word I say. He's looking for cracks.

So I just get it over with.

I slide my arm around her waist, tilt my head close to hers, and aim the camera. She tenses against me, but I whisper "For the story" against her hair. Then, because I need this to look real, I press my lips to her temple just as I snap the picture.

We look . . . convincing. Happy. Like a couple who's been together longer than two weeks.

But looking at the photo, something feels off.

Her smile doesn't quite reach her eyes. Like she's performing too.

Maybe we both are.

I post it anyway.

@CandyKane: Good company, great night.

Generic. Safe. Believable.

It pulls in three hundred likes in five minutes.

"See?" I say, showing her the screen. "People love us."

"Because we're so convincing," she says quietly.

There's something in her tone. Sadness? Resignation?

I can't tell.

By eight o'clock, the party is winding down. Guests are filtering out, saying their goodbyes, thanking Maya and Derek for a lovely evening.

Chloe's helping clear tables—because of course she is, even though there's staff for that. I watch her fold napkins, stack plates, move efficiently through the room like she's trying to be useful.

Trying to earn her place at her own sister's party.

It breaks something in me.

I catch her wrist gently. "Come on. Let's get out of here."

We say our goodbyes—Maya hugs Chloe tight, whispers something I can't hear. Derek shakes my hand, holds it a second too long.

"See you at practice," he says.

It's not friendly. It's a warning.

I nod. "See you."

"Well," I say, pulling out of the parking lot, "that was a disaster."

Chloe looks at me, startled. "What?"

"Oh no, *you* were great." I flash my most reassuring smile. "And I think Maya and your parents are sold. But there's no way Derek believes us. Not to mention I bowled like someone who's never seen a ball before."

"You weren't that bad."

"I was objectively terrible."

She almost smiles. "Okay, you were pretty bad."

"See? Disaster."

"And I think we convinced most people," she offers.

"Most people aren't the problem. Derek is. And the couples shower is in two weeks." I grip the steering wheel tighter. "We need to do this better."

"What do you mean?"

"I didn't know you were good at bowling. I didn't know you went to college here. I don't know your middle name or your favorite movie or—" I stop myself before I say *How to make you laugh every day the way you did while bowling.*

She's quiet.

I continue. "We don't really know each other. Not the stuff real couples know. And Derek's going to figure that out."

"So what do we do?"

I glance at her as I merge onto the highway. "We fix it. A real date. Not a performance. Just us."

CHLOE

We fix it. A real date. Not a performance. Just us.

The word *real* lands in my chest like a stone dropped into deep water, and I'm nodding before my brain catches up to what I'm agreeing to, which is how people end up in cults or time-shares or other situations that are universally assumed to be bad news.

"Okay," I manage. "I'm free Monday."

Earth to Chloe—what part of "fake boyfriend" do the two of you not understand?

He glances at me as we merge onto the highway. "All right, then, Monday it is. I'll pick you up for dinner. Seven."

I turn to the window and thank God for the darkness hiding my furiously blushing face.

Minneapolis slides past in streaks of light and shadow. The skyline glitters against the winter sky. We cross the Mississippi, and the bridge lights reflect off the dark water below. Normally I'd think about how pretty this is, how the city looks like something out of a movie at night. But right now I'm too busy trying to remember how to breathe like a normal human and not think about the fact that we're alone in this car and his cologne smells amazing and I am absolutely not prepared for whatever's about to happen.

The silence stretches.

"You okay?" Brody asks.

I glance back, my hair falling around my shoulders like a curtain.

"Yeah. Just tired." I aim for casual, land somewhere near *desperately trying not to have feelings.* "Long night."

Snow drifts past the windshield in lazy flurries, caught in the headlights. The wipers sweep it away in a steady rhythm.

Now it's quiet. Loud quiet. I should say something. But my brain has apparently clocked out for the evening, leaving me with nothing but the hyperawareness of him beside me—the way his hands rest on the steering wheel, the line of his jaw in the dashboard glow, his left leg propped up slightly, reminding me of his knee pressed to mine at the coffee shop just this morning. How was that less than twelve hours ago—

"Can I ask you something?" His voice cuts through my spiral.

I answer way too quickly. "Sure."

"The bowling. You were incredible tonight. How did you get so good?"

Oh. That's not so bad. Safe territory.

"College," I say, relieved. "Freshman year. My roommate dragged me to league night, and I was surprisingly not terrible."

"What position?" He sounds genuinely curious. "Or is that not how bowling works? I clearly have no idea."

"Anchor. I went last."

"Of course you did." Something changes in his tone. "Most pressure. Most responsibility."

I glance at him. He's watching the road, but there's this expression on his face—understanding, maybe. Like he just puzzled something out.

"Yeah," I say quietly. "I guess."

We stop at a red light. He looks at me.

Really looks.

Not the performance look from the party—the one designed to convince my family we're madly in love. This is different. Searching. Like he's trying to see past all that to whatever's underneath.

My throat tightens.

"Why bowling?" he asks. "Out of everything you could've been good at?"

And there's the real question.

I could deflect. Make a joke about how I have a secret passion for rental shoes and polyester bowling shirts.

But I'm so tired. And he's looking at me like he actually wants to know.

"I needed something that was mine," I hear myself say. "Something I could be good at without—without comparisons."

The light turns green. He drives.

He doesn't push. Just lets it sit there.

"Maya's good at everything," I continue, and I don't know why I'm still talking, except maybe my exhaustion has obliterated my filter. "Always has been. Beautiful, successful, confident. And I'm just the little sister who tried but didn't quite measure up. So bowling was weird enough that nobody cared. I could just be good at it without anyone comparing me to her."

I stop. Bite my lip. That was too much. Way too much. Next time, I should save myself the trouble and just turn over my diary.

"Sorry," I add quickly. "That was—I'm tired. I shouldn't have—"

"Don't." His voice is firm. "Don't apologize."

We drive in silence for another minute. Two. I'm staring out the window again, mortified, wishing I could go back and just say *I liked knocking down pins* like a normal person.

"Can I ask you something else?" Brody says finally.

Oh no. Here it comes. "I think you're reaching your contractual limit soon, so choose wisely."

He chuckles, his lips quirking in that very Brody way. "I don't remember that in the contract."

"Ah, well, it's in the fine print. I had my people add it in," I say, waving a hand flippantly.

"Oh, I see. Well then, I'll try to keep that in mind."

"What's the question?"

"Your family." He pauses, and I can feel him choosing his words carefully as the mood changes again. "Your parents. The way they—" He stops. Starts again. "Your mom redirected every conversation back to Maya tonight. Five times during dinner. Your dad barely acknowledged the decorations you did. And you just—took it. Like you're used to it."

My chest constricts.

"How long has it been like that?"

I still, my heart lurching into my throat. I don't know what's worse—the fact that he noticed it, or that I'm so used to it I didn't.

"My entire life?" And now I sound pitiful. Just toss my pathetic bones on the pile of unpaid bills and send me off in a blaze and call it good at this point. "It's not intentional. Patricia is my stepmom. My real mom died when I was three—car accident. I don't even remember her. Dad married Patty about a year later, and she came packaged with Devon and Maya, who were in elementary school. Devon was already playing hockey. Maya was in ballet, then drama and . . . you know, a star. I sort of tagged along behind."

"Chloe."

The way he says my name—it's suddenly too much. We've jumped off the deep end, from the safe shallows of bowling and fake dates into a deep, dark drop-off. And I so want to trust him. But this is too much too soon, and he's not my boyfriend. Not really.

"Really, Brody, it's okay." I aim for a gentle shutdown. "I've gotten used to being a little . . . invisible."

The car rolls to a stop, the red from the traffic light pouring through the windshield, and Brody looks at me, his lips pressed tight. "You are not invisible."

My throat closes up completely.

"Not to me."

The light turns green, and Brody drags his gaze away as we start moving again, and I try to jumpstart my brain back into survival mode. *Air, Chloe. You need air to live.*

"What about you?" I manage finally, desperate to change the

subject before I do something mortifying like start crying. "What about your family? You never talk about them."

He stiffens slightly. I notice because I'm hyperaware of everything about him right now.

"Not much to talk about."

"That's not an answer."

He glances at me, surprised. Then almost smiles. "Fair enough."

Another long pause. I wait.

"My mom died when I was fourteen," he says finally. "Cancer. My dad's—" He stops. "Well, I told you all about his stuff. We're not close."

"I'm sorry."

"Don't be. Not your fault." He pulls up to a stop sign, then continues through the quiet neighborhood. "Point is, I get the family stuff. I get wanting to be someone other than who they made you."

The words permeate the air between us. We're both carrying family wounds, just different shapes.

The car slows as he pulls up in front of my building.

He parks. Turns off the engine.

Silence fills the car in that heavy, fuzzy way. Like Christmas snow falling. Meaningful but somehow completely ordinary. We stay like that for a minute, neither of us willing to end the moment.

"I'll walk you up," he finally says, his voice soft.

"You don't have to—"

But he's already out, coming around to my side.

The cold hits me like a slap when I step out of the car. Fifteen degrees, maybe less. My breath comes out in visible puffs, and the snow is falling harder now—light flurries catching in the porch light above my second-floor door.

We climb the exterior stairs together. His hand hovers near my back—not touching, but close enough that I can feel the warmth.

I fumble with my keys. My hands are shaking, and I'm telling myself it's the cold, but we both know that's a lie.

"Chloe."

I look up.

He's standing close. Too close. Our breath mingles in the frigid air between us, little clouds of white that disappear as quickly as they form.

His eyes meet mine.

And then he leans in.

Time stops.

His gaze drops to my lips. And then—

He stills, lets out a resigned sigh. His lips brush my cheek. Soft. Quick. Over before I can fully process it's happening.

"Seven o'clock Monday," he murmurs.

Then he's gone, taking the stairs two at a time, and I'm standing on my doorstep in the cold, frozen, one hand still clutching my keys, the other touching my cheek where I can still feel the ghost of his lips.

I hear the car engine start. See the taillights disappear down the street.

Finally—finally—I get my key in the lock and stumble inside.

Warmth hits me. The smell of cinnamon candle and coffee. Jessa's on the couch with her laptop, working late as usual.

She looks up. "How was it?"

I close the door. Lean against it.

"Dangerous."

BRODY

I MAKE THE DEFENSIVE PLAY LOOK EASY—READ-
ing Tyler's approach two steps ahead, positioning myself where the
puck's going to be before he even releases it, cutting off the angle
with the kind of precision that's been eluding me for weeks.

"Nice, Kane!" Coach Jacobsen calls from the boards.

I tap my stick on the ice, already tracking the next play.

My reads are sharper today. Positioning's more solid. The defensive slump that's been plaguing me since November?

All right, that's still there.

But something's different.

I can feel it—the way I'm reading the ice better, moving with
more confidence, no longer second-guessing every decision. It's
not fixed. Not even close. But it's . . . better.

Maybe I'm more relaxed. Maybe having one less crisis to manage—the image crisis finally down to a dull roar—freed up enough
mental space that I can actually focus on hockey.

Or maybe it's something else entirely.

Something I'm not ready to examine too closely.

I execute another decent defensive sequence. Not perfect, but competent. Wyatt makes the save behind me, nodding approval through his mask. Tyler skates past, grinning.

"Looking good out there, Kane."

I don't respond. Just reset for the next drill.

Practice continues. Drills, scrimmages, the familiar rhythm of skates against ice, sticks hitting pucks, Coach's whistle cutting through it all.

By the time practice is called, I'm feeling something I haven't felt in weeks.

Capable.

Not great. Not dominant. Not the player I used to be.

But capable.

It's a start.

"Kane!" Coach waves me over as we're clearing the ice. "Got a sec?"

I skate over, pulling off my helmet. "Yeah, Coach?"

"Whatever you're doing, keep it up." He's got that look—stern, but approving. "Your gap control is still too loose, among other things, but it's an improvement."

"Thanks, Coach."

"Still a ways to go, but"—he pauses—"you're looking a little more settled. Less . . . in your own head."

Settled.

Interesting word choice.

"I've been working on it," I say. How exactly is having a fake girlfriend helping my real hockey game? Your guess is as good as mine.

He claps my shoulder. "Well, keep working. We need you sharp for playoffs."

"Yes, sir."

The locker room is the usual chaos—guys stripping off gear,

heading for showers, arguing about last night's NFL game. I'm pulling off my jersey when Tyler drops onto the bench beside me.

"So. Chloe."

"What about her?"

"She coming to Friday's game?"

I hesitate. Chloe's not exactly the sports kind of girl. But then again . . . that's what a real girlfriend would do . . . right? Feels like a trap. I flash a smile. "Yeah, I don't know. She's got a lot going on with her sister's wedding."

"Well, tell her she should come." He grins. "You've been less miserable lately. Whatever she's doing, it's working."

I stuff my jersey in my locker without response.

"Seriously, man. You've been wound tight for months. It's nice to see you loosening up."

"I'm still the same person, Torch."

"Yeah, but you're not walking around like the world's about to end anymore. So . . . are you really?"

"Ouch." I grimace, feigning injury.

He chuckles as he heads for the showers.

I sit there with my gear half off, his words sitting uncomfortably in my chest.

Am I different?

Less miserable?

I haven't thought about it. Haven't had the time. I've been too busy trying not to set my career on fire, juggling the constant calculation of what's real and what's tactical between Chloe and me.

But maybe he's right.

Maybe something is working.

Now I just need to make sure, when things with Chloe come to a crashing halt, that it doesn't disappear.

I pull off my skates. Toss them in my locker. Head for the showers too.

The hot water feels good against sore muscles. I let myself stand under the spray, let the water rush over me, quiet my mind. I let the game fade away, the contract, my renewal, my reputation . . . all of it. And then I'm back to Chloe . . .

To our date, tonight.

Seven p.m., Barcelona Wine Bar. Reservation for two.

A real date. That's what I called it, but it's more like recon work. A chance to get to know Chloe on a deeper level. Make us convincing enough that Derek backs off and our next event doesn't turn into an execution.

And maybe—maybe—figure out what I'm actually doing here.

I'm dressed and heading out—jeans, Henley, leather jacket—when someone steps into my path.

Derek.

"Kane." His voice is flat. "We need to talk."

My stomach drops, but I manage to keep my expression neutral. "Yeah? About what?"

"Don't play dumb with me." He steps closer. "This whole thing you've got going on with Chloe, it's got to stop. I don't know what kind of scheme you're running—"

"Scheme?" My voice is level, but my heart is pounding. "What are you talking about?"

"You show up out of nowhere with Maya's sister, and suddenly you're this devoted boyfriend?" His voice drops low, seething with disdain. "A week after the news breaks that you're not the charmer everyone thinks you are? You need her. I'm not an idiot, Kane."

"There's no scheme, Derek. Chloe and I are together. We reconnected a few weeks back and—"

"Save it." He cuts me off. "I don't know what your angle is, but I'm watching. And if you hurt her—if this is some publicity stunt and she gets caught in the crossfire—I will make your life miserable. On the ice and off it."

The threat hangs in the cold air between us.

I fight the urge to push back, tell him to back off. But the words die in my throat.

He's not wrong.

This *is* an arrangement. A mutually beneficial agreement with contracts and NDAs and payments.

And if he knew that, well, you saw the contract. My career would be over.

So I lie.

Sort of.

"I'm not playing games with her," I say quietly. And that part, at least, feels true. "I care about her. I'm not going to hurt her."

That one is true.

"You better not." He steps past me, heading back toward the locker room.

I should let it go, but—

"What's your problem, Derek? Why are you so against this?" I keep my voice low, but it holds an edge. "Did I do something to you in a previous life?"

Derek stills, glancing over his shoulder, his eyes dark in the tunnel light. "The fact that you don't know is exactly why."

He keeps walking. Leaving me standing in the empty tunnel with my heart still racing and absolutely no idea what just happened.

What don't I know?

What am I missing?

I stand there for another minute, trying to piece it together. Nothing.

Finally, I give up, head out the tunnel. I'm almost to my car when the Blue Ox social media and PR coordinator, Felicity, calls from behind me. It's never a good idea to stop and acknowledge her. Trust me on this. "Brody! Got a second?"

I don't stop, just turn around and keep walking backward. "Yeah, what's up?"

She's running up to me. "I saw the photos from Saturday night. You two look great together." She's got her tablet out, scrolling. "Very natural. The bowling pictures especially—people are eating it up."

I slow. "That's good."

"It is. And I've been thinking . . ." She looks up. "Chloe's event planning business. I did some research. She's got a great eye—those decorations Saturday were professional level. But she's struggling to break through, right? Small client base, not a lot of visibility."

I nod slowly.

"I'd like to help," Felicity says. "I have a few friends in the wedding and events industry who could shine a light on her business. Maybe give her a boost."

I study her, looking for the catch.

But her expression is genuine. Professional.

Kind.

"That would be great," I say finally. "I'm sure she'd appreciate it."

"Perfect. I'll reach out to her directly." She smiles. "Have a good night, Brody."

She's gone before I can respond.

I throw my gear bag in the Shelby's trunk. Slide into the driver's seat.

Just sit.

The leather is cold. Dashboard dark.

My phone buzzes.

Multiple texts.

<u>Rick</u>

Saw the party photos. Good work.

Yeah, well, what can I say? I'm good at this game.

Right. But Chloe makes it easy.

Another text.

Ashley Morrison's lawyer sent another letter. Wants public apology and admission of wrongdoing. They're threatening to file if you don't comply. DO NOT apologize. It'll just create more tabloid drama and make you look guilty. Keep the relationship with Chloe solid. That's your best defense.

My chest tightens.

A public apology.

An admission of wrongdoing.

For something I *didn't do.*

If I apologize, it validates her lie. Makes me look guilty. The tabloids will destroy me.

If I don't, she files suit. A lawsuit means depositions, discovery, media circus. She doesn't have a case. But sometimes that doesn't matter.

I let my head fall back against the seat.

I've got four hours until my date with Chloe. And I gotta make this one count.

I start the engine. Drive home through the gray January afternoon.

All I can think is *Don't screw this up.*

CHLOE

This is a terrible idea.

I'm standing in front of my closet, staring at hangers holding approximately three outfits that could maybe pass for "date night," and wondering what possessed me to agree to this.

Oh, right.

Twenty thousand dollars and crushing financial desperation. Very romantic.

"I can hear you thinking from here," Jessa calls from the couch without looking up from her laptop. "Stop spiraling."

"I'm not spiraling."

"You're absolutely spiraling."

I pull out a black dress. Put it back. Pull out a burgundy sweater. Put it back.

"It's just dinner," I say. More to myself than to her. "Casual. Low-key. A basic first date, except with less pressure . . . because it's not real. So. What's there to spiral about?"

"Uh-huh." Jessa's still typing. "And the fact that you've been standing in front of that closet for twenty minutes has nothing to do with Brody's kiss the other night?"

My face goes hot. "No! It. Does. Not."

"Oh, please, you came in here like you'd just stolen your first kiss, all grinning and breathless."

"I did not."

"Touching your face like 'I'll never wash this cheek again!'" Jessa goes full Victorian, pressing her wrist to her forehead as she faints against the couch.

"Ew, Jessa." I laugh, tossing one of the rejected outfits at her. "Stop. I'm trying to think, and you're not helping."

"Overthinking is more like it."

I shoot her a scowl. That's it. I reach back without looking and grab a dress at random. "This one," I say.

See? How's *that* for not overthinking?

Okay, wait—on second thought, that maybe isn't the best way to make this possibly life-changing decision. Oh heavens, please don't let me have grabbed something horrible. Nothing orange.

Jessa looks up. Surveys the dress. Nods approval. "It's perfect."

"Really?" I glance down to find my emerald-green dress. One of my favorite Goodwill finds and one I've been saving for the right occasion. I let out a relieved sigh.

Jessa presses her wrist to her forehead again. "Oh dear. I've found my dress, but goodness, how will I ever decide on hosiery on time?"

"Stop!" I cry as Jessa breaks down laughing.

We both go still at the sound of a knock at the door.

"Is that—that can't be him. It's too early!" I say, frantically gathering all the dresses into my arms.

"Oh, relax," Jessa says, pushing her laptop aside. "It's probably Mrs. Swenson from downstairs asking us to keep it down again. I'll get it."

Jessa vanishes down the hall, comes back a moment later holding an envelope.

A large manila envelope with my name typed on the front.

My stomach drops.

"This was in our mailbox," Jessa says, handing it to me. "Looks official."

I know what it is before I open it. The return address confirms it: Starlight Publishing—Children's Publishing Division.

I submitted my manuscript three months ago. A children's book about a dragon who wants to fly and the little girl who helps him find his wings. All twenty-eight pages are filled with whimsical illustrations I drew myself. It's twenty-eight pages of the most vulnerable thing I've ever created.

I've been checking my email obsessively for weeks.

Apparently they went old-school.

Snail-mail rejection.

"Want me to open it?" Jessa asks gently.

"No. I've got it."

I tear open the envelope. Pull out the letter.

Dear Ms. Dawson,

Thank you for submitting your manuscript, "The Dragon Who Wanted to Fly," to Starlight Publishing. While we appreciated the creativity and heart in your story, we regret to inform you that it does not fit our current publishing needs . . .

The rest is standard rejection boilerplate.

We receive thousands of submissions. This is a subjective business. We wish you the best in your future endeavors.

Something falls out of the envelope.

One of my illustrations—the dragon from Barcelona. The one I'd sketched out that morning in Park Güell, just before Brody saved my purse.

Only that dragon had been different—sharper, harsher. Beautiful and expressive, but unafraid.

And then Brody showed up. Burst into my life and made me believe in a different kind of hero . . . even just for a moment. From then on, my dragon looked a little different. No matter how many times I sketched him. He wasn't ferocious anymore, not crouched over his hoard of treasure. He was just . . . alone. Hiding.

In this version, the dragon peers out from the depths of a dark cave, his eyes bright in the inky black.

I stare at it.

Jessa picks it up carefully. "Chloe. This is beautiful."

"It's not good enough, apparently."

"One rejection doesn't mean—"

"It's fine." I fold the letter. Shove it back in the envelope. "It's just a silly dream anyway. I should focus on event planning. Stick to what I'm good at. That's the practical thing. The realistic thing." Never mind that my event planning business is circling the drain as well. But with Maya's wedding coming up, at least there's hope for it.

"Chloe—"

"I'm fine." I force brightness into my voice. "Really. It's fine. I have a date to get ready for. Let's just—let's focus on that."

Jessa watches me for a long moment.

Then she sets the illustration down carefully on the coffee table.

"All right," she says. "Let's fix you up."

Three hours later, I'm staring at myself in the bathroom mirror, barely recognizing the person looking back.

The green dress fits perfectly—vintage seventies-style with bell sleeves and a wrap waist that's somehow both bohemian and elegant. Jessa convinced me to wear my hair down in loose waves instead of my usual ponytail. Minimal makeup but enough to make my eyes look less like I've been fighting back tears over rejection letters.

I look . . . good?

Not Maya-level stunning. Not "professional hockey player's girlfriend" polished.

But good.

Like maybe I could pass for a girl who deserves to be on Brody's arm.

Maybe.

"You look amazing," Jessa says from the doorway. She's holding my coat. "Seriously. He's going to lose his mind."

"It's just dinner."

"Right. Just dinner." She winks dramatically.

The doorbell rings.

My stomach flips.

"That's him." Jessa grins. "Deep breaths. You've got this."

I grab my purse and head for the door.

Deep breaths.

It's just dinner.

Professional.

Transactional.

Nothing to panic about.

I open the door.

Brody's standing there in dark jeans and a moss-green sweater that makes his eyes look impossibly blue, holding flowers—actual flowers. Not just a sunflower this time, but a small bouquet of white roses and eucalyptus—and he's so gorgeous I can't breathe.

"Hi," he says.

My brain short-circuits. "Hi."

He's staring at me. Not saying anything. And something painfully delicious and not at all professional flashes in his eyes.

Stop that!

"You look—" He stops. Swallows. "Wow."

My face flushes. "Thanks. You too. I mean—not wow. Well, yes, wow. But—you look nice."

Smooth, Chloe. Very smooth.

He holds out the flowers. "These are for you."

"Oh. Thank you." I take them, and our fingers brush for a half second. An electric zing shoots up my arm, stealing my breath for a heartbeat. "They're beautiful."

"I wasn't sure if flowers were too much. Or not enough. Or—" He stops himself. "I'm overthinking this."

"No, they're perfect." I step back. "Come in. Let me just put these in water."

He follows me inside.

Jessa is standing by the couch, trying very hard to look like she wasn't eavesdropping.

"Hi, Brody," she says brightly. "Chloe, I'll just—" She makes this very pointed eye gesture. Like *Wow, he looks niiiiiice. Don't you think so?*

I shoot her a look that hopefully conveys *Stop that immediately.*

She grins innocently. "Have fun, you two!"

And then she disappears into her bedroom.

Leaving us alone in the tiny living room.

I find a vase—actually a mason jar, because I don't own vases—and fill it with water. Arrange the flowers. Set them on the counter.

When I turn around, Brody's looking at the dragon illustration Jessa left on the coffee table.

My heart stops.

"Is this yours?" he asks quietly.

"Oh. Yeah. It's just—something I was working on."

He picks it up carefully, his gaze falling over every line, taking it in like some sort of fine art.

The silence stretches.

"It's incredible," he says finally.

"It's just a silly doodle."

He looks up at me, and his eyes catch mine in that sort of unescapable way. That way that makes me feel seen . . . and so vulnerable. There's something in that look—something I can't quite read. Like he wants to say something. Like he's deciding whether to say it.

Then he sets the illustration down carefully. "It's really good, Chloe."

His voice is so genuine it makes my chest ache.

"Thanks," I manage.

He doesn't know it was rejected today. Doesn't know that publishers think my "creativity and heart" aren't enough. Doesn't know that this silly dream of mine just got professionally dismissed.

And I'm not going to tell him.

"Ready to go?" I ask, grabbing my coat before he can ask more questions.

"Yeah. Of course."

He helps me into my coat—his hands gentle on my shoulders—and I try very hard not to think about how good he smells or how close he's standing or how my heart is doing that weird flutter thing again.

We head downstairs and out to the street. The Shelby is parked at the curb, gleaming under the streetlights.

"So," Brody says as he opens the passenger door for me. "How was your Sunday?"

I slide into the car. The leather is cold but familiar now. "It was good. Went to church. Had lunch with Jessa. Worked on some business stuff."

He gets in the driver's seat. Starts the engine. "Church?"

"Yeah. My church does this thing where they go through books of the Bible slowly. We're in 2 Corinthians right now."

I'm rambling. I always ramble when I'm nervous.

And what's there to be nervous about? Oh, I don't know. Maybe the fact that this fancy little car smells just like him and there's a very real possibility that it overrides my brain's ability to be rational and I end up throwing myself at him over the middle console during the next red light, and now all I can seem to think about is just *not* doing that . . . Yeah, I think I'm nervous about that.

And so I keep going, boring him with details about the morning's sermon. "Yesterday was about not losing heart. How God is at work in us even when we don't understand what's happening. When everything feels hard or confusing or like it's falling apart."

I stop.

That got way more personal than I intended.

"Sorry. You probably don't care about—"

"No, I—" He's quiet for a moment. Pulls out into traffic. "Do you go to church? Regularly?"

"Most Sundays, yeah. Unless I have an event." I glance at him. "Do you?"

"We did. When I was a kid. My mom had faith."

His voice changes.

Softer. Quieter.

"It sort of died with her."

The words hang in the air.

"I'm sorry," I say.

"It's fine. It was a long time ago."

But it's not fine. I can hear it in his voice. The way he's gripping the steering wheel a little tighter. The careful control.

"You know, she got me into hockey," he continues. "My mom. She was sick most of my childhood. Cancer. That's why we moved to Minneapolis, actually. Shorter commute to Mayo for her treatment. Anyway, hockey was the one thing that was just mine. She'd come to my games when she could. Sit in the stands wrapped in blankets, even when she was exhausted. She never missed a game if she could help it."

The pale streetlights pour through the window, softening the hard lines of his face. My heart aches at that faraway look in his eyes. He's back there now, with his mom.

"Hockey saved me," he continues. "Gave me purpose. A future. A way out. After she died, my dad started drinking. A lot. Home was chaos. But hockey had rules. Structure. If I worked hard enough, played well enough, I could control the outcome."

He pauses.

Glances at me.

"That's why I can't lose it. Hockey is everything. It's all I have."

It's all I have.

The words sit heavy between us.

He doesn't have people. Doesn't have family he can count on. Doesn't have anything except the game and the performance and the careful control he's built to survive.

And now I'm taking twenty thousand dollars from him to help him keep the only thing he has left.

Great.

Cool.

Love that for me.

"You're not alone," I hear myself say. "I know it feels like hockey is all you have. But you have people. Even if you don't see it yet."

You've got me I want to say. But I can't promise that. I shouldn't promise that.

Brody doesn't respond. Doesn't take his eyes off the road.

I can't tell if he's being mysterious or is suddenly thinking this is a bad idea.

Then he pulls up in front of a restaurant—dark brick exterior, warm lighting glowing through windows, elegant signage that reads *Barcelona Wine Bar* in script letters.

I stare at the sign.

"I thought we weren't supposed to talk about Barcelona," I say slowly.

He looks at me. All innocent confusion. "What?"

"The restaurant. It's called Barcelona."

"Is it?" He glances at the sign like he's noticing it for the first time. "Huh. Would you look at that."

I narrow my eyes at him. "You didn't know?"

"Total coincidence." His face is perfectly neutral. "I just picked it because the food's supposed to be good."

"Brody."

"What?" He's fighting a smile now. I can see it at the corners of his mouth. "It's a popular name. Lots of places are called Barcelona."

"In Minneapolis?"

"Sure. Probably." He's fully grinning now. "Statistically speaking."

"You absolutely knew."

"I have no idea what you're talking about." But he's laughing. A deep, warm rumble that instantly fogs my mind. "I'm just a simple hockey player who wanted to take a beautiful girl to dinner and—"

"You're lying."

"—happened to pick a restaurant with a completely random name that has absolutely nothing to do with—"

"Brody Kane."

He holds up both hands in surrender.

And then he smiles.

Not Candy Kane. Not performance. Not careful control.

Just him.

A real, devastating, knee-buckling smile that makes my heart forget how to beat properly.

"Okay," he admits. "Maybe I knew."

My stomach flips. "Why?"

"Because—" He stops. The smile softens. "Because I needed a do-over."

Oh.

Ohhh.

And now my heart is doing extremely unauthorized things.

The contract said we weren't supposed to talk about Barcelona outside of our official story. Section something-or-other. *Prior romantic history remains confidential . . .* We were supposed to pretend that some things from that night never happened.

"So this was"—I can barely get the words out—"intentional?"

"Completely intentional." He's still smiling *that* smile. Oh, he's good. "Is that okay?"

Is it okay?

Is it okay that he remembered Barcelona enough to pick a restaurant with the same name?

Is it okay that he's totally breaking the rules?

Is it okay that I really don't care?

Absolutely not okay. *Danger. Danger!*

"Yeah, it's okay." Oh, I'm in trouble.

"Good." He gets out of the car. Comes around to open my door. "Because I'm really hoping this night ends better than the last one."

He offers his hand.

I take it, and we walk toward the restaurant entrance together. The winter air bites at my cheeks. Somewhere behind us, the Shelby's engine ticks as it cools. Ahead of us, the restaurant glows with warm light and the promise of Spanish wine and tapas and conversation.

And second chances.

And rules that need breaking.

And I think: *Maybe this isn't such a terrible idea.*

Maybe.

BRODY

THIS MIGHT HAVE BEEN A BAD IDEA.

Scratch that. It was definitely a bad idea.

Because sitting across from Chloe in the soft glow of Edison bulbs with a Spanish guitar playing somewhere in the background, the scent of olive oil and garlic wafting from the kitchen, it feels a little too much like Barcelona.

Only this time, I'm not running. Not on your life.

"The patatas bravas look good," Chloe says, glancing up from the menu. "And the croquetas. Oh, and calamari. Is it weird to order all the appetizers?"

"Tapas, and not weird at all." I close my menu. "Let's do it."

She smiles. That genuine smile that makes her whole face light up. "That was easy."

This girl has no idea how devastating she is with that green dress that brings out flecks of gold in her brown eyes. Her hair falls in waves over her shoulders, catching the light every time she moves. She could ask for everything on the menu and I wouldn't argue.

A male server comes by, takes our order, and recommends a spiced vermouth to pair with the patatas. I couldn't tell you what else he says because my head is completely wrapped up in Chloe Dawson, who's tracing patterns on the tablecloth with her finger.

Is she nervous?

Or maybe her heart is racing, like mine. Maybe she feels the electrical charge between us. I almost jerked away when our fingers brushed earlier.

And this is supposed to be a simple get-to-know-you date.

I'm in deep trouble.

The server leaves, and silence settles between us.

I should ease into this. Play it cool. Charm my way through this conversation.

Instead, I lead with panic. "I think we're in trouble."

She blinks. "What?"

"Derek. He blindsided me after practice today. He's onto us."

Her eyes grow wider. "What do you mean?"

"I mean, he basically accused me of using you to boost my reputation . . . which is only off base because he doesn't know how true it really is. We gotta know everything about each other if we're going to survive the next few events."

Chloe straightens, a slight blush creeping into her cheeks. She brushes her hair behind her ear. "Um, all right then. What do you want to know?"

"Your middle name. How you take your coffee. Your biggest fear. What you do when you're stressed." I lean forward. "For starters."

The waiter stops by, dropping off the patatas and vermouth. Chloe picks at the food, dishing some onto her plate before diving into answering my questions.

"Middle name's Rose. Chloe Rose Dawson," she says, covering her mouth with a hand.

"Chloe Rose," I say, pulling out my phone to take notes. "That suits you."

She smiles. "Does it? I didn't like it so much when I was younger. But it's grown on me the last few years."

"It does." I scoop a forkful of patatas and keep going. "Coffee order?"

Chloe's lips part, but I jump back in—

"Wait, don't tell me. I already know this one. Candy cane latte."

She chuckles a little, and my chest tightens at the sound. "Well, now it is. I used to be all about oat milk lattes, but then—" She stops. Colors slightly. "You bought me that candy cane latte after the coffee shop collision, and I got addicted. So now that's my order."

I can't help but grin. "Maybe I got a little too confident about that one. I think it still counts for a point though."

She raises a brow. "There are points?"

"Oh, there are always points." I take a sip of the vermouth. It's good. Warming. "Biggest fear?" I ask, setting down my glass.

"Being run over." She says it matter-of-factly.

"Like, literally? By a car? Train? Bus?"

"My family."

I pause, recalling her words from Saturday night. *I've gotten used to being a little . . . invisible.*

She's paused too, looking at me with that vulnerable expression, and it does something to me. Something primal, like when I see an enforcer go after one of the rookies. Even if I don't like them, I don't like to see them crushed.

"What do you do when you're stressed?" I continue, needing to keep moving before this gets too heavy.

She pulls her gaze away, shrugging off the heaviness of the moment. "Oh, you know, the usual. Bread. Cookies. Just about any carb will do the trick. Ironclad's velvet smash cookie is particularly soothing after a stressful day."

I grin, trying to envision her buried in a cookie skillet after a hard day's work. Maybe we'll have to get dessert after this.

I try to think up another question, keep things light. But instead, I hear myself say, "I saw the dragon."

Chloe freezes. "What?"

In hindsight, without context, that didn't make a whole lot of sense. "In your sketchbook back in Barcelona." It's not breaking the rules—the topic's not anywhere near the kiss that shall not be named. But still, my pulse leaps as I keep going. "It fell open for a second after I got your purse back. I saw your drawings. They're really good."

Her face flushes. "You never said anything."

"You closed it so fast, I figured it was private. But I remembered it when I saw the sketch in your apartment earlier." I pause. "What's with the dragon?"

Chloe is quiet for a long time. "Don't laugh."

I scoff. "I would never!"

She takes another sip of her drink, pushes the patatas around with her fork. "I spent a lot of time in the library as a kid. After school, on weekends. Reading and drawing and making up stories about princesses and warriors and magical creatures."

"Like the dragon."

"Like the dragon." She meets my eyes. "I have this crazy dream about becoming a children's book author and illustrator."

"What's crazy about that?"

She tilts her head. "It's not super practical. Doesn't exactly pay the bills."

There's something in her voice. Resignation. Defeat.

Like she's already given up on the thing that makes her eyes light up when she talks about it.

"Practical is overrated," I say.

She laughs. But it's hollow. "Says the professional hockey player with the guaranteed contract."

I pretend to wince. "Ouch."

The moment settles like dust in water, her laughter fading into a quiet smile.

I reach across the table. Not thinking. Just moving.

My hand covers hers.

She doesn't pull away.

"You shouldn't give up on being a children's author," I say quietly.

"I don't know," she says, her expression wry. "I got a rejection letter today. The publisher said it didn't fit their current publishing needs. Translation: Not interested."

"Aw, Chloe. That's one publisher—"

"It's fine. It's just a silly dream."

"Stop." I squeeze her hand. "Stop calling your dreams silly. They're not. You're—"

I stop, because what I want to say is *You're incredible. Your art is incredible. And anyone who can't see that is an idiot.*

But that's dangerously close to real-boyfriend territory. So instead, I say, "You're talented, Chloe. Don't let one rejection letter convince you otherwise."

She's staring at our hands. At the way my thumb is tracing circles on her palm without my permission.

"Thanks," she whispers.

The server arrives with the other food—croquetas (as golden as I remember them from that night in Barcelona) and perfectly fried calamari with lemon wedges—followed by the delicious redolence of garlic and lemon and parsley.

Chloe glances at our hands, her fingers trailing mine as she finally pulls away. But a magnetic force remains.

"This is amazing," Chloe says around a bite of croqueta. "Why is everything in this restaurant perfect?"

"Barcelona magic."

"Is that a thing?"

"It is now."

She laughs. Real laughter. The kind that makes her nose scrunch up, her brown eyes twinkle. I want to make her laugh like that every day for the rest of my life.

The thought hits me like a slapshot to the chest.

Oh no.

I'm in trouble. Real trouble.

She has her phone out now and is holding it up to take a picture of the food.

"What are you doing?"

"Phone always eats first."

Right then, of course, the waiter swings by our table. "How's the food?"

Before I can answer, his eyes fall to Chloe's phone. "You want me to take a picture?"

I glance at Chloe. Do we?

"Sure," she says, handing over her phone. I lean in close and, okay, the smile comes easy. Too easy. Chloe's hair brushes my shoulder, and I resist the urge to pull any closer. The server snaps the picture, then hands it back to her. My phone dings a moment later when she texts it to me.

"Okay, my turn for invasive questions," Chloe says, stealing a piece of calamari from the shared plate. "Let's start with . . . what's the hardest thing about hockey?"

The hardest thing about hockey?

"The reading," I say after a moment. "Plays, formations, defensive strategies. Everything's written down. Game plans, scouting reports, coach's notes. And I can't—" I stop. Take a breath. "I have to memorize everything. Every single play. Every formation. Every adjustment. Because I can't rely on reading them in the moment."

Chloe tilts her head a little, her brown hair tumbling over her shoulder.

I hesitate before explaining. This is the part I don't talk about. The part that feels like weakness. "I struggle with it. Dyslexia. Makes reading plays, contracts, anything with a lot of text . . . hard."

Her lips part, understanding dawning.

"So I spend hours before every game going over everything with my coach. Having him explain it verbally. Draw diagrams. Working it out until it's committed to memory." I'm surprised by how easy this is to say. How she makes it feel less like weakness. "But that's not the hardest part."

"What is?"

"Making it make sense. Hockey isn't just memorization. It's angles. Physics. Geometry in motion. You have to read where the puck is going, where your opponent is moving, how to position yourself to cut off their options. It has to click. Has to make sense spatially. It's about seeing the space. Understanding how bodies move through it. Anticipating flow."

"That's incredible."

"It's exhausting."

"But effective. You're one of the best defensive players in the league."

I pause. She's been doing her research.

I fight a satisfied smirk. "Well, I used to be."

"Your coach says you're improving. You told me that."

There's something in her eyes—pride, like she's behind me. On my team. Not Candy Kane's team. Mine. Someone who sees past the performance. Past my careful control.

I remember that feeling . . . from Barcelona. It's addicting.

My phone rings.

I glance at the screen.

Dad.

My stomach drops.

It's almost ten p.m. My father never calls this late unless—

Unless something's wrong.

"I'm sorry," I say to Chloe. "I have to—"

I answer. "Dad?"

But it's not my father's voice.

It's a woman. Professional. Calm. "Is this Brody Kane?"

"Yes. Who is this?"

"This is Hennepin County Medical Center. Your father, Robert Kane, was brought in about an hour ago. You're listed as his emergency contact. We need you to come to the hospital as soon as possible."

The world tilts.

"What happened?" I ask.

"He was in a car accident. You should come. Soon."

The line goes dead.

I'm staring at my phone. My hand is shaking.

"Brody?" Chloe's voice is gentle. Worried. "What's wrong?"

"It's my dad. He's in the hospital. I have to—" I'm already standing. Throwing cash on the table. Too much, but I don't care. "I'm sorry. I have to go."

"Okay." She's grabbing her coat. Her purse. "Let's go."

"You don't have to—"

"I'm going with you."

"Chloe—"

"Brody." She takes my hand again. Firm. Grounding. "I'm going with you. We'll figure out the rest later."

I should argue. Should tell her this isn't her problem. Should maintain the careful distance between professional arrangement and whatever this is becoming.

But I can't.

Because my father is in the hospital.

And I don't want to face it alone.

"Okay," I manage.

We leave the restaurant together, the Barcelona magic dissipating into the cold February night and the smell of car exhaust and the sound of my heart pounding too fast in my chest.

The perfect evening is over.

And I have no idea what's waiting for us at the hospital.

But Chloe's hand is in mine.

And somehow, that makes it bearable.

CHLOE

Hennepin County Medical Center smells like antiseptic and bad coffee and anxiety in the way only emergency rooms can.

I'm standing next to Brody in a temporary ER bay—curtains for walls, beeping monitors, the constant shuffle of nurses and doctors moving between patients—watching a young doctor with cartoon penguins on her scrubs explain Brody's dad's discharge instructions.

"Broken collarbone," she's saying. "It's a clean break, so it should heal in six to eight weeks with rest and physical therapy. We're prescribing pain medication and a follow-up appointment with orthopedics."

Robert Kane is sitting on the edge of the hospital bed, looking significantly smaller than I expected.

I don't know what I imagined. Some larger-than-life figure, maybe. The kind of father whose shadow you can't escape.

But he's just . . . a man. Mid-fifties, graying hair, weathered face, wearing a hospital gown, and looking deeply, profoundly embarrassed.

"Was he drinking?" Brody's voice is carefully controlled.

The doctor's expression shifts. Sympathetic but honest. "His BAC was point-one-two. Just over the legal limit. He drove into a light pole. It could have been much worse." She glances at Robert. "You'll be hearing from the police about charges. But medically, you're clear to go home."

Brody's face goes carefully blank.

That Candy Kane expression I'm starting to recognize as his default when emotions get too big to handle.

"I can get dressed," Robert says quietly. "Give me five minutes."

The doctor nods and disappears through the curtain.

Silence.

Brody is staring at the floor. Jaw tight. Shoulders rigid.

I want to say something comforting.

I have no idea what that would be.

Your drunk father wrapped his car around a light pole, but hey, he's not dead doesn't exactly inspire warm fuzzy feelings.

"I'm sorry," Robert says finally. His voice is hoarse. "I know you've got better things to do than—"

"Just get dressed, Dad." Brody's voice is flat. "I'll bring the car around."

He walks out before Robert can respond, leaving me standing there awkwardly with his dad.

"Brody didn't really get a chance to introduce us," I say, trying my best to fill the silence. "I'm Chloe, the girlfriend."

The word rolls off my tongue. I like the sound of it a little too much.

"Ah, it's nice to meet you, Chloe," Robert says, wincing as he extends a hand. I take it. He pulls back, reaching for the clothes hanging on the chair. "I'm sorry you had to see this. Not exactly the best first impression."

"It's okay."

"It's not." He meets my eyes. "But thank you for being here anyway."

The drive to Brody's childhood home is silent.

Robert sits in the back seat, arm in a sling, staring out the window. Brody drives with both hands on the wheel, jaw clenched, not speaking.

I'm in the passenger seat, trying to figure out what my role is here.

Supportive girlfriend? Professional arrangement fulfillment? Random person who decided to insert herself into family drama?

All of the above?

We pull up to a house that makes me blink in surprise.

Because this is not at all the house I imagined.

I don't know what I pictured—maybe something small and run-down, a bungalow barely holding together, evidence of years of struggle and chaos.

Which would have been just fine.

But this?

This is a historic brick Victorian—probably 1920s, based on the architecture—with arched windows and a covered front porch and this beautiful gabled roofline that makes it look like something out of a storybook.

Small, yes. Modest too.

But gorgeous.

The kind of house that has character. History. Bones.

"Wait." I'm staring. "You grew up here?"

"Sure, if you count middle school as 'growing up.'" Brody's voice is flat. Embarrassed, maybe. "It's not much."

"Are you kidding? This is beautiful."

He glances at me. Surprised.

"I saw the magazine spread," I continue. "The one with your penthouse in Minneapolis. All glass and steel and minimalist furniture. Very fancy."

"That's for show." He turns off the engine.

The words sit in my chest.

Because of course Brody Kane would grow up in a house like

this, then end up somewhere sterile and modern for his public image.

Because nothing about his public life is real.

Brody helps Robert inside while I stand by, trying my best to be helpful without getting in the way.

The interior is dated—wood paneling, worn hardwood floors, furniture that's seen better days—but clean. Organized. Lived-in.

Not the chaos I expected from Brody's description of his father's drinking.

Just . . . a house where someone's been trying.

"Couch," Robert says. "Can't deal with stairs right now."

Brody gets him settled. Pillow, blanket, TV remote within reach, and with every passing moment, I'm feeling more and more useless. So I do the only thing that makes sense to me. I head to the kitchen and start rummaging.

The kitchen is small. Galley-style. White cabinets that could use a fresh coat of paint. Brody's head pops through the door a moment later, brow cinched. "What are you doing?"

"Looking for hot chocolate." I open another cabinet. "Found it!"

"You don't have to do this."

"I know." I keep stirring. "But it's hot chocolate. Universal comfort food. And also, I don't know what else to do with my hands right now."

He almost smiles.

Almost.

"Thank you," he says quietly, his head resting on the doorjamb. "For coming. For staying. For—" He stops. "For not running away screaming."

"The night's not over yet."

That gets a real smile. Small, but real.

"How is he?" I ask.

"Embarrassed. In pain. Trying to pretend he's fine." Brody steps farther into the room, leaning up against the counter. "Standard Dad behavior."

"You can't control what other people do," I hear myself say. "You know that, right? His choices aren't your responsibility."

"I know."

"Do you?"

He's quiet for a long moment.

"I feel like I've been trying to fix him since I was fourteen," he says finally. "Since my mom died. Hasn't worked yet. But I keep trying anyway."

My chest aches. "That's not fixing. That's loving someone even when it's hard."

He looks at me. Something vulnerable in his expression. "When did you get so wise?"

I shrug. "Sunday? Just plagiarizing my pastor."

"Well, your pastor's smart."

I pour three mugs of hot chocolate, hand one to Brody, and pick up the other two. "Come on." I nod toward the door.

Robert is grimacing when we enter, trying to adjust his position on the couch. Clearly struggling with the sling.

Brody sets his mug down.

"Here." He reaches down. Helps him reposition. Adjusts the pillow.

The gentleness surprises me.

All that careful control, all that hard Candy armor, and underneath, he's just a son taking care of his father. Something about the moment gives me pause, and I stop at the door, giving them some space.

"Thanks," Robert says. Then, looking at Brody, "I'm sorry. I know I keep saying that, but I mean it. I'm sorry you had to—" His voice catches. "I'm trying. I know it doesn't look like it, but I'm trying."

"I know, Dad."

"I hadn't had a drink in three weeks. That's something, right?"

"Yeah, Dad. That's something."

"But I screwed up. Again." His dad shakes his head. Lets out a weighted sigh. "Story of my life."

Brody doesn't respond.

Just stands there, his shoulders rigid, his whole frame controlled.

I don't know what possesses me. Call it cliché. Or maybe the Holy Spirit. Or maybe just a blip in my ability to read the room.

"Would it be okay if I prayed?" I ask quietly. "For both of you?"

Both men turn to stare at me. Robert glances at Brody. Then back at me. What in heaven was I thinking? No, of course they don't want me to—

"Actually, that'd be nice—yeah," Robert says.

Oh. Okay then.

I set down the hot chocolate. Close my eyes.

"God, I don't really know what to say here. This is messy and complicated and probably way above my pay grade. But I'm asking—please be with Robert. Lay a healing hand on him, Father, and give him strength for whatever comes next." My voice suddenly feels raw as I continue. "And be with Brody. Give him peace. Help him know he's not alone. Please, Lord, help both of them know they're loved. Even when things are hard. Especially when things are hard. Amen."

The room feels quiet, still. My eyes feel heavy when I finally open them.

Robert is staring at me, eyes shining.

"Thank you," he says quietly.

"You're welcome."

Brody is looking at me with this expression I can't quite read.

I reach out, thread my fingers through his, and squeeze. *You are not alone, Brody Kane.*

Another heavy beat passes, and suddenly I remember—

"Oh, the hot chocolate!" I retrieve the mugs I'd set down on the nearby table and hand one to Robert. "I know it's a little adolescent, but there's something about hot chocolate. A good warm mug in my hands can make any moment feel bearable."

Robert looks at the mug with curiosity, turns his gaze back to me, his eyes twinkling. "I can see why Brody was so smitten with you after Barcelona."

Brody's head snaps up, no longer focused on his mug of cocoa.

"You are the Chloe from Barcelona, aren't you?" Robert asks.

"How do you—" I turn to Brody. "How does he know about Barcelona?"

A mortified look washes over Brody's face. "You know what, Dad? I think it's time for you to get some rest." He gives his dad a look as if to add *Before you stir up any more trouble.*

"Right," Robert says, apparently taking the hint. "I'm all set here. Why don't you two get back to your date. I'm sorry I held you up."

Brody places a hand on my lower back, heat immediately soaking through, and leads us toward the door.

"Good night, Robert. It was really nice to meet you. Get some rest."

"Thank you, Chloe."

The house feels quiet, the old floorboards creaking beneath our feet as we move out to the front hall. Brody takes a seat on the carpeted stairs, cupping his mug. I sit down beside him, our shoulders brushing.

"So . . ." I say, looking into my milky-brown mug. "How is it that your dad knows about me?"

Brody smiles, shaking his head.

"Did ya tell him all about me?" I tease, bumping his shoulder.

"Well, I sort of had to," he admits. "The only reason I was in Barcelona was to bail him out at the casino, which I was spectacularly late for. Because I was with you." He finally looks up. Sheepish.

I let out a gasp. "Brody! You left him waiting that whole time?"

"I had to! I was with this amazing girl. Beautiful. Funny. I wasn't going to pass that up."

I give his shoulder a little smack, laughing. "You're terrible."

Brody is smirking, the hard lines of his face melting away. "I am. But luckily for me, my dad sort of owed me one, so when I told him about the girl whose laugh made me completely forget where I was supposed to be, he gave me a pass for being late."

He's really smiling now, his gaze dipping to my lips, and my breath hitches.

"I know I already said it, but I'm really sorry about Barcelona, Chloe."

My eyes find his, those ocean-storm eyes. Blue, gray, blue again. We could have had something real . . . "I really thought that night didn't matter to you. That I didn't matter."

"Chloe." He sets his drink down, turning his body toward me. "You have no idea how much you mattered. I left because my life was a disaster and you deserved better. Not because you didn't matter."

He's leaned in closer, his fingers grazing my chin, tilting my face back to look at him. "I never forgot about you. Not for a single day."

Vaguely, I'm aware of sirens going off inside my head. Wee-ooo. This is bad.

This is so bad.

Because he's looking at me like the man I knew in Barcelona. Which is bad in itself, if you're trying very hard NOT to think about dancing by the fountain. Kissing under the orange trees. Then again . . . the contract didn't say I couldn't *think* about the kiss.

Except I know without a doubt that I'm looking at him the same way.

"Chloe," he says again. Softer this time. His thumb grazes my jaw, sending my brain into a full meltdown. His gaze drops to my lips again, and he leans in. And I don't pull away. In fact, I think you could construe what I'm doing (with my hands apparently moving of their own accord to touch his face) as leaning as well. His fingers thread through my hair, pulling me closer—

A car horn honks outside.

We both freeze.

Brody blinks. Pulls back slightly. "Who's that?"

"Jessa." The words come out breathless. "I texted her to pick me up."

"Why?"

"Because you should stay here." I pull back. Put necessary space between us. "With your dad. And maybe it's not a great idea for me to . . ." I trail off. The weight of what I'm not saying hangs heavy in the air. ". . . also stay."

Understanding dawns in his eyes.

"Chloe—"

"Thank you for tonight. For Barcelona the restaurant. For trusting me with"—I gesture around—"all of this."

I step down from the stairs, my knees still a little weak, and move toward the door.

He catches my hand. "Wait."

I stop. Don't turn around. Can't turn around.

Because if I look at him, I'm going to kiss him.

And that's not in the contract.

That's real.

And real is terrifying.

"Thank you," he says quietly. "For coming. For staying. For praying. For being here when I—" His voice catches. "When I needed someone."

"Anytime," I whisper.

The horn honks again.

"I have to go."

"I know."

I pull my hand free. Head for the door and run down the front steps to Jessa's waiting car.

"Drive," I say the second I'm in the passenger seat.

"Are you okay?"

"Drive first. Questions later."

She pulls away from the curb. I watch Brody's house disappear in the side mirror.

We drive in silence for three blocks.

I press my hands to my face, my palm cold against my super-heated skin.

Jessa glances over, does a double-take. "Oh no . . ."

"Don't."

"Do you need me to go over the contract details with you again?"

"Probably."

"Section Four: No romantic involvement outside of public appearances. Section Seven: Relationship terminates after final wedding event. Absolutely one hundred percent no falling for him allowed."

"It might be too late," I whisper.

BRODY

MY BACK IS KILLING ME.

Not the good kind of hurt—the post-game, worked-hard, earned-it kind. The bad kind. The "sleeping on a couch designed for looks not comfort for three straight nights" kind.

The brown leather monstrosity in my father's living room was probably trendy in 1997. But now it's lumpy, sagging in the middle, and makes ominous creaking sounds every time I change position. Which is often. Because I haven't slept more than three hours straight since the night we brought my dad home from the hospital.

The night with Chloe.

Which I'm not thinking about.

I'm standing at the stove in my childhood kitchen, making scrambled eggs at nine a.m. on a Thursday because that's my life now—playing nurse-slash-chef to my father, who can't lift his arm above his shoulder without wincing.

I always forget how small this kitchen is. Outdated. Old cabinets that should have had a fresh coat of paint years ago. Linoleum floors patterned with what's supposed to look like hardwood but absolutely does not. An ancient refrigerator that hums from the corner like it's planning a revolt.

Everything in this house is frozen in time.

Including me, apparently. I'm a child, still trying to keep everything calm and happy.

My father isn't handling his sudden withdrawal from alcohol too well. Not since I went through the house and poured all his bourbon, whiskey, and even a half pint of Macallan down the drain.

The eggs are cooking too fast. I turn down the heat. Scrape them around the pan with a spatula that's missing half its rubber edge.

My phone buzzes on the counter.

Again.

It's been buzzing all week. Texts from Chloe that I've been answering with increasing brevity.

Chloe
How's your dad?

Brody
Better. Thanks.

Chloe
How are you holding up?

Brody
Fine. Busy with the team.

Chloe
See you Saturday?

Brody
Yeah.

One-word answers. The conversational equivalent of a brick wall. Because if I write more than that, I'll say something I can't take back.

Like *Please come over.*

Or worse. *I need you.*

My defensive game has gone back to being garbage too. So all around, things are just . . . great.

The toast pops up. Burnt on one side, pale on the other. Naturally. I scrape the black parts into the sink. Plate everything. Pour coffee that's been sitting in the pot for forty minutes and is now thick enough to be a biohazard.

"That smells good," my dad says from the doorway.

I turn.

He's dressed—barely. Gray sweatpants with a hole in the knee. Ratty Minnesota Blue Ox T-shirt that should have been thrown out years ago. Arm still in the sling, hanging at an awkward angle. Hair uncombed. Face unshaven. Looking like he aged five years in the past week.

Looking like me, probably.

He lowers himself carefully into a chair at the small Formica kitchen table.

The same table where my mother sat before she got too sick to come downstairs, when she'd wrap herself in blankets and sip ginger tea and try to pretend she wasn't dying.

The same table where my father and I have sat a thousand times, not talking, just existing in the same space because that's what you do when you don't know what else to do.

I set the plate in front of him.

"Thanks," he says quietly.

"No problem."

I make my own plate. Sit across from him.

We eat in silence.

Just the scrape of forks on plates and the hum of the ancient refrigerator and the ticking of the wall clock that's been stuck at 3:47 for as long as I can remember but still makes ticking sounds.

This house is full of things that don't quite work but refuse to quit.

Feels appropriate.

My dad sets down his fork. "I think it's time for things to get back to normal." His voice is rough. Tired. The voice of a man who's been apologizing his whole life and is exhausted by it. "I'm glad you've been here. But I know you've got your own life. The team. Your girlfriend. You don't need to be babysitting me."

"I'm not babysitting you."

"Feels like it."

"You broke your collarbone. You need help. I'm helping." But my back twinges. A reminder that the couch and I are not friends.

"I'm okay, Brody. Really."

Except he's not. And I'm done letting it go.

"I think you need help," I say. The words come out harder than I intended. "Real help. Treatment. And not just for the drinking."

He twists his glass. Won't look at me.

"I've tried it." His voice is flat. Defeated. "AA. Rehab. Therapy." He waves his good hand vaguely. "Doesn't take."

"Dad—"

"No, Brody. I can't—I . . ." He pauses, staring at his plate with a completely defeated look, refusing to meet my eye. "I can't even get past Step Three."

"Step Three . . . ?"

"Accepting that there's a higher power in my life and surrendering to it." He lifts his gaze, his face etched with hurt. "I used to believe in something like that . . . your mother—" His voice cracks. "She believed. And look what happened."

My chest tightens. That feeling like someone's pressing on my sternum with both hands. Like the air in this kitchen is too thick to breathe properly.

"I would have lost everything if it weren't for you." He finally looks up. His eyes are bloodshot. Red-rimmed. The eyes of a man who hasn't slept well in years. "You paid for this house. Got me out of debt—I don't know how many times. Cleaned up every mess I made." His voice breaks again. "You are the best thing I ever did."

My throat is tight. Burning. I don't want to hear this. Don't want the weight of being the one good thing in his life.

I've heard it before, frankly. Sometimes it feels like part of the game. Still, every time, a slapshot to the chest.

"It's fine," I say. I start clearing plates even though we're not done eating.

"It's not. Brody, I know it's getting to you. You're not playing well—"

"I'm just in a slump." I start washing the dishes, the water scalding. "My luck will turn around. You'll see. Always does."

Wait.

No.

That's not—

I freeze.

Hands in the soapy water. Staring at the window above the sink. At the smudged glass that needs cleaning. At the view of the backyard with its overgrown grass and the rusted hockey net I used to practice on.

Those are *his* words.

Every time he loses at poker. Every time he drains his bank account at the casino. Every time he shows up asking for money to cover gambling debts with that sheepish, embarrassed expression that makes my chest hurt.

I'm just in a slump. My luck will turn around. You'll see. Always does.

And I just said them.

Like I actually believe that's how life works. Like if I just keep trying, keep controlling, keep performing, keep pretending, everything will magically fix itself.

"Brody?" My dad's voice is gentle. Worried. "You okay?"

No.

I'm not okay.

Because I can't control my father's addiction. Can't bring back my mother. Can't fix the defensive slump that's threatening my contract renewal. Can't make Ashley Morrison and her lawyer disappear. Can't stop myself from falling for a woman I'm supposed to be using for image repair.

Can't control any of it.

And pretending I can is just—

It's gambling.

Same as my father.

Different stakes, same lie.

But I can't seem to stop trying anyway.

I turn off the water. Grip the edge of the sink hard enough that my knuckles go white against the stainless steel.

Stare out the window.

And I see her.

My mother.

Just a memory. The kind that shows up when you're exhausted and overwhelmed.

But for a second, she's there.

Sitting on the porch swing. Wearing that floral cancer scarf she used to tie around her head when the chemo took her hair—blue with little yellow flowers, the cheerful pattern a stark contrast to what it represented. Wrapped in the old afghan she crocheted herself before she got too weak to hold the needles. It's summer in the memory, but she's bundled up because she was always cold those last few months. Always shivering. Always small.

Watching me.

I'm maybe twelve. Skinny. All elbows and knees and too-big

hands I hadn't grown into yet. Shooting tennis balls into the net I'd set up in the backyard. Practicing my aim. My form. My control.

Over and over and over.

Because if I could just get good enough—

And she's singing. Some old hymn I don't remember the name of. It carries across the yard like a promise.

If I get good enough, if I make it to the NHL, I can pay for better treatment. Better doctors. I can fix this.

I close my eyes.

The phone buzzes again.

This time I look.

Chloe
Everything okay? You've been quiet
this week.

I stare at the message.

She doesn't deserve this. She walked into my life, my mess, and . . .

No. I pick up the phone.

Brody
Yep. Fine. I'll see you at the couples
shower.

And now my back isn't the only thing that hurts.

CHLOE

This has to go well.

I'm standing in Maya's kitchen—which is basically the kitchen equivalent of a luxury car commercial, all white marble and glass-front cabinets and appliances that probably cost more than my entire apartment—arranging cupcakes on a three-tiered stand and trying very hard not to spin out. Mentally speaking.

It's not working.

The couples shower starts in forty-five minutes, and I've been here since noon setting up, directing catering to the kitchen, staging the bar down the hall (accessible, but not a focal point), setting out favors and supplies for the plethora of wedding-themed games between rounds of gifts (of which there is bound to be a disgusting amount). I hurt just thinking about the number of gifts I can look forward to hauling back to the guest room throughout the night.

The house is gorgeous. Of course it is. Derek bought it for them just a few weeks after the engagement, with plans for them to move in together after the wedding. And of course, like everything else in Maya's life, it's perfect. A lakefront property on White Bear Lake, with a massive deck and floor-to-ceiling windows. It's modern farmhouse meets Scandinavian minimalism meets "we have more money than taste but hired a designer to fix that."

Meanwhile, my apartment is going for that "I have no money and no designer to fix it" vibe. So . . . samesies.

Actually, that's not entirely true anymore.

For the first time in my adult life, I'm not panicking about rent. I paid up last month. This month. Next month. Three months ahead. The landlord did a double-take when I handed him the check.

I also made a massive payment on my student loans. Didn't clear them—because that would require winning the lottery or a small miracle—but I made a dent. The kind of dent that means I might actually pay them off in this lifetime.

Thanks to the contract.

Thanks to twenty thousand dollars for playing pretend girlfriend.

It should feel like a victory.

Instead, it feels like I sold something I can't get back.

My phone buzzes on the counter.

Jessa
How's it going? You freaking out
yet?

Chloe
No. Not freaking out.

Jessa
That's a lie. You used a period. You
never use periods unless you're
lying.

Chloe
I'm FINE. The cupcakes look great.
The games are set up. Even the
bartenders are set up. Everything
is great.

Jessa
So he hasn't texted . . .

And there it is.

The question I've been avoiding all day.

No.

Brody hasn't texted.

Well, that's not entirely true. He texted exactly three times this week. Each one shorter than the last.

Monday: Dad's doing better. Thanks for asking.

Wednesday: Practice has been intense. Talk soon.

Friday: Should I pick you up tomorrow? 6 p.m.?

And I said no.

I don't even know why. Pride, maybe. Or self-preservation. After our near kiss, I'm not sure I can be trusted alone with him.

Maya's giving me a ride. See you there.

His response: Okay.

One word.

That was it.

No "Are you sure?" No "I don't mind picking you up." No attempt to push back or insist or act like he wanted to see me before the party.

Just: *Okay.*

Cool.

So lucky me got to ride with Maya, who spent the entire drive lecturing me about needing a car.

"You can't keep relying on Uber and the kindness of friends," she said, merging onto the highway with the confidence of someone who's never had to check her bank account before filling up with gas. "If you're going to be a professional event planner, you need reliable transportation."

"I know. I'm working on it."

"Are you though? Because you've been saying that for the last year."

"I paid off three months of rent and made a massive loan payment. The car fund is next on the list."

She glanced at me. Surprised. "Really?" Another glance, a flash of confusion. "That's amazing. Business must be picking up."

"Something like that."

Lie.

Business is not picking up. Business is barely limping along.

But the contract money is keeping me afloat.

Which makes me feel simultaneously relieved and completely gross.

I watched his game last night. Staying up late with the excuse that I was going to multitask and work on last-minute shower details. And then I sat on my couch in my pajamas with a bowl of popcorn and my laptop open to the livestream, my last-minute shower details in a forgotten pile on the floor.

And maybe—*maybe*—I was wearing the jersey I bought.

Number 7. Kane.

It was a splurge, ordering the official Blue Ox merch, but I told myself it was a business expense. I had to look the part. Show off a little for social media, right? How could I play the part of devoted girlfriend of Minnesota's favorite defensive player without wearing his number?

So I took a picture.

Me in the jersey. Hair down. Smiling at the camera with my best "celebrity girlfriend" smile. I took thirteen selfies before settling on one that didn't make me look completely deranged and posted it to Instagram with the caption:

@BleedingBlue: Cheering on my favorite player tonight! Let's go Blue Ox! 🩵 🏒

The likes came pouring in. Comments from people I barely know.

@Sherriontheshore: So cute!

@LuvCats39: You guys are perfect together!

@Momsquad: Relationship goals!

But Brody didn't like it.

Didn't comment.

Didn't acknowledge it at all.

And I told myself it was fine. He was probably focused on the game. He probably didn't even see it.

Except I know he saw it. Because his agent commented.

@RCastellano: Great support, Chloe! Keep it up!

They lost, by the way. 3–2 in overtime. Brody was on the ice for the winning goal against them. Not his fault—the forward blew past their left wing, and Brody was caught out of position trying to cover. (Someone please be impressed that I know this about hockey.)

But I saw his face after. That careful, blank expression that means he's beating himself up inside.

And I wanted to text him. Tell him it wasn't his fault. Tell him one game doesn't define him.

But I didn't.

The last thing he needs is a pep talk from his fake girlfriend.

"Chloe?" Maya's voice pulls me back to reality. "You okay? You've been staring at that cupcake for, like, two minutes."

"What?" I blink. Look down. I'm holding a cupcake with pink frosting, frozen mid-placement on the tower. "Oh—yes. I'm good. Just doing the final touches. Making sure everything's perfect."

"All right, stop. It's perfect. You're a miracle worker." She's leaning against the doorframe, wearing a white dress that probably cost more than my three months of rent combined. "Seriously. This is exactly what I wanted."

"Good. That's good."

She quirks a brow, pinning me down with that big-sister look that tells me she's about to ask invasive questions.

Great. Here we go.

"So. Brody."

There it is.

"What about him?"

"How are things? Really?"

I set down the cupcake. Act natural. "They're good. Great, actually."

"Really?" She walks into the kitchen. Leans against the marble island like she's settling in for a long conversation. Like it's the sort of thing we do all the time. "Are you sure? Because you've been acting weird all week. Distracted. And Derek says Brody's been off lately . . ."

My chest tightens. "He's dealing with a lot. His dad just went through—" I stop. I don't know what about Brody's personal life is public knowledge. "He's been stressed."

"Yeah, it's too bad about his dad's accident. Derek told me all about it." She's watching me carefully, her gaze piercing. "I'm glad he has you."

Heat rises to my cheeks. I never was great at lying.

"Yeah. Well, I'm glad I have him too." I'd be even more glad if I had him *here*. I could really use some backup right about now.

Maya tilts her head. "You really like him, don't you?"

"What?" Nervous chuckle. "I—of course. We're together. Obviously I like him."

"No, I mean *really* like him. You're falling for him."

I swear, if there were anything flammable nearby, my face could set fires. "I—yeah. I guess. Maybe."

"Listen, Chloe, I don't want to butt into your love life, but I feel like you're not getting the whole truth about Brody."

I freeze. "What about him?"

She takes a breath. Glances toward the living room like she's making sure we're alone. "Well, Derek's known him a long time. They played on the same team back in college—"

"I didn't know that."

"It was only for a year. Derek transferred after that. But while Derek was there, he saw a different side of Brody."

My lungs seem to tighten, waiting for her to drop whatever terrible bomb she's dangling.

"Apparently, there was this girl they both liked—I know, drama—but she chose Brody, who supposedly wasn't even all that interested. It rubbed Derek the wrong way."

Losing to Brody? I want to say. Who would have thought?

"And he got it in his head that Brody's some sort of womanizer. So when that thing between Brody and Derek's cousin happened—"

"What thing?"

Maya pauses, her head tilting. "You didn't hear about that? Derek's cousin, Ashley, is this wannabe influencer. Honestly, she comes off a little desperate for attention to me, but Derek's got a soft spot for her. So he got her this social media job at a Blue Ox charity event a few months ago, and that's when she met Brody."

My stomach drops.

Ashley Morrison.

The girl with the viral post about Brody.

"Ashley got Brody's number—said it was for work, social media stuff for the team. She started texting him. I'm not sure if Brody led her on or what—"

"He didn't."

Maya's voice is careful. "Well, *she* says he used her. And Derek believes her version." *And I believe Derek.* I can read between the lines.

"But that's not what happened."

She lifts her hands, as if to say *Who knows what's true?*

I do. I know what's true.

"Derek only sees that his cousin got hurt and humiliated online. And he blames Brody."

"So Derek thinks Brody is some kind of serial heartbreaker."

"Exactly. And now Derek thinks Brody's doing the same thing to you. Using you for his image repair and that he's planning to dump you when the press dies down."

If my stomach sank before, it's bottomed out now.

Because that's exactly what's happening.

I think.

I don't know anymore, because that almost-kiss at his house made things so much more complicated than they were supposed to be, and the way he held my hand at Barcelona felt so real, and I'm so confused I could scream.

"Derek's wrong," I say. The words taste like ash. "Brody's not— he wouldn't—"

"I just don't want you to get hurt." Maya's voice is soft.

Huh. For once, it doesn't feel like condescension. She's really worried about me.

She meets my eyes. "So I'm giving him a chance," she says firmly. "Despite Derek's opinions. Despite the history with Ashley and college and all of it. I'm reserving judgment." She reaches across the island. Takes my hand. "And I think you could be really good for each other."

I can't speak. I mean, what would you say?

"Thanks," I manage. My voice sounds strangled. "That means a lot."

She squeezes my hand. "Just promise me you'll be careful. I've seen how he looks at you, but I've seen how you look at him too. Like he's the answer to a question you've been asking your whole life."

What question is that?

The sound of a car in the driveway breaks the moment.

"I'll get the door," I say.

I walk to the front door. Take a breath.

Open it.

And there he is.

Standing on Maya's sprawling front porch in dark jeans and a gray sweater that makes his eyes look like oceans of blue. Looking unfairly gorgeous in that casual, effortless way that should be illegal. His hair is slightly damp like he just showered, and he's holding a bottle of wine in one hand.

And when he sees me, he smiles.

That Candy Kane smile. Charming. Perfect. Completely performative. And I can't help but feel just a little disappointed.

Don't get me wrong, it's a great smile. It's the smile that's launched a thousand endorsement deals and made him Minnesota's most eligible bachelor.

But that smile doesn't reach his eyes. It feels different now. Like there's a wall between us that wasn't there before.

My chest tightens.

"Hi," he says.

Or maybe it was always there, and I'm just noticing it now.

"Ready?" he asks.

I open my mouth to respond. Nod instead.

"Good," he says, stepping forward. Brushing past me into the house. "Let's get this over with."

And he walks inside.

CHLOE

IRING SOMEONE TO PLAN A COUPLES shower they will also be attending as a guest is a lot like making a murder victim dig their own grave.

In hindsight, I probably didn't do myself any favors.

Maya and Derek are in matching white wicker chairs—decorated with *Mr.* and *Mrs.* sashes that I burned my thumb hot-gluing this afternoon—finishing up their round of the newlywed game.

The room's packed. Twenty-five people. Maybe thirty. Most of them guys Derek plays hockey with. I don't recognize any of them, but they all fill the room with a sort of bravado and competition. And they're all watching as Derek reveals his answer to the last question.

"Biceps," he says, grinning as he holds up his whiteboard.

Maya flips hers. "His smile."

The room erupts in laughter, and Maya doubles over. It's a quick recovery, and she leans over to kiss Derek's cheek, laughing.

"Close enough!" she declares. "How'd we do?"

There's a chorus of wildly inaccurate scorekeeping. "Ten out of ten!" "Nailed it!"

I try my best to join in, but my heart is racing.

Because I know what's coming. And maybe a week ago, after spending a day with Brody, I might have felt a little more confident that we could survive this. But today . . . there's something off.

His words are still ringing in my ears from earlier. *Let's get this over with.*

Over with. The way you do chores. Or hospital paperwork. Like I'm a dirty pot that you've just got to knuckle down and take care of before the fruit flies show up.

Very romantic.

Maya stands, smoothing down her dress. She's got that mischievous look. The one that means she's about to do something that will make me want to crawl under the furniture and die.

"Okay, okay!" She claps her hands and the chatter dies. "That was fun, right? But now"—she pauses for dramatic effect, because she's Maya and everything must be done with ✨*flair*✨—"we're going to do something a little different."

Here we go.

"Let's see who's got what it takes to become the next newlyweds!" She's practically bouncing. I'd like to mention that this was all her idea, by the way. The whole dragging unwilling participants into the spotlight with you. Not my idea of fun. "We're getting other couples in on this!"

The room goes wild. There's cheering. And whooping. Actual whooping. Tyler's girlfriend squeals so loud I think my eardrums might actually rupture.

Maya grabs the basket I prepped earlier and tucked under her seat—wicker, lined with tissue paper, filled with name cards of every couple here. She reaches in without looking. Dramatic pause.

Please not us. Please not us. Please not—

"Lauren and Brad!"

Thank You, God.

Lauren—blonde, perfect highlights, probably has never had a bad hair day in her life—squeals and drags her boyfriend to the center. I recognize him from the meet-and-greet party and the Blue Ox team roster. Brad's laughing, shaking his head like he already knows this is going to be a disaster.

They're pulling up chairs. Setting up. Everyone's laughing.

Maybe we're safe. Maybe Maya will pick another couple, and we can just watch and—

Derek takes the basket.

Oh . . . no.

His hand pauses inside. Fishing around. He pulls out a card.

Unfolds it.

His eyes meet mine.

And there's something in his expression—calculating, testing—like he's waiting to see if we'll pass whatever test he's set up.

"Brody and Chloe."

Of course.

Of *course*.

The room absolutely loses it. Cheering. Whistling. Someone shouts, "Let's go, Candy!" And I'm going to die. Right here. We're in deep . . . deep trouble.

I know it's not right to pray for God to help you lie . . . but I'm half tempted to toss a prayer up for good measure.

Brody's hand finds the small of my back. The touch sends electricity up my spine, jumpstarts my racing heart.

His voice is low next to my ear. "You okay?"

I nod because what else am I supposed to do? Say no? Explain that I'm legitimately having a minor panic attack because we're about to be tested on how well we know each other? Our get-to-know-you date was cut short because of his dad's hospital visit. Give a girl a break!

We make our way to the center.

Pull up chairs.

Sit.

Lauren and Brad are to our left, Maya and Derek facing us like game show hosts, the entire room watching.

Cool. Just relax.

Maya is practically vibrating with excitement as she pulls out index cards. At least someone's enjoying this. "Okay, here's how this works. There are five questions. Two for the boys, two for the girls, and one last one for you both. When I ask you the question, you'll both write down your answer. You get points if you match. Most points wins."

Someone hands us small whiteboards and markers. The kind teachers use. Very official. Very terrifying.

Brody's knee presses against mine. Warm. Solid. He gives me this look—quick, assessing. *How much do you remember from Barcelona? From Monday night. From* any *of the conversations we've had.*

Spoiler: probably not enough.

"First question!" Maya announces, holding up a card. "Ladies, this one should be easy for all of you. What is your partner's jersey number?"

Oh. Easy.

I write down: *7*

Brody's already done, his handwriting neat and slanted. Confident.

"Reveal!" Maya shouts.

We turn our boards.

Mine: *7*

His: *7*

The crowd cheers, hungry for something a little more challenging.

"Next question!" Maya's grinning. "Gentlemen, what is your girlfriend's comfort food?"

I hesitate.

Did we talk about this? I'm searching my memory—we've talked about food a lot, actually. Over tapas, coffee, dinner . . .

It doesn't matter. I have to write something down.

I scribble on my board.

Brody's done before me. Again. Not even hesitating.

"Reveal!"

Mine: Carbs.

His: Bread. Cookies. Carbs.

The room erupts, cheering.

And I'm just staring at his board. That is almost exactly what I said. I remember now, Monday night. What do you do when you're stressed? That had been the question.

He remembered.

I spare a glance at Lauren and Brad. She's looking at his haphazard scribble of "salad" with a look of absolute disgust. I don't blame her. Nobody's comfort food is *salad*. Come on, Brad.

"Ooooh." Maya winces, her nose scrunching in that perfectly modelesque way I've always been a little jealous of. "You'll get the next one, guys. Ladies, what's your boyfriend's guilty pleasure TV show?"

I smile. This one I definitely know.

Saturday morning at the coffee shop. He admitted it almost sheepishly, like it was this secret he didn't usually share. I almost feel bad letting the secret out, but . . .

"Reveal!"

Mine: Cooking competitions

His: Cooking competitions

Again, the crowd goes wild. Lauren looks like she's about to walk out of here because she wrote *K-dramas* (which feels like wishful thinking on her part), and all he wrote was *cheese*, all of which the crowd finds very amusing.

But I can't laugh.

Because Brody's looking at me with this expression I can't read. And Derek's watching us both. Really watching. Like he's cataloging every microexpression.

"Seriously, Candy? Cooking shows?" Tyler shouts from the audience.

Brody pulls his gaze away, grins at the crowd, and gives a quick shrug. "You should give it a try."

Maya cuts in, waving a hand, and the audience dies down for the next question.

"Fourth question!" Maya says, and there's something mischievous in her smile now. "Gentlemen, what was your girlfriend wearing the first time you met?"

My stomach drops.

Barcelona was six-ish months ago. There's no way he—

I can barely remember what I wore yesterday, let alone six months ago.

I'm frantically trying to recall. It was hot. Summer. I was wearing . . . a dress? Shorts? Did I have a sundress?

I write: *Sundress (yellow?)*

The question mark is doing a lot of work there.

Brody's already done. Not even a pause.

"Reveal!"

Mine: Sundress (yellow?)

His: Blue sundress with white polka dots. Brown sandals.

The room absolutely *erupts*.

I'm staring at his board. My heart is racing. I think I can hear those little sirens again.

He remembered the polka dots.

"Oh my word," Maya squeals. "That's SO romantic!"

Meanwhile, this might be the only question Lauren and Brad got right, having both written *white puffer jacket.*

Brody smiles at the crowd, hamming it up, but there's something in his face—soft, maybe a little embarrassed that he revealed just how much attention he was paying that day.

Oh, Brody.

"Final question," Maya announces. "This one's worth double points. And it's for *both* of you—you each write your answer. Where did you two have your first kiss?"

My stomach drops.

Straight to the floor.

Through the floor.

All the way to the earth's core.

Because I know the answer. The *real* answer.

In Barcelona.

Beneath the orange trees off Plaça Reial. After we danced under twinkling lights. After he looked at me like I was the only person in the entire world. After everything felt real and honest and like maybe—just maybe—this wasn't a mistake.

But that kiss isn't part of our official story.

I glance at Brody.

He's already writing. Face carefully neutral. Giving absolutely nothing away.

Right. Stick to the script.

I write quickly: *The coffee shop where we ran into each other again.*

Safe. Consistent. A complete lie.

"Reveal!"

Mine: The coffee shop where we ran into each other again.

His: The coffee shop.

Match.

Another lie we're telling in perfect sync.

The room goes wild. Tyler's yelling "SWEEP!" Someone's demanding we get a trophy. Lauren and Brad are dramatically bowing out, retreating to the safety of the crowd.

"WINNERS!" Maya grabs our hands, lifting them like we're championship boxers. "Five for five! Undefeated!"

Everyone's clapping. Cheering. Derek's nodding slowly—thoughtfully—like maybe we just passed his test.

And all I can think about is the way Brody remembered the polka dots.

We return to our spots as the party continues around us.

Catering brings out another round of hors d'oeuvres. Little bruschetta with tomatoes and basil. Bacon-wrapped dates. Those grilled cheese triangles that are basically comfort food in formal wear.

The energy shifts. Relaxes. People are mingling, refilling wine glasses, laughing about the game.

Maya and Derek settle onto the couch. Someone brings over a pile of wrapped gifts.

"Gift time!" Maya's back in hostess mode.

And honestly? It's sweet. Watching them.

Derek's hand on Maya's knee. Casual. Affectionate. She leans into him when she laughs. When she opens matching robes with *Mr.* and *Mrs.* embroidered on them, he actually blushes.

They're good together.

Real.

You can see it in the way he looks at her—like she hung the moon and personally arranged all the stars. The way she touches his arm when she's excited.

This is what actual love looks like.

Unlike whatever performance Brody and I just gave.

He's standing next to me now, playing his role perfectly. Arm around my waist. Smiling at the right moments. Laughing at Derek's jokes about honeymoon plans.

Every inch the devoted boyfriend.

But I can feel the tension. The coiled energy. His hand on my waist is just a fraction too careful. His laugh doesn't quite reach his eyes.

He's performing.

And I'm starting to hate that I can tell the difference.

One of Maya's bridesmaids—Hayley, I think—corners us by the bar.

"You two are so cute together!" she coos, like we're fuzzy zoo animals. "I follow you on Instagram." This to Brody. "The way you post about Chloe is so sweet. That picture of you two at that Spanish restaurant? Very cute."

Wait. What?

I glance at Brody. He looks uncomfortable for half a second before the Candy Kane smile returns, brighter than before.

"She makes it easy," he says, pulling me closer.

Hayley practically melts. "You guys are relationship goals. Seriously."

She floats away to talk to someone else, nearly bumping into a side table in her champagne-induced haze.

I turn to Brody, keeping my voice low enough that the couple standing three feet away can't hear. "You posted about our date?"

"Rick handles most of my social media." He's not meeting my eyes, instead watching the happy couple as they tear open another gift they really don't need. "He's just making it look authentic."

The words sting more than they should.

Authentic.

"Right. Okay." The word is salt and lemon on my tongue.

Maya tears into another gift—a large box from Tyler and his girlfriend.

She gasps. "A karaoke machine!"

Oh no.

I turn. Maybe I can take it from her, tell her I'll stash it with the other gifts before she can—

She's already pulling Derek to his feet. "We have to try it right now!"

Tyler moves to help set it up. Plugs it in near the fireplace, where I'd arranged the makeshift stage area. The little TV flickers to life.

Maya scrolls through songs. Lands on "Call Me Maybe" by Carly Rae Jepsen.

Of course. Very on-brand.

She hands Derek the other microphone, and they launch into it.

And of course, she's good. Confident. In tune. Working the room.

Derek, however, is . . . less good. But he's smiling, laughing as Maya draws him in. And when he jumps in, it's all ham, all goof. Gone is the stoic team captain, replaced by a googly-eyed, lovesick fool with a microphone. And I feel like I'm getting an inside look at the cute little world the two of them live in.

The room's clapping along. Filming. It's chaotic and fun and exactly what I hoped for when I planned this party.

And then the song ends.

Maya's breathless, laughing, trying to hand the microphone to Tyler. "Your turn!"

But Derek intercepts.

Takes both microphones.

Turns to face us. "Wait."

The room quiets.

"The winners of the newlywed game need a song too." He's looking directly at us. "Come on. It's only fair."

Absolutely not.

No way.

Not happening.

The room erupts. Chanting. "DO IT! DO IT!"

I spin, looking for a retreat, and run straight into the rock-solid chest of my fake boyfriend. Brody's got a mischievous look in his eye.

"Brody..."

He scoops me up—I'd call it sweeping me off my feet, except that it's the opposite of what I want at this exact moment.

"Brody, no!"

He carries me to the stage, spurred on by a chorus of cheers, and leans in, his breath grazing my neck. "Come on, Chloe. Show 'em what you've got."

Oh yeah. Thanks. Here's the problem.

What I've "got" is a terrible voice and even worse stage fright. So...

Derek hands us the microphones, a challenge issued.

Brody scrolls through songs. Pauses. "You know this one?"

I look at the screen.

"Like I'm Gonna Lose You" by Meghan Trainor

Oh.

Oh.

That's a love song. A *real* love song. For *real* couples.

"I know it," I manage.

The music starts. Light guitar, a simple beat. And then it's my line.

I panic, watching the lyrics scroll across the screen. I open my mouth and ... nothing.

Brody's hand slips into mine, his gaze ducking into my line of vision. He takes a step, blocking out the rest of the crowd, filling my view, and suddenly it's just the two of us.

And somehow, I find my voice just as the chorus begins.

> *"So I'm gonna love you like I'm gonna lose you*
> *I'm gonna hold you like I'm saying goodbye ..."*

Brody nods, encouraging me as I find my footing with each note. And when the second verse begins, Brody takes over.

And—

Wait.

He can *sing*.

Not professional or anything. But his voice is warm. Rich. And the lyrics—

> *"I'll kiss you longer, baby, any chance that I get*
> *I'll make the most of the minutes and love with no*
> *regret . . ."*

A song about love and loss. About holding on to each moment while it lasts, even while the end is barreling toward you.

I think I could cry.

The chorus comes back around, and I join back in.

We're not looking at the TV screen.

We're looking at each other.

And the room disappears.

Just vanishes. Gone.

It's just us. Just this song.

> *"Wherever we're standing, I won't take you for granted*
> *'Cause we'll never know when, when we'll run out of*
> *time . . ."*

My voice is failing by the end, rasping out each word. It feels like Barcelona all over again, that heavy heartache, knowing all of this is temporary. It's not even real.

Except, I think . . . maybe it is.

The song ends.

He still hasn't looked away. The room is so quiet, I think you could hear my heart pounding.

And then—

Brody's hand cups my face. Gentle. Careful. Like I'm something that might break.

And then he kisses me.

In front of everyone.

On this makeshift stage with twenty-five people watching and at least five phones recording.

His lips are soft. Warm. Moving against mine like he's been thinking about it. Like maybe he's been falling apart the same way I have. Like maybe all that distance these last two weeks was him running from this exact moment.

His other hand finds my waist. Pulls me closer.

Not for show.

Not calculated.

This feels—

Real.

My hands find his sweater. Grip the soft fabric. The microphone falls from my other hand—*thunk*—but I don't care.

The room is losing it. Cheering. Whistling. Tyler's yelling something. Lauren's actually crying. Someone's chanting "KISS! KISS! KISS!" even though we are literally already doing that.

He pulls back. Slowly. Reluctantly.

His forehead rests against mine for just a second.

"Chloe—" It's so quiet I almost miss it when he breathes my name.

But then the cheering breaks through.

Reality.

The room.

All of it rushing back like cold water.

He steps back.

Smiles at the crowd.

Waves the microphone—which he somehow didn't drop, unlike me.

The perfect performer. Back on stage.

And just like that, the wall is back up.

The party continues.

More karaoke. Tyler and his girlfriend massacre something

country. One of Derek's teammates attempts "Bohemian Rhapsody," and it's objectively terrible, but everyone loves it anyway because we're all happy and having fun.

Brody stays close. Plays his role. Arm around my waist. Laughing. Chatting about upcoming games.

But he's distant.

Careful.

Like the kiss broke something instead of fixing it. Like he gave too much and now he's pulling back twice as hard.

Like he's scared of what happens if he stays in that vulnerable place for too long.

People start leaving. Grabbing coats. Calling Ubers. Promising to see everyone at the wedding.

I slip away to start cleanup.

Collecting champagne glasses. Tossing paper plates. Organizing leftover food by catering into containers.

I'm in the kitchen, wrapping the last of the bruschetta, when Maya finds me.

"Chloe." Her voice is soft. Happy. She catches my elbow. Turns me to face her. "I need to tell you something."

I set down the container. "What?"

"I was wrong about Brody."

My stomach drops.

She takes my hands. Squeezes. "About being worried. About thinking he might be using you."

"Maya—"

"That kiss?" She's beaming. "That was real. The way he looked at you during the song? The way you two know each other so well you won every single round?" Her eyes are shining. "That's not something you can fake, Chloe. I think he's a keeper. I'm so happy for you. You deserve someone who looks at you like that."

I try not to look stricken.

I try so hard.

Because I have absolutely no idea what's true anymore.

Was the kiss real? Or was it just another box checked on the contract to-do list? *Kiss girlfriend in public to sell the story.*

How am I supposed to know the difference when Brody's so good at performing that even *I* can't tell what's an act?

"Thanks, Maya." My voice sounds normal. Cheerful, even. "That really means a lot."

She hugs me tight. Then floats back to Derek.

And I'm standing in the kitchen, surrounded by dirty dishes and leftover food, trying to figure out what just happened.

Trying to figure out if Maya's right.

If that kiss was real.

If any of this is real.

We say our goodbyes.

Brody helps carry chairs. I hand out tip envelopes to the bar staff packing up.

Derek watches us both with that assessing expression, but he's less hostile now. Maybe the party softened him. Maybe seeing us win every game convinced him.

Or maybe he's just biding his time.

And finally, it's just us.

The cold air feels almost refreshing after a long day. Brody walks me to the passenger-side door, opens it for me.

We drive in silence. The streets are quiet. Dark.

"That went well," I say finally. "Everyone seemed to have fun."

"Yeah. You did a great job."

More silence. Just the engine and the tires on pavement and my heart beating too fast.

We're almost at my apartment when he finally speaks. "We're on the road for the next two weeks."

"Okay."

"So I'll see you in Maple Lake. For the wedding."

Oh. My heart sinks. That's it?

We're not going to talk about what's been going on with him. We're not going to address that kiss back there. Heck, I guess we're not even going to talk about winning that stupid game.

I don't know why I thought that kiss meant anything in the first place.

He pulls up in front of my building.

Parks. Doesn't turn off the engine.

Leaves it idling. Ready to escape.

I should get out. Thank him. Go inside. Process this disaster.

But I can't.

"Did I do something wrong?" The words just come out. No filter. No dignity. What is wrong with me?

His gaze snaps up. "What?"

"I just . . . feel like something's off between us." I sound pitiful. *Get out of the car, Chloe.* For the love . . .

"No. We're good." His voice is rough. And then he sighs, the kind that feels like I'm annoying him.

Right.

My hand finds the door handle.

"I'll see you in two weeks, Chloe."

"Yeah." I'm already getting out. "See you then."

Door closes. Maybe with more force than necessary.

I walk up the steps without looking back.

He drives away, tires squealing slightly.

Roadrunner cloud of smoke.

Gone.

I'll admit, he really had me going at the party.

Someone give that man an Oscar.

BRODY

YOU WANT ICE FOR THAT?"

I look up from my bruised knuckles. The bartender is standing across from me, pointing at my right hand with a bar towel that's seen better days. Purple-and-yellow bruising is spreading across my knuckles like a storm system. Swollen. Throbbing. The result of introducing my fist to a helmet during tonight's game.

"No," I say. "I'm good."

He raises an eyebrow but doesn't push. Just goes back to polishing glasses.

I flex my hand. Pain shoots up my arm, sharp and immediate. Good.

Better to feel this than the other thing.

I'm sitting in the hotel bar in Seattle—one of those chain places where every city is identical. Same dark-wood tables with brass fixtures. Same laminated, sticky drink menus and fake plants in the corners. The air smells like stale beer with a hint of someone's leftover burger and fries.

I'm nursing a Coke because I'm not drinking. SportsCenter is playing on the mounted TV above the bar, volume low. They're replaying our loss. Seattle 3, Blue Ox 1. I watch myself take a hit into the boards. Get up slowly. Skate away with my jaw clenched.

We got destroyed.

I played like a man possessed. Blocked six shots—felt every single one of them. Pucks hitting shin pads and shoulders, and once, terrifyingly, my inner thigh, just above the knee. Threw three hits that rattled teeth. Then spent five minutes in the penalty box for roughing after their center said—I don't even remember what— and I just . . . snapped.

Coach Jacobsen wasn't happy. I got an earful in the tunnel after the game about the difference between intensity and recklessness.

I didn't care, but I said all the right things. Showered and got out of there.

Condensation pools around my fingertips as I rotate my glass. I don't know why I'm here. Feels better than alone in my room.

"This seat taken?" The voice is familiar. Steady.

I look up. Conrad Kingston is standing there, wearing jeans and a Blue Ox hoodie. Hair still damp from the shower, droplets darkening the fabric on his shoulders.

Great. The team's unofficial therapist is here to fix me.

"It's all yours," I say.

He sits on the stool next to mine. The leather creaks under his weight. He signals the bartender with two fingers, the universal sign for "one for me."

We sit in silence while the bartender pours Conrad a Coke too.

He takes a drink. Sets it down carefully on his own coaster. The TV's moved on to highlights from some other game. Someone scores a beautiful goal, the announcers losing their minds over it.

"You want to talk about it?" Conrad asks finally, his voice gruff over the music.

"About what?"

"Whatever's got you playing like you're trying to kill someone." He pauses. Takes another drink. "Or yourself."

"I'm fine."

"You know, you've said that a lot lately. I'm starting to wonder if you know what it means."

"I'm playing hard. That's what you're supposed to do."

"There's playing hard, and there's playing angry." Conrad turns on his stool to face me fully, one elbow on the bar. "You blocked six shots tonight. Six. And you fought a guy who outweighs you by forty pounds."

"He was running his mouth."

"About what?"

I don't answer. Can't answer. Because I don't actually remember what he said. I just remember needing to hit something. Someone. Anything to release the pressure building in my chest over the last week.

Conrad's quiet for a moment, studying me. Then, "It feel good? Throwing that punch?"

I look at him, surprised by the directness.

"Yeah," I admit. "It did."

"I get it." He takes another drink. "Sometimes punching something is easier than dealing with whatever's actually wrong."

I look away. Wow, he's lethal.

"Kane. What's going on?"

"Nothing," I say. "Just focused on the game."

He doesn't believe me. I can see it in his face, in the way his eyebrows rise slightly and his mouth tightens. Yeah, I don't believe me either.

Mostly because that kiss with Chloe won't stop looping in my head. What. Was I. *Thinking*?

I wasn't. And that's the problem. I wasn't thinking, just feeling. And it felt good.

"This have anything to do with Chloe?" he asks.

My hand tightens on the glass, condensation making it slippery. "What makes you say that?"

"Because you've been staring at your phone all week, and you haven't sent a single text."

Nothing gets past Conrad Kingston.

"It's complicated," I say finally.

"Relationships usually are."

"We're not—" I stop. What are we? "It's not that simple."

"Why not?"

Because it started as a business arrangement. Because there's a contract with an end date. Because that's what is best for her. And probably me.

Because I'm terrified.

"We had a fight," I say. It's not exactly true, but it's close enough. "Sort of. I don't know."

"Did you say something stupid?"

"I said nothing. That's the problem." I run my good hand through my hair, still slightly damp from my own shower. "I've been avoiding her. Ignoring her texts." *Being a coward.*

"Why?"

The question is simple. The answer isn't.

"Because I don't know how to do this," I admit, staring at my bruised knuckles instead of at him. "I'm not good at this."

Conrad is quiet for a moment, the ice in his Coke shifting as the bubbles settle. "Hard to live up to your own press."

I glance at him. "Something like that."

Conrad turns to face me, leans forward. "I'm going to tell you something, and you're going to listen. Okay?"

Whatever.

"Pushing someone away because you're scared doesn't protect

you. It just makes you alone." His voice is steady, sure, the voice of someone who's been there. "And being alone because you're terrified of being hurt? That's not strength. That's just fear wearing a different jersey."

The words hit like an elbow to my face.

"She deserves better," I say quietly, "than someone who's a mess. Who comes with baggage."

"Maybe. But that's her choice to make, not yours."

My jaw pulses, and I take another sip of my Coke.

Conrad sighs. It's a big sigh, like I'm thick in the head. Maybe I am. "Look, I can't tell you what to do. But I can tell you that running away because you're scared is a coward's move. And you're not a coward, Kane. You block shots with your face. You fight guys twice your size. You're just scared of something you can't punch."

I almost smile. Almost.

"Make up with her," Conrad says. "Before you lose something real."

Ha. If he only knew. Except, "How?"

"Be real. Admit you're wrong. Ask how you can fix it." He shrugs, the gesture simple, like he's explaining how to tie skates. "It's not complicated. It's just hard."

I think about her texts. The ones I haven't answered. The way she still reached out even when I was pulling away, asking if I was okay after the Seattle game.

Conrad stands, the stool scraping against the floor. He claps me on the shoulder—carefully, avoiding my bruised areas. "For what it's worth?" He's got this half smile. "I think you two are good together. It's been a long time since I saw a glimpse of the old Brody. Whatever you did, whatever fight you had? Fix it."

He leaves, weaving between the scattered tables toward the elevators.

And I'm left sitting there with a truth I can't avoid anymore.

I might be in love with her. And I'm terrified of losing her.

The bartender comes back over, wiping down the section of bar Conrad vacated. "Another drink?"

"No. I'm good." I stand, leaving a twenty on the bar. I head toward the elevators, doors sliding open with a mechanical hum. I step inside and press the button for the seventh floor. My reflection stares back at me from the mirrored walls—bruised, tired, looking every bit as wrecked as I feel.

I unlock my room with the key card—it takes two tries, the light blinking red before finally turning green. The door clicks open.

Beige walls, two queen beds with burgundy comforters that match every other hotel room I've stayed in this season. Curtains drawn against the Seattle skyline—just distant lights and darkness beyond the window. Standard hotel art on the walls, abstract prints that mean nothing.

Tyler's bed is empty. He's out with some of the other guys, probably at a bar that's not attached to the hotel. His duffel bag is thrown on the luggage rack, clothes spilling out in organized chaos.

I should sleep. We have an early flight to Vancouver tomorrow. A five a.m. wake-up call. Another city. Another game. But I sit on my bed and stare at my phone.

Three unread texts from Chloe over the past week.

Monday:

Chloe

Hope the road trip is going well! Saw highlights from Denver - that assist was beautiful. Stay safe out there.

Wednesday:

Chloe

Watched the Seattle game. Are you okay? That looked rough.

Friday:

<u>Chloe</u>

Heading to Maple Lake this
weekend for wedding prep. See you
in a week? Let me know if you need
anything.

I didn't respond to any of them. Because I'm an idiot.

I groan, lie back on the bed and open Instagram instead. Her profile appears—obviously, because I follow a handful of people, but she's the only one I care about.

The last post is from a week ago. The one in my jersey. Number 7. Her smile genuine and bright and everything I don't deserve. The lighting in the photo is warm, making her freckles stand out.

The comments are mostly positive. Supportive. People who think we're cute together.

But there's one comment that makes my blood run cold.

Ashley Morrison.

Posted two days ago.

@AshleyMorrison: Watch out honey 🏃‍♀️ **Candy Kane has a habit of disappearing when things get real. Ask me how I know. #BeenThereDoneThat #YoureTooGoodForHim**

My jaw clenches so hard it hurts. I scroll through the replies. Most people are defending Chloe. Telling Ashley to move on. Calling her out for being bitter.

But there are enough supportive comments on Ashley's post to make me sick.

@kira.K.33: For real girl, you tried to warn us

@AJOutdoors: He seems shady tbh

@L.Evergreen: Poor Chloe, she seems so sweet

Chloe doesn't deserve any of this.

This is my mess. My past. Following Chloe into her present. She doesn't deserve Ashley's bitterness. Doesn't deserve to be collateral damage in someone else's vendetta.

What was I thinking? I should have responded to her texts. Should have told her what that kiss meant instead of running like a coward.

My phone is in my hand, and I'm scrolling to her contact before I can stop myself.

This is a bad idea. Terrible idea. It's eleven p.m. She's probably asleep. Or busy. Or over me.

I call anyway.

It rings. Once. Twice. Three times. Maybe she won't answer. Maybe she's finally moved on from my—

"Hello?" Her voice. Slightly breathless. Like she ran to get the phone.

And just like that, I can breathe again.

"Hey," I say. "It's me."

"Hey." There's something in her voice. Careful. Guarded. "What's up?"

Right. I've been ignoring her for a week, and now I'm calling at eleven p.m. *Hey! It's me.* Smooth, Kane.

"I just—" I stop. Conrad said to be real. I drag in a breath. "I wanted to hear your voice."

There's silence on the other end. I can hear something in the background. Music, maybe. Or a TV.

Then, "Are you okay?"

Be real. Be honest.

"Yeah. Fine." He shoots. He misses.

"Brody." She says my name like she can see right through me. "I watched your games. You got into two fights in three games. That's not fine."

I close my eyes. Of course she watched.

"It's been a rough week."

Her voice softens slightly. "Are you hurt? That hit tonight looked bad."

I look at my wrapped hand. The bruised knuckles. Touch my left eye gently—still tender, still swelling. "Nothing serious. Just bumps and bruises."

"You don't have to pretend it's all okay, you know." She pauses. "I'm still bound by our contract. Your secrets are safe with me."

I can't tell if she's kidding. It doesn't feel funny. But then she laughs. Soft. Warm. "Loosen up, Brody. I'm not going to leak your medical records to *TMZ*."

And just like that, the tension breaks.

I lean back against the headboard, the cheap hotel pillow bunching behind me. My shoulders relax for the first time in days. *Admit you're wrong.* "I'm sorry, Chloe. I—"

"My brother used to get in a little funk after losing a game. I get it."

That's not what I was apologizing for, but she continues, and I let her. "How's Vancouver looking?"

"Cold. Wet. Canadian."

She laughs again. "Wow. You really know how to sell a city."

"I'm a man of many talents."

"Clearly."

We fall into sudden, weird silence. Like maybe she's thinking about the kiss—I know I am. I clear my throat. "How's the wedding prep going?"

"Good. Chaotic. You wouldn't believe it. I went with Maya to pick up her dress from the bridal shop, and they *didn't* have it. Apparently, their seamstress had it sent to a facility to be pressed, and it somehow didn't end up on the truck to be sent back. Took five hours for them to track it down, during which Maya just about imploded. I think fifteen minutes and we'd have needed to sedate her." She's smiling, I can hear it in her voice. "It's terrible. I shouldn't laugh. It wasn't funny at the time . . . but now that we've got the dress back, I can't help it. Other than that, it's pretty much your standard prewedding chaos." She pauses. "Oh, and I got a call from the Blue Ox publicist. She asked if I'd be interested in doing an interview with someone about the wedding and the company."

Felicity. The conversation in the car park. She must have followed it up.

"That's great," I say, trying to sound casual.

Chloe stops. "Did you have something to do with that?"

"She asked me about your business a few weeks ago. Offered to get in touch with some people who could boost your visibility. That's all."

"Oh." She sounds surprised. Pleased. "Well, thank you. Both of you."

I shrug, still trying to play it cool, even if she can't see me. "You're talented. You deserve the exposure."

She's quiet for a moment. "Thank you."

The words hit different. Softer. Deeper. Like she's thanking me for more than just the interview.

"Always," I say, and I mean it more than she knows.

Another pause. "What are you doing right now?" I don't want this conversation to end. Don't want to go back to the silence of this generic hotel room, with its beige walls and meaningless art.

"Drawing."

"Yeah?"

"Yeah. I've got a new story in my head. I'm trying to sketch it out before I lose it." She sounds almost embarrassed. Self-conscious. "It's probably silly."

"Tell me about it."

Hesitation. And then, "It's about a dragon. He's a special dragon. He's got these beautiful scales—iridescent, blues and greens, all sort of colors—that make him stand out." Her voice picks up, relaxing a little as the story pours out of her. "But everyone's always trying to steal his scales. Take pieces of him. So he hides away in his cave, keeping everyone away. They think he's this grump, but he's just protecting himself."

I may not be a genius—if my behavior the last week is any indication—but it doesn't take a lot to see where she got her inspiration. A grump dragon with flashy scales that everyone seems to want a piece of.

I may not breathe fire, but if it looks like a dragon and sounds like a dragon . . .

"That's not silly," I say quietly.

"I don't know where it goes from there. Just that image. The dragon alone, because he's too scared to let anyone in."

I swallow hard. "Well . . . it sounds to me like he needs someone to find a way into his safe little cave . . . draw him out into the sun."

"Like . . . a warrior princess."

"Yeah. But . . . someone who can't see his scales." I prop an arm behind my head, trying to envision the sketch in her hands.

"What? Why not?"

"I don't know . . . maybe she's blind?"

Silence. Then, "Really? That's your pitch?"

"Okay, magically blind or . . . colorblind. Enchanted by a spell or something," I say, chuckling. "The point is, she can't see the scales everyone else wants. Not until the spell is broken. By then, she's seen who he is without the scales. Just . . ." *Me.* "Him."

There's a long pause, and I suddenly want to take it all back, stuff it down. But I can't, it's already out there. When she finally speaks, the sound is full and bright. "That's . . . kind of perfect."

"Yeah? I mean—yeah. Well, I'm full of great ideas."

She laughs, lighting up the whole room. "I know."

When the silence settles again, it's warm and heavy. Like a weighted blanket.

"Brody?"

"Yeah?"

"You're a good man. On the inside and out. And you need to know that."

The words fill my chest. I can't speak. Can't breathe. Can't process what she just said. Because she just saw through every wall I've built. Every carefully constructed lie I tell myself about being all show and no substance, and . . .

And she thinks I'm good.

"I gotta go," I manage. "I've got an early flight tomorrow to Vancouver."

"Right. Of course. But, Brody?"

"Yeah?"

"Go big, Number Seven."

I think I love her.

I set down the phone. Stare at it for a long moment. Conrad's words echo in my head. *Be real. Admit you're wrong. Ask how you can fix it.*

I've been running because I'm scared. But maybe—just maybe—it's not too late to turn around.

I get up, grab the ice bucket, and head out into the hall. Pile ice from the machine into it, return to my room, and shove my swollen knuckles into the cold.

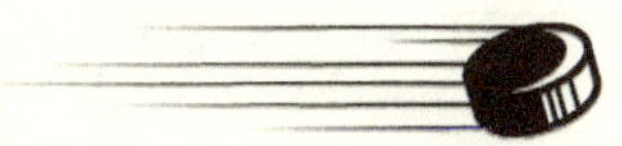

CHLOE

Of all the ways I imagined spending my sister's wedding weekend, sitting alone in a honeymoon suite wasn't one of them.

And yet, here I am. A complete fraud with my fake relationship, unpacking in the Lakeside Suite—king bed, stone fireplace crackling away, rose petals scattered across white bedding like someone's Pinterest board exploded. There's champagne chilling in an ice bucket. Chocolate-covered strawberries on the nightstand.

The whole nine yards of romance.

For me.

Alone.

Apparently, there was a little mix-up with my reservation. Maya booked the reservation as part of her room block, and the check-in lady thought it was her room. But she'll be glamming it up with her bridesmaids down in the Oak Cottage—all five of them squeezed into three bedrooms, which apparently left no space for the bride's sister. Hence the honeymoon suite.

I set my suitcase—my sensible, decidedly unfancy suitcase that probably cost less than one of those throw pillows—on the bench at the foot of the bed and can't help but laugh.

This room is ridiculous.

Floor-to-ceiling windows overlook Maple Lake, where late-February sun glints off patches of ice still clinging to the surface like it's not quite ready to let go of winter. The bathroom has a jetted tub and heated floors. Heated. Floors.

If I wasn't so embarrassed about being *literally* single in the honeymoon suite, I'd think I'd died and gone to heaven.

I start unpacking. Hang up the dress I brought for the rehearsal dinner. Set my toiletries in the bathroom that's roughly the size of my entire apartment bedroom. Toss my giant tote filled with all the contracts, files, and timelines for the wedding onto the bed, and a manila folder skids across the duvet.

For a moment, I just stand there, staring at it.

The return label reads *Stratton Publishing*.

I don't know why I even brought that thing along, except that it was sitting outside my door when I went to pack Jessa's car, and I couldn't bear the thought of opening another rejection in front of her, so I stuffed it into my tote and let it burn a hole in my brain for the next three hours and seventeen minutes while Jessa drove me to Maple Lake.

The envelope stares at me, waiting.

Fine. Let's just get it over with.

I lean across the bed, snatch the envelope, and plop down on the edge of the bed. The envelope is heavier than I expected. Thick. Official. It makes a very crisp tearing noise when I slide my thumb under the flap.

The letter is printed on heavy cream-colored cardstock—the expensive kind that makes you feel important just holding it. Stratton Publishing logo embossed at the top.

> Dear Ms. Chloe Dawson,
>
> I am writing to personally extend an offer for your manuscript, *Sparkle, the Dragon*. Your voice is exactly what we've been searching for in our children's literature line, and I believe your work has the potential to resonate deeply with both parents and children alike.
>
> After careful consideration, Stratton Publishing would like to discuss the potential of a five-book deal with the following terms:
>
> Advance of $5,000 for the first book, payable upon contract signing
>
> • $10,000 per book upon successful completion and acceptance
>
> • Eight-month delivery schedule for the finished collection
>
> • Standard royalty terms as outlined in the attached contract
>
> • World English rights with subsidiary rights to be negotiated separately
>
> We envision releasing your books in rapid succession to build momentum and establish your presence in the market. The first book would be scheduled next fall, with subsequent releases every four months.
>
> While this is an aggressive timeline, we believe

your talent and the commercial appeal of your writing style make this an achievable goal.

Please review the attached contract proposal and reach out to us with any concerns you may have. We would appreciate your response within the next two weeks, as we are hard at work acquiring titles for our upcoming publication year.

I look forward to welcoming you to the Stratton family.

Sincerely,

Milo Brooks

Chief Executive Publisher

Stratton Publishing

I blink. Hard. Read the letter again. This is . . . this isn't real, is it? And it's signed by Milo Brooks himself. The CEO.

That's weird, right? You'd think an acceptance letter would come from an editor. Or an agent liaison. Someone whose job is actually dealing with aspiring authors. But no. CEO signature. In actual ink. Is that a good sign or a red flag?

I read it again, this time combing through for anything that could possibly hint that this is some sort of sick, terrible joke.

There's none.

I let out a laugh. They want my book. They want more than that—they want *five* books! I laugh again. Pull out my phone to text Brody—and stop.

All that excitement rushing in my blood slows. Cools. Hardens to a pit in my stomach.

Here's the thing. It took me two years to write and illustrate the first book. Two years of nights and weekends and lunch breaks, fitting it into the margins around jobs that barely paid enough to cover rent and student loans. To meet an eight-month deadline for five books? I'd need to quit my job.

Could I even do that?

Before the contract with Brody came along, absolutely not.

And now . . . ? I don't know. Can I write that fast when I know the money is dwindling? Oh, the pressure!

I tuck the letter back into the folder without looking at the official contract proposals. Stuff it back into the tote of doom.

I'll deal with it later. After the wedding. When I can think clearly and not while sitting in a honeymoon suite that's mocking my entire life.

My phone buzzes.

<u>Brody</u>
Just passed Elk River. Be there
soon. Miss you.

Miss you.
Two words that shouldn't mean as much as they do.
I type back.

<u>Chloe</u>
Drive safe. We're meeting at the
hotel restaurant at 7. See you there!

And my heart does that silly little flip when I hit Send.

But—complete transparency—I'm getting used to that feeling, because things have been different. Better. (So much better.) Since his game in Seattle.

We've been texting every day (real texts, not those one-word responses he was giving me before), talking about everything. His games. My new book idea. The crazy thing he overheard in the Starbucks line at the airport. Everything and nothing.

He's playing better too. I've watched all three of his games this week (not obsessive at all), and there's something different about him on the ice. Calmer. More focused. Like whatever was chasing him finally slowed down.

And after every game, he calls before bed. And we talk on the phone, filling in the gaps that we forgot to text about.

He's the last person I want to talk to every day and the first person I want to talk to when I wake up. Which feels . . . really dangerous.

Because I can't see the lines anymore, where fake-boyfriend Brody stops and Barcelona Brody begins.

And that's—

Yeah.

I'm not going to think about that right now either.

I shove it into the mental drawer, right next to the Stratton Publishing letter, and start getting ready for dinner.

Le Papillon is exactly what you'd expect from a resort restaurant trying very hard to be fancy. Warm wood. Soft lighting. White tablecloths. Fresh flowers on every table. The smell of butter and herbs, garlic and rosemary, wafts in the air, mingling with the classical music playing overhead.

We're all seated at a long table—wedding party at one end, family at the other. It's maybe twenty people total. Derek's parents are at the head, speaking animatedly with my mom. My brother is right at home, talking hockey with the boys. And somehow, I got myself sandwiched in the middle of Maya's bridesmaids, trying to look even remotely engaged in the conversation while my gaze keeps going back to the entrance.

The door opens.

And there he is.

Brody strolls into the restaurant wearing dark jeans, a blue polo, and a gray sports jacket that complements those gray-blue eyes I can't seem to get enough of. His hair is slightly windswept, jaw dusted with stubble. He looks more relaxed than I've seen him in weeks.

His gaze finds mine immediately.

Something in his expression shifts. Softens.

He crosses the restaurant in long strides, weaving between tables. I stand without thinking about it, my chair scraping against the floor.

I'm only halfway to my feet when he pulls me into a hug.

His arms wrap around me, solid and warm. He smells like winter air and his woodsy cologne. His chin rests on top of my head for just a second.

"Hey," he says quietly. Just for me.

"Hey."

We pull apart. He looks at me like he's seeing me for the first time, his gaze taking me in.

"You look beautiful."

Heat instantly rises to my cheeks. "Thanks. You look"—I gesture vaguely at him—"surprisingly great. For someone who just drove three hours."

He grins, and I just . . . melt. "High praise."

Maya waves from down the table. "Brody! Come sit!"

There's a newly empty chair next to me, and Brody takes it without hesitation. His knee bumps mine under the table. He doesn't move it away.

A waiter appears with menus. Starts explaining the specials in accented English.

Brody listens, then responds in French.

Actual French.

This elicits a chorus of starstruck oohs and ahhs from around the table.

The waiter lights up, responding enthusiastically. They have a whole conversation—I catch maybe three words total—and the waiter practically floats away, promising to bring the chef's recommendation.

I know I'm staring, but seriously, who just *knows* French?

"What?" he asks.

"You speak French?"

"You speak Spanish," he counters.

"Not like that!"

Brody chuckles. "I took it in high school. Spent a summer in Quebec for hockey camp." He shrugs like it's nothing. "It's rusty but functional."

"That was not rusty. That was fluent."

"You're easy to impress."

"Apparently."

We're grinning at each other like idiots, oblivious to anyone else at the table.

The meal unfolds around us. Courses arrive—some kind of French onion soup that tastes like heaven, duck confit that melts off the bone, roasted veggies with pureed parsnips. Wine is poured, my dad stands to pray over the meal, and conversation quiets down as everyone digs in.

And through it all, Brody and I never stop talking.

I give him the lowdown on some of the family he'll meet at the wedding. And he tells me the story of a time in high school when he forgot his hockey jersey on an away game day.

"My coach told me just to grab an extra one from the box in his office as we left." He's laughing before he even gets to the punch line. "I pulled from the wrong box. Wound up wearing a middle-school jersey to the game."

I gasp, covering my mouth with a hand.

"I could hardly move my arms it was so tight!"

I can just see it—Brody squeezing himself into a jersey half his size, just so he can play. It's funny. But also . . . a little sad. That was after his mom passed away. He was probably on his own as far as laundering his uniform and packing his equipment.

His hand finds mine under the table at some point. Intertwines our fingers.

I don't pull away.

The contract feels very far away right now.

After dinner, and then dessert and coffee, we make our way back toward the main lodge. The group splinters off. The bridesmaids head toward their cottage, down by the lake, the groomsmen toward their lodge. Derek's parents to their room.

Leaving Brody and me walking alone through the quiet resort.

The path is lit with lanterns, their warm glow reflecting off patches of snow. The air is cold but not brutal—a crisp February night. It smells like pine and wood smoke. Stars are starting to appear overhead—more than you can ever see in the city.

That's one thing I miss about Maple Lake.

Ahead, the main building comes into view. The main lodge is massive—dark wood and stone, built in that classic 1930s North Woods style, with steep rooflines and enormous windows. Three stories, maybe four, with a wraparound porch dotted with Adirondack chairs and firepits. Behind it, the lake stretches out, still partially frozen, the surface reflecting sunlight like shattered glass.

"I should check in," Brody says as we reach the massive oak doors. "Get my key."

"Right. Yeah." My stomach drops a little at the thought of turning in for the night.

We walk into the lobby together. The evening light makes the lobby even more impressive. Vaulted ceilings with exposed beams. A stone fireplace so large you could park a car in it, flames crackling and throwing dancing shadows across the hardwood floors. Leather furniture arranged in conversation clusters. Vintage skis and snowshoes mounted on the walls, alongside black-and-white photos of the resort from decades past.

It smells like wood smoke and cinnamon and expensive candles.

The front desk attendant stands behind a massive wraparound desk, looking a little frazzled after what was likely a very busy day. She gives a little start when we step up to the desk.

"Hi," Brody says, flashing that easy smile that probably makes people forget their own names. "Checking in. Brody Kane."

The woman types on her computer.

Frowns.

Types some more.

The frown deepens.

Oh no.

"Is there a problem?" Brody asks.

"Um." She glances between us, looking genuinely pained. "Mr. Kane, I have a reservation for you, but . . . it's for next weekend."

Silence.

"Next weekend?" Brody repeats.

"February nineteenth through the twenty-first."

I watch Brody's face. He's trying to hide it, but I can see the frustration. The embarrassment. His jaw tightens. Shoulders tense.

And then I remember.

The dyslexia.

Numbers get jumbled sometimes. Dates. Addresses. It's not his fault. It's just how his brain works.

"That's my mistake," he says, forcing a laugh that doesn't reach his eyes. "Must have mixed up the dates when I booked."

"I'm so sorry," she says, and she actually looks sorry, "but we're completely booked this weekend. Multiple weddings, family reunions—there's not a single room available."

"It's okay. I get it." Brody pulls out his phone. "I'll text the guys. Maybe someone has space in their room."

He types quickly.

We wait.

His phone buzzes.

His expression says it all.

"They're all full," he says. "Four guys per room already."

The attendant winces. "There are a few hotels in town. Let me check availability for you—"

But Brody's already pulling up his phone. Scrolling through booking sites. His expression gets grimmer with each swipe.

"Everything's booked," he finally says. "Within twenty miles."

Which makes sense. Maya's wedding is kind of a big deal. And this isn't exactly Minneapolis—it's a small town that probably has, what, three hotels total?

I take a breath. "You can stay with me."

The words come out before I can think about whether they're a good idea.

Brody looks at me. "Chloe—"

"The room has a couch that pulls out. It's big. There's plenty of space."

"I can't ask you to—"

"You're not asking. I'm offering." I try to sound casual. Like this isn't making my heart race. "Besides, it's either that or you drive three hours home and three hours back tomorrow morning. Which seems excessive."

He hesitates.

Because he's a gentleman.

Because this is complicated.

Because we've been walking a fine line between friends in a fake relationship and more than friends in a doomed one.

Another beat passes before he gives in. "All right, then."

"All right?" The receptionist lets out a relieved breath as though she'd been bracing for a disgruntled customer. "Great. I'll make you a set of keys."

A few minutes later, Brody's grabbed his bag from the car, and we're headed up to the honeymoon suite.

"Wow." Brody sets his bag down inside the suite. "I didn't realize we'd be staying in the Taj Mahal."

I didn't pick the room, but I'm embarrassed just the same, as though I somehow dragged him into the fever dream that is the honeymoon suite. There's still a trail of petals leading from the door to the bedroom.

"I should have asked housekeeping to come by and pick this up."

"What?" An amused smile plays at his lips. "You don't want flower petals all over your room? I can't imagine why not."

I give his shoulder a little smack. "Stop it, you."

He laughs, catching my hand.

And I'm suddenly hyperaware of how small the room feels with both of us in it. "I feel bad. You've been traveling almost all day. I should . . . Let me take the couch," I offer, gesturing to the sofa.

"Absolutely not."

"Brody—"

"Chloe." He looks at me. Really looks at me with those stupidly blue eyes. "What kind of gentleman would I be if I let you take the couch?" He's already moving toward it, testing the cushions. "I've slept in worse places. Team bus after a double overtime game in Dallas? This is luxury." He's already flopping down on the couch, tossing his feet up on the coffee table. "Surely you wouldn't take this away from me."

"All right, fine." I roll my eyes. "I'll allow it."

He smirks, and my heart does a full pirouette.

A beat passes while I'm still standing there, staring at him, my brain turning to mush, and Brody clears his throat. "So, are you gonna turn in, or . . ." He pauses, and I swear I see something hopeful flicker across his face. "We could hang out? If you want."

My heart does something complicated in my chest.

There is quite literally nothing I'd like more than just a few more minutes together.

"Okay," I hear myself say. "Yeah. Let me just . . . I'm gonna go change."

His smile is worth every bit of confusion currently rioting in my chest. "Take your time."

I grab my pajamas and practically flee to the bathroom.

Very dignified.

I change into flannel pants and an oversized sweatshirt. Nothing even remotely romantic. Practically armor. Brush my teeth. Wash my face. Stare at my reflection in the mirror and give myself a stern talking-to about not doing anything stupid.

The mirror doesn't respond.

Helpful.

When I come out, Brody's on the couch again, leaning back against the cushions. He's changed into sweatpants and a T-shirt, which looks both effortlessly comfortable and unfairly attractive.

The fireplace is still going, casting flickering shadows across his face, and Brody's holding the remote, flipping through the channels.

He looks up when I appear, and something warm crosses his face. "Hey."

"Hey." I move toward the couch, and he scoots over to make room for me. The TV cycles through channels—a home renovation show, a true-crime documentary, what appears to be a very dramatic reality dating show—

Then he lands on a cooking competition. Two chefs in white coats working frantically while a timer counts down. The chairman's voice booms dramatically about a secret ingredient.

I remember what he told me. Back at the beginning of all this. How cooking shows are his guilty pleasure.

"*Iron Chef*?" I ask, settling onto the couch beside him.

He glances at me. "Is this okay?"

"Absolutely."

His smile could power the entire resort.

I curl up next to him, and somehow—naturally, easily, like we've done this a thousand times—his arm comes around my shoulders. I fit against his side like I was made to be there.

The show plays on. He tells me about the chefs, explains the judging criteria, gets genuinely excited when someone pulls off a particularly impressive technique. "Look at that perfect sear."

We settle deeper into the couch. Into each other.

It feels romantic in a way that has nothing to do with the fireplace or the rose petals or the honeymoon suite. It's just . . . us. Watching TV. His thumb tracing absent patterns on my shoulder. I feel completely safe under his arm.

This is what it would be like, I think. If this were real. If we were just two people who chose each other. Quiet nights in. Cooking shows and comfortable silence. His arm around me like it belongs there.

The show ends. Another one starts.

Neither of us suggests moving.

At some point, I tilt my head up to look at him and find him already looking down at me.

The air changes.

His eyes drop to my lips.

He leans in.

Just slightly.

My breath catches.

Closer.

I can feel the warmth of him. My heart hammers in my chest. I can't hear the TV anymore. And then, something flickers across his face. Some thought. Some reminder.

He pulls back.

Just an inch. But it doesn't feel like the last time we almost kissed. There's nothing cold about it. Just careful. Wistful. A moment held between us.

"You should probably get some sleep," he says quietly, his breath brushing my skin. "Big day tomorrow."

"Right," I manage to breathe. I pull away and stand on unsteady legs. "You're right."

I cross to the door and pause. "Good night, Brody."

"Good night."

I step into the room and close the door behind me, leaning back against it, my head spinning. I press a hand to my cheek, my cool palm soothing against my scalding skin.

We're playing with fire.

There've been too many close calls.

If we keep going like this, we're bound to fall.

And neither of us can afford to fall, because in two days, we're going to break up—disastrously, publicly, heartbreakingly.

And if we don't? It's not the first time the thought has crossed my mind.

I pull out my phone, swiping into the photos app, and find the screenshot I took of the contract clause.

> Both parties agree to maintain the appearance of a genuine romantic relationship through all wedding events. Upon completion of the Wedding (Event #4), both parties will execute a staged public breakup at the Wedding Reception (Event #5), with Party B (Chloe Dawson) initiating the breakup and Party A (Brody Kane) positioned as "at fault," followed by a mandatory thirty-day no-contact period. Any premature breakup, exposure of the contractual nature of the relationship, or other deviation from this termination plan will result in forfeiture of all benefits: Party A loses NHL contract renewal, and Party B forfeits all payment and owes financial penalties.

If we don't break up, I lose all the money, and he loses . . . everything.

I turn off the light and head to bed.
Two more days.
We can do this.

BRODY

I DON'T SLEEP.

Not really.

I lie on the sofa, my feet dangling off the end, blanket pulled up to my chin, staring at the ceiling beams while the fire crackles and pops and slowly burns down to embers. Whoever picked out the furniture for the honeymoon suite obviously didn't anticipate anybody sleeping on the sofa, because it's about as comfortable as rocks, but I've slept on worse. Airport floors. Team buses with broken suspension. That hotel in Calgary where the heater died and we all huddled in our winter coats until maintenance showed up at three a.m.

This isn't about the couch.

This is about the fact that Chloe is just on the other side of that door, sleeping in a bed covered in rose petals, completely unaware that I'm lying here having what Conrad would probably call an "emotional crisis."

The dragon with the sad heart.

That's what she called it. The grumpy dragon who keeps everyone out because he's too scared to let anyone see the real him.

She sees me.

And for some reason, that doesn't terrify me like it did.

In fact, I ache for it.

At some point, I give up on sleep. The fire has died down to glowing coals, casting barely any light. I sit up slowly, quietly, muscles protesting the hours of contorting my body to fit onto the small couch. But when I stretch, I can still feel the phantom warmth of her head against my shoulder, my arm wrapped around her, pulling her in.

I want to spend every night like that for the rest of my life.

The thought hits me like a body check I didn't see coming.

Who are you kidding, Brody? The contract ends tomorrow, after the wedding reception.

After which, Chloe has to dump you . . . or you lose out on the money.

My chest tightens.

I need coffee. And air.

I grab my phone—6:17 a.m.—and slip out of the room as quietly as possible, pulling on my hoodie and shoes in the hallway. The resort is silent at this hour, just the hum of heating systems and the distant clatter of someone setting up breakfast in the restaurant downstairs.

The lobby is empty except for a young guy behind the front desk, who looks like he's been up all night, scrolling through his phone with the glazed expression of someone counting down the minutes until shift change. The massive fireplace is cold now, just ash and the smell of yesterday's wood smoke.

I follow the signs to the coffee bar—a small counter near the restaurant entrance with an espresso machine that looks like it probably takes an engineering degree to use. But there's also a regular coffeepot, thank you, and I pour myself a large cup. Black. Hot enough to burn.

"You're up early."

I turn. Derek is standing there in athletic gear, clearly just back from a run. Sweaty. But looking less hostile than usual, which is saying something.

"Right back at ya," I say. "Wedding nerves?"

"Nope." Derek pours himself coffee. Adds cream and sugar. We stand there in awkward silence for a moment, two guys who should probably be friends—teammates, after all—but aren't.

"Listen," Derek says finally. Turns to face me. "I owe you an apology."

I wasn't expecting that.

"For what?"

"For being a jerk. About you and Chloe." He runs a hand through his sweaty hair. "Maya and I were talking last night, and she sort of pushed back. Told me I was being weird and suspicious and probably too hard on you because of my own issues."

"Your issues?"

Derek hesitates, glancing down at his coffee as though he'd like to drown himself in it rather than have this conversation. "Ashley Morrison is my cousin."

I blink at him. "Wait—what?"

"Yeah. I'm the one who invited her to that charity event. She wanted to be an influencer, so I thought it might be good for her." He takes a sip of his drink, glancing away. "Looking back on it, I probably could have seen it coming. They don't call you Candy for nothing. You can be a charmer."

I'll try not to let that sting.

"And Ashley . . ." He grimaces. "I've always known she was . . . a lot. But when she told me about you, I believed her. Maybe because I wanted to believe the worst. Because it fit the narrative I already had about you."

"What narrative?"

"That you coast on talent and good looks and your stupid smile. That you're a player."

My mouth sort of twists at that.

He takes a drink of his coffee. "But seeing you with Chloe the last few weeks, I'm starting to think maybe I was wrong." He pauses, and something gives in his expression. A weight between us lifting. "I hope so."

My throat tightens.

"So"—Derek extends his hand—"truce?"

I shake his hand. "Truce."

He meets my eyes. "Don't prove me wrong." He releases my hand. Nods. Then leaves, taking the stairs two at a time.

And I'm standing there with my coffee, my stomach knotting. *Don't prove me wrong.*

When I get back to the room, Chloe's awake. She's sitting on the edge of the sofa in black leggings and an oversized cream sweater with a red heart on the front. Hair pulled into a messy bun. No makeup. Looking soft and sleepy and so beautiful it hurts.

"Hey," she says, her voice still rough with sleep. "Where'd you go?"

"Coffee run." I hold up both cups. "One boring mocha latte for you, made by yours truly. I apologize in advance—it's not a candy cane mocha, just plain ol' milk and chocolate sauce swiped from the breakfast bar."

"Please. You don't do anything halfway."

She takes the cup like I just handed her the Holy Grail. Takes a sip. Closes her eyes and makes a sound that probably shouldn't be legal before seven a.m.

"This is perfect. Thank you." She takes another sip, cradling the cup in both hands. "How'd you sleep?"

"I've slept in worse places."

"That's not an answer."

"It was fine." Aside from the part where I didn't sleep. But I can't tell her that. Not without admitting that it was the thought of losing her in twenty-four hours that had me lying awake all night.

She gives me a look that says she doesn't believe me but isn't going to push it. "Well, thank you. You're a real gentleman."

The morning light is stronger now, streaming through the windows and making the lake visible—patches of ice and dark water, pine trees framing the view.

"Want to go for a walk?" I ask. "Before the wedding chaos starts?"

"You read my mind. I need to move before Maya finds me and starts panicking about something."

We grab our coats—hers a puffy jacket that makes her look tiny, mine the standard wool coat I use all winter—and we head downstairs together, coffee cups in hand like we're a normal couple doing normal couple things.

The lobby is starting to wake up. A family with small kids heading toward breakfast. An older couple reading newspapers by the fireplace that's been relit. The smell of bacon and coffee drifting from the restaurant.

"Excuse me?" A woman's voice stops us near the entrance. "Are you Chloe Dawson?"

We turn. She's maybe forty, dressed in a way that's giving off a covert-professional vibe. Slim jeans, sweater, expensive boots. Holding a tablet and wearing a press credential on a lanyard.

"Yes?" Chloe says, sounding uncertain.

"I'm Jennifer Hartley, from *Minnesota Bridal Magazine*. I'm here to cover the Dawson–Munson wedding." She's smiling, friendly. "Felicity Grant mentioned you're the event planner who planned not only the wedding but also the prewedding events? I'd love to chat with you about your business while I'm here. Get your perspective on what makes a great wedding."

Chloe's eyes widen. "Oh. Um, yeah. Sure. I'd love to."

Jennifer's gaze falls on me. Studies me for a moment. "Oh my goodness, you're—"

"Brody Kane." I extend my hand. "I'm with Chloe."

The words come out before I can think about them. *I'm with Chloe.* Not "I'm her date for the wedding." Not "We're seeing each other." Just . . . I'm with her.

It feels right.

"Oh!" Jennifer's smile widens. "I'd heard you two are dating. What a great story—the event planner and her hockey player. Would you both be willing to sit for a quick interview?"

Chloe looks at me. I nod. Why not?

"Sure," Chloe says.

We end up in a corner of the lobby, sitting in leather chairs arranged around a coffee table. Jennifer pulls out her tablet, opens a recording app, and launches into questions. I settle in, ready to face the usual onslaught I've come to expect during interviews— anything to get me off-kilter, reveal something I didn't want to share. But today, I'm not being asked anything. Jennifer seems focused entirely on Chloe.

Which feels weird, but I'm not complaining.

"So tell me about your business. How did you get started in event planning?"

Chloe sets down her coffee cup. Takes a breath. And starts talking.

And I watch her transform.

Gone is the nervous, self-deprecating woman who apologizes for taking up space. Instead, she's confident. Passionate. Talking about how she started planning events for her family, Maya's engagement party, the bridal-cation, how she learned to see what people really wanted versus what they thought they should want, how every event tells a story about the people at the center of it.

"The best weddings aren't about perfection," she says, gesturing with her hands in that animated way she has when she's excited.

"They're about authenticity. About creating moments that feel true to the couple, not just true to Pinterest boards and wedding magazines." She pauses, then grins. "No offense."

Jennifer laughs. "None taken. That's a refreshing perspective."

"I think people get so caught up in the performance of weddings—the Instagram photos, the perfect details—that they forget to enjoy the day. To be present with each other and their loved ones." Chloe leans forward. "My job isn't to create magazine-perfect events. It's to create events where people feel seen and celebrated for who they really are."

She's glowing. Animated. Completely in her element, even if she doesn't know it.

And I'm falling for her all over again.

"That's beautiful," Jennifer says, typing notes. "And Brody, you must be so proud of her work."

I look at Chloe. She's watching me, curious what I'll say.

"I am," I say. And mean it. "She's incredible at what she does. She sees people—really sees them—and creates experiences that bring out the best in everyone. She did that for Maya's events. She did that for—" I stop before I can say it, *me*. "She's very talented."

Chloe's cheeks flush pink.

Jennifer is eating this up. "You two are adorable. Can I get a photo? For the article?"

"Oh, um—" Chloe looks uncertain.

"Sure," I say. Standing. Offering Chloe my hand.

We stand together in front of the massive fireplace while Jennifer frames the shot on her phone.

"Perfect. Now smile—not too posed, just natural."

I look at Chloe. She looks at me. And we smile. And for the first time, I'm not showing off my media-perfect smile. Jennifer's getting the real me.

"Can I get one, for us?" Chloe says and hands her phone to Jennifer.

"Sure." Jennifer takes the photo. "Got it. Let me just check—" She looks at the screen. Frowns slightly.

"Everything okay?" Chloe asks.

"Oh, yes. You two look great." Jennifer hands back the phone. "Beautiful shot."

But there was something in that frown. Something that makes my instincts prickle.

"Thank you so much for this opportunity," Chloe says, and pockets the phone.

"My pleasure. I'll send you a copy of the article when it comes out." Jennifer gathers her things, smiling again. "Enjoy the wedding weekend!"

She disappears toward the restaurant. Chloe immediately opens her phone, pulling up the photo.

We're standing close, my arm around her waist, her hand on my chest. Both of us smiling like we're actually in love. Like this isn't a business arrangement. Like we're a real couple at a real wedding, celebrating real feelings.

"We look good," Chloe says softly.

"Yeah. We do."

We stand there staring at the photo for a long moment.

"Ready for that walk?" I ask, needing to move, needing the cold air to clear my head and remind me where this whole thing is headed.

"Yes. Please. That was a lot first thing in the morning."

We head outside into the sharp February air. It's crisp, hovering just below freezing, the kind of cold that makes your lungs burn in a good way. The sun is higher now, melting the frost on the pine trees, making everything sparkle. The resort grounds stretch out before us—paths winding through the woods, the lake visible through gaps in the trees.

We walk in silence for a few minutes, our footsteps crunching on the gravel path. Our breaths come out in white clouds.

"That was really cool," Chloe says finally. "I've never been interviewed about my business before."

"You were amazing."

"I was nervous."

"You didn't seem nervous. You came off passionate. Confident." I glance at her. "You should do more of that. You're a natural."

"Ha. Hardly."

But I stop her. "Listen. You're honest. And real. And not caught up in worrying what people think of you." The words come out before I can stop them. "I admire that about you."

She is looking at me, nonplussed. "You admire me?"

"Yeah. I do."

"Brody Kane, hockey's golden boy, admires me?"

"I'm not—" I stop. "I'm not a golden boy. That's just a persona. A performance. Candy Kane isn't real."

"I know."

"You're the only person who sees that. Who sees me." My chest is tight. And then I say something completely corny. "You see the dragon underneath the scales everyone else wants."

Oh brother. On the list of most cringeworthy moments in my life, I think that one will be holding a top spot for a while. But she doesn't laugh. Doesn't cringe. She just nods.

Then, "And the princess needs the dragon too. Because while her blindness lets her see beyond his sparkle, he makes her laugh and helps her to feel . . . safe. And maybe special."

And right then I know.

I'm in love with her. And this isn't a game, and . . .

The words fill my lungs. "Chloe, I—"

"Chloe!" Maya's voice carries through the trees. She's jogging down the path toward us, still in her pajamas but with a coat thrown over them. "I've been looking everywhere for you! We have final dress fittings in an hour, and the florist called and the flowers have arrived frozen—"

"Calm down—we'll fix it." Chloe takes her hand, then looks at me apologetically. "Duty calls."

"Go. I'll see you later."

I'm left standing alone in the woods with the crushing realization that I have approximately twenty-four hours left on this contract.

Twenty-four hours to figure out how to tell her that this has stopped being fake—has never been fake.

I don't want us to break up. Which means, of course, I'll break the contract.

Lose everything.

I'm no longer the dragon in the cave, too scared to let anyone in. And the blind princess isn't the one who needs him.

He's the one who needs her.

CHLOE

He admires me.

The thought has been playing on repeat in my head for the last four hours.

I'm lying on a heated massage table in the resort spa, wrapped in a plush white robe, while someone named Svetlana works lavender-scented oil into my shoulders with the kind of pressure that borders on aggressive. Maya insisted on a full spa day for the wedding party—massages, facials, mani-pedis, the works. Her gift to her bridesmaids and, apparently, to me.

"You are very tense," Svetlana says in a thick accent that could be Russian or possibly just very rural Minnesotan. "You must relax."

Easy for her to say. She's not the one whose fake relationship ends tomorrow and who just realized she's completely, hopelessly, irreversibly in love with her contractually obligated boyfriend.

Which wouldn't be terrible except the contract includes the epic fight.

The breakup.

And if we break the contract, well . . .

Who decided a contract was a good idea anyway?

The spa smells fresh, like eucalyptus and mint. Very spa-ish. Soft music drifts overhead, playing some sort of pan-flute monstrosity that's been drilling into my brain since I stepped into the room. Candles flicker in glass holders, casting a dim, eerie glow from under the massage tables.

"Breathe," Svetlana commands.

I breathe. Or at least, I try to.

I try to focus on the sensation of her hands working out the knots in my shoulders. On the warmth of the heated table against my stomach. The rich smell of oils. Anything other than the roiling anxiety bubbling up through my chest.

This is supposed to be relaxing.

Why isn't it relaxing?

Oh, I don't know, maybe because every time I close my eyes, I see Brody. Standing in the morning light, looking rumpled and soft and like he didn't sleep well. Speaking French to waiters. Holding my hand under the table. Looking at me in the woods like he was about to say something important before Maya interrupted.

You see the dragon underneath the scales everyone else wants.

Who says things like that?

Brody Kane, apparently.

The man I thought was all performance and charm and carefully constructed image. The man who turned out to be vulnerable and scared and kind and real underneath all of it.

The man I'm absolutely, completely in love with.

"You are tensing again," Svetlana says disapprovingly. "What is wrong?"

"Nothing. Everything. I don't know."

"Man problems?"

"How did you—"

"Is always man problems." She digs her thumbs into a particularly stubborn knot near my shoulder blade, making me wince. "You love him?"

"Yes," I admit. "I think I do."

"Then tell him."

"It's complicated."

"Is always complicated." She moves to my other shoulder, giving me a brief reprieve before starting in again. "But life is short. You tell him. He loves you too, probably. Men are stupid but not blind."

I want to laugh. Or cry. Or both.

When she finally finishes—patting my shoulder in what I think is meant to be an encouraging way but feels more like a warning—I'm ushered into another room for the facial. This one smells like cucumber and roses, the air humid from the facial steamers. Maya's already there, lying on a table with her face covered in what looks like green mud, cucumber slices over her eyes.

Maya lifts one of the slices and peeks out as I settle onto my own table beside her. An aesthetician, who introduces herself as Amber, starts cleansing my face, applying some kind of exfoliating scrub with her fingers. I close my eyes, trying very hard to focus on relaxing, keeping my mind from wandering back to—

"So," Maya says from her table, "I didn't tell Mom, but you and Brody . . . in the same room?"

"He slept on the couch, so don't go crazy."

"Well, for the record, I'm happy for you, Chloe. You deserve someone who chooses you. Who makes you feel like you're the most important person in the room." She's quiet for a moment. "That's how Derek makes me feel. And I think Brody does that for you."

Brody doesn't just make me feel like the most important person in the room. He makes me feel like the *only* person in the room.

Amber wipes off the exfoliating scrub and starts applying a mask that smells like honey and lavender.

"Can I tell you something?" Maya asks.

"Of course."

"When Derek proposed, I was terrified. Not of marrying him—I wanted that. But of the wedding." She laughs softly. "Sometimes I feel like Mom and Dad . . . and just about everyone else, put me up on this pedestal. Expect me to be picture perfect." She pauses, letting out a breath. "It's a lot sometimes. And I was so nervous about the wedding. I just wanted it to be . . . different. Not something for anyone else, but something for Derek and me." She reaches out, her fingertips brushing my wrist. "I couldn't have pulled any of this off without you. Everything you've done, from the bridal-cation to the meet-and-greet party to the couples shower, you somehow managed to make them truly about us. About our story. It means so much to me."

My chest tightens.

"You're really good at what you do, Chloe. I know I don't say it enough, but I'm proud of you. Of your business. Of how hard you've worked."

I'm going to cry. Right here. With a honey-lavender mask on my face and cucumber slices I haven't even gotten yet.

"Thank you," I manage. Barely.

"I mean it. You're talented. And you're brave. And you deserve all the good things." She pauses. "Including Brody."

"Oh, this is wonderful," someone says, though I know the voice instantly. Our mom appears, settling into the chair next to me with a contented sigh. Like us, she's got on a plush white robe, her hair wrapped in a towel. But unlike me, she looks like she's actually gotten some relaxation in. "It's so nice to see my girls together, getting pampered before the big day."

My girls. She said *my girls.* Plural. Including me.

Something in my chest loosens.

She reaches over and squeezes my hand. Smiles, warm and genuine. "Everything is perfect, by the way. All the events you planned were beautiful. You really outdid yourself. I think you've finally found your calling."

And there it goes again. Whatever just loosened tightens right back up. A few months ago, I would have given anything to hear her say that. But now . . . there's a scared dragon and a blind princess calling too . . .

She squeezes my hand again. "I'm proud of you, sweetheart. Really proud."

Thank goodness for the cucumbers Amber presses to my eyelids, because I was about to be known as that one guest who cried during her facial.

The rest of the afternoon passes in a blur of beauty treatments and girl talk. We get our nails done—I choose a soft pink that makes my hands look elegant. We sit in the relaxation room afterward, sipping cucumber water and eating those fancy tiny sandwiches you only see in movies. The bridesmaids show up too, chattering about the wedding and their dresses and their dates.

And through it all, of course, I'm thinking about Brody. About the way he said "I'm with Chloe" to Jennifer like he meant it.

About how the contract ends tomorrow.

And about Svetlana's words. *Life is short. You tell him. He loves you too, probably.*

Maybe she's right. Maybe I should tell him. Maybe there's a world in which Brody and I get the happily ever after.

By the time we're getting ready for the rehearsal dinner, I'm a new woman. My skin is glowing. My nails are perfect. My hair is done in loose waves that one of the bridesmaids helped me with, soft and romantic and nothing like my usual messy bun. I'm wearing a navy-blue dress—simple, fitted, hitting just above the knee. And most of all, I've got that confident glow that comes with being so sure that love has finally found you.

And I know what I'm going to do.

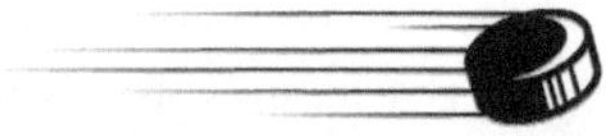

The rehearsal dinner is in the resort's private dining room—a space with floor-to-ceiling windows overlooking the lake, long tables set with white linens and candles. It's warm and romantic and perfect. It smells like winter, and I spot pine garland someone draped along the windowsills.

I walk in and immediately scan the room for Brody. He's near the windows, talking to a couple of Derek's groomsmen—guys from the team. He looks good. Relaxed. Happy.

And then he sees me.

His whole expression changes. Softens. He excuses himself from Tyler and crosses the room toward me with purpose.

"Hey," he says when he reaches me.

"Hey."

We're standing close. Closer than necessary. The room is filling up with people—family, wedding party—but I barely notice them. My heart is already pounding, and I haven't even gotten to the scary part yet.

"You look beautiful," Brody says quietly. His fingertips brush my arm, sliding into my palm.

Something in my chest expands, warm and bright and terrifying.

This is what love feels like.

"Thank you," I manage. "You look pretty good yourself."

"Dinner's starting," Maya calls from across the room. "Everyone, find your seats!"

Brody offers me his arm. "Shall we?"

I take it. Let him lead me to our assigned seats—next to each other, naturally.

The meal unfolds around us. Speeches from Derek's dad about

love and commitment. Toasts from the best man about hockey metaphors that mostly don't land. Laughter and clinking glasses and the kind of warm chaos that comes from gathering people who love each other in one room.

And through it all, Brody, his fingers intertwined with mine under the table, holds on like he's not planning to let go.

Between the main course and dessert, when people are mingling and the formal part is over, he leans close. His breath is warm against my ear.

"Can we talk later? After this?"

"Yes." My voice comes out breathier than intended. "I need to talk to you too."

"Good." He squeezes my hand. "It's important."

"Mine too."

We sit there with the weight of unspoken words between us, both of us knowing that something is about to change. That tonight, after this dinner, we're going to have the conversation we've been avoiding for weeks.

That the contract ends tomorrow, but whatever this is between us—this real, terrifying, beautiful thing—doesn't have to.

We just have to play it right.

BRODY

IN HOCKEY, THERE'S A MOMENT RIGHT BEFORE you take a shot when everything slows down. You see the angle. You know what you need to do. And you either take it or you miss your chance.

Walking back from the rehearsal dinner with Chloe's hand in mine, more stars overhead than I've seen in months, I can see my shot. It's clear as day. The perfect angle. The open net.

Just take the shot, Kane. Just tell her: *I'm in love with you. This stopped being fake weeks ago. The contract ends tomorrow, but we don't have to.* Simple. Direct. Honest.

Except my throat feels like I swallowed sandpaper, and my heart is doing things that would concern a cardiologist, and every word I've carefully planned disappears the moment I look at her.

"So," Chloe says, her voice soft in the cold air. "You wanted to talk?"

"Yeah. I did. Do." Smooth, Kane. Very articulate. "What about you? You said you needed to talk too."

"I do. I did. I mean—" She tucks a loose strand of hair behind her ear, nervous. "Wow, we're bad at this."

"Spectacularly bad."

She laughs. She's beautiful in the starlight, her dress dark blue against the snow, her hair catching the light from the lanterns lining the path. She looks confident. Happy. Like the woman who talked about event planning this morning, passionate and sure of herself.

Like someone who deserves better than a guy who's spent over a month pretending and is only now figuring out it stopped being pretend somewhere along the way.

"Brody—" she starts.

My phone rings.

Of course it does.

I pull my phone out, thumb hovering over the voicemail button, and stop.

The number is local. Unfamiliar. But something in my gut twists.

"I should—" I gesture to the phone. "Sorry. Just let me—"

"It's okay. Take it."

I answer. "Hello?"

"Is this Brody Kane?" A man's voice. Professional. Clipped. The kind of voice that deals with unpleasant situations regularly.

"Yes."

"This is Michael O'Ryan, security manager at Grand Pines Casino. We have a situation here involving a gentleman claiming to be your father. He's accumulated some debts and is asking for you. Says you'll cover him."

The world narrows to a pinpoint. My father. Gambling. Again.

I turn my back to Chloe, and the cold rushes in, pricks the back of my neck.

"Is he—" I stop. Clear my throat. "Is he safe?"

"He's intoxicated and becoming disruptive. We'd like to resolve this quietly, but we need someone to come get him and settle the immediate situation."

Translation: Pay what he owes, or we call the cops.

I glance back at Chloe. She's watching me, concern etched across her face.

"Where do I need to go?"

"Grand Pines Casino, just south of Maple Lake. I can meet you in the lobby when you arrive."

"I'll be there in thirty." I hang up. My hand is shaking as I shove the phone back in my pocket.

"Brody? What's wrong?"

"It's my dad." The words taste like failure. "He's at a casino. Gambling again. I need to—" I run a hand through my hair. "I'm sorry. I have to go."

"I'll come with you."

"No." The word comes out harsher than I intend. "No, you should—Maya might need you. I promise, I'll be back."

"Brody—"

"Please." I'm already backing away, already shutting down, the walls slamming into place like blast doors. "I'll be back soon. We'll talk then. I promise."

I leave without looking back, so I don't have to see that abandoned, left-in-the-starlight look I've seen before. This isn't like Barcelona.

The drive to Grand Pines Casino is a blur of dark highway and my own spiraling thoughts. The heater blasts hot air that dries out my eyes. Oldies play on the radio, Elvis crooning "Viva Las Vegas," and I turn it off because I can't handle the irony.

My hands are tight on the steering wheel. Knuckles white.

I don't know why I believed him when he said he'd be better. Stupid.

The casino appears like a mirage in the darkness. Bright lights and neon signs advertising cheap buffets and loose slots, it glows with false promise. The parking lot is half empty on a Saturday night. Cars scattered across spaces marked with fading paint.

I park. Sit for a moment. Try to breathe.

Conrad's words from Seattle echo: *Pushing someone away because you're scared doesn't protect you. It just makes you alone.*

But I'm not pushing anyone away. I'm just dealing with my father. Again. Like I always do. Alone. Because that's how this works.

I get out of the car, the cold air biting, the wind clawing at my face. The casino entrance smells like cigarette smoke and hope that's gone rancid—desperate. Inside, it's worse. Stale air thick with smoke, faded carpets stained with use, the electronic chime of slot machines, flashing lights everywhere—reds and blues and golds—designed to disorient and excite and keep people gambling past the point of reason.

The security manager is waiting near the entrance. He looks tired, his hair thinning, deep lines across his face. He extends his hand.

"Mr. Kane. Thank you for coming."

"Where is he?"

"Blackjack tables. Section C. We've asked him to stop playing, but he's insisting he's about to win it all back."

Of course he is.

We weave through the casino floor. Past elderly people feeding quarters into slot machines like it's their job. Past a bachelorette party laughing too loudly at a craps table. Past a man who looks like he's been sitting at the same poker machine for three days straight.

And there, at a blackjack table with two other players who look deeply uncomfortable, is my father.

He looks terrible. Worse than at the hospital in Seattle. Rumpled suit jacket. Tie loosened and crooked. One arm still strapped with a sling. Hair uncombed. Face flushed—drunk, definitely drunk. His eyes have that manic brightness that means he's convinced himself that the next hand will fix everything.

"Dad."

He looks up. His face transforms—relief, joy, desperation all at once. "Brody! I knew you'd come. Listen, I just need a small loan. Tiny. Five thousand. I'm so close to breaking even. One more hand—"

"How much does he owe?" I ask the manager, ignoring my father.

"Twelve thousand. Credit line he opened tonight using your name as reference."

My jaw clenches so hard I might crack a tooth. Of course he did.

"But we need it settled before we can release him."

My father is standing now, unsteady on his feet. "Brody, son, please. It's just bad luck. It happens. You understand—"

"No." The word comes out cold. Hard. "I don't understand."

"Your mother would have—"

"Don't." I step closer. Lower my voice. "Don't you dare bring her into this. Mom would have wanted you to get help. Real help. Not enablement."

He flinches like I hit him. "I'm trying. You don't know—"

"I know you're drunk. I know you're gambling. I know you used my name to open credit you can't pay back." I'm shaking. From anger or hurt or exhaustion, I don't know anymore. "I know you called me here to clean up your mess. Again."

"I'm your father—"

"Then act like it." The words explode out. Louder than I intended. A few people at nearby tables turn to look. "Act like a father instead of a disaster I have to manage. Act like someone who cares about something other than the next bet."

The silence that follows is thick enough to suffocate in. The slot machines keep chiming. Someone at another table whoops with excitement. The world keeps spinning, moving faster and faster, but mine has stopped, leaving me dizzy. Sick.

"Mr. Kane," Michael says quietly. "Can we settle this?"

I pull out my wallet. Hand over my credit card. Watch Michael walk away to process the payment that will drain another significant chunk of my savings. Money I was planning to use for—what? What was I planning? A future? With Chloe? After the contract ends?

Doesn't matter now.

My father sits back down at the table, defeated. That gleam in his eye, that manic glint he gets at the table, is gone now. And he's somehow smaller. Older. "I'm sorry. I'm so sorry, son."

"You always are."

"I'll pay you back—"

"No, you won't. We both know you won't." I'm so tired. Bone-deep tired. "I'm done, Dad."

His head snaps up. "What?"

"I'm done. Cleaning up your messes. Bailing you out. Pretending this is normal." I crouch down so we're eye level. "You want help? Real help? Call me when you're ready for treatment. Otherwise, I can't do this anymore."

"Brody, please—"

"This is it. This is the last time." I stand. My legs feel unsteady. "Get yourself home. Don't call me unless you're really ready to change."

"You think you're better than me?" His voice rises, anger replacing the pleading. Heads turn again, a few looks of recognition flickering across their faces. "Mr. Perfect? Hockey star? You're just like me. Running from everything that matters. Hiding behind that fake smile and perfect image. You're just a liar, like your old man."

The words hit like a physical blow.

"Maybe," I say, swallowing the ache in my throat. "But at least I'm trying to change. Are you?"

I stand and walk away, leaving him there, calling after me. I can't save someone who doesn't want to be saved.

It's after midnight by the time I get back to the resort. The lobby is dark except for emergency lighting and the glow from the dying fireplace. My footsteps echo on the hardwood floors, too loud in the silence.

My key card beeps against the lock as I enter the honeymoon suite as quietly as possible.

The lights are low. Just the fireplace, burned down to embers that cast barely any light. The room smells like the lavender candles someone keeps lighting and the faint scent of Chloe's shampoo—something floral and clean.

I stop.

Chloe is lying on the sofa, her eyes shut, her hair pouring around her shoulders. Asleep.

The glow of the dying fire catches her face, and for a moment, I just look.

She is beautiful.

The door finally clicks behind me, and I let out a hiss as she stirs.

"Brody? You're back."

"Shhh, it's okay, go back to sleep." But it's too late. She sits up, her hair falling around her shoulders, wearing an oversized T-shirt that says something I can't read in the dim light.

"I thought maybe you weren't coming back," she says softly.

"Yeah. I'm sorry." My voice sounds wrecked. I clear my throat. "It was my dad. He was . . ." I can't finish the sentence. Can't explain the whole disaster.

"Is he okay?"

"He will be. Eventually." *I hope.*

"Are you okay?" she asks, her voice like velvet in the dark.

No, I'm not. I run a hand through my hair. "Yeah, I'm all right."

"Do you want to talk about it?"

I glance up at her again, my chest aching. "Not really . . . I just . . . I'm tired." Dead tired.

Chloe's lips part. "Oh, sure. Of course." She stands hurriedly, wadding up the blanket she'd been using and draping it over the coffee table. "I'll just—"

"Would you stay with me?" The words escape from my lungs like a breath.

Chloe stills.

"Just . . . for a while," I clarify. "I don't want to be alone."

I know how it sounds. Pitiful. Weak. Like a kid afraid of the dark. Like that dragon, hiding in his cave. But I'm too tired to care.

Chloe's gaze softens, her lips parting in surprise before, "Of course."

I nod. "Okay. Don't . . . don't go anywhere." I toss my jacket on the nearest chair, grab my overnight bag, and head to the bathroom to change.

When I come back out, she's made room for me in the corner seat, just like last night. But this time, the TV is off, the glowing embers the only light in the room. I slide into the space beside her, and Chloe nestles in, resting her head on my shoulder. I breathe in the scent of her, relaxing one muscle at a time.

"Brody?" Her voice is soft in the darkness.

"Yeah?"

"What did you want to talk about earlier?"

Everything. Nothing. *I love you. I'm terrified. I don't know what I'm doing.*

"Tomorrow," I say instead. "Let's talk tomorrow. After the wedding."

"Okay. Tomorrow."

Silence again. The fire crackles softly, a log settles and sends up a shower of sparks. Somewhere outside, an owl hoots. And for the first time in what feels like months, sleep washes over me.

CHLOE

I wake up to the sound of steady breathing that isn't mine.

For a moment, I'm disoriented—why is there breathing? Why is my pillow so warm and solid and . . . why does it have a heartbeat?

My eyes crack open, and my heart leaps at the realization.

We fell asleep on the couch. Brody's arm wrapped around me, pulling me close. My head, which started out on his shoulder, somehow migrated to his warm—very solid—chest. And while I'm not complaining, it definitely wasn't how I expected to be waking up this morning.

Brody stirs, his thumb stroking my arm.

Oh, this is . . . this is bad.

I might never get up. I'll miss the whole wedding, and it might just be worth it.

I close my eyes again, weighing today's responsibilities against how much I really, really, *really* want to stay here. He's so warm. And he smells good—that woodsy cologne I've grown familiar with.

And what's worse—I lift my head just slightly to look at him— yeah, what's way worse is that he's beautiful.

I know that sounds dramatic. Men aren't supposed to be beautiful. They're handsome or attractive or hot. But Brody asleep, with his face relaxed and his guard completely down, is beautiful. The morning light filtering through the curtains catches his features—the line of his jaw, the dark stubble, the way his eyelashes rest against his cheeks. I want to reach up and touch them.

He looks peaceful. Younger. Like the weight he carries when he's awake has lifted.

But . . . I have a wedding to run, and I'd never hear the end of it if I was late.

I attempt to extract myself slowly. Carefully. Trying not to wake him.

His arm tightens around me. His eyes open—those always-changing blue-gray eyes that make me forget how to form sentences.

"Hey," he says, his voice rough with sleep.

"Hey." My face is approximately three inches from his. "I fell asleep—I mean, we fell asleep. I didn't mean to—"

"It's okay." He's not letting go. Not moving away. Just looking at me like he's memorizing my face. "How'd you sleep?"

"Good. Really good, actually." Better than I've slept in weeks, but I'm not admitting that. "You?"

"Best I've slept in a long time." He smiles. It's one of those lazy-day smiles, easy, rested, and it does things to my heart. How I love that smile.

Still, he doesn't let go, just props his other arm behind his head, bringing him closer. Close enough that I can count the flecks of darker blue in his eyes. Close enough to that dangerous territory where one of us could lean forward just slightly and—

I pull away. Sit up. Run a hand over my tangled hair. "I should—I need to go. Maya's probably freaking out. Valentine's Day"—I can't help the little flutter in my stomach thinking about us, together, on Valentine's Day—"and wedding day and all."

"Right. Yeah." He sits up too, the throw blanket pooling around his waist. His T-shirt is rumpled, his hair sticking up on one side.

"What did you want to talk about?" I ask, pulling on a cardigan over my pajamas. "Last night. Before everything."

He's quiet for a moment. Then, "I'll tell you after the ceremony. Is that okay?"

"After the ceremony?"

"Yeah." He smiles, warm and sure. "It can wait a few hours. Let's get through the wedding first."

I'll admit, I had a lot of time to think about it last night. Maybe too much time, because I've got it all planned out. The moment when I tell him the truth, that this isn't fake anymore, that I'm totally, hopelessly in love with him, and that I want to try to make it work for real. I'm going to wait for dancing to start, for that first slow song to play—call it corny, but I used to think that kind of movie moment didn't happen to girls like me, but I'm starting to believe, so you'll excuse me if I get a little cliché—that's when I'll tell him. That's when it's supposed to happen. The perfect moment.

So, really, waiting to talk until after the ceremony works perfectly.

"Okay," I say. "After the ceremony."

"It's a date." He winks. Actually winks. Who winks? Main characters, that's who. I told you! I'm starting to believe.

"A Valentine's date." I brush my hair back behind my ear, oddly nervous. Something's different between us. Something is new. "I need to go help Maya." I'm backing toward the door, grabbing my bag of toiletries and the dress I brought for getting ready. "I'll see you at the ceremony?"

"I'll be there."

The cottage is already full steam ahead when I arrive, bridesmaids buzzing from room to room. The cottage looks like a 2011 JC Penney post Black Friday, clothes strewn haphazardly across furniture, dresses hanging in doorways, food left half eaten on the counters. Music drifts from every room—different music, I'd like to add—creating a cacophony of sounds.

"Is that Chloe?" I hear Maya's voice from somewhere inside the mess. There's a hint of nerves to it. She's on edge, and the morning's only just begun.

"Chloe! Thank goodness." Lauren shuffles into the room carrying a large box, her hair twisted up in one of those no-heat curlers across the top of her head. "This just arrived at the hotel. The front desk had it delivered." She drops the box on the counter, sliding it toward me. Inside, about ten billion crisp sheets of paper lined with names stare up at me. "They're the escort cards."

My stomach plummets. "What?—no. We ordered the escort cards from a specialized printer. They're supposed to alphabetize and cut them."

Lauren shushes me, glances toward the door to Maya's room. "I wouldn't bring that up with Maya. Apparently . . . your dad saw the bill and about had a heart attack when he realized how much he was paying for the bells and whistles."

"He did not." But even as I'm saying it, that doesn't surprise me. My dad has never been one to pay for a job he could do himself . . . or in this case, a job I'll have to do. I slump down in the open seat at the counter and drape myself across the box.

It's gonna be a long day.

But a day that ends with me telling Brody that I love him.

A day that maybe ends with the beginning of our own happily ever after.

"I'm gonna need scissors, zip lock bags, and a big cup of coffee. Stat."

I spend the next three hours in crisis-management mode. Slicing, creasing, and alphabetizing the three hundred Valentine's-themed escort cards, placing each letter of the alphabet into its own little baggy. Once that's done, I try my best to wash the glitter off my fingers (I really didn't think that through when I was ordering the cards—but then again, I didn't anticipate needing to hand-crease every single one of them, so . . .). Then I pop out of the cabin to check the ceremony site and lay assigned seat cards on the first rows, along with tissues and programs for Derek's parents and mine. I do a once-over of the space. Chairs in perfect rows facing the lake, white fabric draped just so, the arch decorated with pine branches and winter flowers. Make sure the candles are ready to light.

On my way back, I stop in at the reception, which is coming along. The linens are draped, the florists bustling here and there with centerpieces and greenery. The catering manager meets me at the bar to confirm our timelines.

It's all perfect.

It's after lunch when I finally make it back to the cottage, and the energy has shifted. Maya sits gracefully in a white director's chair, having her makeup done. The other girls are all lounging around, drinking mimosas in their matching pink robes, their hair and makeup already finished. The music has died down, only one speaker crooning now.

"You're back!" Maya says, peeking at me while her makeup artist works on her other eye. "How does everything look?"

"It's all running exactly as planned." Which is a relief, because this is one thing in my life I cannot afford to mess up. The money from Brody won't be able to save my business if my wedding failure is plastered all over magazines and social media.

I'm pulling on my dress—a frosty blue that Maya picked, fitted and elegant and making me feel like a slightly more sophisticated version of myself—when a hush falls over the room.

The kind of hush you just know is about you.

Maya is staring at her phone, her face pale. Lauren is reading over her shoulder, her expression somewhere between shock and pity. The other bridesmaids are exchanging glances, their gazes flickering toward me but not making contact.

"What?" My heart is already racing, because there's really only one thing this could be . . .

Maya looks at me, her face a wash of emotions—hurt, confusion, disappointment maybe? She walks over, phone in hand. Turns the screen to face me.

It's an article. *Minnesota Bridal Magazine*. Posted two hours ago.

The Not-So-Perfect Wedding Date: When Hockey Romance Meets Cold Reality

By Jennifer Hartley

And there's a photo. The one from yesterday morning. Me and Brody in front of the fireplace, smiling like we're really in love.

I scroll down, my hands shaking.

> This weekend, I had the pleasure of covering the Dawson–Munson wedding at the beautiful Maple Haven Resort. During my stay, I met event planner Chloe Dawson and her boyfriend, Minnesota Blue Ox defenseman Brody "Candy" Kane. They seemed like the perfect couple—attentive, affectionate, clearly smitten.
>
> But something didn't add up.
>
> And then sources close to Dawson revealed the suggestion of a contract, with terms.
>
> Including a public breakup.
>
> Further investigation revealed that Kane has been embroiled in controversy recently, with accusations of manipulation from social media influencer Ashley Morrison. Dawson's sister is marrying Kane's teammate Derek Munson. The timing of their relationship—conveniently coinciding with Kane's image crisis and Dawson's need for a wedding date—raises questions.
>
> I reached out to both parties for comment. Neither responded.
>
> Is their romance real, or is this hockey's latest publicity stunt? You be the judge.

Alarms start blaring inside my head. *Code red, code red!*

"Is it true?" Maya's voice is hollow, steady.

My head is spinning, working overtime to remember the details of the contract.

Listen, I'm no legal expert, but I'm pretty sure the contract said if our relationship is proven to be fake, we both lose everything. And even if I'm planning to break the contract anyway by telling Brody I want to be with him, I don't want to do it like this. By shouting to the world while he's out of the room that this whole thing was a sham.

So, I close my ears to that little voice telling me to come clean. And I lie.

"I can't believe someone would post this. No, it's not true."

Maya's brows pinch. "Really?"

"Maya, no. None of this is true." I scowl at the phone, as though this is the most absurd thing I've ever read. "This is crazy." I scroll a little. "Hold on. 'Sources close to Dawson'?" Now that part *is* crazy. Who would . . .

And that's when the pieces fall together. It's me. I'm the source close to Dawson. The screenshot of our contract was right in my photos, unlocked, practically waiting for Jennifer to find.

Which means . . .

Option 1: We go through with the contract. I dump Brody at the reception, make him look like the villain and myself the victim—and prove Jennifer right. It was all fake. Every moment, every touch, every smile. Just actors following a script to the bitter, contractually obligated end.

Option 2: I tell him I love him instead, refuse to follow the script, try to make this real—and we violate the contract. Brody loses his NHL renewal. His career. Everything he's worked for. And I lose the money that releases me from college debt prison, saves my business, and gives me a real shot at being an author.

Option 3: We come clean together and ride into the sunset, broke and jobless. Perfect.

We're trapped. Completely, utterly, devastatingly trapped.

"Chloe?" Maya's voice breaks through my spiral. "Are you okay? You look like you're going to pass out."

"I'm okay," I say, my voice coming out a little higher than normal. I glance at the time, partly for somewhere to look other than her knowing eyes. "You gotta get into your dress. Photos start soon."

"You sure?"

"Yeah, I'm okay." I paste on my best people-pleaser smile. "I guess this is just something I have to get used to dating a celebrity."

Surprisingly, Maya grins, a breath of relief slipping from her lips. "Welcome to the club, sis."

The rest of the afternoon goes just as planned. The photographer shows up, snaps some pictures of the bridal party in their robes, the girls waving their mimosas, cheering when Maya steps out in her dress—absolutely stunning. All lace and beading, and a train that goes on for days. Then we head out to the resort's massive balcony overlooking the lake for a first look, after which Derek and the groomsmen join us for full party photos.

It's all a blur—a tempest of timelines and simmering anxiety—but we all wind up back in the bridal suite, waiting for the last guests to arrive, and Maya seated beside me, holding my hand.

I can't tell you which of us needs it more.

Finally, I peek my head into the hall. Everyone is seated, and the musicians are in place. The rest of the wedding party has lined up outside the ceremony space. We're ready. I give the quartet a thumbs-up, and the music starts playing.

This is it, the point of no return.

I turn back to my sister. "It's time."

I help Maya to her feet, place the bouquet in her hands, and escort her to our dad, who's waiting at the back of the lineup.

The music changes. Derek's taken his place at the altar.

I move to my place beside the door, my heart hammering as I signal for the wedding party to start walking. The music sweeps over me, swelling as Maya steps up to the door, her eyes already brimming, and looks to me. Waiting.

"Walk slowly. Enjoy it," I whisper. "I love you."

"I love you," she says, giving my hand a squeeze.

And she starts walking.

I step through the door, watching as she makes her way to the altar, but my gaze falls on Brody seated on the aisle. He's looking past Maya, right at me, smiling that private smile. The one that says *I see you. I choose you. Just a little longer and we can talk.*

It might be too late for that.

BRODY

N APPROXIMATELY TWO HOURS, THIS CON-
tract between Chloe and me is coming to an end. But I've already
set my mind on it. I'm not letting her go.

Chloe catches my eye as she slips into the room, wearing the blue dress. Just like Barcelona. This girl kills me in blue. Her hair tumbles in a half do over her shoulders, and the music swells as she leans back against the doors, like a dream I didn't know I was having.

A dream I didn't know I wanted so badly.

But I want this. I want a future with her. I want to look out over the ice and see her wearing my number. I want Friday nights curled up on the couch, talking about anything and nothing. Saturday mornings at Brew & Rumor, watching her sketch out another story and bring it to life. I want us.

And I think she wants that too.

So tonight, when the contract ends, before she can break it off with me like she's supposed to, I'll whisk her away. Find a way to pull her aside, like our first kiss under the orange trees, and tell her how I feel. *This stopped being fake for me. I'm in love with you. The contract says you're supposed to break up with me tonight, but what if we don't? What if we tear up that clause and make this real instead?*

It's not public yet. No one knows about the contract except me, Chloe, and Rick. Okay, and maybe the Blue Ox team manager and Chloe's bossy roommate, Jessa. But true love will save the day, and we'll just change the terms. Mutually agree to void the staged breakup clause. Just . . . not do it. Stay together. Make it official. Make it real.

No harm, no foul. Everyone (especially us) lives happily ever after.

The thought makes my chest feel too small for my heart. I pull my gaze away, turning back toward the procession as Maya reaches the arch. Her father lifts her veil, kisses her cheek, shakes Derek's hand. The moment is sweet, genuine, the kind of thing that makes even cynical hockey players believe in forever.

The officiant starts talking. Something about love and commitment and choosing each other every day. The words wash over me because even fifty feet apart, with three hundred people in between, I feel connected to her in a way I've never felt connected to anyone.

My phone trembles in my pocket.

I ignore it. Because I'm at a wedding, and checking your phone during the ceremony is the kind of thing that gets you dirty looks.

It vibrates again.

I glance again at Chloe. She's still standing in the back of the room, focused on the ceremony.

More buzzing. A phone call this time, vibrating insistently against my leg.

Okay, okay.

I slip away from my spot near the side door, push out of the room, wait until I'm a good six feet from the door before pulling out my phone. Seven missed calls from Rick. Six texts, two from Conrad, who's still sitting in the audience.

Rick

Call me NOW

Rick

Have you seen this? (Link attached)

Rick

We have a SERIOUS problem

Conrad

Answer your phone

Conrad

You need to see this. It's bad.

Rick

I'm not kidding Kane. Call me immediately.

My stomach drops. That feeling you get when you're about to get checked into the boards and you see it coming but can't avoid it.

I open the link Rick sent.

Minnesota Bridal Magazine. Posted three hours ago.

The Not-So-Perfect Wedding Date: When Hockey Romance Meets Cold Reality

By Jennifer Hartley

And there's our photo. The one from yesterday morning. Chloe and me in front of the fireplace, smiling like lovesick fools.

My blood turns to ice as I skim the article. Sources close to Chloe. The contract. The staged breakup that's supposed to happen tonight. The accusations about Ashley. The convenient timing. Every detail we thought was private, now exposed for the world to see and judge.

The plan I had—the beautiful, simple plan where we just mutually agree to tear up the breakup clause and make this real—shatters like glass.

Because it's not private anymore.

> Is their romance real, or is this hockey's latest publicity stunt? You be the judge.

The article ends there. Short. Devastating. Leaving just enough unsaid to let readers fill in the blanks with their worst assumptions.

And the comments below—I shouldn't read them, but I do—are exactly what you'd expect:

> "I KNEW something was off about them."

> "Poor Chloe, he's using her."

> "Typical athlete behavior."

> "Wait, they're supposed to break up tonight? This is going to be messy."

> "If there's a contract requiring a breakup, how was ANY of it real?"

That last one hits the hardest. Because it's the question I'm asking myself. How do you prove something became real when it started fake? How do you convince anyone—including maybe Chloe herself—that feelings evolved when there's a contract saying it was supposed to end tonight anyway?

The section I was planning to ignore. The section I thought we could just void because no one knew it existed.

Except now everyone knows.

My phone rings. Rick.

I answer, my voice coming out rougher than intended. "I saw it."

"Finally. I've been trying to reach you for an hour."

"I'm at a *wedding*. The phone was on Do Not Disturb, thank you."

"Well, it's a disaster. The article dropped three hours ago, and it's everywhere. Sports media picked it up, social media is having a field day, the team management has called twice, asking for an explanation." He's talking fast, the way he does when he's in crisis-management mode. "We need to get ahead of this."

"Get ahead of it how? The contract is exposed. Jennifer has sources."

"Sources that 'suggest' a contract. That's vague. We can claim—"

"We're gonna come clean, Rick. Chloe and I, we don't want to do this."

The line goes quiet for a long time. "You can't do that, Brody."

Something in his voice makes my stomach drop. "Why not? It's already out there. People already know."

"People don't know anything. So long as you make this convincing." His voice is steady, solid, leaving no room to argue.

"Rick, I don't—"

"You both signed an NDA. And I got off the phone ten minutes ago with the NHL. They don't want any part of this coming back to them. If you guys come clean, they won't just null the contract—they'll come after you both for breach of contract. We're talking serious legal action against you both."

My head is spinning, like I took a hard hit.

I drag a hand through my hair. "So what are you saying?"

"I'm saying…" He pauses. "Tonight at the reception, you need to convince people that your love is real—so real there's no way this article can be true. And then you need to break up and make that look real too."

The words hang in the air like smoke.

"I'm not breaking up with her."

"You don't have to. *She's* supposed to break up with you. That's what the clause says."

From inside the ceremony area, I hear applause. The vows are done. Maya and Derek are married.

The end is near.

I hear Rick let out a sigh. "Do you love this woman?"

The question stops me cold. "Yes."

"Then don't kill your future. Or hers." His voice softens. "I know this isn't what you want. But sometimes, protecting someone means making the hard choice. Even if it breaks your heart. You need to fulfill the contract as specified. That means making sure this breakup is believable. Make everyone see that you love her—really love her—and then let her break your heart. That's the only way you both come out of this intact."

He hangs up.

Inside, music is starting to play, and any moment, the newlyweds will come bursting through that door.

The choice is obvious. Terrible, but obvious.

I have to let her break up with me tonight.

Or more accurately—I have to *make* her break up with me.

And then I have to hope—pray, really—that in thirty days, after I've ghosted her, after the media buzz has died down and we're allowed to "reconcile," she'll forgive me. She'll understand. She'll take me back.

I feel like my father. Taking a gamble and losing. Except the stakes aren't money or pride—they're the woman I love and any chance we had at a real future together.

Best performance of my life. Here we go.

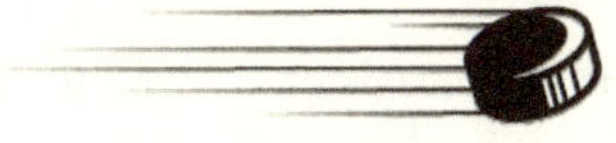

CHLOE

This morning, I woke up in Brody Kane's arms thinking maybe we had a chance.

Now I'm hiding behind an ice sculpture at my sister's wedding, trying to avoid eye contact with him while simultaneously wondering if there's any possible way out of the disaster we're both trapped in.

Brody is standing near the massive floor-to-ceiling windows, chatting with his teammate, Tyler, looking unfairly good, gesturing with a glass in a way that suggests he's telling a story. Our eyes meet across the terrace.

I panic.

I nearly take out a server as I crouch-run through the crowd and duck behind the bar. In hindsight, it wasn't my best moment.

"Can I help you, miss?" the bartender asks, a pretty redhead in a black button-up uniform.

"Oh no, I'm just hiding from the man who's probably the love of my life so that I can avoid making decisions that could alter the course of our entire lives, possibly ruining them if I make the wrong one."

The bartender raises a brow, her gaze skittering over the crowd. "Mr. Handsome, gray suit, chatting near the windows?"

"That's him."

She nods. Pours a glass of wine and hands it to me under the bar. "Stay strong, babe."

There's no time to enjoy my drink, however, because moments later, someone clamps onto my elbow, hauling me out from below the bar with surprising strength.

It's Maya—curse that cardio-regimented queen and her vice grip.

"Maya—what's—" But I can't get a word in as she drags me toward the staff door at the back of the reception hall.

She pushes through the doors and finally turns to face me. "Chloe Dawson, you tell me the truth this time. Are you in a fake relationship with Brody Kane?"

My stomach drops, and all the air leaves my lungs. I open my mouth to deny it, but looking at Maya's face—not angry, just concerned—breaks something in me.

"Yes," I whisper, my voice cracking.

All at once, my sister's hard exterior, that Wonder Woman shell, evaporates. Her expression softens, and suddenly I'm in her arms, wrapped in a tight hug. It's unfamiliar territory for us. "Oh, hun," she whispers. "Tell me what's going on."

And so I spend the next ten minutes telling her everything. About our kiss in Barcelona and running into him at Ironclad—how we hadn't been dating at all when the viral photo was taken—and finally the contract. But I don't stop there. The words are pouring from me like I'm parched for the truth. I tell her about our date—the real one—and the late-night calls, and falling asleep on the couch together, and about the looming breakup that I can't seem to find a way out of.

"Chloe, you don't have to do this." Her grip on my arm tightens. "Forget the contract. Forget the penalties. I'll help you—Mom and Dad will help you pay whatever you owe—"

"I can't let you do that."

"Why not? You're my sister. You think I'm going to stand here and watch you destroy your own happiness because of some stupid contract you signed when you were desperate?"

"It's not just about me," I say quietly. "If I don't follow through, Brody loses everything too. His contract renewal. His career. Everything he's worked for." I grab her hands. "I can't do that to him. Not when I—" I can't finish. Can't say *Not when I love him* out loud.

"So you're sacrificing yourself to save his career?" Her voice rises slightly, and she immediately lowers it, glancing around to make sure no one heard. "After he got you into this mess in the first place?"

"It's not like that. It's more complicated than the article made it seem. We both agreed to this. We both signed." I squeeze her hands. "Maya, please. You've got to trust me on this. Just . . . don't tell anyone. I mean it." I fix my eyes on hers. "Nobody can know the contract is real. Please."

She looks at me for a long moment, her eyes shining with tears. Then she nods, pulls me into a hug.

"I hate this," she whispers. "I hate that you're hurting and I can't fix it."

"You're helping by letting me do my job. By trusting me." I pull back, swipe at my eyes. "Now go. Your guests are waiting. And your day is perfect. Let's keep it that way."

She hesitates, then nods. "Okay. But, Chloe, if you change your mind, if you need help, you come find me. I don't care if I'm in the middle of my first dance. You're more important than any of this."

She walks away before I can respond, and I'm left standing there, trying not to cry and ruin my makeup.

The ballroom is perfect. Months of planning came together—white and gold everything, centerpieces with winter flowers, pops of Valentine's red, subtle but sweet, candles, and elegant drapery creating a canopy overhead. The sweetheart table is centered on the massive windows, the ceremony arch now set up to frame the table behind them, the cake on display, the dance floor open and waiting.

Guests are filing in for dinner. And I'm seated at table three, beside Brody.

Table three includes Conrad Kingston and a woman I recognize from photos I've seen online—Penny Pepper, the true-crime podcaster. She's pretty. Dark hair, brown eyes, and the way Conrad's hand rests on her back suggests they're definitely together.

"Nice to finally meet you, Chloe," Penny says, shaking my hand with genuine warmth. "I've heard so much about you . . . well, about you and Brody. From what I hear, you've really brought out a different side of him."

I try my best to chuckle. Ignore the churning in my stomach.

The other guests at our table—more of Derek's hockey friends and their dates—are chatting cheerfully, oblivious to the tension.

Dinner is served. Some kind of chicken with roasted vegetables, all the standard wedding food, and I spend the duration of the meal pushing it around on my plate. Brody does the same.

Neither of us is eating.

Neither of us is talking.

Under the table, his knee brushes mine. I don't move away.

"You two all right?" Conrad asks quietly. He's watching us with the kind of attention that suggests he knows something's wrong.

"Fine," Brody says.

"Great," I add.

It's not our best lie. I guess we're both a little off our game. Conrad exchanges a glance with Penny.

She leans forward slightly. "I'm sorry about that article in *Minnesota Bridal*."

My fork clatters against my plate. "You saw that?"

"Everyone saw it," she says gently. "But for what it's worth, I believe you guys. Give it some time. In a few days, everyone will forget all about that article."

I can't respond. Can't process the kindness in her voice when I know what's coming in less than two hours.

The toasts begin while dessert is being served. The maid of honor goes first with a funny, loving speech about Maya and their friendship and all the adventures they've had. Followed by the best man—one of Derek's hockey teammates—who makes jokes about Derek's terrible cooking and worse fashion sense before getting sincere about what a loyal friend and good man he is.

And finally, our dad. His voice is raw as he gets up to speak. He tells stories about Maya as a little girl and how proud he is of the woman she's become. And then he turns to Derek, charges him with being the kind of man that Maya deserves. Derek stands, taking his hand in a heartwarming exchange.

Then the DJ announces: "Now, as you know, our groom tonight is a member of the Blue Ox"—a chorus of whoops and cheers rattles the floors—"and Derek wanted to give a special opportunity to share this moment with his team. So he's asked that we open the mic up for a few words from some of the people he's spent blood, sweat, and years with."

Wait, what? I didn't okay this. It's just asking for creepy Uncle Austin to take over the mic, drunk, and make really cringy speeches. Nope.

But before I can intervene, Conrad stands. Walks to the microphone with easy confidence.

"I've known Derek for a few years now," he says, "and I can tell you right now, he wasn't always the man he is today. When Derek met Maya, we all saw something in him change. She brings out the best in him." His gaze flickers to our table for a heartbeat, landing on Brody and me before continuing. "That's something I've learned in my own life, that love can be terrifying and wild, but when it's real, true love, it brings out the best in you." He lifts his glass. "To Derek and Maya."

The room applauds. But I catch the look Conrad gives Brody.

Brody's jaw tightens.

Another teammate goes up—Torch, I think—keeps it brief and funny. He tells the story of Derek's first away game after meeting Maya, how the bus broke down on the way home and Derek almost pulled a *Planes, Trains and Automobiles* to get back to their first date. Everyone chuckles. He lifts a glass, and then says, "To the kind of love you fight for."

More applause.

Then Brody stands.

My stomach drops. He's walking to the microphone. He didn't tell me he was planning to give a toast. Why is he giving a toast?

He takes the mic. Smiles that easy, charming smile that I know is a mask. "Hey, everybody, I'm Brody, one of Derek's teammates." The room quiets. Maya is watching him with interest, her hand clutching Derek's. "I wasn't planning to give a speech tonight, but Conrad said something that really stuck with me. Love worth fighting for."

He glances over his shoulder at the happy couple. "Derek and Maya are one of those couples that make you believe in love," he says. "The real kind. Not the performance we put on for social media or the version we think we're supposed to want. But the kind that changes you."

He's not reading notes. Just talking, his voice steady and clear.

"See, I've been learning something about love lately. It makes you feel terrified and hopeful at the same time. It makes you want to be better than you thought you could be." His eyes find mine across the room. Hold. "It sees all your worst parts—the things you try to hide, the flaws you're ashamed of—and doesn't run away."

I can't breathe. The entire room is listening, but I feel like he's talking only to me.

"As some of you might know, I go by another name on the ice. *Candy Kane*," he continues, still looking at me. "That's the name people gave me because I'm that guy who plays nice with the media, smiles for the cameras, says the right thing. Polished. Fake." He shrugs, flashes a smile. "All sugar, if you will."

That earns a few chuckles from the crowd.

"And maybe that's who I was. But lately I've found someone who makes me want to be more than that." His voice softens. "Someone who sees the real me—the scared, flawed, imperfect version I try to hide. Someone who sees the dragon underneath the scales. And who loves me anyway."

Maya is crying. I can see her from the corner of my eye, tears streaming down her face, looking between Brody and me with this expression that's half hope, half heartbreak.

"That's how love feels when it's real," Brody says. Still looking at me. Still holding my gaze like we're the only two people in this room. "The kind of love that's worth the risk. The kind that's terrifying and raw and changes everything. The kind that makes you want to be brave enough to be honest. The kind that makes you want to tear down every wall you've built and just be . . . you."

My vision blurs, tears pricking my eyes.

He's not making this easy for us.

Then he pivots, turning to the head table. "And I know that's how Derek and Maya feel about each other. That's what we're celebrating tonight—two people brave enough to choose each other, to be vulnerable, to believe in forever." He raises his glass. "To Derek and Maya. To true love. To taking the risk."

"To Derek and Maya!" the room echoes, glasses rising.

The applause is deafening. People are crying. Dabbing eyes with napkins.

Brody walks back to our table. Sits next to me.

Penny is staring at us with tears in her eyes. "That was beautiful," she whispers.

Conrad nods, his expression serious. "Real recognizes real."

I'm going to hyperventilate. I can't be here.

The DJ announces the first dance. "Ladies and gentlemen, please welcome Derek and Maya to the dance floor for their first dance as husband and wife!"

Everyone's attention shifts. Maya and Derek walk to the center of the floor, and some slow, romantic song starts playing. They're holding each other, swaying, lost in their own world.

I stand abruptly. "Bathroom."

I'm moving before anyone can respond, weaving between tables, heading for the exit. My heart feels like it's going to explode.

The hallway outside the ballroom is blessedly empty—just

cream-colored walls and sconces and the sound of my own rag-ged breathing.

I lean against the wall, trying to get my heart rate under control. Trying to think.

What was that? *That's how love feels when it's real.*

"Chloe."

I open my eyes. Brody stands in front of me, looking at me with those stormy eyes. The door to the ballroom drifts shut behind him, muffling the sound of the music.

We're alone.

"Did you mean it?" The words burst out before I can stop them. "What you said in there. Did you mean it?"

He steps closer, his expression serious, none of the Candy Kane charm. Just Brody. Real Brody.

"Yes." His voice is rough. "Every word."

Another step. He's close now. Close enough that I can see the rise and fall of his chest, smell his cologne. "I love you."

"Brody—"

"I love you, Chloe. I'm in love with you. I have been for weeks." His hand comes up, cups my face. "I don't know when it happened. Maybe that first day in Ironclad. Maybe it was that night you went with me to the hospital. Maybe it was Barcelona. I don't know. All I know is that I love you, and I can't keep pretending. I can't unlove you."

My eyes are burning. "I love you too."

"Say it again."

"I love you." The words feel like freedom. Like breaking through the surface after being underwater too long. "I love you. Not Candy Kane. You—Brody."

He kisses me.

And it's nothing like the careful touches we've practiced for cameras. Nothing like the sweet, tentative kiss in Barcelona under the twinkling lights when we were still strangers.

This is Brody pouring six months of wanting and weeks of falling and every single moment of pretending that became real into this one kiss. His hand slides from my face into my hair, fingers tangling, tilting my head back. His other hand finds my waist, pulling me closer—not gentle, not asking permission, just *needing*.

I make a sound—something between a gasp and his name—and he deepens the kiss. His mouth moves against mine like he's memorizing the taste of me, like he's trying to say everything he can't put into words. *I love you. I'm sorry. I don't want to let you go.*

My hands are in his hair, gripping his jacket, pulling him closer even though there's no closer to get. I can feel his heart hammering against mine, or maybe that's my heart, or maybe we've just become one desperate, aching thing that doesn't want to end.

Time stops. The world narrows to just this—his mouth on mine, his hands holding me like I'm something precious and breakable and worth fighting for. The hallway disappears. The reception disappears. Everything disappears except the feeling of being completely, devastatingly in love with someone you're about to lose.

When we finally break apart, it's only because we need air. His forehead drops to mine. We're both breathing hard, shaking slightly, neither of us willing to create more distance than absolutely necessary.

"Chloe," he whispers against my lips, but it's sad. Like a broken promise. Like an apology.

His thumb traces my cheekbone, gentle now, reverent. I can feel him trembling. Or maybe that's me.

"Yowza." We both freeze, still tangled together, as Penny comes down the hallway—out of the restroom, clearly. "Well, that's the most real kiss I've ever seen."

Oh.

And we're guilty. Brody's hands in my hair, mine gripping his jacket, both of us flushed and breathing hard and clearly having just been thoroughly kissing.

She smiles as she walks past us, heading back toward the ballroom, and throws over her shoulder, "Whatever that article says? It's wrong."

The door to the ballroom closes behind her.

Brody and I are still frozen, staring at each other. The interruption broke whatever spell we were under. Reality is creeping back in—the contract, the consequences, the impossible choice.

"Brody?" My voice is small. Scared.

He takes a breath. Steps back. Creates distance that feels like miles even though it's only inches.

And then he says the words that shatter everything. "You have to break up with me."

BRODY

THE WORDS HANG IN THE AIR BETWEEN US.

"What?" Her voice is small. Broken.

"You have to break it off. Now." I step back—creating distance that feels like miles.

Chloe blinks at me, eyes watery and brimming. "No."

"Chloe—"

"You just told me you love me." Her voice cracks, and I die a little inside. "I'm not going to break up with you just because some contract says I'm supposed to."

She walks away from me, back toward the reception hall doors.

"Chloe, wait—"

But she's already gone, disappearing through the doors into the reception.

I stand there for a moment, alone in the hallway. The ghost of our kiss still lingering in the air. The weight of what I'm about to do crushing my chest.

Then I follow her.

The reception is in full swing when I walk back in. Music playing, guests laughing, fairy lights overhead making everything look soft and romantic. Maya and Derek's perfect wedding, exactly as planned.

Chloe is across the room, talking to a waiter near the dessert table. She's gesturing to the cake station, pointing at something, her coordinator persona firmly in place.

But I can see the tension in her shoulders. The way she's not quite looking at anyone. The slight tremor in her hands.

I watch as she tells the waiter something about the chocolate fountain running low. He nods, hurries away. She turns to adjust a napkin display that doesn't need adjusting.

Avoiding me.

I head back to my table and sit down. It feels like the penalty box.

Conrad looks at me. Then at Chloe across the room. Then back at me.

"You okay?" he asks quietly.

"Great," I lie.

The DJ's voice cuts through the noise. "Ladies and gentlemen, the dance floor is now open! Let's celebrate Derek and Maya!"

The music starts, kicking off the dance floor with a classic. "Celebration" by Kool & the Gang.

And I wait. Chloe keeps herself busy, focuses on coordination tasks, grabbing Derek and Maya more drinks, keeping tabs on the dessert station. She even stops at a random table to grab empty plates before handing them off to one of the catering staff. Anything to avoid the inevitable.

Because that's what this is. Inevitable.

I won't let her lose everything.

A handful of songs play out while I'm stuck on the sideline. But then the lights change. The strobing flashes of green and pink and yellow fade out, washing over the dance floor with blue.

"It's time to slow things down a little," the DJ says. "Let's get all our sweethearts out there for this one."

The music starts up again, the unmistakable voice of Elvis crooning through the hall.

"Wise men say, only fools rush in . . ."

My eyes catch Chloe's across the room. This is it. I step out of the box and make my way over to her.

"Chloe."

She doesn't look at me. "I'm busy."

I lean in close enough that only she can hear. "Dance with me."

"No."

I reach for her, my fingers brushing her waist, begging her to look at me. To understand. "Please."

She finally looks at me. Her eyes are red-rimmed, mascara smudged. Beautiful and breaking.

"Come dance." It's practically a whisper.

"Brody—"

But I'm already pulling her toward the dance floor. I feel her pulse jumping under my thumb. She could resist. Could pull away. Could make a scene right here.

But she doesn't.

She follows me to the dance floor.

We reach the center, and I pull her into my arms. Chloe melts into me, hiding her head in my chest.

"You need to do this," I say quietly, my mouth near her ear.

"Stop." Her voice is tight. "Just stop."

"Chloe—"

"Why?" She pulls back to look at me. "Why are you pushing

this so hard? If you love me like you said you do, why do you want to break up so badly?"

Because I love you. Because I'm trying to protect you. Because the NHL will sue you into oblivion if we don't, and I won't let that happen to you.

But I can't tell her that.

"It's complicated."

"Complicated." She laughs, but there's no humor in it. "That's your answer?"

"You know why—" I lower my voice, glancing at the nearby couples.

"Forget about that!" Her voice rises before she catches herself. "I don't care about any of that. I care about you. About us. Why can't that be enough?"

"It's not that simple—"

"Then explain it to me!" Tears are streaming down her face now. "Make me understand why you're doing this. Why you're so desperate to end this."

I can see her mind working. See the moment something clicks.

"It's your contract, isn't it?" Her voice gets quiet. Careful. "Your NHL contract. That's what this is about. You don't want to lose your renewal."

"What? No—" I reach for her.

"Hey." Maya is there, stepping between us, her voice low over the music. "Is everything okay?"

Of all the terrible timing. "We're fine," I say.

But Chloe is crying, real tears now. There's nothing fake about the way her heart is breaking. And I hate myself for it. How did this get so turned around?

Maya looks at Chloe, at me, then back. "Chloe? Are you okay?"

Chloe's lips press tight, her gaze falling to the floor, hiding her tears.

Derek steps forward, positions himself slightly in front of Maya. Protective. His jaw is tight. "I knew it was a game."

Something in me snaps. "It wasn't a game!"

"Then what is it?" Derek's voice is hard. Cold.

I turn back to Chloe. She's standing there crying, mascara running, looking at me like I'm destroying her.

I *am* destroying her.

"Please—" The word comes out broken.

She takes a shaky breath. Wipes her eyes. "Fine."

The whole ballroom is watching now, the song long over, silence pushing in on us from every side. I brace myself for the hit.

And then she says the words that shatter me completely. "You're just like your father."

The world stops.

"He chases the rush. The winning streak. Gambling everything for the next big score. And you"—her voice breaks—"you're doing the same thing. Chasing your career, your contract, your success. And anyone who gets in the way—"

"That's not—"

"You'll hurt them." Tears are falling freely now. "You're a charmer, Brody. Just like him. Make people fall in love with you and then leave them picking up the pieces."

I can't breathe. Can't move. Can't process.

My father. The man whose mistakes I've spent my entire life trying to outrun. The gambling addict who ruined everything he touched.

I step back, the distance between us suddenly insurmountable.

My face must show something—betrayal, pain, devastation— because Chloe immediately looks horrified. Her hand flies to her mouth.

"Brody, I didn't—"

But she did. She said it. And she meant it.

I find my voice. It comes out quiet. Wrecked. "Yeah. You're right."

I turn and walk away.

I'm already out the doors when my phone buzzes.

<u>Rick</u>
Did you do it?

Yeah. I did it.

I destroyed the woman I love to fulfill a contract I should never have signed.

CHLOE

THE THING ABOUT DOG WALKING IS THAT dogs don't care if you're heartbroken.

They care about squirrels and fire hydrants and whether that other dog across the street is friend or foe. They don't care that you spent last night ugly-crying into a pint of ice cream while scrolling through Instagram posts that may or may not feature your ex-fake-boyfriend looking devastatingly sad.

Which is why I'm currently being dragged down Hennepin Avenue by three dogs who have very different opinions about which direction we should be walking.

Muffin—a corgi mix with Napoleon Syndrome—wants to investigate every mailbox. Bruni—a Bernedoodle who thinks she's still a puppy despite being seventy pounds—wants to say hello to every human. And Princess—yes, you heard that right, Princess, a tiny Pomeranian with an attitude problem—wants to bark at literally everything that moves.

It's seven in the morning. March in Minneapolis, which means winter is fighting with spring and currently winning. My nose is running, my fingers numb, but the dogs need walking. And I need the money.

Except, I don't need the money anymore. Not technically.

The contract payment came through. All of it. Twenty thousand dollars, what's left of it, burning a hole through my bank account. Bills paid. Rent current. Even my student loan's looking better.

I should feel relieved.

Instead, I feel like I sold my heart for financial solvency.

Great trade.

Princess lunges at a pigeon. I yank her back before she can commit bird murder. "No. Birds are friends, not food, Princess."

She glares at me.

We pass Brew & Rumor Coffee Co. I don't look in the windows. I haven't been back since the breakup. Can't even step through the door without thinking about Brody sitting across from me, that stupid contract between us, back when I thought this was just a business arrangement and not the thing that would completely wreck me.

My phone buzzes in my pocket. I ignore it. Probably another Instagram notification. My account went from 800 followers to 50,000 overnight after the wedding video went viral.

Twenty-nine days ago.

Not that I'm counting.

Social media has divided into camps—#TeamBrody versus #TeamChloe versus #TeamTheyreBothIdiots.

I'm in the third camp.

The only bright spot was Penny Pepper's Instagram post three weeks ago. Long and heartfelt, with a photo of her and Conrad at the wedding. The caption:

@PennyP: I Know What Real Love Looks Like.

She described the kiss she witnessed in the hallway. Called it "the most real thing I've ever seen." She went on to say that she investigates lies for a living, and that kiss was pure truth.

@PennyP: Whatever that contract said, whatever that breakup looked like—I saw them in that hallway, and what I saw was two people who found something rare and precious and are losing it. From the bottom of my heart, I believe these two people are genuinely in love. #TeamLove

Two million likes. Countless shares. The new hot topic on everyone's lips, igniting endless think pieces about "performative relationships" and "finding real love in fake situations."

It should make me feel better.

It doesn't.

Because Brody hasn't said a word. Not one. Twenty-nine days of complete radio silence.

The contract specified thirty days of no contact post-breakup. "Maintaining the breakup narrative." Both of us playing our roles right up until the end.

One more day.

Then the contract is fulfilled. We're both free.

Except, after what I said to him at the wedding, I don't think I can expect a phone call when this is all over. Maybe I shouldn't want one either.

After all, he pushed me away. He chose his career.

Made the decision for us.

We turn onto Lyndale, and I trudge up the slushy steps of Mrs. Butler's house—the sweet seventy-year-old who pays me to walk Bruni three times a week. Her house is one of those charming bungalows with a front porch and flower boxes that will be full of tulips in another month.

"Thank you, dear," she says, taking Bruni's leash. Bruni immediately flops onto her living room rug, becoming one with the floor. "Are you all right? You look tired."

"Just busy. You know how it is."

"Hmm." She gives me that look. One that says she knows I'm lying but she's too classy to push. It's one of the many things I like about her. "Well, take care of yourself. You're no good to anyone if you're running on empty."

I smile, nod, make an empty promise, and head to the next doggy drop-off.

I'm worn out by the time I get home, my face wind-chilled but somehow still warm from the rising sun.

The mailbox in the lobby catches my eye. I almost never get mail. Just bills and junk and the occasional Christmas card.

But seeing as it's March, I wasn't expecting Christmas cards. Or anything else for that matter.

But there's something there.

A manila envelope. My heart somersaults as I flip it over to see the return address for Stratton Publishing.

I take it upstairs. Set it on the kitchen counter. Stare at it like it might explode.

Then I open it.

It's a letter. Professional letterhead. Stratton Publishing.

> Dear Ms. Dawson,
>
> After further consideration and internal discussion, we'd like to present a revised offer that better reflects the value of your work and the realistic timeline needed to produce quality illustrations.
>
> Revised terms:
>
> Five-book series, timeline extended to twelve

months

$15,000 advance on signing (not $5,000)

$10,000 per book on delivery

Total advance potential: $65,000

Royalties as previously discussed

We believe in your talent and want to make this work for you. Please contact me at your earliest convenience to discuss.

Best regards,

Milo Brooks

Executive Publisher, Stratton Publishing

I read it twice. Then three times.

Sixty-five thousand dollars. Twelve months. My actual dream.

I don't understand what I'm looking at, because I turned this offer down. Twenty-nine days ago. The morning I woke up in Brody's arms.

Why?

Because the only way I could dream of finishing five fully illustrated books in eight months was if I was out of debt. If I had the money from our contract to hold me over while I wrote the books. And I was going to break that contract.

Lose the money.

And it would have been worth it.

But now?

Now the wedding is over. The contract has expired. I have time.

And someone—somehow—negotiated better terms.

I pull out my phone. Text Jessa.

Chloe

Did you negotiate with Stratton
Publishing?

Her response is immediate.

Jessa

What? No. Why? I'm at the coffee
shop btw, needed to escape the
apartment.

Chloe

I got a revised offer. Way better
terms. $15K on signing, 12-month
timeline.

Jessa

WHAT. That's amazing!

Chloe

You didn't reach out to them?

Jessa

Seriously, I didn't do anything.
Maybe they just reconsidered? Or
someone told him he was lowballing
you? Does it matter? CALL THEM.
Accept it. This is your dream, Chloe.

I set the phone down. Stare at the letter.

Someone fought for me. Someone told Stratton Publishing
that I was worth more than five thousand dollars and a crushing
timeline.

But who?

By six o'clock, I've accomplished exactly nothing productive.

I showered. Made coffee. Stared at the publishing letter for an
hour. Scrolled Instagram (mistake). Tried to sketch (bigger mistake—everything I draw looks sad). Made more coffee. Stared at
the letter some more.

The apartment is quiet. Too quiet. Jessa's still out—she texted
that she's meeting with an interviewee and won't be home until
late.

So I'm alone with my thoughts and a frozen pizza and the TV that I turned on for background noise.

Except it's not background noise anymore.

Because it's a hockey game.

Blue Ox versus Chicago.

And there he is.

Number 7. Brody Kane. On the ice.

The camera follows him for a moment, and I forget how to breathe. Yeah. He still has that effect on me.

I pick up the remote, my thumb hovering over the button to change the channel. I should turn it off. Really, I should. But . . .

He's in his defensive position. Skating with that focused, controlled power I saw against Vancouver. Except something's off. When the puck comes his way, he makes the hit against the boards, but the puck is passed off.

The ref blows the whistle, and Brody skates to the penalty box, looking fierce.

The camera zooms in on his face.

And he looks absolutely wrecked. Dark circles under his eyes. Jaw tight. A darkness in his expression, one I don't recognize.

No more Mr. Candy, clearly.

The announcer's voice cuts through my spiral. "Kane's defensive game has been brutal this past month."

The color announcer says, "Yeah, but he's racking up penalties, and now Chicago has a chance to score. He needs to learn to balance if he hopes to stay an asset to this team and close the deal on his contract renewal."

My throat is tight. Eyes burning.

I know exactly why he's playing as if he's got nothing to lose.

Maybe because he's already lost everything?

I abandon the pizza. Walk to the couch. Sit down.

Can't look away.

Blue Ox loses. 4–2.

The announcers are already talking about the next game. "They face Chicago again tomorrow night in the second game of this back-to-back series. Let's hope Kane can shake off whatever's bothering him and get his head back in the game."

I turn off the TV. Silence rushes in, pricking my ears.

I look at the publishing letter still sitting on the counter.

Look at my sketchbook on the coffee table. It's sitting on top of my Bible.

Which of course tugs at me. I pick it up, and it falls open to where last Sunday's bulletin is marking the page with this week's verse printed at the top:

"My grace is sufficient for you, for my power
is made perfect in weakness." 2 Corinthians 12:9

I read it once. Then again.

Give up.

"All right, God, what are You trying to show me here? Because I'm lost."

The silence stretches, fills the room with a holy stillness. And I listen. I wait.

I close my eyes, my heart slowing, settling. My fingers trace the edges of my Bible, fidgeting while I wait, then catch on a sharp edge.

My eyes open. I'm looking at a weathered piece of paper tucked between the pages. It's folded and creased, lined pink paper—a remnant of the early days. From that summer after high school, when I first started taking my faith more seriously.

I unfold it carefully.

God doesn't love you because you're good enough. He loves you because you're His.

I stare at the words, and that's when I feel it—that little tug again.

My power is made perfect in weakness.

Not in strength. Not in performance. Not in earning it or deserving it or being good enough.

In *weakness.*

Well, goody, because I have that in spades.

Except I think about the publishing offer. Better terms. More money. Without me doing anything to earn it.

I think about Brody. Loving me when I was broken and struggling and falling apart.

But what if all of that was grace?

What if that's the point?

I've spent a lot of my life trying to prove I was worth loving.

But what if I simply stop being afraid of being rejected? Stop trying to earn love and be brave enough to give it. Unconditionally.

A little like Jesus did.

I know what I have to do.

I open my laptop. Buy two tickets for tomorrow night's game. Lower bowl, near the penalty box. Close enough that he might see me.

Then I pick up my phone. Text Jessa.

Chloe

When you get home, I need your
help with something.

Jessa

Anything. What's up?

Chloe

I'm going to make the biggest
spectacle of my life.

BRODY

I HAVE A GAME TONIGHT.

I should be thinking about defensive formations, Chicago's offensive strategy, how to shut down their power play.

Instead, I'm sitting in my car outside Serenity Hills Treatment Center, staring at my phone, wondering if it's possible to die from missing someone.

Probably not. But it feels like it might be.

My dad is getting released today. Thirty days sober. Completed the program.

And I should be celebrating that. Should be focused on him.

But all I can think about is that today is also day thirty of not talking to Chloe.

Day thirty.

The contract is officially over at midnight. Thirty days of mandatory silence. Thirty days of torture.

I've written and deleted the same text message forty-seven times this morning.

The message keeps changing:

"I'm sorry" (too simple)

"Can we talk?" (too casual)

"I miss you" (too weak)

"I love you and I'm an idiot" (too desperate, also true)

My thumb hovers over the Send button for the forty-eighth time.

Then I delete it again.

Instead, I do what I've done every morning for the past month: open Instagram. Find Chloe's personal profile. Stare at her latest post like it might give me answers.

I'm not following her anymore. I had to unfollow after the breakup, couldn't handle seeing her face in my feed, smiling at events I wasn't part of.

But I check her profile every day. Sometimes multiple times a day.

Like an addict.

Today's post is from this morning. A photo of her sketchbook. A dragon with scales falling away, revealing something soft and vulnerable underneath. The caption:

@Chloe.D: Sometimes the armor has to come off.

I've stared at this post for twenty minutes. Tried to figure out if it means something. If she's trying to tell me something.

Or if I'm just a desperate idiot, looking for signs that don't exist.

The dragon. Just like the one in Barcelona. The day we met. When everything was possible and nothing was complicated.

Is she thinking about that night too?

Or has she moved on?

My phone buzzes.

<u>Dad</u>
Ready for pickup. Last day.

Right.

I pocket my phone, get out of the car, and trudge through the cold March morning toward the building that's supposedly given my father his life back.

The Serenity Hills Treatment Center smells like industrial cleaner and hope.

I'm not sure which is more overwhelming.

The visitors' lounge has uncomfortable chairs, motivational posters about "one day at a time," and a coffee machine that dispenses something that's technically coffee but tastes like regret.

My dad is waiting by the window, holding a small duffel bag—everything he came with plus some workbooks and a thirty-day chip.

He looks better than I've seen him in years.

Clearer eyes. Steadier hands. Actually present.

"Hey, son." He walks over, and for a second I think he's going to do the awkward shoulder-pat thing we usually do.

Instead, he hugs me, his arms enveloping me like I'm a kid again.

I'm so surprised, I almost don't hug back.

"You ready?" I ask when we pull apart.

"Not yet." He sets the bag down. "There are some things I need to say first. Walk with me?"

"Yeah. Sure."

We head outside. It's one of those mid-March days that feels like a promise—the sun bright and almost warm, melting snow dripping from the building's eaves. The air still has that sharp edge of winter, but there's something softer underneath. Spring, maybe. Hope.

The facility grounds are quiet. A paved path circles the main building, lined with bare trees and dormant flower beds. Patches of dirty snow cling to the shaded areas, but the sidewalk is clear, wet with melt.

Dad starts walking. I follow, hands in my pockets, watching my breath cloud in the air.

For a minute, we just walk. The only sounds are our footsteps on wet pavement and the drip-drip-drip of melting snow.

Then Dad says, "I've been thinking about what happens next. After I leave here."

I've been planning this for weeks. "I was thinking I'd move back to the house for a while. Keep an eye on things—"

"I think it's time you stop babysitting me," Dad says.

I glance at him. "What?"

He pauses on the path, turns to face me fully. "Son, I can't tell you how much it's meant to me all the times you've come to my rescue. But . . . that's got to stop."

He drops his gaze, clearly reciting something practiced. "I've spent thirty days learning about myself. About my addiction. About the lies I told myself and everyone around me. And one thing I know for sure—you can't control me into sobriety."

The words sting. "I'm not trying to—"

"Yes, you are. And I don't blame you. I put that on you." His voice cracks. "I made you responsible for my mistakes. Made you grow up too fast."

A bird lands on a nearby branch, sending down a small shower of water droplets that catch the sunlight.

"I want you to know how sorry I am," he says quietly. "I'm so sorry, Brody. For all of it. For every time you had to bail me out. Every time you had to lie about why you were late. Every dollar you spent cleaning up my messes."

We start walking again, slower this time.

"In treatment, they made us recite the Twelve Steps every morning," Dad continues. "And for the longest time, I couldn't get past Step Three. 'Make a decision to turn our will and our lives over to the care of God.' I kept thinking, 'I don't need God, I just need to be better. Stronger. More disciplined.'"

He laughs, but it's not a happy sound.

"Your mother used to say the same thing to me. Before she got sick. I was always chasing the next big thing—the business idea that would make us rich, the investment that couldn't fail, the dream that was just around the corner. She'd say, 'Robert, you can't outrun reality. You can't charm your way into success. You have to do the work.'"

The path curves around a stand of pines, and we follow it.

"She was right. But I didn't listen." He looks down at his hands. "Then she got sick. And the medical bills piled up. And I couldn't fix it. Couldn't charm it away. Couldn't dream it better."

"Dad. That wasn't your fault—"

"I know. But grief doesn't care about logic. I blamed myself. Started drinking to numb it. And then I couldn't stop."

We pass a bench, and he gestures to it. We sit.

"Then I came here," Dad continues, "and something changed. I realized I can't control this. I can't white-knuckle my way to being okay. I can't dream my way out of addiction. I need help. From God, from counselors, from AA meetings, from people who understand. And it's okay to need that help. It's okay to not be okay."

He looks at me, and I feel my throat go dry.

"But here's what I learned—we don't need to hide anything from God. We're already broken, and He loves us anyway. That's what grace means." He pauses. "Your mom understood that."

"Mom?"

"She knew I was a dreamer. Knew I was selling her castles in the sky when I could barely afford a one-bedroom apartment. But she loved me anyway." He smiles. "I asked her out seven times before she finally said yes. She kept saying no because she wasn't sure I was serious. But finally she said, 'Okay, Robert. But promise you'll never stop trying. Not for the dreams. Just to be a good man.'"

I've never heard this story.

"She was something, your mom."

"I know." My voice comes out raw.

"We went to one of your games," Dad says quietly. "You remember? Junior year, state championship. She was so sick by then, I had to carry her into the arena—wheelchair wouldn't fit in our section. We sat there and watched you play. You scored the winning goal."

I remember that game. Remember seeing them in the stands, Mom wrapped in blankets, Dad holding her hand.

"After you won, she looked at me and said, 'We did this. We made him.' And I said, 'He's nothing like me, thank God.' And she grabbed my face—weak as she was, she grabbed my face—and said, 'Don't give up on God, Robert. Don't give up on yourself. The only thing that matters is what He thinks of us. And He already loves us.'"

He looks at me.

"I lost sight of that." His voice breaks as he puts a hand on my shoulder. "And I think I made you lose sight of it too."

"Dad . . ."

"I wasn't a good father, Brody. I know that. But I want to be. I have to ask, can you forgive me?"

My eyes are burning, throat stinging. "Yeah, Dad. I forgive you."

Dad gives me a watery smile. Wipes his eyes. "I love you, son."

"I love you." In that moment, I don't care that I'm a twenty-eight-year-old man. I hug my dad. I hold on to him, bury my face against his shoulder.

God, please let this be real. Please let this last.

At last, he pulls away, clasping a hand on the back of my neck. "All right, now I think it's time we talk about you."

I frown. "What do you mean?"

"The girl," he says, standing up. "I heard about what happened at that wedding. There are a lot of stories going around. Why don't you tell me about it?"

We start walking again, and his words echo back inside my head. *I lost sight of that, and I think I made you lose sight of it too.* "I pushed her away. I told myself it was to protect her, but I wound up doing the one thing she was most afraid of. I ran her over. Made the decision for her instead of letting her in, letting us figure it out together."

Dad winces as we round a corner. "So what'd she do?"

"She . . . uh." I run a hand over the back of my neck. "She told me I was just like you. Said I was a charmer who makes people love them and then leaves them to pick up the pieces."

"That's fair," he says. "That's exactly what I taught you to do. To protect yourself. To charm people so you can keep your walls up. So you don't get hurt." We stop at the entrance. Dad picks up his bag from where he'd left it. "So you hold all the control."

He stops outside the facility. Turns to face me again.

"Do you love her?"

I nod. Can't trust my voice.

"Then stop protecting her from yourself. Stop performing. Stop trying to be perfect." He smiles. "Stop thinking you have to earn love. Stop controlling everything because you're afraid of being hurt. You're already loved. By God. By me. By that girl who's probably sitting at home right now thinking you don't want her. I think it's time you go win her back. Now, come on. Don't you have a game tonight?"

I check my phone. 11:23 a.m. Game starts at seven.

"Yeah. But I was going to help you get settled at home—"

"Absolutely not." He grabs his duffel. "You're going to that game. And you're going to play like you used to play—not because you're trying to be perfect or impress anyone or prove something. But because you love it. Because it's who you are. Because it's a gift God gave you, and you're going to use it."

"Dad—"

"I'm not asking, Brody. I'm telling you. Go to the game. Play your heart out. And after"—he claps a hand on my shoulder—"you find that girl, and you tell her the truth. That you love her. That you're sorry. That you're done running."

"What about you?"

"I'm going to an AA meeting. Already looked up the schedule—there's one at two o'clock at the church down the street from the house. I've got a ride coming. I'll be fine." He tosses his duffel over his shoulder and starts walking back toward the facility. "I'm proud of you, son. Your mom would be too."

The doors shut behind him, leaving me to process . . . a lot of things.

My phone is still in my hand.

I open it. Pull up Chloe's contact.

My thumb hovers over the Call button.

Then I put the phone away.

I'm not texting her.

I'm not calling her.

I'm going to play the best game of my life.

And then I'm going to find her.

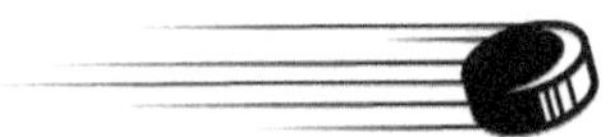

The game goes sideways in the first period.

Two penalties. One offside. Coach Jacobsen benches me halfway through.

I sit there, watching through the plexiglass, replaying every conversation with my dad. Every word about dreams and control and being human.

Stop protecting her from yourself. Stop performing.

The problem is, I don't know who I am when I'm not performing.

Second period starts. Coach puts me back in.

"Kane," he says. "Get your head in the game or get off my ice."

I skate out. Take my position.

But my head isn't in the game.

It's thinking about Chloe. About armor coming off. About dragons and vulnerability and the fact that she posted that this morning—the day our contract ends.

Sometimes the armor has to come off.

Is she thinking about me too?

Stop protecting her from yourself.

The puck drops.

Chicago charges down the ice. Their left wing breaks free, heading straight for our goal.

I'm supposed to block him. It's my job. My position.

Instead, I see Chloe's face. The way she looked at me before everything fell apart.

I love you. Not Candy Kane. You—Brody.

The crowd noise fades. The ice disappears. There's just that moment. That truth.

She loves me. The real me. The messy, imperfect, terrified-of-failing me.

And I pushed her away because I thought I was protecting her.

But I was really just protecting myself.

The Chicago player blows past me.

Shoots.

Scores.

The crowd groans.

Coach is yelling something.

But I'm not listening. I'm done pretending.

I'm done doing the right thing.

Intermission can't come fast enough.

I skate off the ice, helmet in hand, heading straight for the tunnel with the other guys.

Derek catches up with me. "Kane, where are you going? We've got—"

"I need five minutes."

"We're down by one—"

"I know." I keep walking. "Five minutes. I promise."

I burst into the locker room. Everyone's scattered—some guys getting water, others checking their equipment.

I grab my phone from my locker.

Open Instagram.

Find Chloe's profile.

The dragon post is still there. *Sometimes the armor has to come off.*

My fingers hover over the keyboard.

Then I notice she's posted again. Two minutes ago.

A photo of her sitting next to Jessa in what looks like a hockey arena. Behind her, I spot a section number. It's section 104 in our arena. No caption.

My heart stops.

Section 104.

She's *here.*

I look up at the clock. Three minutes until we're back on the ice.

Derek appears in the doorway. "Kane, Coach is—" He stops. Sees my face. "What?"

"She's here."

"Who's—" Understanding dawns. "Chloe?"

I nod. "Section 104."

Derek grins. Shakes his head. "Whoa, whoa, whoa. Slow down there, lover boy."

"I've got to—"

"And you will." He claps me on the shoulder. "But do it after we win. You owe us a decent third period after that disaster you just pulled."

"Derek—"

"Save it. Get your head together. Win the game. Then go get your girl." He heads back toward the tunnel. "In that order, Kane!"

I look back at my phone. At the photo of section 104.

She came.

After everything. After the contract. After I pushed her away.

She came.

And she's wearing—I zoom in on the photo—is that a *glittery* jersey?

A laugh bursts out of me. It feels like a weight lifted, floating like light.

Conrad pokes his head in. "You good, man?"

"Yeah." I'm grinning like an idiot. "Yeah, I'm good."

"Then get back on the ice. We've got a game to win."

Third period.

Before we take the ice, Coach Jacobsen stops me.

"Whatever's going on with you," he says, "figure it out. Now. I need you present."

"Yes, Coach."

"Good." He starts to turn away, then stops. "Also—section 104. Blue glitter jersey. Foam ox horns. That your girl?"

Heat floods my face. "How did you—"

"I'm a coach. I see everything." He smiles. Barely, but it's there. "Nice taste. Now go play hockey."

We take the ice for the third period.

I scan the stands as I skate to position.

Section 104.

And there she is.

Chloe Dawson. Wearing a bedazzled Blue Ox jersey that catches the arena lights like a disco ball. Foam ox horns on her head. Holding a giant sign that says *GO BIG 7* in glitter letters.

She's not subtle.

She's perfect.

Our eyes meet across the ice.

She grins.

Waves the sign.

And then she blows me a kiss.

Actually blows me a kiss. In front of eighteen thousand people.

My chest is so tight I can barely breathe.

Derek skates past me, heading for the tunnel. Sees where I'm looking. Sees Chloe in her glittery jersey and ridiculous horns.

He grins. Shakes his head. "Eyes on the puck, Candy."

I play like I've never played before.

Not trying to prove anything. Not performing. Not being perfect.

Just being.

Every blocked shot. Every defensive play. Every split-second decision.

I'm not thinking. I'm just moving. Trusting my body. Trusting my training. Trusting that this—hockey, the ice, the game—is what I was made for.

And knowing that she's watching.

That she came. That she's here. That she's wearing the ridiculous getup and waving a sign like this is game seven.

Cheering for me.

We score again. And again.

Chicago can't touch us.

Final score: 5–2.

The crowd is on their feet. Chanting. Celebrating.

The team mobs me on the ice—pounding my back, yelling, congratulating.

"Best game of the season, Kane!"

"That's what I'm talking about!"

"Candy Kane is BACK, baby!"

But I'm not listening. I'm scanning the stands.

Section 104.

She's there. Running down the steps toward the glass. Pushing through people, apologizing, still wearing that ridiculous glittery jersey, her foam horns crooked now.

She reaches the boards. Presses her hands against the plexiglass.

I'm on the other side. Separated by three inches of reinforced plastic and every rule about player-fan interaction.

We stare at each other.

She's crying. I'm probably crying too, but the helmet hides it.

Her lips move. I can't hear her through the glass and the crowd noise, but I can read the words:

I'm sorry. I love you.

That's it.

I'm done with things keeping us apart.

I look at the bench. At Coach Jacobsen who's watching with raised eyebrows.

Then I climb over the boards.

Not the normal exit. Right over the plexiglass between the bench and the stands, using my stick for leverage.

My teammates are shouting. The crowd is screaming. Security is probably having a heart attack.

I don't care.

I drop down into the stands—awkward in skates, nearly losing my balance. She's right there.

I reach for her, but she holds up a hand.

"Wait." She's crying and laughing at the same time. "The contract doesn't end until midnight."

I stare at her. "Are you serious?"

"The thirty-day period. It's technically—"

"Chloe." I step closer. "It's midnight somewhere."

Her face breaks into the biggest smile I've ever seen.

And I kiss her.

Pull her into my arms and kiss her like I've been wanting to for thirty days. Like I'll never let her go again. Like she's the only thing that matters.

She kisses me back. Hands in my hair. Tears on both our faces. The foam ox horns fall off her head and tumble down the steps.

The crowd loses their minds.

Chanting. Clapping. Stomping.

Someone's playing "We Are the Champions" over the loud-speakers.

The Jumbotron is showing us—I can see it out of the corner of my eye. The kiss. Us. Together.

My teammates are leaning over the boards, whooping and hollering.

"Way to go, Candy!" Torch yells.

Derek is grinning. He catches my eye and gives me a thumbs-up.

I pull back just enough to look at Chloe's face. She's wearing sparkly eye makeup and her mascara is running and there's glitter everywhere.

"You look ridiculous," I say.

"I just didn't want you to miss me," she says, laughing through tears.

"How I missed you." I kiss her again. Softer this time. "I'm so sorry. For everything. For asking you to break up with me. For the contract—"

"Stop." She puts her hand over my mouth. "I'm sorry too. For what I said. For comparing you to—I didn't mean it."

"You were right," I interrupt. "I was running. Just like him. Trying to control everything instead of trusting. But I'm done running. I'm done hiding. I'm done pretending."

"Good. Because I'm done hiding too." She grins. Touches my face. "I love you, Brody Kane."

"I love you too." I'm grinning like an idiot. "Also, is that glitter on your jersey?"

"Yes. I made Jessa help me bedazzle it. It took four hours and six containers of craft glitter."

"It's perfect."

"It's hideous."

"It's perfectly hideous." I kiss her forehead, her nose, her cheeks.

"You smell," she says, wrinkling her nose.

"I just played three periods of hockey—"

"Shower. Then meet me at Ironclad. Jessa's gonna drive me." She grins. "I need a giant chocolate chip cookie and a late-night latte. And you. Not necessarily in that order."

"I'll be there."

"You better." She picks up the fallen ox horns, puts them back on her head. Crooked and ridiculous and perfect.

I kiss her one more time—quick, sweet—then climb back over the boards.

My teammates are waiting, all of them grinning like idiots.

Conrad skates over first. "Sheesh. I guess absence makes the heart grow fonder."

Derek follows, shaking his head. "Thirty days and you climb into the stands. Could've just texted her, Kane."

"Where's the fun in that?" I'm grinning so hard my face hurts.

"Fair point." Derek claps me on the shoulder. "Welcome back, buddy."

Coach Jacobsen is waiting at the bench, arms crossed, trying to look stern. "Kane. My office. Tomorrow morning."

"Yes, Coach."

"But good game." The corner of his mouth twitches. "Best I've seen you play all season."

Conrad appears at my elbow. "You good?"

"Yeah." I'm still grinning. Can't stop. "I'm really good."

We skate toward the tunnel. My teammates are still ribbing me, still laughing, still making jokes about climbing into stands and midnight and glitter.

I don't care.

For the first time in my entire life, I feel like I'm exactly where I'm supposed to be.

Not performing. Not pretending. Not hiding behind charm or control or fear.

Just being.

And in about thirty minutes, I'll be at Ironclad Desserts with the woman I love, eating cookies and drinking terrible coffee and figuring out how to build a life together.

No contracts. No performances. No rules.

Just us.

Finally.

EPILOGUE

CHLOE

THREE HOURS AGO, I WAS A REASONABLY anonymous (outside the hockey world) event planner with a failing business and a broken heart. Now I'm "Glitter Jersey Girl," and there are already memes.

I checked Instagram while waiting for Brody at Ironclad. Someone created a GIF of me waving my GO BIG 7 sign with the caption: "When you're extra but he's worth it." It has 47,000 likes.

I showed it to Brody as he slid into the booth. He almost smacked his face on the table, doubling over in laughter.

"You're never living this down," he said, wiping his eyes.

"Neither are you. Someone made a clip of you climbing over the boards with the *Mission: Impossible* theme song."

"How many views?"

"Two million."

"Bam. That's how it's done."

And now we're at Ironclad Desserts—the place where this whole ridiculous, beautiful, complicated mess sort of started.

Or restarted.

The place smells like butter and cinnamon and happiness. Vintage lights cast warm shadows across the brick walls. A couple at a nearby table keeps glancing over, whispering, probably wondering if we're who they think we are.

Spoiler: We are.

Brody sits across from me, freshly showered, wearing jeans and a sports coat (of course), hair still slightly damp. He smells like soap and aftershave. Fresh, clean. Like a new start.

"You have glitter on your face," he says, reaching across the table.

"I have glitter everywhere. I'm pretty sure there's glitter in places glitter should never be."

He grins. "Yeah, you're not bringing that jersey in the car with you. I'm not getting glitter in the seats."

"What? I'm keeping it forever. I'm gonna wear it to every game." I'm grinning too. Can't stop.

Marcie approaches our table. "Chloe!" She's beaming. "Girl, I saw you on the Jumbotron tonight. That was incredible!"

My face heats. "You watched the game?"

"Everyone watched the game. We had it on the TV behind the bar. The whole place erupted when he climbed into the stands." She looks at Brody, still grinning. "You're definitely an upgrade from the sketchbook. No offense to the sketchbook."

"None taken," I manage.

"The usual?" Marcie asks.

"You know what? Surprise me."

Marcie grins. "You got it."

The college kids two tables over are definitely filming us again.

"We can leave—"

"No." I reach across the table, take his hand. "I don't care."

The cookies arrive a few minutes later—two Midnight Eclipse

cookies. Cast-iron skillets with dark chocolate brownie cookies. Sea salt caramel is drizzled across the top, the bourbon vanilla ice cream slowly melting into creamy pools.

I take a bite. Close my eyes. Let the chocolate and caramel and butter work their magic.

"This is what happiness tastes like," I say when I open my eyes.

Brody is staring at me instead of eating his cookie.

"What?" I ask.

"Just memorizing this. You. Here. Happy."

My throat tightens. "I am happy."

"Good." He finally takes a bite of his own cookie. His eyes close. "Oh, this is dangerous. I'm going to gain twenty pounds if this becomes *our place*."

I blush at that, but I like the idea of it. "Worth it?"

"Absolutely."

We eat in comfortable silence for a moment. Then Brody sets down his fork.

"So. My contract extension came through."

I look up. "Yeah? That's great!"

"Three more years. Maybe longer if they like what they see." He's smiling, relief clear in his expression. "They were waiting to see how I'd finish out the season. Tonight's game helped."

"You were incredible tonight."

"I had good motivation." He reaches across the table, brushes glitter off my hand. "So, it looks like I'm staying in Minneapolis. For the foreseeable future."

"Good," I say. Okay, that isn't at all what I mean, but it's hard to vocalize the feeling of confetti exploding in your soul.

"What about you?" he asks. "How's the event planning business?"

"It's good. Really good." I take another bite of cookie. "The wedding magazine spread brought in three new clients. One of them is a corporate event for a tech company—huge budget, lots of potential for referrals. And . . . I'm out of debt."

"That's amazing, Chloe."

"It is. But—" I pause. Set down my fork. Look at him. "I have bigger news." I can't keep the smile off my face. "I got a publishing offer. For a five-book illustration series. Children's books. Dragons and adventure and—it's everything I've wanted."

Brody's face does something complicated. A smile that's equal parts pleased and . . . something.

"What?" I ask.

"Just about time." He's still smiling. "I hope you're taking it."

"I am. I mean, I'm going to. Now that . . ." I stop. Laugh. "Well, let's just say I happen to have come into some money recently."

He laughs too. Winks.

And right then, I realize—it's past us. We can laugh about it. Tell our . . . kids? Yes, maybe, someday.

"Also," Brody says, his expression shifting to something more serious, "my dad went to treatment. He's thirty days sober."

"Brody." I squeeze his hand. "I'm so glad. How is he?"

"Better. Really better. Clear-headed. Present. He's going to AA meetings, has a sponsor, the whole thing." He pauses. "I think we're going to fix up the house, spend some time together in the offseason."

"Brody, that's great."

"I think it'll be good for us. He needs support. And honestly, I think I need it too. We have a lot to work through." He grins. "Plus, I'm thinking about doing some upgrades to the house. New kitchen, renovated bathroom, maybe adding a deck. Give me something to connect with him about."

My heart flutters. "Of course you are."

"What?"

"Nothing. Just—you're a good son."

We finish our cookies slowly, savoring every bite. Talk about the upcoming games and my ideas for another book. Whether the NHL will start selling glitter jerseys.

Brody says doubtful, but I think I'm really on to something.

The door opens, and someone walks in—a man in his thirties, dark hair neatly combed, wearing a blazer.

Brody's face lights up. He stands immediately.

"Hey, Milo!"

I turn. The man—Milo—sees Brody and grins. Crosses the coffee shop with his hand extended.

"Brody Kane! Didn't expect to see you here. Good game tonight."

Brody nods, smiles. "You're a little ways from Iowa."

"In town on business."

Then it hits me.

Milo.

Milo Brooks.

From Stratton Publishing.

Oh my . . . *Seriously*?

Milo notices me. His eyes widen. "And you must be Chloe."

My face is on fire. "That's me. Chloe Dawson."

He extends a hand. "Nice to put a face to the name."

I shake his hand, still processing that Brody apparently knows my publisher.

He glances at his watch. "I'd love to stay and talk. But I'm meeting someone here—one of our authors. She should be here any minute. You probably know her, Brody—Everly Hart."

What? I love Everly Hart. I have a shelf of her books.

Stay calm. Do not be awkward!

Brody nods. "Yeah, I know Everly. Assistant Coach Hart's daughter. We met once at a Blue Ox event."

The door opens again, and I practically leap from my chair to get a look. A woman walks in—late twenties, dark-auburn hair, confident stride, carrying a laptop bag. She's pretty in an understated way, like she doesn't try too hard because she doesn't need to.

"Everly!" Milo says.

She sees him and then beyond him to Brody. "Brody Kane. I should've known you'd be here. Saw that Jumbotron kiss—very smooth."

"Thanks." Brody gestures to me. "Everly, this is Chloe. Chloe, Everly Hart."

Standing to shake her hand, I say, "I love your books. The one about the cold-case detective—I stayed up all night reading it."

"Thank you." She seems genuinely pleased. "That's always nice to hear."

Milo gestures toward a table in the corner. "We should let you two finish your date. Everly and I have a series to discuss."

I sink back into my seat, staring at Brody as they walk away.

"You know Milo Brooks," I say slowly.

"I know Milo Brooks." He's suddenly very interested in his cookie.

"My publisher."

"So it would seem."

I blink at him, still reeling from the shock. "How? How on earth do you know Milo Brooks?"

Brody smirks, shrugs a little. "He's my cousin."

"Brody."

He looks up. "If you must know, I called him. A few weeks ago."

My heart stops. "You what?"

"During the thirty days. I called him and told him you were incredibly talented and he was getting a bargain, that he should reconsider his offer." The words come out in a rush.

I'm staring at him. Tears forming.

"You did that? While we weren't even speaking?"

"I wanted you to have your dream. Even if—" He stops. Swallows. "Even if you ended up hating me. Are you mad?" he asks, looking genuinely worried.

"No." I reach across the table, take both his hands. "Thank you. For coming to my rescue."

His face softens. "Always."

The word hangs between us—a callback to Barcelona, to the beginning, to when he was just a stranger being kind.

Someone approaches our table—a young woman with her phone.

"Excuse me, are you two the couple from the game tonight?"

I look at Brody. He looks at me.

"That's us," I say.

"Could I get a photo?"

We stand. Pose together. Brody's arm around my shoulders, both of us smiling.

We leave together eventually—hand in hand, walking out into the cold Minneapolis night. Past the vintage photos on the walls. Past the other customers, who smile at us with knowing expressions. Past Milo and Everly, who wave as we go.

Outside, the air is crisp and clear. Stars are trying to break through the city lights. We walk slowly, not in any rush. My hand in his, our breath forming clouds in the cold air.

"I love you," he says. Simple. Clear. Real.

"I love you too," I say.

Then he leans over, kisses me. Soft and sweet and tasting like chocolate and caramel and promises.

Because sometimes, the best stories start with a lie and end with the truth.

THANK YOU

Thank you so much for reading *The Not So Neutral Zone*. We hope you enjoyed the story. If you did, would you be willing to do us a favor and leave a review? It doesn't have to be long—just a few words to help other readers know what they're getting. (But no spoilers! We don't want to wreck the fun!) Thank you again for reading!

We'd love to hear from you—not only about this story, but about any characters or stories you'd like to read in the future.

Contact us at www.sunrisepublishing.com/contact

THE BLUE OX BOYS
Don't Cross
THE BLUE LINE
SUSAN & SARAH MAY WARREN

He's the hockey player she can't stop writing about. She's the author he's been anonymously writing to. When a blizzard traps them in a mall with thieves, the truth comes out—and so do the feelings.

Everly Hart lives a double life. By day, she's E.J. Hartley, bestselling thriller writer. By night, she's Sutton Blake, author of sweet hockey romances. Her latest project? A book about Beckett 'Blue Line' Brooks—the disgraced Blue Ox center she can't stop thinking about. He's her ultimate book boyfriend.

Beckett's secret: for six months, he's been pouring his heart into anonymous fan mail to Sutton Blake, the only person who makes him feel seen beyond his stats.

Then a blizzard traps them in an abandoned mall—with thieves. Suddenly they're living their own romantic suspense novel, and he's the hero. She'll have to figure out how to rewrite the plot without giving away her secret. But when you're trapped with the man you've been writing about—and he's been writing to you—some secrets refuse to stay hidden.

Can two people who've been writing each other's stories survive the plot twist neither of them saw coming?

A hilarious, heart-pounding hockey rom-com about book boyfriends coming to life, secret identities, and falling in love while dodging thieves.

ACKNOWLEDGMENTS

Writing this book has been one of the most joyful creative experiences of my life, and that's entirely because I got to write it with my daughter.

There's something magical about collaborating with someone you love—especially when that someone challenges you, inspires you, and makes you laugh until you cry.

This story is close to our hearts for so many reasons. We wanted to write about two people who are tired of hiding—tired of pretending to be perfect, tired of keeping parts of themselves locked away out of fear. Brody, with his carefully curated "Candy Kane" persona and the secrets he carries about his dyslexia and his father's struggles. Chloe, the sister who's always felt invisible, always working behind the scenes, always wondering if anyone would choose her first.

We wanted to explore what it means to be truly seen—not just the highlight reel version of yourself, but the messy, complicated, beautifully imperfect reality. Because that's where real love lives. Not in the neutral zone where you play it safe and keep your distance, but in that vulnerable space where you risk everything to let someone in.

And we wanted to write about family, about the relationships that shape us, and make us better versions of ourselves.

But mostly? We just wanted to write a swoony, funny, heart-tugging romance about a hockey player and a wedding planner, which felt right in our wheel-house as our first-time gig.

To my daughter: Thank you for being my favorite writing partner, my brainstorming buddy, my fellow romantic at heart. Thank you for every comment (and making me laugh!) This book exists because of your brilliant ideas, your humor, your heart. I'm so proud of the writer you are and so grateful I got to create this story with you.

To the incredible team at Sunrise Publishing—Rel, Sarah, Katie, Kristyn, Caroline, Tari and Lisa—thank you for scrambling whenever I say, "Hey, I have an idea…" You guys rock, and really, Sunrise would be lost without you!

Especially Kristyn Fortner: Thank you for your insight, your encouragement, and your expertise. Your feedback strengthened this story in ways we couldn't have imagined, and your support has been invaluable. We're so grateful for you.

And to you, our dear reader: Thank you for picking up this book. We hope Brody and Chloe's story makes you laugh, makes you swoon, and reminds you that the bravest thing you can do is step out of the neutral zone and let yourself be fully, beautifully seen.

Go Blue Ox Boys!

Susie May

Like mother, like daughter! **Susan and Sarah May Warren** are proof that the writing gene runs strong in this family. With nearly 2 million books sold and 100+ published novels, USA Today bestselling author Susan May Warren has been spinning faith-filled tales of romance and adventure for decades, collecting RITA, Christy, and Carol awards along the way. Her daughter Sarah grew up surrounded by story magic and, despite her best efforts to resist, caught the writing bug while falling in love with her own real-life romance hero. When they're not crafting swoon-worthy stories of faith and love, you might find this dynamic duo plotting their next novel over coffee, debating character arcs at family dinners, or thanking God for the gift of storytelling that brings them together - proving that the greatest story of all is the one God writes in our lives.

WELCOME BACK TO
Jonathon Island

where you'll find the magic of small town happily ever afters.

"Cozy, heartfelt, and irresistibly romantic—Jonathon Island is my new happy place."

–SUSAN MAY WARREN
USA Today bestselling author

We solve the problem of what to read next.

Created by New York Times bestselling author

RACHEL HAUCK

Welcome

Home to Hearts Bend

for sweet stories of romance, faith, and happy endings.

We solve the problem of what to read next.

YOU MAY ALSO LIKE...

When Noah Hebert inherits the struggling Blue Pirogue Inn, he must solve a puzzle left by his grandfather to save it from his family's nemesis, Isaac Bergeron. Teaming up with Elisa Bergeron, the café manager and his rival, they must navigate family feuds—and unexpected sparks—while racing against time.

***Where I Found You* by Besty St. Amant**

Grace Howell leaves her life as a ballerina and returns to Heritage, Michigan, to heal. Teaching dance is just a temporary gig, until she finds herself unexpectedly charmed by small-town life and her growing attachment to Seth Warner, a man from her past with a troubled history of his own.

***You're the Reason* by Tari Faris**

Dani Sullivan is determined to revive Jonathon Island's fading charm and reunite her fractured family. Her plan? Reopen the Grand Sullivan Hotel. But without the funds to restore the hotel, Dani's forced to accept help from Liam Stone—a big-city hotel developer whose sleek, modern vision is everything she's trying to avoid.

***Meet Me at the Grand* by Lindsay Harrel**

We solve the problem of what to read next.

WHERE EVERY STORY IS A FRIEND,
AND EVERY CHAPTER IS A NEW JOURNEY...

Subscribe to our newsletter for the latest news, weekly giveaways, exclusive author interviews, and more!

follow us on social media!

 @sunrisemediagroup

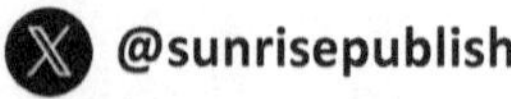 @sunrisepublish

 @sunrisepublishing

Shop paperbacks, ebooks, audiobooks, and more at
SUNRISEPUBLISHING.MYSHOPIFY.COM